SPEAKING
SCIENCE FICTION

Dialogues and Interpretations

Edited by
ANDY SAWYER and
DAVID SEED

LIVERPOOL UNIVERSITY PRESS

First published 2000 by
LIVERPOOL UNIVERSITY PRESS
4 Cambridge Street
Liverpool L69 7ZU

© 2000 Liverpool University Press

British Library Cataloguing-in-Publication Data
A British Library CIP record is available

ISBN 0-85323-834-0 (hardback)
ISBN 0-85323-844-8 (paperback)

Typeset in 10/12.5pt Meridien by
XL Publishing Services, Lurley, Tiverton
Printed by Bell & Bain, Glasgow

U H University of Hertfordshire

College Lane, Hatfield, Herts. AL10 9AB

Learning and Information Services

For renewal of Standard and One Week Loans,
please visit the web site **http://www.voyager.herts.ac.uk**

This item must be returned or the loan renewed by the due date.
The University reserves the right to recall items from loan at any time.
A fine will be charged for the late return of items.

Liverpool Science Fiction Texts and Studies
General Editor DAVID SEED

Series Advisers I.F. Clarke, Edward James, Patrick Parrinder and Brian Stableford

Contents

Speaking Science Fiction: Introduction

BRIAN W. ALDISS

The papers collected here represent the fallout from a very successful conference held in Liverpool in 1996, under the aegis of the University of Liverpool and the Science Fiction Foundation.

They indicate, I believe, the way in which the science fiction field continues to diversify and departmentalize. This process is not, perhaps, to everyone's taste; but these papers demonstrate encouragingly how intelligence and perception have crept in. In the earlier stages of its growth, the genre or mode of sf was weirdly homogeneous. Brian Attebery puts the matter clearly, when speaking of issues of *Amazing Stories* or *Thrilling Wonder*. He says that to scrutinize these magazines 'from cover to cover, complete with ads, editorials, and letters from readers, reading the hacks along with the more ambitious writers, one gets the sense that it is all one thing. Rather than being self-sufficient objects of art, the individual stories are part of a continuous stream of discourse.'

Of course it is so. And I remember my blessedly naïve days when I liked it that way. Liked it until I came to write myself, and wanted every story to aspire to Attebery's definition, a self-sufficient object of art.

Those old days when *Amazing* was available and not much else presented the tempting possibility to its adherents of being able to read everything published. Scarcity of material lead to such litanies as I witnessed at the first World SF Convention to leave the shores of North America, held in London in 1957.

A major part of the entertainment consisted of a panel – or perhaps one should say convocation – of people such as Sam Moskowitz, Robert A. Madle and Forrest Ackerman asking each other such questions as 'Who wrote the lead serial for the first issue of Gernsback's *Air Wonder Stories*?' and, 'In which issue *of Fantastic Adventures* did Tarleton Fiske's story "Almost Human" appear?' coupled with 'Who wrote under the pen name of Tarleton Fiske?'[*]

Since those days, sf and its allied fields have become more various and more sophisticated. It is no longer possible to read everything, to see everything. New departments have sprung up. Star Trek has been around for thirty years; saved from obscurity by the fans, it enjoys various incarnations: four TV series, eight films (so far), countless novelizations, books on the Klingon language, autobiographies, conventions, toys and insignia, as well as expositions on Trek physics. There are articles on the composers who wrote the music for the various 350 episodes. Plus that hallmark of an earlier fandom, fanzines. *Star Trek* alone, and all that therein is, commands a wider public by far than did the seminal *Astounding* in its palmy days.

Of course, this development reflects a great change in public taste. The daring hypothesis a few of us held, back in the forties or even earlier, that whole civilizations lived in the remote heart-stars we saw above our heads on a clear night, is daring no longer. The alien has now become, thanks to *Star Trek* and *Star Wars* and *The X-Files*, commercial coin.

Yet we are wise to have reservations about this sweeping success of sf. As Pamela Sargent pointed out in a recent issue of *Science-Fiction Studies* (July 1997), 'Visual science fiction is almost a virtual museum of the forms and ideas found in written sf, dumbed down to varying degrees and with occasional flashes of originality'.

Much of the vitality of written sf lay in its conflict of ideas. Humanity was a descendant of some superbeings' escaped laboratory animal. Or we were going to inherit the stars. Or we had once owned a huge galactic empire which had collapsed. Or we were imprisoned on Earth, the Hell Planet, by a galactic culture, as measurably insane.

These ideas may not have been especially overwhelming in themselves: but placed cheek-by-jowl within the pages of a magazine such as *Astounding* they raised a fructifying debate. All attempt to digest some of the grand if unpalatable ideas informing our culture: that we have evolved from the humblest of origins, that empires come and go, and that Freudian analysis reveals some instability of mind in many people.

That these ideas have now become part of common perception has robbed them of their original challenge. What is easily forgotten is that pressure on magazine space once meant compression of ideas. They were presented and received in the form of short stories. In her acute examination of an early Heinlein story, Farah Mendlesohn makes the point that only by studying the earlier shorter work can we perceive Robert Heinlein's shifting views of state and corporate monopolies, and so understand his political position as a whole.

It would be valuable to have a study of the short stories of other authors who were considered important at that shaping time, such as Robert Sheckley, William Tenn and (*par excellence*) Frederik Pohl. A volume entitled *The Meanings of the SF Short Story* would be a grand contribution to sf studies.

If, as I suspect, Pamela Sargent is correct in her description of visual sf as a museum of past ideas, it behoves those writers who still write for the printed page to look forward rather than back, and to keep one step ahead of the *zeitgeist*. I confess I have not always looked far ahead myself; despite our best intentions, we cannot always practise what we preach. While preparing this introduction, it happens that I am reading Jean Heidmann's book, *Extraterrestrial Intelligence*. Heidmann devotes some sections to Titan, the largest satellite of the planet Saturn (almost the size of Mars). Titan may be in the prebiotic stage, a deep-freeze version of earth during its first few hundred million years.

I was haunted by a vision of an Earth vehicle hovering in orbit about Titan, preparing to despatch men down in a lander through that nitrogenous atmosphere to the surface. Having checked back, I find that there is no word picture of this event in Heidmann's book. My imagination had conjured it up, aided and abetted by artists who have painted cosmic scenery for magazines, books, movies and elsewhere, over many years. An article discussing such artists, whose predictive work has largely been taken for granted, would be welcome.

A spaceship nosing about a strange planet is one of sf's lasting icons – so much that it has become hackneyed. Yet as a symbol it stands for much that is essential to science fiction: the excitement of probing the unknown, of forcing ourselves to dare to think ahead. The practical-minded may ask why we should visit Titan. It is part of our quest for wisdom, and perhaps for an answer to the great question, posed, I seem to recall, by Victor Frankenstein: 'Whence, I often asked myself, did the principle of life proceed?'

Questions of the origins of life and of the necessity for space exploration are hardly the province of critics. Their trade is with texts. But is not the business of sf critics somewhat more complex than that—to comment on writers' current work, and to be informed to some extent on scientific advances—perhaps at the expense of combing once again through the lucubrations of Hugo Gernsback?

Is not one of the chief attractions of sf to present us with a leap into the conjectural—via hard sf or soft—so that we are forced to decide whether we believe this conjectured event to be possible or not?

Most of the contributors here are not scientists. Yet of the two opposing sides who read sf, the scientists and the general literate public, it is the scientists, I'd say, who generate most enthusiasm and have most influence on the field.

The scientists are keen to explain that the alien life we may find elsewhere, on Titan or elsewhere in the universe, cannot look remotely like us. They may not be bipedal, they may dwell in seas, they may have extraordinary life-cycles. However, scientists are not story-tellers. We story-tellers need readers to empathize with characters who must lead us into the realms of speculation. Or, as Gwyneth Jones puts it in her paper, 'Humanoid aliens certainly make life easier for the science-fiction novelist.' More than that, the writer herself may be unable to transmit her feelings through something divorced from human life, our intense physical existences here on this planet.

I strongly endorse Jones's statement, 'The control our physical embodiment has over our rational processes is so deep and strong that it's excruciating trying to write about intelligent plasma clouds.'

Pace the scientists, there is recent support for the Jones statement. For instance, Antonio Damasio, in his brilliant book *Descartes' Error*, points out that 'the body, as represented in the brain, may constitute the indispensable frame of reference for the mental processes that we experience as the mind'. It's hard to imagine us striking up a conversation on Titan with the local plasma cloud. It goes against, not only the grain of science, but the grain of our imaginations.

The lesson of these essays is that we need to be better informed, in order to help us play the serious game of science fiction better than before. This is one of the objectives of the renewed SF Foundation.

* For those who cannot supply the answers to these questions, they are noted here:
   1) Victor MacClure; 2) July 1943; 3) Robert Bloch.

Who Speaks Science Fiction?

ANDY SAWYER

'Speaking Science Fiction' began as a way of celebrating the new life of the Science Fiction Foundation Collection at the University of Liverpool. The Collection, developed by the Science Fiction Foundation as a research library for the benefit of those engaged in the study and scholarship of sf, is now the largest publicly available collection of science fiction and material about science fiction in the UK, given new impetus by Liverpool's MA in Science Fiction, the first in the country. It contains material in many languages, as well as specific sub-collections such as the Myers Collection of Russian science fiction, and numerous manuscripts and collections of papers deposited by authors and editors such as Ramsey Campbell and Colin Greenland. Together with the Eric Frank Russell and Olaf Stapledon Archives, it forms one of the largest resources of sf-based material anywhere. We are grateful to the University of Liverpool and the Friends of Foundation for ensuring the survival of the Collection at a moment of crisis, to the Higher Education Council for England for funding a two-year cataloguing project, and to the Heritage Lottery Fund for recently enabling Liverpool University to purchase the John Wyndham Archive.

A library of science fiction is a library of Babel: a collection of fictions classified as 'science fiction' because someone, somewhere, has decided that they reflect, somehow, one of the many definitions of sf. One of the implied themes of 'Speaking Science Fiction', held in Liverpool in July 1996, was this underlying debate about the field: a debate which has in recent years become more intensified as more attention is given to the body of literature called—or miscalled—'science fiction'. The conference was to some extent a celebration of Liverpool University's rescue of the Science Fiction Foundation Collection, but it came at an auspicious time. The previous year had seen one of the rare British hostings of a World SF Convention (Glasgow, 1995), and 1996 was also to see another major academic conference devoted to the field (Luton's 'Envisaging Altern-atives'). The following year was also to see the annual Easter SF Convention held in Liverpool and here many of the conference delegates met again to continue discussing some of the implications thrown up by 'Speaking Science Fiction'. The conference, organized by the University of Liverpool with the support of the Science Fiction Foundation, was thus part of an ongoing dialogue between various 'wings' or 'tendencies' of those involved in researching, studying and writing science fiction.

This brief description suggests some of the themes which became apparent through the three days of the conference. 'Who,' asks Roger Luckhurst, 'has the right to speak (of/with/for) science fiction? Who holds the authentic, self-proximate voice of the genre? Is it the writers themselves? Or is it the phalanx of fans who surround the writers? One which is otherwise degraded, rendered impure, by the secondary, inauthentic speech of academia?' The only possible answer is, of course, 'all (or none) of the above'. Science fiction is one of the few literary forms— it has been claimed, the only one—about which such a question can be asked. Its readers have never been content to remain passive consumers, and have for decades constituted a forum for intelligent criticism and informed discussion which has bred writers and scholars alike. Science fiction fanzines (the term was first coined by sf fans) are still the only source of information for discussions of many major writers and themes: one might point to the puzzled enquiries I receive from academic libraries who can find no trace of periodicals which turn out to be amateur productions circulated among at most a hundred or so fans and which were never intended for deposit in scholarly libraries. Science fiction conventions are very different from academic literary conferences (in some ways) but share this: people attend them because they work in, or are passionately interested in (even both!) a particular field of literature. Many of the editors and contributors to these fanzines, and those attending conventions, are now writers, critics, even academics. The result is what I believe to be an interesting and significant blurring between these groups.

'Speaking Science Fiction' was by no means a homogeneous gathering. As well as established scholars from the academic field, such as Brian Attebery (co-editor of *The Norton Book of Science Fiction* and *Strategies of Fantasy*), Istvan Csiscery-Ronay Jr and Veronica Hollinger (co-editors of *Science Fiction Studies*), Edward James (Editor of *Foundation: The International Review of Science Fiction*), and George Slusser (Curator of the Eaton Collection of Science Fiction at the University of Riverside, California, and author/editor of a number of critical works), we saw a number of writers. Brian Aldiss, Candas Jane Dorsey, Josef Nesvadba, Gwyneth Jones and Sue Thomas attended either as guests or delegates, bringing a refreshing variety of viewpoints. (Another writer, Stephen Baxter, had to pull out for the best possible reason: he was summoned to Kansas to receive the John

W. Campbell award for his novel *The Time Ships*.) Brian, Candas and Gwyneth provided stunning readings after the conference banquet. One of the most interesting exchanges in the conference itself came when Sue Thomas, who had previously spoken about her forthcoming novel set largely among the strands of the World Wide Web, said that she did not think of herself as a 'science fiction writer'. Someone agreed, but remarked, 'You are a mainstream writer whose work is read by a lot of people who read science fiction and some of whose work might be thought sf by people who don't read it': a comment which has interesting implications about the networks which make up the British science fiction community today. Several of the 'academic' contributors to 'Speaking Science Fiction' (Andrew Butler and Farah Mendlesohn come to mind) are almost as likely to be seen at British sf conventions as at academic conferences. Andrew Butler is co-editor of *Vector*, the critical journal of the British Science Fiction Association, and co-founder of the Academic Fantastic Fiction Network, which itself has held two highly successful conferences. Farah Mendlesohn is assistant editor of *Foundation: The International Review of Science Fiction*, which has long prided itself on its contributions from authors and non-academic critics as well as those who are based in universities. On the other hand, a great deal of support was given to 'Speaking Science Fiction' from the Science Fiction Foundation's largely fan-based support group, the 'Friends of Foundation', and Caroline Mullan and Roger Robinson provided both much-appreciated moral support and incisive, informed comment to the many debates which ebbed and flowed throughout the conference.

Science fiction fandom has long been used to the equality between the producers and consumers of the literature: the fact that the person you are arguing with at the bar might have published a dozen highly regarded novels or not yet have produced her first fanzine. Helen Merrick's essay 'Fantastic Dialogues' considers the notion of feminist science fiction and the different discourses and dialogues implicit in the various critical modes, and highlights, for example an approach which goes beyond the canonically, critically approved 'feminist sf' to take issue with the assumption (by feminists and non-feminists alike) that sf was almost entirely male-dominated until the 1970s—a point also emphasized by Brian Attebery in his examination of the 1937 issues of the early pulp *Amazing*. Merrick ends her essay by suggesting some ideas on the relationships between fandom and academia—a relationship which has been marked over the years by suspicion and ideological disdain on both sides but which is now, thankfully, becoming less of a barrier.

Speakers and guests at 'Speaking Science Fiction' represented some of the various strands which go up to making the field we know as sf. Brian

Aldiss, of course, is the most distinguished figure in British science fiction, one of the few British writers whose central corpus of work is unashamed and unambiguous science fiction but who has never limited himself to any of its subgenres and who is part of that vein of science fiction writing which cannot be divorced from the wider literary mainstream: one thinks of writers as diverse as H.G. Wells, Olaf Stapledon, C.S. Lewis and Kingsley Amis. Central to the 'New Wave' of the 1960s, Aldiss was writing before it and after it. He is one of the great writer/critics of the field: his *Billion Year Spree*, later revised with David Wingrove as *Trillion Year Spree*, brought about a renaissance in sf studies. He was also guest of honour at the 1997 Easter SF Convention,

Josef Nesvadba's most illustrious predecessor in Czech sf was the writer who gave the field one of its earliest neologisms and most abiding images. The existence of the Czech author Karel Capek, whose play *R.U.M.* (Rossum's Universal Robots) gave generations of sf writers something to copy, reminds us that science fiction has roots beyond the Anglo-American tradition. Even (perhaps particularly) when the Iron Curtain fell over post-war Europe, science fiction writers behind this barrier were developing their own national and political traditions. Nesvadba is one of the few current Czech writers with an audience in the West. His collection *In the Footsteps of the Abominable Snowman* was published in the USA and Britain, his stories have appeared in *The Magazine of Fantasy and Science Fiction* and, more recently, *Interzone*. He has been a guest at science fiction gatherings in Britain before: his talk for 'Speaking Science Fiction' was a partial exploration of themes raised in that given at the convention Wincon 2 in 1991.

Candas Jane Dorsey also encapsulates more than one strand in the dialogues of sf. Her much-reprinted story '(Learning About) Machine Sex' is where feminist sf and cyberpunk fuse, but she is also associated with a group of fine Canadian writers centred around Tesseract Books and the magazine *On Spec* and her contribution to 'Speaking Science Fiction' was a meditation on her role as a Canadian urban writer. Canadian sf has made great strides in its endeavour to be something other than Anglo-American sf with a slightly different accent, and at its best connects interestingly with the sense of place (or various senses of places) of the country itself: urban/rural, Old World/New World, an eternal borderland, meditating on its very existence. Candas Jane Dorsey brought this interior dialogue to her address for 'Speaking Science Fiction'. Her latest publication, the novel *Dark Wine*, has won the Crawford Award for the best fantasy novel of the year, given by the International Association for the Fantastic in the Arts. (Despite the nature of the award, this lyrical, oblique work is science fiction: but *that* is another debate.)

Edward James is Professor of Medieval History at the University of Reading, and has been editor of *Foundation* for over ten years. He is also author of *Science Fiction in the Twentieth Century* (OUP) and Director of Reading University's MA in Science Fiction. If that sub-genre of science fiction known as 'alternative history' can be borne in mind, Professor James is its living practitioner: he is so well-known among the British science fiction community that it is sometimes hard to remember that he leads a double life as a historian. In another time-line, perhaps, a Professor of Future Studies edits *Foundation: The International Journal of Medieval History* and writes about that ambiguous form of scholarship which delves into the past.

Gwyneth Jones takes up the theme of communication as reworked in her 'Aleutian' trilogy and examines it to provide a fascinating interrogation of her own creation: how an sf writer speaks to and for the complex web of spoken and unspoken dialogues which surround her, and in the process does peculiar things like reinventing poststructuralist psychology. José Manuel Mota reflects not on *who* speaks sf but on *what* speaks it, and looks upon sf as part of the discourse between modernism and postmodernism. George Slusser and Danièle Chatelain examine how an sf narrative functions as narrative: how, for instance, the techniques used by sf writers to describe alien worlds are part of the range of 'travel' narratives used by realist and fantastic writers alike, and how sf creates particular relationships between narrator and narratee, author and reader. Ross Farnell discusses a phenomenon to which commentators often apply the rhetoric or imagery of science fiction, but which is in many ways far from it: the 'posthumanism' of performance artists such as the Australian Stelarc. Terms used within the sf field for decades—such as 'cyborg'—are given new meaning as Stelarc examines the relationship between machinery and his own body. Stelarc himself—rightly—insists on the distance between his motives as ideological 'body artist' and those of traditional (or even current) science fiction, but nevertheless we can see how his own techniques have been 'spoken' by science fiction writers, and how his technological strategies can be seen as literalizations of the science fiction metaphor.

Other essays, such as those by Andrew Butler and Farah Mendlesohn, express the various debates between 'classical' and 'modern' sf, between the literary-theoretical and literary-historical approaches, and the form-centred approach which sees the novel as privileged over the short story. Yet others look at the narrative stances which establish the debate on how a story should be told.

What comes out of the debate is the strength of the differing stances towards science fiction. The popular literary press, overwhelmed by the way science fiction has become part of popular culture, insists upon a monolithic interpretation of science fiction, to the extent that the sf of J.G. Ballard, William Gibson and even Philip K. Dick is increasingly seen as, in some mysterious way, *not* science fiction at all. A conference such as 'Speaking Science Fiction' reflects the various strands and strains at work in the field: the fact that there are different, even ideologically opposed approaches to the field and that this source of creative tension is one of the field's strengths. The fact that sf criticism comes from a wider basis than most other fields of criticism in the late twentieth century is not always a source of creativity. Often acute insights into an unexplored or neglected text are marred by the process of reinventing the critical wheel (or as Gwyneth Jones puts it in another context, suddenly realizing that you have come up with poststructuralist psychology), while attempts to incorporate suddenly-fashionable writers into an academic canon may distort their actual place in the traditions within which they have been writing. Nevertheless, these caveats are only mentioned because serious sf criticism is well aware of them. We speak sf in many dialects because sf is spoken by many of the most creative artists of the century: not as marketing category but as a natural mode of expression.

Science Fiction Dialogues

DAVID SEED

In the course of her analysis of *The Lord of The Rings*, Christine Brooke-Rose draws a distinction between realist and science fiction narratives whereby the former maximizes familiarity: 'the realist narrative is hitched to a megastory (history, geography), itself valorised, which doubles and illuminates it, creating expectations on the line of least resistance through a text already known, usually as close as possible to the reader's experience'. By contrast, 'in the marvellous, there is usually no such megatext, at most a vague setting (Baghdad, a city, a village), in no specified time. Sf usually creates a fictional historico-geographico-sociological megatext but leaves it relatively vague, concentrating on technical marvels.'[1] So works like *Dombey and Son* and *A Portrait of the Artist as a Young Man* would be read within framing grand narratives of the history of railway expansion or of Irish Catholicism; but Brooke-Rose dismisses the corresponding 'megastory' for science fiction rather too easily. Wells's *War of the Worlds*, for instance, is packed with descriptive data testifying to Britain's military prowess and economic prosperity, a historical moment against which a different grand narrative—that of evolution—can pull through the means of the invasion story. Or, to take a more recent example, Octavia Butler's *Parable of the Sower* draws on a whole history of inner-city neglect and ethnic tensions to set up its narrative. In many science fiction novels the realist megastory is neither ignored nor replaced, but selectively installed.

Brooke-Rose problematically links *The Lord of the Rings* to science fiction through the specific case of a mega-narrative which the author cannot assume is already known by readers and which therefore has to be explained at greater length than in realist fiction; and here the appropriate works for comparison would be not science fiction in general but those sequences of novels and short stories which place themselves within an epic frame. Patrick Parrinder has argued that much science fiction can be read as 'truncated epic' because in dealing with future or alternative history there is often a disparity between subject and narration: 'If the events that they portray are of epic magnitude, the manner of their portrayal is brief and allegorical, reminiscent not of the poem in twelve books but of the traditional fable.'[2] It is unusual for a writer to cover such vast tracts of time as Olaf Stapledon does in *Last and First Men,* although here the sheer extent of the narrative questions our assumptions about time: 'the cosmic events which we call the Beginning and the End are final only in relation to our ignorance of the events which lie beyond them'.[3] Stapledon anticipates Walter M. Miller's *A Canticle for Leibowitz* in depicting historical change as cyclical, whereas a writer like Cordwainer Smith planned out a whole epic sequence of the Instrumentality which recapitulates Western history as a progression from early wars through dark ages, renaissance and period of exploration, to an era of revolution by the 'underpeople'. Smith's short stories characteristically have period markers which indicate larger processes at work than the individual works can ever narrate, for example: 'We were drunk with happiness in those early years. Everybody was, especially the young people. These were the first years of the Rediscovery of Man, when the Instrumentality dug deep in the treasury, reconstructing the old culture, the old languages, and even the old troubles.'[4] Like Fenimore Cooper's Leather-Stocking Tales, also modelled on an epic paradigm, there are constant suggestions in Smith's stories of large events taking place elsewhere or at an earlier period which make up a framework for the present action of his narratives.

The existence of these sequences which recapitulate longer or shorter passages of history suggests that, contrary to Brooke-Rose's contention, science fiction megastories are not total inventions, but are imagined permutations or extensions of known history which, as I.F. Clarke's publications have demonstrated, always includes a dimension of expectation. There is nothing unusual, then, in the reading of a science fiction narrative involving acts of historical recognition, whether of American Progressivism as Farah Mendlesohn shows in her discussion of Robert Heinlein in this volume, or of totalitarian currents in twentieth-century history. Philip K. Dick draws attention to the latter in *The World Jones Made* when he depicts the rise of a post-war autocracy in the USA as a replay of the growth of Nazism.

In the article cited above, Brooke-Rose uses the terms 'megastory' (suggesting grand narrative) and 'megatext' as if they are interchangeable, and the latter has been taken up and developed by Damien Broderick to identify the generic nature of science fiction. For him the sf text situates itself within a vast and growing body of other sf texts and its interaction with the latter both determines its meaning and puts heavy demands on the reader's competence to understand the specific practice of the genre.[5] Broderick helpfully alerts us to the need to identify what Samuel Delany calls the generic protocols, and clearly represents a generic application of Roland Barthes and Julia Kristeva's more general argument that intertextuality is an unavoidable fact of life whereby texts can be conceived more helpfully as assemblies rather than creations.[6] It is becoming more and more common not only for sf texts to engage in dialogue with other sf texts but for generic boundaries to be crossed within a single work.

We could take two examples of this: the first from the outside looking in. Towards the end of Alison Lurie's *Nowhere City*, the New Englander Paul Cattleman has a general view of Los Angeles from Beverly Hills and registers its strangeness as an inadequacy in that novel's mode of ironic observation:

> It was a beautiful landscape, in its way, but inhuman, like some artist's vision of the future for the cover of *Galaxy Science Fiction*. People looked out of place here: they seemed much too small for the roads and buildings, and by contrast rather scrappily constructed... very few people were visible. The automobiles outnumbered them ten to one. Paul imagined a tale in which it would be gradually revealed that these automobiles were the real inhabitants of the city, a secret master race...[7]

Of course the tale never gets written and Paul flies back to the accustomed proportions of Massachusetts. Nevertheless, the brief speculation opens up an alternative method of representation which for Lurie would do better justice to California city life. By contrast, Thomas M. Disch's *Camp Concentration* is routinely classified as science fiction although its multiple allusions invite the reader to consider its narrative in relation to an astonishingly broad range of earlier works from Dante to *Faust*, from Dostoevsky to *Donovan's Brain*. Disch engages with the whole Faustian tradition of speculation but the reviewer of the novel for *Analog* declared that it was 'perfectly straightforward science fiction'. Blanking out its narrative complexities, he compared it to Michael Crichton's *The Andromeda Strain* and maintained that it represented the 'epitome of "inner space" science fiction that doesn't discard the tested values of the old. That is, it is really *science* fiction—not just speculative fantasy'.[8] The reviewer uses sheer insistence here to reclaim the novel for a restricted paradigm which Disch is actually confronting within his work. The territoriality of this review is contradicted by the energy and procedures of the novel itself, which constantly moves to and fro across generic borders.

Even within the genre, adaptations of earlier works commonly involve the depiction of a different outward-looking context. The more firmly novels become placed in the science fiction canon, the more likelihood there is of these adaptations—what Barthes would call filiated narratives deriving from these works, such as Brian Aldiss's 1980 novel *Moreau's Other*

Island. To a certain extent Aldiss produces a reprise of Wells's account of a castaway discovering not an island refuge but a secret laboratory for genetic experiments; but then a dialogue takes place between Mortimer Dart (the Moreau-figure) and Aldiss's castaway, a US Under-Secretary of State, about Wells's novel. The former recalls from his reading: 'Wells also wrote a novel about a Pacific island, nameless as I recall, on which a Dr. Moreau practised some unpleasant experiments on animals of various kinds. Any connection?'[9] To which Dart replies that they are indeed standing on Moreau's island at that moment. When the visitor objects that the novel was fiction, the other replies that it was fiction based on an actual island. In this episode Aldiss destabilizes the reader's presumption of a hard and fast separation between fiction and reality, and between the earlier novel and his own. Whereas Wells's narrator undergoes a prolonged crisis of subjectivity as his confidence in his species identity collapses, Aldiss shifts the emphasis by updating his narrative in two respects: to show that Dart and some of his companions are already casualties in being thalidomide babies, and in depicting a shrunken world where the concept of an island existing 'off the map' is no longer tenable. The novel is set in 1996, during a nuclear war, within which context the island's strategic importance as a submarine base emerges. The 'other island' is therefore not Aldiss's retelling but the island which exists in US government files. So, the Under-Secretary's climactic realization consists of a recognition of his own government's secret complicity in Dart's experiments, which are designed to produce a breed of drones ideal for the job of post-war reconstruction. 'If this monster was to be believed', he reflects, 'then I was witnessing the culmination of the Frankenstein process', thereby deriving the action from a proto-text which, Aldiss has argued in *The Trillion Year Spree*, initiated the tandem traditions of Gothic and science fiction.[10]

Aldiss's dialogue with Wells's novel changes the status of the narrator and therefore of the narrative. In this volume Danièle Chatelain and George Slusser discuss ways in which the reader projected by science fiction works can play a crucial role in the transmission and reception of information, particularly in anticipating and negotiating the reader's scepticism. Wells himself anticipates many practitioners of the genre by narrating the reception of his story before we get the story proper. In *The Island of Doctor Moreau* there are two Prendicks, the first being the nephew of the traveller who is editing his uncle's 'strange story' in accordance with his wishes (inferred, since there is no explicit request for publication). Prendick junior records that the general public reaction to the story had been that his uncle was demented. So the maximum doubt is shed on the latter's credibility, an issue which bears not just on the strangeness of the events he recounts but also on the conclusion, where he has withdrawn from bestial society into the solitary comforts of his study. If we identify uncritically with Prendick we find ourselves bizarrely estranged from humanity itself, as happens at the end of *Gulliver's Travels*.

An intermediary text between the Wells and the Aldiss revises both narrator and narratee away from their original. Josef Nesvadba's story 'Doctor Moreau's Other Island' makes the narrator a woman doctor who addresses her story in the form of a letter to a Scientific Council. A number of medical workers have been disappearing mysteriously and the narrator pursues one of these to a point over Noble Island in the Pacific where he has simply vanished. Circling the island in a helicopter, she crashes during a storm only to discover the missing figures presided over by a famous professor of surgery who has been nicknamed 'Moreau' 'after the fictional vivisector in an old book by Wells'. The narrator's crisis comes when she stumbles across a number of amputees whose plight is doubly inexplicable since surgery has been superseded by tissue developments and since they seem to enjoy their predicaments. Like the 'vol-amps' in Bernard Wolfe's *Limbo*, they are participating only too willingly in a programme to produce 'perfect' human beings for sending out in space probes—all brain and modified hands. Brian Aldiss takes this as a parable: 'the unnecessary has been cut away. Art, music, sport, these mean nothing to the amputees; it is science that attracts them.' The narrator's attitude wavers ambivalently. First she is horrified, then she decides to join them, then she leaves. Finally she believes that the group was suffering from a collective infection 'which causes the mutilation of the human organism by its own particular degenerative process'.[11] Her conclusion is to diagnose a sickness 'endemic' in civilization from the very beginning, when the scientific impulse first started to manifest itself, but her diagnosis is framed paradoxically within the values and community of science. At the very point of identifying the sickness she is claiming from her mentors the honour of discovering a new illness.

All three works, Wells's novel and its two subsequent adaptations, take different purchases on science, situating it differently within the contexts of evolution, civilization or contemporary politics. Science is never a static given. On the contrary, Brian Attebery here argues that even those stories which seem on the surface to confirm a male adventure paradigm incorporate within themselves more alternative viewpoints than we might suppose. Surveying examples from 1937, he concludes that the code of the scientific megatext is there to be played with, not simply confirmed. If that is so, then science fiction works contain a dialogue dimension which might turn out to be the rule, not the exception. Stephen Potts, for instance, bases his discussion of the dialogue between idealism and scepticism in Stanislaw Lem on the sweeping premise that science fiction usually shows

the 'triumph of human reason over the irrational, the alien'.[12] By contrast
George Eliot sets a whole imaginative agenda for twentieth-century fiction
in her sketch 'Shadows of the Coming Race' (collected in *Impressions of
Theophrastus Such*) which shows a debate between the narrator and an
optimist named Trost. The latter foresees that science will liberate humanity
from 'grosser labour' while the narrator outlines a rival future narrative
where the machines will displace humanity, producing an enfeebled
degenerate race. The latter wins the argument but there is no closure to
the sketch because Trost's sentiments are circulating in society; so the
debate will continue.

Narratives of alien encounter become the test cases for the dialogic
dimension to science fiction. In Frederik Brown's classic story 'Arena', the
protagonist Carson experiences the alien through two totally distinguished
senses of sight and internal hearing. Regaining consciousness on an
unrecognizable planet during an intergalactic war between humans and a
species named the Outsiders, he 'hears' from an unlocatable source the
dignified cadences of the collective voice of a race nearing its evolutionary
end. This voice, at once choric and godlike, declares that it has intervened
in the forthcoming battle to ensure that one side will gain a decisive victory.
If this voice suggests a higher consciousness, the Outsiders represent a
species lower in the evolutionary hierarchy, near-shapeless creatures with
tentacles and driven by an instinct to destroy; 'creatures out of nightmare,
things without a human attribute'.[13] Carson catches telepathic 'glimpses'
of an Outsider's hatred but the story, like many from the 1940s and 1950s,
straddles the science fiction and horror genres by denying the creature any
point of contact with humans other than a meeting which leads inevitably
to conflict. Murray Leinster transposes this same imperative on to the new
Cold War context of meetings between equally intelligent species in his
story 'First Contact'.

Early versions of the alien, then, can polarize between the horrifyingly
different Other and creatures separated from humanity by transparent
guises. As Walter E. Meyers explains, 'it is only in bad science fiction that
the alien being acts like a costumed human, differing from the familiar
only in appearance. In the hands of the masters of the genre we are
constantly reminded through the new terms, new metaphors, and the very
turns of phrase that our accustomed ways of thinking are not the only
ones.'[14] To refocus attention on habits of thought, a kind of narrative has
grown up to a greater or lesser extent using the frame fiction of anthropological investigation. These works are characterized by their provisional
nature and by the ways in which the exercise of observing a different
species bends back on the observers. Michael Bishop's 'Death and
Designation Among the Asadi' (collected in *Transfigurations*) is a narrative

assembled from reports by an investigator who has since disappeared into the wilds of the planet Boskveld. The status of the text is ambiguous in so far as it has been assembled by a friend of the investigator and evidently viewed with scepticism by its implied readers who have already decided that it is a work of fiction. Anthropology is used more satirically in Ursula Le Guin's *The Word for World is Forest*, where the inclusion of an anthropologist among the colonizing team on the Athshean planet gives a benign façade to what is essentially an act of conquest. Thus the discourse of cultural analysis is totally contradicted by other Terrans referring to the indigenous race as slaves or livestock. Judith Moffett's first novel *Pennterra* similarly takes up the theme of colonization, but presents a more complex account of interaction between a small human group and the native 'hrossa'. Part 2 of the novel again pieces together fieldnotes in which the group members find themselves comparing notes on the extraordinary heightening of their own sexuality during their visit; and so once again detachment breaks down.

In all these cases the focus falls on the process of investigation. Many critics have suggested that the alien should be imagined as a distorting mirror of humanity and so Gregory Benford has written: 'For me, the unexamined alien is not worth meeting'.[15] To examine the alien is to examine our presumptions about our own species. This is an issue addressed in this volume by Gwyneth Jones, who explains how she took particular care not to distance the reader in her depiction of the humanoid Aleutians. Because the language of aliens can be a minefield, she wisely avoids clichés by concentrating instead on communication through body language.

An alternative strategy is followed by Orson Scott Card in his Ender novels, which have been criticized by Carl Malmgren for 'anthropomorphizing the universe'.[16] In the second novel of the sequence, *Speaker for the Dead*, we are presented with four distinct forms of sentient life: Catholics from Earth who have partly colonized the planet Lusitania; the 'piggies' or diminutive indigenous creatures of that planet; the hive queen of a temporarily extinct species; and a supercomputer facility called Jane who 'speaks' through a jewel implanted in Ender's ear. Speech, and therefore dialogue, is the defining mode of the novel. Every creature has a voice, and a forceful one at that. And every position expressed has a counter-position. One of the first casualties in these constant debates is the anthropological principle of minimum intervention when a piggy questions a settler near the opening of the novel: 'You watch us and study us, but you never let us past your fence and into your village to watch *you* and study *you*.' The nature of xenology is brought into question not only because, as a character later observes, 'the observer never experiences the same culture as a participant', but because the conditions of observation put the observed in a quasi-colonized position.[17] By foregrounding voice, Card minimizes the appearance of his aliens who as a result seem no stranger than different human cultures from each other. The novel introduces such differences by the Whorfian strategy of citing examples of 'foreign-terms' from different languages, in the process relativizing the concept of alienness. *Speaker for the Dead* therefore narrates an open-ended multi-vocal dialogue on this concept, demonstrating that it is formulated out of a whole religious, social and cultural context.

In a rare instance of a science fiction work being organized explicitly around the notion of dialogue, Poul Anderson's volume of stories *Dialogue With Darkness* explores ways in which humans attempt to make sense of their predicaments or their place in the cosmos. The opening piece, 'A Chapter of Revelation', looks back to an alternative Korean War which is escalating towards total nuclear holocaust. Seemingly there is no way out of the spiral of events, no political solution at least. An American who appears on a TV chat show declares that these events are happening because 'we don't know God' and these sentiments are echoed by others. One character quotes Joshua 10:12 in pleading 'Sun, stand still', and sure enough it does. For one day the motion of the Earth relative to the Sun is suspended and as a result a wave of religious mania sweeps through the world, compelling the superpowers to make peace. The event stays an enigma throughout the story, occasioning endless unresolved debates on free will, miracles and the existence of God. Although one war is avoided, social breakdown is increasing and the story ends with the onset of a new Dark Age. Darkness in this series, then, connotes the void left by the disappearance of religious belief and cosmic space. It is inner and outer. Indeed the collection is at its most powerful when dramatizing the dread induced by visions of the stars, the sublime landscape of Venus, or the possible encounter with intelligent beings from other planets. Anderson takes a whole series of science fiction motifs—such as the rupture of the natural order, planetary colonization, and time travel—and in each case denies consolation within the theme. The story about time travel, 'Time Heals', describes the experience as being like dying. The traveller finds that the speech of the people of the future is distorted as if by an impediment or illness, and is gradually reduced to near-imbecility by the dystopian order of the future Scientific State.

Throughout these stories Anderson dramatizes *attempts* at communication, not meaningful dialogue. One narrative finishes with the plea *'Oh God… please exist. Please make hell for me.'* Another describes the horrific impact of going on the first manned spaceflight. One of the astronauts experiences a loss of self and then a solipsistic crisis: 'He had slipped into darkness, and now he fell, while an eyeless face that was his own receded before him, then came back swelled until it filled the universe, swelled until it was the universe...'. Although he has companions, McAndrew carries on a 'mono-dialogue' in his own head, having a nightmare vision of his wife, the cherished partner who might respond to his need, who is seen as a corpse with her slashed throat mocking his solitude in a travesty grin. McAndrew therefore cannot even focus his words on an absent spiritual figure like some of Anderson's speakers; instead, his attempted address slips into self-description: 'blackness, nothingness, oh, help me, I am so alone. I cry and there is no voice.' Even when there *is* a voice in response the result is usually unsatisfactory and a matter of misunderstanding. The story 'Dialogue' explores the possible problems of communications with other intelligent beings. 'Conversation in Arcady' ironically depicts the inhabitants of a future pastoral world as so infantilized that when an astronaut reaches them from some 300 years in the past (that is, from the reader's present) the Arcadian very quickly gets bored with the visitor's words because 'he had wanted to hear about romantic adventures on foreign worlds'.[18] The whole sequence concludes rather blandly on the symbolism of the day/night cycle which plays down darkness to a manageable temporary phenomenon, whereas the stories repeatedly dramatize it as an absence or space challenging rationality itself.

The essays in this volume all examine such dialogues within and between science fiction works. They demonstrate that it is a mode constantly engaging with other areas of enquiry, whether of body technology, the political control of language, or telepathy. Gary Wolfe has proposed a complex interaction in the title of his study of science fiction iconography, *The Known and the Unknown*, arguing that the barrier performs a central symbolic function; and each essay here testifies to the sheer speculative energy of a genre which constantly delights in challenging or crossing bounds.[19]

Notes

1 Christine Brooke-Rose, *A Rhetoric of the Unreal* (Cambridge: Cambridge University Press, 1988), p. 243.

2 Patrick Parrinder, 'Science Fiction as Truncated Epic', in George Slusser et al., eds., *Bridges to Science Fiction* (Carbondale: Southern Illinois University Press, 1980), p. 96.

3 Olaf Stapledon, *Last and First Men* (New York: Dover, 1968), p. 229.

4 James A. Mann, ed., *The Rediscovery of Man: The Complete Short Science Fiction of Cordwainer Smith* (Framington, Mass.: NESFA, 1993), p. 375.

5 Damien Broderick, *Reading By Starlight: Postmodern Science Fiction* (London and New York: Routledge, 1995), pp. 57–63.

6 Samuel Delany, 'Generic Protocols: Science Fiction and Mundane', in Teresa de Lauretis et al., eds., *The Technological Imagination: Theories and Fictions*

(Madison: Coda Press, 1980), pp. 175–93.

7 Alison Lurie, *The Nowhere City* (London: Minerva, 1994), p. 231.

8 P. Schuyler Miller, 'The Reference Library', *Analog* 89.1 (March 1972), p. 171.

9 Brian Aldiss, *Moreau's Other Island* (London: Jonathan Cape, 1980), p. 39.

10 Aldiss, *Moreau's Other Island*, p. 154.

11 Josef Nesvadba, *In the Footsteps of the Abominable Snowman* (London: New English Library, 1979), pp. 139, 9.

12 Stephen W. Potts, 'Dialogues Concerning Human Understanding: Empirical Views of God from Locke to Lem', in Slusser et al., eds., *Bridges to Science Fiction*, pp. 41–52.

13 Anthony Cheetham, ed., *Bug-Eyed Monsters* (St. Albans: Panther, 1974), p. 76.

14 Walter E. Meyers, *Aliens and Linguistics: Language Study and Science Fiction* (Athens, GA: University of Georgia Press, 1980), p. 9.

15 Gregory Benford, *In Alien Flesh* (London: Victor Gollancz, 1989), p. 31.

16 Carl Malmgren, 'Self and Other in Science Fiction: Alien Encounters', *Science-Fiction Studies* 20.1 (1993), p. 23.

17 Orson Scott Card, *Speaker for the Dead* (London: Legend, 1992), pp. 4, 36.

18 Poul Anderson, *Dialogue With Darkness* (New York: TOR, 1985), pp. 135, 154, 160, 231.

19 Gary K. Wolfe, *The Known and the Unknown: The Iconography of Science Fiction* (Kent, OH: Kent State University Press, 1979), pp. 30–51.

Speaking of Homeplace, Speaking from Someplace

CANDAS JANE DORSEY

I came here charged with a task: to talk about where some of my work in particular, and speculative fiction in general, might have come from: I was particularly guided toward two pieces, the urban 'Living in Cities' and its pastoral precursor 'Willows'. These pieces have come to represent the manifestation of homeplace in my work, and so I decided to speak of the places from which they came, and, in general, speak about how our work speaks of, if not 'homeplace' then *some*place', even when we write the most speculative of fictions.

But as I began to examine this task, I realized, as I always do, that in some ways a writer is the worst judge of where the work comes from: in the general sense we learn to talk about our field with remarkable fluency yet in the personal sense we very seldom actually understand the intuitive source of the decisions we make. So I discovered that I was to come thousands of miles, into a country where I do not know the landscape or, in the heartfelt way that leads to comfort and confidence, the language to talk about a set of decisions which are so far under the surface of the slough of a writer's unconscious that they are completely obscured by mud, algae and weeds.

What is a slough? On the prairies we pronounce it 'slew' but here I think you may call it a 'slaow'.

Let me tell you about a prairie slough for a minute. Officially I suppose they are called 'wetlands'. They often form temporarily at first, in the corner of a farmer's field, a low area which was too muddy to plough that year. Maybe after a few years there is some particularly heavy rain and the pond stays there all winter. In the spring a pair of ducks settles there, a momentous event I have commemorated with a line in one of my stories, and they stay and raise a bunch (a brood, a passel, a waddle?) of ducklings. Next year they all come home to the growing pond, which has managed to last the winter again. By now the farmer has given up, and has left the muddy verge unploughed. A few bulrushes self-seed and begin to grow. The next spring two seasons of ducks have brought mates, and a red-wing blackbird is singing his territorial little heart out as he swings on a bulrush head. Over on the other side, pussy willows are spreading out by the spot where the fenceposts are now submerged and starting to lean slightly. And so it goes, until three decades down the timeline, ducks, geese, grebes, shrikes and the occasional heron or whooping crane are using the place as a nesting ground or way station. The night is alive around the slough with the chorus of frogs, and an owl's startlingly human-sounding 'who?' is a common night sound. Days, raptors cruise the skies, and coyotes, gophers, cattle, elk and deer—and perhaps, in some areas, the occasional moose and wolf—come to drink or even to wade into the water and chow down on the inhabitants or the weeds and shoreline grasses, each according to their nature.

Now, there's microscopic and not-so microscopic life in these waters that I prefer not to imagine. Of course mosquitoes, and perhaps bloodsuckers—leeches—and certainly algae and swimming insects and insects that alight on the water, and eventually fish. How do fish get there? Darned if I know, except that if the slough gets big enough it gets promoted to a lake and stocked with fish for sport fishermen by a special branch of the provincial government that actually hires people to raise tame trout.

This is a slough, and having a prairie dweller's awareness of sloughs, I had a firm vision in my mind of what the landscape was like when the guy in *Pilgrim's Progress* went through the Slough of Despond. (Except that to make it Despond-like, I had to up the mosquito quotient and think of it on a cold wet autumn day at about an hour after dusk, and me with a close-up view of the duck-shit, a pair of leaky rubber boots on, and a companion with a big mouth and a bad attitude about gun control and 'queers'. Otherwise, I would have found the idea of a slough too likeable.)

In every creator's unconscious, there's a slough which is wider than Despond and not as miserable, and contains every experience, every feeling, every thought, every understanding in that person's life, and from this Black Lagoon rises periodically, dripping and unpredictable, a Creature, brought into existence in the organic soup at the bottom, and coming into the light new and awful and exhilarated, to become that creator's idea, inspiration, or perhaps even Great Work.

And how is that work formed? Sometimes we creators are the least able to tell you. We can guess, but it is often up to critics and academics to find themes, tropes, metaphors and allegories among the eclectic stuff of which the Creature is made, or the various matter with which it is decorated.

Lately my slough has resembled the Slough of Despond in some wise.

For one thing, the social Darwinists are taking over where I live, which means that the growth of meanness (what I believe is sometimes called 'man's inhumanity to man') and fear is astronomical. In order to feed the Creature a certain confidence in its right to existence is necessary, but I have been more tempted recently to skim the surface of the water for diatribes than to let the time pass which allows life to be created far under the surface. Still, my first love is the Creature in all its forms, and I always go back to the soupy depths for what I think of as my real work.

Now, before I continue with this agrarian metaphor I must say here that I'm a city dweller. Although I was born of parents who were born in small towns and country, I was born in a city hospital and I grew up loving the way a city looks and lives. I've written about that in a story, too, in which my city, Edmonton, becomes a future collector's historic site restoration project, and I finally get to protest the twenty-some year ago decision to make my favourite bridge one-way, which I do by routing fictional travel the wrong way across it, which drives other Edmontonians crazy. They keep thinking, purely reflexively, that a bus is coming to wipe out my protagonist.

But even a city dweller, paying attention, hears the migrating geese honk, sees the brightest of the Northern Lights, and knows which way the weather comes from (west, by the way, the only correct source direction for weather, at least according to my prairie instincts). And even a city dweller can learn to stop several times each day and look above the power lines and through the buildings and away from the streetlights and into the sky. Sky does not belong to the city or the country.

Where we come from influences where we can go. Place is not just physical, we all know that, but physical place often forms and informs psychological place, conceptual place, ideological place, theological place, sociological place. Sf writers often forget that science and technology are primarily a *place*, not a bunch of toys nor a set of theories. Even language, so often framed as a tool, a technology or a virus, is a place to locate expression and experience.

Rhetorical and not-so-rhetorical question: why should we locate ourselves and, as writers, how do we locate our stories?

The best science fiction is placed in a physical place which evokes and sometimes stands as analogue of all those other places I have mentioned. This may sound like a given, but I have been teaching a lot of speculative fiction writing classes and the thing that is the greatest weakness of many of my students is that they have no idea what ground their characters or their stories stand upon.

They cannot describe the landscape. They cannot place macro *or* microflora in the Slough of Despond or the outer asteroid belt. They cannot even imagine the rooms in which their characters sleep and wake. Yet we know that the best, most memorable sf in our personal histories gave us an immediate and concrete place to be, no matter how *someplace else* it was. Whether the work's place in the Delany taxonomy of subjunctive tension is fantasy's 'could not happen' or science fiction's 'hasn't happened', we never remember anything that happened *nowhere*.

Nor can they describe the ethical, moral, social place where their characters stand. They cannot imagine the journeys taken to get there. They place 1950s-foolish 'women with big busts and men with big lusts' (as a student of mine neatly summarized it recently) tens, hundreds or thousands of years into the future and imagine that they will behave like people in bad novels of forty years ago. Yet any thinking person needs only to sit down and think about the changes of the last decade or two to realize that profound ethical, social and cultural changes have overtaken us even in this part of our lifetime. If we were to write our own stories, we would see we have gone through more in ten years than these characters and their societies have been allowed to go through in centuries.

I said several times just there, 'they can't imagine'. Is it truly a failure of imagination? Lately I have come to think of it more and more as a failure of place.

Let us go back for a moment to the slough where the duck are at this moment raising their ducklings. Why can I describe this micro-ecology so evocatively? I'm not from the country. I haven't seen a slough grow in my backyard. I have paid attention to a certain pattern of occurrences that I have seen from a distance, visited as a tourist, read about and synthesized, and I told them to you in a certain way, and you bought the sense of place that I gave you.

It wasn't false. I'm from there, I really am: the prairie forms part of the landscape of my heart. But I'm also, as I said, from the city: from straight, grid-patterned streets so different from your anarchic British webs of pathways and roads, straight streets whose perspective-illustrating parallel boulevards and sidewalks are shaded with Dutch elms which haven't yet fallen prey to Dutch elm disease, from concrete playgrounds with hop-scotch grids painted on by school board maintenance people and shunned by children who draw their own in chalk, from slummy university 'co-op houses' allowed to run down by block-busting landlords and rented to hippie students who painted the doors with the Eye of Horus; from a whole lot of places where ducks don't go (voluntarily).

And yet, ducks fly into my science fiction stories. Ducks fly there because there is something important to me about ducks on the surface of mirror-water sloughs in spring after a long winter, and there need to be ducks and sloughs in the future. So I allow them to scramble into the air of the future on their short wings, and bring with them an ideology of landscape, an ethical ecology.

I also write about cities, and this is as it should be, because I love and fear and understand cities with an intuition which I know tells me a great deal about my culture. When I move these cities forward into the future, it is with the solid stance of the shot-putt athlete who stands within a certain circle which limits her footing as she makes her throw.

All of my personal starting places are limited: everyone's are. I think it was Karl Marx who said every man is a product of his time. Allowing for the pronoun, I have to agree that I am a product of my time: time *also* being a place. I am a product of a certain family place, a certain attitudinal place, a cultural location, a language, and a presence at a certain time in a certain century. When I write, I try to move beyond these personal places into shared and imagined space. That is part of the appeal of writing: transcendence. But words like transcendence are relative: in order to transcend, we have to come *from* somewhere. That place informs how we see our experience and arguably allows our epiphanies, maybe even our satoris.

When readers of science fiction or fantasy in particular, speculative fiction in wider frame, and literature in general read, they want to be taken to a new place. But they consciously or not want, or more accurately need, to be grounded too. They stay grounded in their own place, which formed their ability to understand their new experiences. They also want to feel grounded in their new place, and that is where writers giving them these journeys must understand the enormous responsibilities upon us.

These readers are no Accidental Tourists of the page. (Remember Anne Tyler's evocation of people who are looking for the nearest thing to the food of home in some foreign marketplace?) They want adventure. They want to be able to taste the strangest sauces, participate in the strangest local customs. But whether they are aware of the need or not, they need to be assured of a certain level of what I might call personal safety. What reads as safety when you are on Mars, when you meet the aliens, when you find a far alternate future where all the rules are different, or a far past where none of the rules have been made yet?

I think what counts as safety is simply the multiplex ability to recognize the landscape. And this recognition has nothing to do with whether they have been there. It has to do with whether and how they *understand* it. As readers, we have this same challenge with each piece of writing into which we travel. I have a fascination with religious tracts, for instance, the really lunatic ones, because in those pieces of writing I find what comes close to an alien landscape, one I truly don't know, yet with horrified fascination I can learn to understand it. It may be the same fascination, *sans* the horror,

with which I met the text of Kim Stanley Robinson's *A Short, Sharp Shock*
or Joanna Russ's 'When It Changed', Ursula Le Guin's *Always Coming Home*
or Susan Palwick's *Flying in Place*, Rebecca Ore's *Becoming Alien* series or
M.J. Engh's *Arslan*, Samuel R. Delany's *Triton* or *Dhalgren*, or any of the
other (many/brilliant) texts which have used the tropes of speculative
fiction of one kind or another to bring me to a new understanding.

This is all very well as a reader, but what is the writer to do? The Creatures
we create are not always within our control, even when we think we
sculpted each dreadlock lovingly and consciously. Our 'responsibility to
the reader', our 'intention in writing the piece', our 'control of the material'
or our 'placement of the characters in time, space and cultural matrix' are
much more accidental than we would like to admit or, at least, they are
grounded in something different than we would like to admit.

We would like the people we talk with about our work to see us as
artisans, hammering and shaping the text into place in a process of layering
that is fully under our control, sort of like the making of *mille-feuille* pastry
or a Damascus steel blade, by an ancient and honourable process. We would
like the source of our power to be that control.

The reality is, the source of our power is more often the giving up of
control, the reliance on faith and dreams to carry us, the ability to trust
that our feet really are planted in the circle of place and that we are strong
enough to throw the story away from us into our future and the readers'.

Or, to go back to the Creature from our private Black Lagoon, the source
of our power is a trust that the material which arises from our personal
slough has been shaped on its way up by our perceptions, which are shaped
by our place in the universe, and that no creature can emerge which is not
indirectly influenced by that shaping. It is the rare person in whom the
unconscious is totally dissociated from the conscious, and usually that
person has developed analogous ways of duplicating the missing
connection, at least as a matter of social necessity if not of artistic integrity.
The rest of us are in relation of some kind, be it bondage or co-operation
or love, whether we like it or not, to our place.

I am a Canadian, and you know by now that I live on the prairies, in
what is called 'the parkland' terrain, which means that it isn't like the vast
buffalo plains where, in the words of the Saskatchewan joke, you can sit
on the porch and watch your dog run away for three days. In fact, I live
in an area which is more like a demonstration project for glacial process
remains: moraine, knob-and-kettle topography, erratics, drumlins and
eskers spring out of the textbooks and have a direct influence on where
the ducks live, where the rivers run, and where gravel for road and railbeds
comes from. The prairies are a delicate and subtle land, without the
pyrotechnics of mountains, the density of Old World landscape; our

horizon is lower than yours here in Britain: yours is about two thirds of the way up the canvas, whereas our painters tend to reserve at least the top two thirds for sky. (As an aside, that gives prairie artists and writers a special relationship with space: in fact, a painter in my area has turned the word 'landscape' around and calls what he paints 'landspace'. I like to think that my relation with the night sky has something to do with the way I see space, while my relation with the daytime sky and what it domes helps inform my ideas of place.)

I also live on the 53rd parallel, 53° north latitude. In winter, days are short and cold; in summer, there can be over seventeen hours of sunlight, and at night, it never gets really dark. When I came to Britain for the first time, I felt most at home in the Highlands, where the days were as long and the nights as nippy as at home. The sea stood in for the long low land, and the weather, coming from the west here too, made sense. But even in London, the evenings are as long as at home: Britain is at the same latitude as Labrador.

Recently I received a note from an American writer who had just read my book of stories—some of which, I must tell you, are set on the Moon, on other planets, in spaceships, and in the mountains of a completely different planet—and she wrote that she loved the 'northernness' of them. I was quite taken aback. To me, 'northernness' means boreal forest or, further north, tundra. It means wild rivers flowing north across Cambrian and pre-Cambrian rock. It means musk ox, dog teams, Inuit, the men of the lost Fraser expedition found again buried preserved in permafrost: it means extremity. I think of north at least as the abode of my friend who lives and teaches school in a predominantly aboriginal community two hundred and fifty miles north of my home city; I think of my own canoe trip north down the Athabasca River, which began three hundred miles from home and ended one hundred and seventy-five miles north of that point, at a tiny trailer-and-microwave-tower town named Fort Chipeweyan, which two hundred years ago was the first fur-trading settlement in my province of Alberta.

North? *That's* north.

Furthermore, I live in a city of 700,000 people: bigger than a lot of famous old cities like New Orleans, about the same size as Liverpool, and with, at the time I learned this statistic, more professional theatres per capita than any other city on the continent (for example), yet still seen by some snobs as a frontier town and still sensitive about the image. North? Not us. It's defensive and semi-automatic to place ourselves in the southern strip of Canada through which the stream of culture flows more thickly and turbulently.

But after I received the message I looked out of my office at a June sunset sky, at around ten at night. I looked at the weather, the spectacular thunderstorm clouds blowing in from the west to cool down our 23° (Celsius) day—seasonably warm: people had complained to me—and I realized that yes, I live north. It's just that, as a flippant friend of mine says, 'wherever you are, there you are'. North and south, east and west, are directions relative to the centre, and we are always at the centre.

This is where we begin: where we begin.

Earlier I asked how, as writers, we locate our stories. This of course is a much harder question than why we should, and I was tempted not to try to answer it at all. Certainly the most real and concrete answers are technical, and are the stuff of editors, writing workshops, classes and long dark nights (or tea-times, for morning people) of the soul. But the sweet burden of my argument makes the conceptual answer almost simpler than the technical, because of course we are being led to say, 'We locate our stories by landscape.'

What is landscape? Yes, it's where we are: it's also where we were, where we're from and where we are going. It's an outlook, a state of being as well as a place. It's natural and constructed, intuited and conceived, dreamed and planned, delighted in and despoiled. It is individual and yet shared, private and yet collectively owned, rich and yet simple, multiplex and yet plain. How do we get from there to the future: how do we get from there to space? It is easy to use a Zen mind to resolve these paradoxes: what is not so easy is to transform paradigms of landscape as we try to transform our ideas, as we speculate in fiction.

Joanna Russ wrote, in an essay called 'SF and Technology as Mystification' (1978), a succinct summary of Rebecca West's re-definitions of lunacy and idiocy:

> By 'lunacy' I mean the attitude of those who consider abstractions apart from the specific conditions of people's lives. Lunatics do this because they are insulated from the solid, practical details of their own lives by other people's labor; they therefore begin their thinking about life by either leaving such practical details out or by assuming that they are trivial. ... Idiocy is the refusal to go beyond the specific details to any larger pattern.

In this context, a lunatic ignores landscape, an idiot believes the world is flat because it looks flat from here.

Inexperienced, unconscious or thoughtless sf writers make their failure of place when they become Accidental Tourists themselves, when they—when we—through clumsiness or arrogance, turn the process about and instead of standing on the basis of landscape and hurling the story away from us we try instead to take our landscape with us, and with utmost idiocy impose it on what is really there. Consider the tenacity in fiction (and in real life) of the naïve and optimistic notion that technological problems can be solved by technological solutions. Consider recent temptations to stories about body modification and the terraforming of Mars (and Venus, and the asteroids... and, in Heather Spears' recent and, actually, quite excellent *The Taming*, the Moon).

As it happens, Joanna Russ was talking about academe's flirtation with technology when she wrote about lunacy and idiocy. Reading the essay almost twenty years after she wrote it, I was more reminded of the flirtation of the New Right (which is neither) with social Darwinism and deficit-myth-based economics. And of course, there is a field rife with both lunacy and idiocy about technology, and it is the field of science fiction.

Ideologues of any stripe are dangerous. We already know this. We have seen ideological battles played out among the Titans of this century's speculative writing field: as some demonstration pairs, let's set Robert Heinlein against Philip K. Dick or Theodore Sturgeon; David Brin versus Joanna Russ or Samuel Delany; let's compare Ursula Le Guin or John Crowley with Larry Niven on the one hand or, oddly, Kim Stanley Robinson on the other. Robinson gets on that list for his Mars series which seems to hold, despite his ability to see more clearly than his genre predecessors, the same tech-will-fix-the-planet notion, and I contrast that with *The Word for World is Forest* or the lovely anecdote in Crowley's *Engine Summer* where the child says, 'What was that [highway] for?' and the parent replies, 'To kill people.' Consider: the writers in this hasty list are the cream of the crop, and a much longer list could be made; I also see egregious lunacy in the aspiring beginners.

The most dangerous ideologue, of course, is the one who doesn't know s/he is one. The one who, thoughtless, imposes the rules and exigencies of their place upon the landscapes of others. We know a lot about imperialism now, and xenophobia, and terraforming, and so on, so aside from the mentions above I'm not going to belabour those topics. I move instead to the dangerous but unfortunately pervasive belief about sf writing (which I have come across among students, colleagues and editors as well as among the non-sf-reading public) that none of this, including what they are doing, matters. That these writings are entertainment, these characters unworthy of respect, these locations bogus and these activities mere play with toys, be they ray guns or unicorns. They have put themselves off their own land, they have refused to allow their ducklings or their raptors to fly, they cannot see their own skies and so they cannot believe in, let alone describe, alien ones.

Remember the last book of C.S. Lewis's Narnia series? In *The Last Battle* there is a time when the children are imprisoned in a squalid little hut in the middle of a dark battlefield. In there with them have been thrust some squalid little enemies. The children find inside this dark prison a landscape bright with sun and full of nourishment. They offer some of their food to the hungry dwarves, but their enemies are still in thrall to the powers of darkness, and they see the food as dung and soiled stable straw, the light as darkness, the space and health as limitation and darkness. Putting aside the Christian imagery and taking the metaphor more literally, it still seems to me one of the most powerful encapsulations of how some people, and certainly in context of this essay I mean some writers, can be spiritually bankrupt in the midst of plenty. What kind of Creatures do their swamps spawn? Poor cringing anorexic ones with an apology for being there at all on their lips rather than a lusty shriek of joy at being alive. They are not allowed to mention the swamps they come from, and if they do they are beaten. Abused children of emotionally incapable parents, they try to say they carry no burden, no meaning.

They are wrong. They carry a message of hopelessness, of conformity, of anomie. They come from nowhere and they wander eternally in search of the land which should have provided them with a central organising principle.

Let me make certain things very clear. I obviously do not mean here that every spaceship must have ducks on its cargo manifest. We furnish our worlds from different swamps. In like wise, not every creation is serious, is earthshaking in its intention. But every authentic Creature who can be proud of the landscape which spawned it has the potential to make meaning far beyond its original intention. I often tell the story from Terry Pratchett's book *Mort* where the man afraid of Death makes a multi-layer vault and hides in it at the time his death is forecast. Nothing can get in or out, not even air, and as he lies alone in the darkness thinking about this oversight, he hears a voice saying, 'DARK IN HERE, ISN'T IT?' It's a very funny piece, but it's also a very strong parable. Because it is authentic, it holds a great deal more weight than perhaps even Pratchett would say he intended if we asked him (assuming we could get a straight answer out of him!). Contrast it with the land of bad puns and bubble-breasted (and brained) women which crowds the A section of the chain bookstores in the name of humour. Will stories from Xanth ever teach a teenage boy something important about death? Unfortunately not. My bias is that such writing is lazy and irresponsible, and that whatever the lightness of the froth we produce, we should locate it in authenticity.

There is one last caveat here. I tell my students, and I tell myself, that on no account must they—must any of us—think about these uplifting, moral and idealistic things when they—when we—sit down to write. As another friend quotes, that way lies madness and rump of skunk or, if not skunk, then sanctimoniousness, which smells just as bad. The absolute enemy of a successful Creature is a sense of moral superiority. Remember, these creations come from sloughs, from lowlands, from the depths of a murky, cloudy, organic soup. They come from confusion, chaos, paradox and even slime. They come from where we really live, not our castles in the air. They are part of us. To our well-mannered, insincere, social, buttoned-down Dr Jekyll, they are the organically connected Mr Hyde.

What we must do is make a place for the Creatures of our creation, make them welcome, and trust in the process that created them out of our control and our conscious sight. We must trust that they are not monsters; trust in 'the ingested metaphor', as a friend calls it, the principle (the very one I have developed here) that our swamps are life-giving, imbued with our essential beliefs, redemptive, and cannot spawn evil. And we must be proud of our Creatures, and groom them as they need to be groomed, and accept their existence with an attutide unwarped by our prejudices against serendipity. We must honour our Creatures: we must make friends with Mr Hyde.

Each time the Creature emerges, we must do this. Sometimes we can let them go on their way as is. Sometimes we must clean them up, comb out their tangled sentences, put braces on their snaggletoothed metaphors until we have given the Creature some bite, improve their manners and give them etiquette lessons, but always we must strive to leave them with their essential selves retained or, more accurately, enhanced. Then we must send them into the world—or worlds—to make their own way in the community, as honest a representative of our home landscape as we have been able to make them: as honest an ambassador for our place in the universe as we have been able to create them and refine them to be.

Then we must do it all again. But every now and again, let's take a break (on the holodeck perhaps?) to enjoy the ducks.

Speaking Science Fiction—Out of Anxiety?

JOSEF NESVADBA

I was of course delighted when I got your invitation to attend this meeting. And because of its theme I thought that perhaps a case from my medical practice would interest you.

It was in the middle of the 1970s when a colleague from the clinic phoned my sanatorium in the country and invited me to visit him and see a patient whom I could help.

'How?' I asked, presuming that I could not be better than the professor and his colleagues.

'By answering him. You know, he seems to be talking to you. He seems to be hearing the voices of your literary hero, Captain Feather, out of your story "The Planet Kirké". Could you please come as soon as possible?'

My sanatorium was situated fifty kilometres from Prague and I did not get to the old building of our clinic until the next morning. My colleague led me to an isolation room. There I saw a young man who stood in the middle of the place, supporting his body with both hands and scratching his hair with the right now and then, as apes do in the zoo.

'Captain Feather?' he asked me. 'I have returned from the planet Kirké.' And he gave some ape-like grunts. Now I have to admit that I really did write a sequence of stories about the cosmic adventures of the Captain, whom I called 'Feather' to stress his non-heroism. One of them really took place on the planet called Kirké, which was so well automated that its inhabitants didn't need to work at all. Therefore they slowly devolved back to apes and later to pigs.

'You certainly didn't read my story properly,' I answered, trying to argue in accordance with his delusion. 'Planet Kirké was destroyed by the same Captain at the end of the story.' He only laughed. I began to recognize him. It was that same boy, George M., who had visited me several times in the 1960s with his first clumsy translations of various stories by van Vogt. He did not want to admit his mistakes at that time, and had insisted that his work was of paramount importance, as van Vogt was entirely unknown in Prague in the first years of that decade. But so of course were many other writers of greater fame and value, as only a few people knew Anglo-Saxon sf at that time. There were still difficulties even with English mainstream fiction.

But to help you understand all this, I am afraid that I have to inform you about a second case important to this report: namely, my own.

For my whole adult life I have led a double existence as writer and physician, mainly as a psychiatrist. In central Europe this is not such a rare case. Before the information explosion started, medicine was a sort of craftsmanship that could be 'learned' like other skills, and which brought a lot of experience with interesting patients. In Anglo-Saxon countries, especially the States, I have often been told that I must be a poor doctor if I have to earn my living through writing. But we are not yet that far advanced.

After the war I was nineteen years old and I deliberated for a long time what profession to choose. I had already, as a pupil of the Prague English Grammar School before the war, translated Coleridge's 'Rime of the Ancient Mariner' and some new English poets, at that time unknown in my country, such as Auden, Spender and Cecil Day Lewis. I started studying medicine and philosophy simultaneously, but only until the year 1948. In February of that year the Stalinists took over and the humanities especially had to undergo purges reminiscent of wartime. For the whole of the 1950s I devoted myself to medicine and wrote only during the weekends or in the army, where I had to serve with the airforce during the Cold War.

The general situation, especially during the Korean War, seemed the beginning of catastrophe, and with the threat of atomic war another holocaust seemed to be in train. Stalinist thinking began to infiltrate medicine and the natural sciences. The origin of every invention was presumed to be Soviet and Stalin himself was the arbiter on linguistics, physics and biology, evidently thinking that since he had defeated Hitler and since Marxist theory could comprehend economics, it could comprehend everything. An article by a colleague of mine, a Stalinist believer, illustrated this. 'How,' (he said) 'can a team of intelligent men, who call themselves geneticists, devote all their time to the study of a single fly, *Drosophila*, and its genes, when the great Lysenko in the steps of the great Micurin is working on the improvement of wheat and fruit, helping people to live better and fighting hunger? Genetics should be forbidden and their laboratories used for something better.'

There seemed to be no way to argue with these 'campaigns against cosmopolitanism' as they were called, with the resulting criticism and banning of cybernetics, relativity theory and much of modern physics generally. A danger existed that nineteenth-century science would be transformed into something sacrosanct and a new scholasticism established like that of medieval times. The only hope in this situation, which we as young men felt bitterly, was practical need. The Soviets needed their bomb and further development of atomic experiments. They needed to match new American weapons and thus they *had* to study the new physics which ran against Newtonian principles. At that time I wrote a story called 'Expedition in the Opposite Direction' where the inspiration was Heisenberg's Principle, that is, free will. I wrote a story, 'Inventor of His Own Undoing', that describes the drawbacks of the ideal communist society, when man has no motivation for his initiative, as well as a story called 'Pirate Island' that described a company of virtuous men who, with the aim of rescuing innocent inhabitants of an island paradise from pirates, compelled them to defend themselves by methods far worse than those the pirates were using. These stories appeared towards the end of the 1950s and became very popular. In the situation I described above, it was the only way possible of arguing with official ideology. I was stunned by the number of people who bought my books at that time.

Simultaneously with this, literature became important in the Cold War. You could of course have shot down a U2 or killed some intruders at the border, but it is difficult to shoot down ideas, especially those of fictitious science. And to tell the truth, in this way many nonconformist writers from Eastern Europe became popular and far better known than their Western colleagues. They even got more money, as the censors could forbid some lines in a book, but rarely a whole book and its sale if the theme was of an allegorical nature. It is this situation that is sometimes regretted by writers since the Soviet Union's implosion. To continue with my case, I was lucky enough to get my stories translated and published, not only in German, which was easier at that time, but also in English. I even attended my first Convention in Oakland in 1964 and later Hollywood, where my story about a vampire car was planned twenty years before Stephen King's *Christine*. Again the explanation is practical: Eastern European production and labour costs were much cheaper and small firms liked to produce in Prague or Belgrade.

At that time science fiction became popular in Prague. Several Anglo-Saxon authors appeared, Bradbury and Clarke among them, and even my visitor George M. got his attempts published. Science fiction was fashionable and it was understood also as a political protest. Younger writers started to write it. One of my colleagues discovered von Daniken and became popular too. The whole situation seemed to be changing.

Until the Soviets came for the second time, in 1968.

But it was soon clear that the World's End of the 1950s could not be repeated. They themselves had other aims. Neither could there be achieved a homogenization of culture which would match their own. Vital values had to be preserved—and with them, science fiction. As emphasis was given to the so-called 'second industrial revolution', our genre was thought to be indispensible. I myself had to leave Prague and the clinic, with the help of that very colleague who invited me to see George M., but I was not arrested for cosmopolitan heresy or links with capitalism, as would surely have been the case in the 1950s. I simply had to work outside the city. At the same time masses of young writers, especially, started writing science fiction. It was the third generation now. And they were using allegory: ecological, social, biological, what have you. In the 1980s a director of the biggest publishing house complained to me that all new manuscripts coming in from young authors were sf! He could not admit it to the party authorities, he said. Surely this was bad from its viewpoint? The young had found a way to circumvent censorship. 'They say it with flowers,' he said. 'Sometimes very ugly blossoms, believe me.' This was the first indicator of the system's end.

But the meeting with George M. that I want to report on preceded this stage by several years.

In my sanatorium we practised what you would call community therapy, a sort of group psychotherapy with some thirty patients. Here I want to explain that the life of a doctor who was a rather well-known (and sometimes proscribed) writer was not at all easy. Sometimes I thought that I was writing sf not just to let it be suspected that I 'stole' the secrets my patients were giving away. But soon I found out that they were more flattered. And in their fantasies they started to 'decode' the allegories and metaphors, finding out what I never intended. This brought me even to the decision to write a special book, on sf only as the subject of psychotherapy. And I also tried to use literature in the healing process through 'bibliotherapy' where we prepared two kinds of books from which the patients could choose. One was the 'utopian': Thomas More, Bellamy and some idyllic authors of our own. The other was 'dystopian and horror'. The patients, people with stress and psychosomatic symptoms, neurotics, in need of what we call 'little psychiatry', mostly chose the second, the dark set. This could help in the eternal argument: does art corrupt, or rid one of bad intentions? Is the role of literature pedagogical or cathartic? Certainly it seemed that towards the end of the twentieth century people preferred reading about the end of our world and the horrors of the future than about the bright perspectives the next century could bring.

'There is, of course, another kind of science fiction,' my colleague was explaining to me in his room after we left George M. in his cell. My colleague was extremely cordial, as if his criticism of my cosmopolitan heresy was forgotten. He indicated the books on his desk: 'I have become a reader of the genre myself! Don't be surprised. I even read your books,' he said, as if he wanted to flatter me. 'And so I realized that we have always had here a branch of the genre intended for adolescents, a sort of fairy-tale. This has no political meaning and has to be judged ideologically, as fairy-tales are...' He obviously still remembered that even children's tales were banned in the 1950s for cruelty and sadistic tendencies. 'We have no tradition of the Gothic novel and Tolkien would be unthinkable here. From the time of the national rebirth in the nineteenth century, literature and culture have always been political and our language the most valued treasure of the nation... This "sf" is foreign: we don't even have a Czech name for it. I think it belongs to the fashionable Americanization of our culture, as does the word "dealer", "rock" and "McDonald's". Fantasy of this kind cannot therefore be explained as escape from reality or regression...'

He indicated a volume on his desk. 'As you surely know, there exist several studies of sf by psychiatrists, especially those of the psychoanalytical orientation.' A remarkable development from the time that he criticized genetics and Drosophila!

Even if I had never specialized in working with psychotics, it had occurred to me that sf material has often been incorporated in their delusions. People are not being followed and governed by angels or radio waves; they are watched by TV and spoken to by little green men. I even encountered a fellow writer in Moscow, a specialist in the Tunguz meteorite, who believed that he was visited by three little green men—'So big,' he said, indicating twice the height of his desk—who were apparently in the uniform of the Soviet artillery but really this was their green uniform and they used special code, understandable only to them.

The use and understanding of codes plays a big role. At our clinic we had a patient for a year, a member of the Czech counter-intelligence before the war, who insisted that his wife, who had deserted him and was now running a small pub in the country, used her beer tap to communicate with aliens and prepare for their invasion. At the harder times of our lives, in the 1950s and 1970s, when the secret police was all-mighty, we had constant visits by young officers because our patient complained that he was not taken seriously. His case history resembled a medieval hand-written bible and these young officers always spent many hours with it, laughing in the end, as they found written there the names of their superiors, who in their youth had also taken these delusions for the truth. I smiled now myself, as it seemed that my colleague had invited me not because of our George M. but rather to settle old accounts and to show good will in a situation that seemed to be changing once more.

'The truth is that in fantasy our patients express their distorted relation to reality. The Freudians speak of the disappearance of the censorship barrier and regression. A paper by Doctor Franck was published in the year 1960. He tried to document his findings by stressing that the sf of that time had very few female heroes, there was little family life and the heroes lived and fought in a sort of isolation. He also described the phenomenon, typical in psychosis, of omnipotence, where huge armies are available at will and come out of the mind of the hero. Therefore he considered Fantasy as an escape from reality caused by casualties in interpersonal relations. I don't think you can say this today, after Barbarella, Ursula Le Guin and all those female sf writers that have been published. Sf certainly has become aware of sex since that time.'

My colleague was a little uneasy:

'But the lack of communication persists. Our patients as well as your heroes try to express by their fantasies something they don't dare to say in reality, wouldn't you agree? Think only of that famous collection of pictures by psychotics, collected by Dr Hans Prinzhorn of Heidelberg in the twenties! They were so similar to the then modern art that they were immediately adored by surrealists and others, and of course hated by the Nazis in Germany, who called them *entartete Kunst*.'

'To show the reaction of Authority,' I said. 'Today the authorities behave differently. They try to ignore us. Shut us in a ghetto, don't take us seriously. And if we are too noisy, as Dick was, for instance, they call us really mad. I worked with a professor in the States whose favourite saying was "A madman is a man who is disliked by his community." And I can document this myself. During my stay in Vietnam, I was told that they had no psychotics at all and didn't need me. Soon I found out that the village people simply turned these patients out into the jungle, to their voices, they said. There exists a lot of folklore about this, yet little medical study. All primitive communities seem to evict people who are thoroughly disliked in the same way. But tell me, how does our George M. and my story fit into all this?'

'Does he live in your fantasies because of you? Is he afraid of you? As you were afraid of the communist censors, when you wrote your stories?' answered the Drosophila-hater with a wicked smile. 'Perhaps he just wants to triumph. Certainly his hallucinations are not compulsive. They do not direct him anywhere, make him do anything he would not like to do. He came here stuffed with catalogues from the big warehouses, pretending this was the stuff of your automated planet. Certainly they are beginning with the process here, but we still have to pay for their merchandise, we still have to work and look after our families.'

'Perhaps it is because of this that you don't understand him.''

I knew the style of our clinic. They examine every patient thoroughly, in biological terms, but they hardly ever speak to his relatives, in the old pre-Freudian Austro-Hungarian tradition. I therefore decided to visit the family of George M. myself. I was somehow in debt to him.

'I shall never speak to him again,' his father said, when I saw him. 'He is not my son any more...' His hands trembled with emotion. He was already quite grey but still held his body as erect as an officer of the Prussian army. 'I discovered what his so-called studies are, he was lying down all day with those dirty books, some of them by you, Doctor, don't try to deny that. You belong to those who corrupt our youth. I can say that as a specialist, having been a Professor of Literature my whole life. I can read the real meaning of your so-called books.'

I thought I had heard such insinuations already, years before, when the state censor accused me but couldn't prove anything. Our genre makes authorities crazy, censors as much as fathers.

'But I am not here because of a literary argument,' I said. 'It's the problem of your son that brings me to you. He is behaving strangely.'

'He's mocking me, that's all. He is trying to drive me out of my mind. I am the one who has problems, Doctor. My only son behaving like a gorilla! Accusing me of hedonism. Look around. We do have some old furniture here, which I bought with my own money. I have a car and a *dacha*, like every university dignitary. That doesn't make me consumer-minded. I am not changing into an ape or a pig because of that, neither are other members of my family. I burnt all his books, that's the reason he behaves like he does. I threw out his girlfriend from these "Friends of the Earth". I won't speak to my son as long as he behaves like this. He doesn't read science fiction any longer, he tries to live it as in your own story, sir. You should be ashamed of yourself.'

The father was stubborn and sure of himself, like all Authorities used to be. I therefore went to look for the girlfriend. She was a fragile little being with green eyes, busy planning a trip with her friends to southern Bohemia where large circles of unknown origin had been discovered in ripe wheat fields.

'George is not ill,' she said. 'All that he does has a meaning. He is trying to protest, that's all. Using your story because it resembles his family. Playing Excalibur, or pretending to be a hobbit would not get him anywhere. He pretends to have turned into an ape because the needs of his family are animal-like.'

So I had to return to my colleague in the clinic. I tried to change his mind.

'You said yourself that the so-called hallucinations of George M. are not compulsive, that he just plays with his delusions and can tell reality from his fantasies; he has, therefore, what you could call insight. It reminds me of a famous case diagnosed before the war by our previous Professor S. His case was a professor of linguistics who, after his wife deserted him, started a fantasy of his own: that she was a visitor from the planet Astron, a double of our Earth; that she visited him with an encyclopaedia of that planet because he himself was in his previous life one of its inhabitants. The patient was an obsessive writer. He devised not only a geography of the planet, its states and borders, but also three different languages with complete vocabularies, a timetable of Astron's trains and stamps for its postal service. When I met him, shortly after the war, his only complaint was that his writing paper had been rationed and that he could fill far more than those thirty pages a day. When he died, all that he created was inherited by the State archives of literature, because our professor insisted that his fantasies were not delusions. Nor did he suffer from a split personality, but had what he called "his own individual myth". I think that it's the same with George.'

'An individual myth? Common to all writers of science fiction? And admired by their readers?'

'We are discussing a psychiatric case not a literary problem,' I said. But my colleague was far from seeking an argument.

'If you can guarantee that he won't be a danger to his surroundings...'

I promised to talk to George about this.

'Of course I want to be a danger,' said George stubbornly, in his cell. 'I pretend to become an ape only to mirror the behaviour of people around me. Also yours, Doctor...' and for the first time he looked directly into my eyes. He had avoided this at our previous meetings. 'Because a man whose needs are fulfilled will not turn into an ape or a pig, you understand. He will become what he is designed to be: namely a part of the cosmic conscience! That is what we are all about, our being on Earth. This is our destiny...'

And he left the clinic walking on his feet, erect like *homo sapiens*. He left for Southern Bohemia, to study those crop circles with his girlfriend. And I have never heard about him since.

Science Fiction as Language: Postmodernism and Mainstream: Some Reflections

JOSÉ MANUEL MOTA

When one asks 'Who speaks science fiction?' this mode of literary expression which we call science fiction is itself, however metaphorically, assumed to be a language. A 'style', a 'genre', even a 'mode' is in a certain sense a language—it has its codes, its vocabulary, its life: the romantic theory of language as a living organism might suit the purpose of the argument.

Since science fiction is a kind of language, then it is *spoken*; but it is not as a language spoken by *whom* that it should interest us here; it is as a language spoken by *what*—by other languages. What I mean is that different media have taken over science fiction, re-encoding it; and, if not interchangeable, all these call attention to their respective materiality and, by implication, to the material nature of 'writing'. The medium is *not* the message—nor is it the language; but it is the material condition of the language. Black signs on white paper, images on celluloid or magnetic tape or other technological devices, interactive computer games, are media: and they interact for two main reasons, one formal, one material.

Formally, whatever shape a text may take, it is ultimately reducible or at least referable to the same symbolic system: human language. Beyond this formal aspect, which derives from the theory and philosophy of language and thought, there is also another very concrete and material point establishing a bridge between the different media: the commodity nature of everything made in contemporary society, the more or less obscure interests that condition the 'necessary' interplay of mass media. A book is written and, if successful, it will eventually become a film, soon afterwards a home video; the film version will be in its turn novelized;[1] stickers and toys will be sold; a computer game will soon be put on sale— encoded in the different formats required by the different brands of machines—marketing the characters and adventures which have become so popular. One may deplore, criticize, disagree, theorize, but one cannot help recognizing the mutual benefits for the different media[2] deriving from this circumstance. What is then the place of sf in our world as a language? In other words: is sf a language in its own right? Is it just a model, a sort of Whorfian way of organizing reality? And if so, how does science fiction 'organize' reality?

All this brings us to the question of literature. In these days of multimedia, where does science fiction stand as a literary form? In order to attempt to clarify some of these questions, I will start with some preliminary reflections and then proceed tentatively to my line of argument: words, words, words...

1. When, in *Brave New World* (ch. 12), the Savage reads Shakespeare to Helmholtz Watson, there is a very curious aspect in the latter's reaction which I do not recall as being noticed before. Watson is in a certain way an obvious *persona* of the author — but not of Huxley the 'novelist of ideas': rather of Huxley the poet, the creator of literary objects, the word craftsman. But Watson is what he and his fellow World State citizens call an 'emotional engineer': he conceives his word-craftsmanship as a way to generate emotions in his audience (his public). He is the Brave New World's equivalent of our time's literary author: but he has degenerated (as the Brave New World is a degeneration) into what in our days is an advertising agent, inventing slogans in order to make people adopt certain behaviours. He has written a poem—that is, 'rhymes'—moved by a certain state of mind: the emotional sense of emptiness after a sort of Saturday night fever has triggered in Watson the writing of the poem; and he expects that the reading of that poem by others (his students) will trigger the same sort of emotion: sexual and social misery, etc. This is perfectly in tune with the novel's expectations: it is behaviourism (one of the main targets of Huxley's satire) taken to its ultimate consequences.

Now, when Watson comes to Shakespeare, he does not show any understanding of the situations depicted. We may smile, like him, at the rigours of old-fashioned codes of behaviour, be it in *Romeo and Juliet* or in other more incongruous situations, like *The Merchant of Venice*, or *All's Well*, or *Measure for Measure*; we accept the dramatic conventions and we recognize (even when poetically disguised) the historical circumstances of the plays, of Shakespeare and his time. This is impossible for Helmholtz Watson: for he has no sense of history ('history is bunk') and he has no sense of literature either—only a strictly formalistic sense of literariness, one might say. He is, then, a post-historical figure, a post-literary figure: does that make him a postmodern figure?[3]

'History is bunk', by which is meant, in Huxley's book, that history is a story told by His Fordship to the young students in the first three chapters. It also means that Utopia has suspended history: the (nominally Wellsian) World State is here to stay. What of literature, then?

All this could be the fulfilment of the wildest postmodernist dreams, proposals, theses: the end of history *and* the end of literature. It is probably illicit to extrapolate from what is a typical early 1930s book to the postmodernist theory(-ies) of fiction at the end of the century; but it may also be that it is after all legitimate to do it: if *Brave New World* does not partake of 'magic realism' (which appeared at the same time),[4] it may nonetheless be useful to read it as an anticipatory comment of some of the nowadays current literary processes or strategies, particularly in this area of the semiotics of the arts. Brian McHale 'constructs' his theory of postmodernism in this way—reading older texts in an evolutionistic or (as his reviewer Csicery-Ronay[5] terms it) 'developmental' light.

It is a pity to me that McHale does not 'confront' the Helmholtz Watson–John the Savage–William Shakespeare situation. In *Constructing Postmodernism* there is a single reference to Huxley and *Brave New World*, apropos the 'feelies' and the 'simstim' of Gibson's *Neuromancer*.[6] And let me add in an aside that it is precisely about the feelies that, when the Savage says 'They don't mean anything', the World Controller retorts: 'They mean themselves' (ch. 16). The fact (or the point of view) that an alleged work of 'art', or its surrogate, is reduced to signifying itself, its emptiness of other meanings, is in my view also 'postmodernist' in its unabashed reductionism.

I am personally not fully convinced of McHale's theory that postmodernism has an ontological, while modernism has an epistemological stance towards the world, at least in so far as sf is concerned and adopted as a model for postmodernism; I still believe, with Suvin, that science fiction is an eminently epistemological genre. But there is a line of argument in McHale's earlier book, *Postmodernist Fiction*, which could help me understand his theory. I quote, '[s]cience fiction, like postmodernist fiction, is governed by the ontological dominant. Indeed, it is perhaps *the* ontological genre *par excellence*. We can think of science fiction as postmodernism's non-canonized or "low art" double, its sister-genre in the same sense that the popular detective thriller is modernist fiction's sister-genre'.[7] This is all very well, and it will surely work as more than a mere hypothesis, especially as a historical argument.[8] But science fiction and detective fiction share a peculiar way of looking at objects: that is, a pragmatic way of looking at and describing their own objective fictional universe, both genres taking into account the material and technological circumstances (in science fiction, particularly in hard sf, the attention to mechanical devices; in detective novels very careful and detailed descriptions of actions, things, living persons, with obvious relevance to the solving of the mystery).

So I believe that both genres are epistemological in this sense: that they both are eminently cognitive and rational. *But...* there is a but. One may remember that, in his book on 'the Fantastic', Eric S. Rabkin discusses both genres as partaking of that elusive category.[9] I would plead that what makes the difference between the two genres, more than the alleged ontology or epistemology, is their distance from the fantastic. Of course, crime novels have never intended to seem or be fantastic,[10] at least in the sense of pertaining to fantasy; they tend to be 'strictly rational', and it is we who may read a fantastic quality into their world. Science fiction also likes to demarcate its field from that of fantasy. Nevertheless rationality, at least a positivistic rationality, may be discarded at some level; the relationship between sf and fantasy is quite another story.

2. In his *Science Fiction Studies* review, back in 1982, of two books by Patrick Parrinder, Fredric Jameson made this short historico-theoretical reflexion:

> I have myself been attracted to Asimov's stages theory (of American sf): Stage One (1926–38), adventure dominant; Stage Two (1938–1950), technology dominant; Stage Three (1950–?), sociology dominant. Twenty years later we can probably date the end of Stage Three from the mid-'60s, and add a fourth stage ('aesthetics dominant') whose 'new wave' preoccupations with myth and language goes into some kind of crisis in the mid-'70s and leaves the field divided into feminist sf on the one hand and a regressive resurgence of 'fantasy' on the other.[11]

Here the 'new wave' is recognized as a literary coming of age of science fiction. But this coming of age was the consequence of a long march, which had started back in the early 1950s, when *The Magazine of Fantasy and Science Fiction* and *Galaxy* were launched. As James Gunn points out in one of the best chapters of his *Alternate Worlds*,

> *The Magazine of Fantasy and Science Fiction* was based on the belief that science fiction could be literature and that a literary approach that included fantasy would be viable on the news-stands. In the Boucher-McComas magazine, the distinction between science fiction and fantasy was not so great as it would have been in *Astounding*: literary science fiction tends to resemble fantasy. ... Science fiction and literature seem poles apart. Fantasy and literature, on the other hand, are inseparable; fantasy, ...that deals...with myth and legend[,] has

as long a history as literature itself; they are interwoven and in some ways identical.[12]

'Literary science fiction *tends* to resemble fantasy'. Here lies the crux of the problem: an ontogeny and a phylogeny of science fiction are being established on the basis of two fundamental assumptions. First, that in order to become literature, science fiction must come nearer to fantasy; second, that, in spite of the cognitive opposition between science fiction and fantasy, this is perhaps not as impossible as it seems, since, after all, whenever sf attempts self-justification, it usually claims as its forerunners texts like the *Odyssey*, or Lucian's *True History*, or *The Thousand and One Nights* (the first volume of Gunn's anthology *The Road To Science Fiction* is called 'From *Gilgamesh* to Wells', although no excerpt from the Akkadian poem is included): that is, science fiction silently acknowledges its fantastic descent and its origin in canonic literature.

One might speak of 'sf in search of a higher status'. And yet: this invocation of venerable texts goes along, self-contradictorily, with the attitudes of those who glorify sf's marginality *per se* and whose war cry is 'leave it in the gutter'...

Now, again in the words of James Gunn, *Galaxy*, the other magazine relevant for the renewal of sf, 'wanted well-written stories, but it was not willing...to accept literary quality as a substitute for narrative excitement'.[13] Nonetheless, the attitude towards the world, and the type of hero demanded by Horace Gold in *Galaxy* (during the so-called 'sociology dominant' period of Asimov's) paved indeed the way to utopia, anti-utopia, satire, parody—literary forms and processes widely explored in more recent years in mainstream literature. Many justly famous works published in *Galaxy* are fine examples supporting my idea: Bester's *Tiger! Tiger!*, a re-writing of *Monte-Cristo*; Blish's 'Surface Tension', a parody of space opera; Pohl and Kornbluth's *The Space Merchants*, a notorious dystopia (albeit with a genre happy ending, or a partially happy one). And, last but not least, the emphasis laid on the heroes as coherent individuals and as interacting with social forces (even if those forces are technologically oriented) is also an advancement in the literary treatment of character. So, what Asimov contends (and Jameson endorses) to be the sociology dominant, in the 1950s, indeed entails an improvement in 'literary' standards (i.e., the standards of mainstream literature).

All this means that the genre was awakening to a new conscience of itself; sf starts to be aware that it *is* 'Literature'. But how was that to be done? Precisely, by putting into practice an ontogenetic theory—bringing science fiction nearer to fantasy and literature (*mainstream* literature)— whence a self-justificatory phylogeny is made to derive. Or vice versa: starting with a phylogenetic theory of science fiction as descending from fantastic literature, and applying accordingly the ontogenetic view of a hierarchy sf is made to comply with. The two views are intricately mingled. This phenomenon begins *before* the full development of the 'aesthetics dominant'—before the strong literary, experimental thrust of the (originally British) 'New Wave'. In commenting on this aspect of the history of science fiction, I am focusing largely on the American, rather than the British, search for a 'literary awareness'.

This new self-awareness of sf, which had indeed started with the appearance soon after the War of the two first major anthologies (Groff Conklin's, and Healy and McComas's, both 1946), and followed by the publication of the first doctoral thesis on sf (James O. Bailey's, 1947), ends up with the (ontogenetic) theorizing of James Gunn in 1975 (but see also his article 'Science Fiction and the Mainstream' from 1974), and with the idiosyncratic (phylogenetic) theorizing of Brian Aldiss in *Billion Year Spree* (1973).

This rise in literary status, if it has not suffered setbacks, has nonetheless caused negative reactions: it is curious to note the nostalgic pose in the late Kingsley Amis, when he says

> It would be a rash prophet who ruled out any hope of recovery from the present state of the genre. One day, perhaps, the last doctoral thesis on it will be filed away and the Institute of Science Fiction in Higher Education disbanded, the trend will move to the academic study of pornography or of the works of Harold Robbins, and a new spontaneity will become possible. But I am not hopeful. Science fiction has lost its innocence, a quality notoriously hard to recapture.[14]

3. Its innocence lost, science fiction was now, like Adam and Eve, ready for history—and for literature; leaving the shores of the legendary timeless river flowing through Eden and entering the real world of *mainstream* Tigris and Euphrates. That loss of innocence was being acutely felt in those days. Among others, the cases of Kurt Vonnegut, Jr. and Philip K. Dick can be taken as paradigmatic. One by success, the other by frustration, these two important writers (sometimes compared—unfairly,[15] I should say—by academic critics) have maintained an uneasy relationship with mainstream literature. If we substitute 'ghetto' for 'gutter' in the anti-academic slogan, one might say that Vonnegut was the man who managed not to stay in the ghetto, while Dick was the man who (at least during his lifetime) did not quite manage to get out of it.

Vonnegut's fight for respectability in spite of writing what was after all termed sf has brought him its fruits; Dick's attitude is more interesting from an intra-generic point of view. He is the typical sf man: he starts tentatively, has lessons in creative writing, sells his first short stories, then begins an irregular career as a novelist. But he has a secret wish: to become famous as a mainstream writer. And he shares at the same time the notion that we have seen spelled out in James Gunn, that fantasy is 'better than' science fiction. He believes himself a *good* fantasy writer.[16] And so he believes he can make it as a mainstream author—fantasy is just one step removed from mainstream literature.

We all know that it was not that easy for Dick: that he never indeed made it, that he remained an sf author all his life. On the other hand, his science fiction was factually a blend of fantasy, an idiosyncratic literary form opening new ways in science fiction and, more than that, leaving its imprint on mainstream authors (and here we have the usual reference to Pynchon[17]). And, through the movie *Blade Runner* (1982), an interference in the 'cyberpunk' atmosphere of the 1980s. I personally interpret the way Dick violated the conventions of science fiction as a step forward—one of the possible steps forward—in the development of the genre: his is a very personal way of writing science fantasy. When we say that Dick's novels make no sense, it is because the sense of his novels is not in their plots: it is a type of meaning which derives from the fantastic, obeying not the cognitive logic of 'orthodox' sf but the inner, literary logic of fantasy.

This was not always the case. *Solar Lottery* (1955) was one exception; it was solid; Damon Knight said then that it was 'like van Vogt miraculously making sense'.[18] *The Man in the High Castle* was another (although alternate-world stories verge on fantasy). All the rest shows two elements in a strange mixture: a van-Vogtian streak towards muddled plots; and a shift towards fantasy. Given that all the fresh blood in science fiction arriving with the 1950s paid its homage to fantasy, could one say that it was Philip K. Dick's lot to bring van Vogt to mainstream literature?

I am going to try to make my point clear with one example, incidentally not taken from sf. Reading Paul Auster's *New York Trilogy*, I was left with the sensation of having read a pastiche of detective fiction which appears as a labyrinthine collage of words and loose bits of plot leading nowhere. There are plenty of allusions, of innuendoes, but they reveal themselves as gratuitous, meaningless, as if you were trying to extract the square root of a text by Samuel Beckett (and you gave up at the end). All those elements just 'mean themselves', as Mustapha Mond had said to the Savage about the feelies. It could be said that the eminently postmodern work of Auster uses a genre in order to build a story which doesn't cohere.

Conversely, a tremendously successful (inside the ghetto) writer of incoherent story lines, A.E. van Vogt, was consciously being imitated by another writer, who (sometimes) made sense out of it (i.e. of van Vogt's plotting methods).[19] That is to say, Auster takes the ultimate coherent and logical form of mass literature (there are no loose ends in a detective story!) and builds playfully (or irritatingly, according to the reader's taste) a messy plot; Dick, at least in *Solar Lottery*, makes of the messy van Vogt a 'straight' genre novel.

There are of course lots of loose ends and threads leading nowhere in many of Dick's books; one could perhaps say that van Vogt got the better of him. As John Huntington has said, 'Dick, like van Vogt, and like other popular sf writers such as Heinlein or Herbert, has learned how to give the impression of deep understanding simply by contradicting himself. ... In this van Vogtian system the reader is simply yanked from understanding to understanding'.[20] What is real, however, is that even out of those factually crass errors you can make sense; among those chunks put together building either what Kim S. Robinson termed 'broken backed novels',[21] or works where Dick himself 'read it over, and drew a diagram, just to see if by any chance it all cohered. It doesn't. It can't be made to work out',[22] there can be found many little gems which will surely survive the strict condemnation, on formal terms, of the works they are encased in. But I will insist on the fact that many of these texts, which 'do not cohere', can still be saved through the literary logic of (science) fantasy.

4. I have just mentioned the connection of Dick to cyberpunk, via the Dick-based film *Blade Runner*. I feel obliged to make a few passing remarks about the genre, if only because I have mentioned McHale's thesis, and in his later book he explicitly supports the idea that cyberpunk sf shares 'the poetics of postmodernism'. One feels the obvious compulsion to cite once more the first footnote of Jameson's *Postmodernism* about cyberpunk being 'henceforth, for many of us, the supreme *literary* expression if not of postmodernism, then of late capitalism itself'.[23] That titillating or tantalizing remark has been commented upon, interpreted, appropriated by others; its singularity and shortness makes it, more than fruitful, 'enigmatic'.[24]

My greatest doubts concerning the cyberpunk phenomenon come from the *déjà vu* sensation left by such works.[25] I recall Dick's *Solar Lottery*, where people's brains are used (cybernetically) to drive the body of a killer android; or Silverberg's *Tower of Glass* (1970), where an android (Dick-wise, a very human person), connects himself to a cybermachine; Fred Pohl's 'We Purchased People' (1974) or, much earlier, his 'The Tunnel Under the World' (1954); or the many other examples of people's brains made into or wired to machines (the three brains that pilot the ship in Simak's *Shakespeare's Planet* [1976] come to my mind). The now current notion of 'virtual reality' may have been anticipated by these examples; the 'punkishness' was not always there, but it came with the times. There

is nothing strictly cyberpunkish in Ballard's 'The ICU' (1977), and yet...
Ballard's story is a rewriting in the age of mass media of the part of Forster's
'The Machine Stops' (1909) that concerns family ties; the violence and the
virtuality, and the virtualities of violence, are all there.[26]

There is another reason for bypassing the discussion: not only that
cyberpunk is a pseudo-novelty, but that it is a thing of the past. I think
that cyberpunk is going (gone?) out of fashion, and this for the following
reason: that perhaps all this email, surfing-the-Internet craze and what
goes along with it in the realm of computer technology stands to cyberpunk
as the Space Age (from Sputnik I to Apollo XIII) once stood to good old
hard sf. Future has arrived, overtaken cyberpunk, and taken over. And if
there once was a sense of distress at being overtaken by facts which were
the private field of speculation of authors and readers of science fiction
(which may have been the feeling after the first Moon landing), now there
appears to be nothing tragic in it: science fiction is alive and well; it has
survived, it has diversified, it is less and less constrained in a genre category,
it impinges on mainstream literature, on history, on our lives in the
postmodern world of media.

5. So the question to be put here should be about science fiction at large.
It appears that we are finally back at where we have begun: 'What is then
the place of sf in our world *as a language*?' by which will be meant, in a
more cultural context: how is it that our genre is a model for understanding
postmodern society (i.e., a human community generating cultural
artefacts)? Sf's presence is pervasive in our technological way of life; it has
become a crucial reference. It is once more the old dreams of the 'Golden
Age' come true: that science fiction has prepared people for the future, and
we find out that sf was right, and the future is really now. The 'Star Wars'
project petered out, but a more Earth-bound science, centred on
communications and information technologies, has been contributing to
the 'société du spectacle'; and sf has quite a large share in the show.

Now is it time to return to Huxley's *Brave New World*. From the beginning
of the twentieth century, capitalism had evolved towards its monopoly
stage: it was the first phase of the consumer society. When modernism
appears (say, around World War I), Lenin theorizes this new development
of world economy: *Imperialism, or the Highest Stage of Capitalism* dates from
1917, the year of Eliot's *Prufrock*.[27] Fifteen years later Aldous Huxley
summarized what had been happening since the war in his satire—and he
aptly chose Fordism as its central target.

Brave New World is neither 'a mirror' of Fordist society, nor 'a model for
understanding modernist society', at least in the sense that science fiction
is now allegedly a model for postmodernism. Postmodern society, or 'late

& p7-41

capitalist' society, is also post-Fordist: the organization of distribution and consumption does not quite follow the same model. Fordism was totalitarian. Henry Ford's ideal was the complete conformism of consumers: the true freedom of choice in the liberal paradise is that all consumers choose the same (the Ford Model T). Philip K. Dick's obsession with monopolies, cartels, and what Peter Fitting called 'the strange identification of religion and capitalist consumerism'[28] is still one aspect of the metaphorical divinization of industrial capitalism present in *Brave New World*. Today however there is an apparent freedom of choice, a diversified offer: instead of being urged to give up Can-D and adopt Chew-Z, as in Dick's *The Three Stigmata of Palmer Eldritch* (1964), you may choose between Pepsi and Coke (and between straight, decaffeinated or Diet Coke); that is, 'in post-Fordism, as well as what has widely come to be called postmodern marketing, cybernetic and information techniques allow the product *minimally* to be tailored to its consumers' cultural needs and specifications … the new modes of distribution (the fundamental trait of post-Fordism as a concept) can be parlored into a rhetoric of consumption and of the market as an ideological value'.[29]

There is some obvious hermeneutic intention behind theses like 'sf is typically postmodernist', and such theses are then necessarily reductionist, as far as they are a selectively organized consideration of an object for a determinate purpose: science fiction is not just that, it has a long history, through to its present maturity. Sf, be it a genre inside the mainstream, be it a 'non-canonized or "low art' double" as in McHale's words, is a mode of literary expression.

The fact remains that there is no film (even a silent movie), no video-game, that cannot be put into words; and conversely, that any graphic or diagram, with all its strength (the strength of the Chinese saying, that an image is worth a thousand words), is always ancillary or explanatory to some point first made through words. I believe in the pre-eminence of language as such—*words* are such stuff as literature, and sf, is made on. 'Words can be like X-rays, if you use them properly—they'll go through anything. You read and you're pierced', said Helmholtz Watson (*Brave New World*, ch. 4). So there is no risk of loss for literature or sf as literature, even through the jungle of new technologies. Poor Helmholtz's malaise was, among other things, that he could not get beyond his 'rhymes'; thus he missed part of his Shakespeare. We are stuck in a Brave New World of sorts, and it appears to be our duty to keep on, exploring our feelies and simstims for sure, but also not forgetting our Shakespeare: exploiting the new ways and means of expressing ourselves, and holding fast at the same time to the power of words.

Notes

1 There will be 'Movie Novelizations, Novelizations, Re-novelizations, Secondary Novelizations, Semi-novelizations, Spinoff Fiction, Storybooks, Tie-ins' (David Pringle, 'Sf, Fantasy and Horror Movie Novelizations', *Interzone* 80 [February 1994], pp. 40–41).

2 'Benefits' are here to be understood in a strictly material sense: I mean the mutual stimulation of technicians for the solving of conversion problems, new inventions as by-products of the solving of such problems, the new possibilities opened by that interplay, etc.

3 Throughout this essay I will use the word 'postmodern(ist)' both systematically and as vaguely as possible: that is, it will include in its semantic field its artistic, economic, historic and/or philosophic (if any) overtones: late capitalism, post-industrialism, 'société du spectacle', etc. Cf. Fredric Jameson, *Postmodernism, or the Cultural Logic of Late Capitalism* (Durham, NC: Duke University Press, 1991), p. xviii.

4 Borges's *Historia Universal de la Infamia* dates from 1935, three years later than Huxley's work.

5 István Csicery-Ronay, Jr., 'An Elaborate Suggestion', *Science Fiction Studies* 20.3 (1993), p. 458.

6 Brian McHale, *Constructing Postmodernism* (London and New York: Routledge, 1992), p. 259.

7 Brian McHale, *Postmodernist Fiction* (New York & London: Methuen, 1987) p. 59. Incidentally, here (as elsewhere) it is naturally assumed that 'pomo' hasn't after all brought down the barriers between 'high' and 'low' or popular culture.

8 It is remarkable that it was during modernism that the detective story came of age, with Dashiell Hammett, as it was with postmodernism that the same happened to science fiction.

9 Eric S. Rabkin, *The Fantastic in Literature* (Princeton, NJ: Princeton University Press, 1977), p. 136.

10 If we were to accept Todorov's theory of the fantastic, many detective stories (for example, the closed room murders; but *The Hound of the Baskervilles* would be an early example, as would be Poe's Tales of Mystery) would fit into his category of the marvellous, where the apparently fantastic is explained away in rational terms.

11 'Towards a New Awareness of the Genre', *Science Fiction Studies* 9.3 (1982), p. 323. (As a caveat, let it be remembered that Asimov was fiercely anti-'new wave' and is used by Jameson in context as a point of departure for a new periodization).

12 James Gunn, *Alternate Worlds. The Illustrated History of Science Fiction* (New York: A & W Visual Library, 1975), p. 214.

13 Gunn, *Alternate Worlds*, p. 216.

14 Kingsley Amis, sel. & introd., *The Golden Age of Science Fiction. An Anthology* (Harmondsworth: Penguin, 1983), p. 36.

15 When I say unfairly, I do not mean that it is not the right of the critic to say that A is better than (or indebted to) B, and state his/her reasons for the assertion; I mean that the bases of comparison between the two writers are perhaps not the most legitimate, since we are dealing with authors fairly different in temperament, upbringing, career, even (literary) interests.

16 'Okay, I started off as a fantasy writer. I didn't start off as a science fiction

writer. I wrote short fantasies for *F&SF* [*The Magazine of Fantasy and Science Fiction*]. And I only wrote science fiction because there was much more of a market [for it]. And my early science fiction was *very bad*. I was a very *bad* science fiction writer, but I was a very good fantasy writer, but outside Tony Boucher nobody existed to buy fantasy.' Gregg Rickmann, *Philip K. Dick: In His Own Words*, Revised Edition (Long Beach, CA: Fragments West/The Valentine Press, 1988 [1984]), p. 61.

17 Cf. Carl Freedman, 'Towards a Theory of Paranoia: The Science Fiction of Philip K. Dick' and 'Editorial Introduction: Philip K. Dick and Criticism', in R.D. Mullen, et al., eds., *On Philip K. Dick: 40 Articles from Science Fiction Studies* (Terre Haute & Greencastle, IN: SF-TH, Inc., 1992), pp. 117 and 145 respectively.

18 Damon Knight, *In Search of Wonder. Essays in Modern Science Fiction* (Chicago: Advent Press, 1967), p. 229.

19 Dick repeatedly acknowledged his admiration for van Vogt: 'he was my hero as a writer and as a person' (Rickmann, *Philip K. Dick: In His Own Words*, p. 113); 'van Vogt influenced me so much because he made me appreciate a mysterious chaotic quality in the universe which is not to be feared' (Arthur Byron Cover, 'Vertex Interviews Philip K. Dick', *Vertex*, 1.6 [February 1974], p. 36).

20 John Huntington, 'Philip K. Dick: Authenticity and Insincerity', in Mullen, et al., eds., *On Philip K. Dick*, p. 172.

21 Kim Stanley Robinson, *The Novels of Philip K. Dick* (Ann Arbor: UMI Research Press, 1984), pp. 85ff.

22 Dick is referring to *The Simulacra* in Rickmann, *Philip K. Dick: In His Own Words*, pp. 151–52.

23 Jameson, *Postmodernism*, p. 419.

24 McHale, *Constructing Postmodernism*, p. 13.

25 At the end of the 1980s Suvin was doubtful about the success of cyberpunk ('On Gibson and Cyberpunk SF', *Foundation* 46 [Autumn 1988], p. 50); Nicola Nixon demystified it later as old wine in new bottles ('Cyberpunk: Preparing the Ground for Revolution or Keeping the Boys Satisfied?' *Science Fiction Studies* 19.2 [1992], pp. 219–37). More recently, we meet the sensible and judicious appreciation of Edward James in his *Science Fiction in the 20th Century* (Oxford: Oxford University Press, 1994), especially pp. 193–97.

26 For the sake of brevity, I will not expatiate on 'techno-punk' objects like Ballard's (and later Cronenberg's) *Crash*.

27 It has been pointed out to me by my colleague Martin A. Kayman that Lenin's *Imperialism...* was based on (or plagiarized from) J. A. Hobson's *Imperialism*, a work published around 1909—incidentally, the year of Ezra Pound's *Personae*, another landmark of early modernism. This being not the moment for developing the point, whichever version of the temporal facts is accepted, my argument still holds.

28 '*Ubik*: The Deconstruction of Bourgeois SF', in Mullen, et al., eds., *On Philip K. Dick*, p. 44.

29 Fredric Jameson, *The Seeds of Time* (New York: Columbia University Press, 1994), p. 41 (my emphasis).

'Fantastic Dialogues': Critical Stories about Feminism and Science Fiction

HELEN MERRICK

Within the sf field, 'feminist science fiction' is not the misnomer it once was, although its existence still evokes surprise from some (mainstream) quarters. Feminist sf, while subject, as is sf generally, to definitional uncertainty, can now claim its own history, canonical authors, fans and dedicated branch of criticism.[1] Indeed, as Veronica Hollinger observes,

> the large number of feminist science fiction texts produced over the last twenty years or so now comprises a body of work no longer well served by criticism that reads it as a unified undertaking, i.e., individual texts all grounded upon the same ideological foundations and all working together for the promotion of a single coherent feminism.[2]

'Feminist sf' is thus a rather indeterminate and contested signifier, entailing potential disagreement over which texts fall under its rubric. A better approach may well be to focus on the impact of 'feminisms' (varying according to historical period, culture and generation) within sf. Lacking space to explore this further, I continue to employ the term 'feminist sf', while recognizing that it can refer to a broad and disparate range of texts, reflecting multiple articulations of feminism(s).[3]

Despite postmodernist claims for the dissolution of hi/lo culture boundaries, and arguments claiming sf's special status as a literature of the postmodern, within the literary mainstream sf is still devalued as a pop culture product to be consumed by the masses rather than analysed by literary critics.[4] Nevertheless, there is an array of critical stories about feminist sf both within and without the field, although for the most part, dialogue across the genre–mainstream border has been rare.

Feminist sf criticism is the most visible and authoritative discourse to speak of (and for) feminist sf. A less recognized source of critical knowledge within the sf field is the body of feminist authors and fans, who, at least within the sf (fan) community, are intimately engaged in the construction and development of 'feminist sf'. Outside the field, significantly different analyses are found in feminist literary criticism, utopian studies and genre studies, where sf is often incorporated into a more palatable tradition of feminist writing. The lack of interaction between various bodies of criticism engaging with feminist sf is evident in the various canons (of both fiction and criticism) constructed within each discourse, and also in the different intertextual dialogues implicit in each critical mode. Feminist sf criticism has as its context the sf critical community where the value and worth of sf is not questioned, but rather re-interrogated through a gendered analysis. In contrast, feminist literary criticism takes the expression of feminist concerns as a given, but the worth of sf as a mode of feminist expression is open to question. Recently, feminists from other disciplines, such as science, technology and 'cyberculture' studies, have produced critiques which situate feminist sf as an important contemporary cultural artefact, rather than an inferior literary sub-genre. This chapter surveys a number of these approaches to feminist sf, concluding with suggestions for expanded critical dialogues about feminism and science fiction.

While marginalized from the mainstream, feminist sf criticism has remained firmly based in literary critical models, only rarely drawing on other feminist theoretical projects, such as feminist film theory or cultural studies.[5] Feminist sf criticism initially developed from the critiques of fan/critics such as Susan Wood, Mary Kenny Badami and Beverley Friend, as well as authors Joanna Russ and Ursula Le Guin in sf journals and prozines in the 1970s.[6] This work provided an overtly feminist interpretation of an issue that had been debated since the beginning of the pulps—the 'women in sf' question. Russ was certainly not the first to criticise the appalling image of most female characters in sf. From at least the 1960s, critical works by Kingsley Amis, Sam Moskowitz, and Sam Lundwall for example bemoaned the failure of sf's extrapolative imagination when it came to the issue of gendered roles and relations.[7]

Early feminist sf criticism focused on women's portrayal in sf and the neglect of female authors, to support a critique of androcentric sf and its masculinist culture. Critical work developed from the championing of female authors and strong female characters ('women's sf') to a focus on overtly feminist texts and authors. In the process, what Sarah Lefanu termed 'feminized' sf has been somewhat abandoned by feminist sf critics.[8] Accounts of women's involvement in sf have largely been superseded by narratives tracing a history of feminist sf, with a change of focus in the criticism from 'women in sf' to feminism in sf. The resultant critical emphasis on a genealogy of feminist influence in sf has established a canon of texts (for example the works of Russ, Le Guin, James Tiptree Jr., Suzy McKee Charnas, Marge Piercy and Sally Miller Gearhart)[9] which dominates the content of feminist sf criticism, and reproduces a hierarchy of literary value mimicking the relationship of sf and canonical literature.[10] Others who do not easily fit the label of 'feminist author', such as Andre Norton, Marion Zimmer Bradley, and Kate Wilhelm, are neglected despite their importance as predecessors of feminist sf. Indeed, many contemporary feminist authors acknowledge the influence of earlier writers such as Norton and C. L. Moore on their careers. Joan D. Vinge, for example, has written of the deep impression left on her by the discovery that Norton was female:

> In the early mid-Sixties, well before the women's movement became widespread, I read her *Ordeal in Otherwhere*, the first book I'd ever read with an honest-to-God liberated woman as the protagonist. Not only were female protagonists extremely unusual at the time, but this character came from a world on which sexual equality was the norm. I never forgot that, and in the late Sixties, when I began to see articles on feminism, something fell into place for me in a very profound way.[11]

Dissatisfaction with the predominance of feminist accounts of women in sf was expressed by Connie Willis in her 1992 article 'The Women SF Doesn't See'.[12] Willis criticizes what she calls 'the current version of women in science fiction before the 1960s', which held that '[t]here weren't any'. This account, which Willis states she has 'heard several times lately' seems to be a story with no apparent written origin, yet is referred to by a number of critics and authors, including Marion Zimmer Bradley, who similarly describes it as the 'conventional wisdom' concerning women in sf.[13] Interestingly, the 'myth' that women were absent from the field before 1960 can fit both a masculinist and feminist history of women and sf.[14] According to Willis, the feminist version of this history claims that 'in the late '60s and early '70s, a group of feminist writers led by Joanna Russ and Ursula Le Guin stormed the barricades, and women began writing (and sometimes even editing) science fiction. Before that, nada.' In this (feminist) account, the presence and influence of earlier female writers is denied or delegitimated, suggests Willis, due to their use of male pseudonyms, or the perception that they 'only wrote sweet little domestic stories. Babies. They wrote mostly stories about babies.'[15]

Willis argues that authors such as Mildred Clingerman, Zenna Henderson, Margaret St. Clair and Judith Merril should be reclaimed, but for the strength of their stories, and not 'because of their historical importance'.[16] Willis bases her re-evaluation on literary merit alone, in order to retrieve the work of these authors who do not signify in reductive accounts of sf—whether constructed from a masculinist or feminist view of the field. This neglect does not, however, foreclose the possibility of a feminist historical narrative which acknowledges both the quality of writing by authors such as Merril and Henderson and also their influence on later generations of female and feminist writers.[17] Many female authors had participated in the male-dominated field from the earliest years of the pulps and begun to challenge the patriarchal and sexist conventions which excluded intelligent, self-sufficient female characters. Unfortunately, few of these stories were ever reprinted, and are only just becoming accessible to contemporary readers through the publications of anthologies such as Pamela Sargent's new *Women of Wonder* books and the collection *New Eves*.[18]

Yet, analyses of feminist sf based in literary criticism have continued to show antipathy to earlier female-authored works, especially from the 1950s, which are characterized as 'domestic' or 'wet diaper sf', derided as little more than ladies' magazine fiction. Such works are cast as a set-back for, rather than part of the development towards, feminist sf. In her influential article, 'The Image of Women in Science Fiction', Joanna Russ divided women writers into categories, one of which was dismissively termed ladies' magazine fiction: 'in which the sweet, gentle intuitive little heroine solves an interstellar crisis by mending her slip or doing something equally domestic after her big, heroic husband has failed. Zenna Henderson sometimes writes like this.'[19] Most feminist sf critics followed Russ's lead in ignoring pre-1970s female authors (other than Tiptree, Le Guin, and Russ herself). Consequently, a very specific historiography informs most examinations of feminist sf, producing a 'selective tradition' similar to the trend to canonization in feminist literary criticism.[20] Many recent feminist sf studies have employed poststructuralist frameworks to examine the interaction of feminism and postmodernism; however, the project of deconstructing the *subject* of feminist sf (a need identified by Veronica Hollinger) remains largely unfulfilled.[21] Feminist sf criticism has embraced nineteenth-century texts such as *Herland* and *Frankenstein* as legitimate feminist literary forebears, but has often denied and even denigrated more direct feminist sf precursors, such as Judith Merril, Zenna Henderson, and Andre Norton. Yet there are signs, in the more recent book-length studies of feminist sf, that neglected and popular writers are gaining more attention, and that critics are beginning to examine the heritage of women's early writing in the pulps.[22]

While feminist sf criticism is facing the challenge to deconstruct its subject, outside the sf field, 'feminist sf' has barely been constituted as an object of study. In general feminist studies of contemporary literature, sf texts are not well represented and indeed their very existence is often marginalized or obscured. The few works of feminist sf that do appear are usually co-opted for the feminist mainstream by ignoring or minimizing their sf identity. A much greater proportion of feminist sf texts are discussed within the aegis of utopian studies, though with similar problems. Surprisingly, even the more recent genre studies do not always do justice to feminist sf and often implicitly reinstate the cultural hierarchies that continue to mark off the mainstream from the 'ghetto' of sf.

When feminist sf texts *are* discussed within mainstream feminist literary criticism, often the negative connotations of the label 'sf' are avoided by substituting the terms 'speculative', 'fantastic' or 'utopian literature' and by stressing links to a feminist literary tradition through juxtaposition with canonical figures such as Virginia Woolf or Perkins Gilman.[23] Additionally this approach removes feminist sf texts from their historical and generic topos, as a fiction whose re-visions are produced in dialogue with specific generic conventions.[24] The sf field is a necessary context for the analysis of feminist sf;[25] a critic who is unaware of the tradition of 'flasher' or women-dominant stories in sf misses much of the texts' import. Feminist women-only worlds and lesbian utopias are not just expressions of contemporary feminism, but also a rewriting and critique of 'evil matriarchy' stories. Thus, critics ignorant of sf will miss much of the impact and humour of a story like Russ's 'When it Changed'.[26]

Often, the only sf or speculative texts analysed in feminist literary criticism are those written by mainstream authors, such as Marge Piercy, Margaret Atwood and Angela Carter. Their presence within mainstream criticism is fairly unproblematic, for although they may produce sf or 'fantastic' texts, in terms of publication and reputation, they are not marked as 'genre' authors.[27] The only genre sf writer to appear with any frequency is Joanna Russ; and critics undertake some interesting negotiations to draw her work—more specifically *The Female Man*—out of the entanglement of genre and into the mainstream of feminist fiction.[28] Other writers such as Tiptree and Charnas are rarely referred to, and (despite the common assumption that she is one of the few sf writers to receive critical appraisal outside the genre), Le Guin also receives very little attention in feminist literary studies.

With the development of feminist cultural studies, and an increasing focus on popular culture, feminist sf is often analysed as an example of feminist genre fiction. The texts that represent feminist sf in such studies usually include the novels of Russ, Le Guin, Charnas, Piercy and Gearhart in addition to sf texts by 'mainstream' authors not always found in sf criticism (such as Anna Livia's *Bulldozer Rising*, or Zoë Fairbairns' *Benefits*).[29] Critics of 'genre fiction' often assume rather rigid models which emphasize the essential conservatism of genre writing, which is more or less successfully subverted in feminist appropriations of the genre. Even those who are more open to feminist genre writing, such as Anne Cranny-Francis, emphasize the 'dangers' of conservatism and phallocentrism that lie 'embedded' in the very forms and codes of genre.[30] This is a familiar feminist dilemma, of course, the question of whether feminist discourse is constricted or even undermined by the very structures of language and literary forms inherited from an androcentric tradition. It is not, however, a problem specific only to genre or 'popular' fiction, but to *all* forms of writing. The tendency in feminist criticism of genre is to see such forms, including sf, as the repositories of the most extreme limitations on feminist strategies of deconstruction and re-visioning. Of course, there are significant differences in the way, for example, Joanna Russ and Anne McCaffrey utilize sf, and some feminist interventions are more 'radical' or successful than others. My concern, however, is with the recursive argument which aligns 'conservative' and collusionary practices with a particular 'form' of writing such as sf, so that successful feminist appropriations, by their very nature, cannot therefore 'be' sf. I would challenge the notion that certain modes of writing can *in themselves* be inherently radical or conservative. The codes and conventions of genre (indeed all writing) are not static—to ignore the fluidity of genre over time (and cultures) is also to deny the transformations brought about, for example, in sf by feminist interventions.

Nevertheless, a number of genre critics seem to retain the belief that the popular is necessarily (and intrinsically) conservative, that genre 'conventions' and codes are more constricting (and phallocentric) than the codes of 'literature', and that the market for genre remains 'consumers' rather than 'readers'.[31] Thus Nicci Gerrard asks, 'can a novel that is popular entertainment and *therefore* confined by intrinsically conservative rules be converted to political ends?'[32] Similarly, a clear demarcation of genre and feminist writing is provided by Patricia Duncker: 'Most of the consumers of genre fiction eat the novels like a favourite meal. They want to know what they are buying, even if it is junk food. Feminism, on the other hand, should always be disruptive, unsettling.'[33] Duncker's opinion of popular fiction is openly disparaging:

> All the women's presses, in the last days of the 1980s and on into the 1990s, have been engaged in promoting women's genre fiction because the combination of feminist textual noises and a brisk escapist read sells extremely well. It is clear ... that I am not a convert to this kind of writing.[34]

Duncker is interested in more subversive (and thus feminist) fiction, which she claims can only occur in genre writing when the 'form of the genre breaks down. And we are reading a new kind of political fiction: feminist fiction'.[35] Thus for Duncker, feminist fiction and genre fiction are mutually exclusive categories, and feminist genre fiction is thus an impossibility. In this formulation genre and sf remain devalued—a truly feminist text which breaks the confines of genre conventions passes over the literary borderland into 'real' literature.[36]

The model of literary criticism, which has served as the primary mode for analysing sf and feminist sf, has been seen as a limited approach by a number of sf critics.[37] Sf in particular is not well served by a traditional literary model which has 'divorced the study of ideas and language from social conditions'.[38] Alternative perspectives on feminist sf are provided by historical and cultural studies, in particular, the expanding field of feminist cultural studies of science and technology. As Hilary Rose has argued,

> the current recovery of sf by literary criticism and cultural studies, which is part of an important and welcome attempt to dissolve the divide between popular and high culture, has often underplayed the close relationship between science criticism and sf, not least within feminism. It is as if, while taking down that cultural divide, another between the arts and the sciences is allowed to reproduce itself uncriticised. It is this division, a sort of replay of Snow's two cultures, even though the categories themselves constantly shift, that I want to see removed.[39]

A number of feminist science theorists, including Rose and Donna Haraway, situate feminist sf as an important point of dialogue between feminism and science. As feminist cultural studies of science and technology increasingly adopt a multi-discursive approach, feminist sf is positioned as one of the pivotal sites where gendered relations of science and technology are reflected, constructed and reconstructed. Donna Haraway has consistently argued for 'a comprehensive feminist politics about science and technology',[40] and has valorized feminist sf for its potential to provide ways of imagining new possibilities of engagement between women and technology, and thus generate new technological discourses and systems of meaning.[41] Haraway's ongoing project to expose and re-vision Western narratives of science has often proceeded by recounting alternative stories, from feminist primatologists to sf writers such as Octavia Butler. In Haraway's words, feminist sf writers are 'our storytellers exploring what it means to be embodied in high-tech worlds', whose narratives problematize the status of men, women, humans, races, individual identities and bodies.[42]

Similarly, Rose situates feminist sf texts as vital participants in contemporary feminist debate, arguing that 'it is not by chance that

feminists writing or talking about science and technology constantly return
...to these empowering alternative visions'.[43] Reflecting the views of
feminist sf critics, Rose argues that 'feminist science fiction has created a
privileged space—a sort of dream laboratory—where feminisms may try
out wonderful and/or terrifying social projects'.[44] One literary critic who
has also explored the relation between feminist science theory and sf is
Jane Donawerth, who argues that both are based on a common utopian
project—the need to design a feminist science for the future and to offer
contesting scientific origin stories.[45] In a final example, the editors of a
recent feminist cultural study of science and technology, *Between Monsters,
Goddesses and Cyborgs*, position feminist sf as a legitimate expression of
feminist thought that predates the establishment of feminist science and
technology studies as an academic research area.[46]

Another thread in feminist and cultural studies of science is the focus
on the figure of the cyborg, informed by Haraway's famous 'Manifesto for
Cyborgs' and the cyberpunk movement in sf usually represented by
William Gibson's *Neuromancer* trilogy. The exponential growth of
'cyborgology' and studies of cyberpunk and cyberspace suggests an
environment more suited to polysemic and cross-textual dialogues about
feminist sf. It signals, I believe, a welcome change in critical emphasis, from
sf as literary text to that of cultural artefact, a vital part of contemporary
Western cultural history. There may be an element of 'fashion' in the
sudden avalanche of critical analyses of 'cyberstuff' (when within the sf
field, writers and critics have been declaring cyberpunk's death since the
late 1980s); nevertheless there have been a number of extremely
interesting studies which integrate sf into this broader framework of
techno-cultural development.[47] The introduction to the eclectic collection
The Cyborg Handbook claims that

> The compleat cyborgologist must study science fiction as the
> anthropologist listens to myths and prophesies. Science fiction has
> often led the way in theorising and examining cyborgs, showing their
> proliferation and suggesting some of the dilemmas and social
> implications they represent. And several important critics—Kate
> Hayles, Scott Bukatman. Fredric Jameson, Anne Balsamo, and
> Donna Haraway...have used these fictional resources to explore the
> cyborg and the ways he/she/it affects our ideas of the 'human'.[48]

Indicative of the leaky boundaries of cyber-discourse, some insightful
analyses of feminist sf have resulted from these cultural studies which use
sf to inform and reflect cyborg feminisms, cybernetic theories and feminist
critiques of technology. A compelling example is Anne Balsamo's
Technologies of the Gendered Body, which employs feminist sf as a 'cultural

landmark', drawing on Pat Cadigan's *Synners* to explore contemporary feminist articulations and reflections of techno-social relations.[49]

Another area of cultural studies which has the potential to provide interesting perspectives on feminist sf are those focusing on audiences, readers and fans.[50] A number of works on media sf dealt with fandom, the most pertinent being those examining the predominantly female fandom of *Star Trek*. Following the work of Henry Jenkins and others,[51] Constance Penley in particular has provided insightful analyses of slash fan culture, raising questions about feminist approaches to popular culture and its audiences, and the problematic intersections of identity between fan/critic, observer and observed in ethnographic studies of audience.[52] These media sf studies highlight the presence of another vital participant in the discourses of feminist sf: readers and fans.[53]

To date there are very few accounts of women's involvement in sf literary fandom, and no academic studies similar to those of female Trekkers and slash writers. Yet, from the 1970s, feminist fandom not only provided some of the earliest feminist sf criticism but actively set out to change the environment in which sf was produced. The voices and actions of feminist fans were vital to the development and encouragement of feminist sf and its criticism. In her 1978 article 'A Feminist Critique of Science Fiction', Mary Kenny Badami considered women's place in sf as characters, fans and writers and mentioned some of the feminist developments in fandom, including publications such as the fanzine *The Witch and the Chameleon* and the *Khatru* symposium on women in sf.[54] Badami's critique of the sf community has had few successors, however, as most feminist sf scholarship remains firmly based in literary criticism, and rarely discusses fan readings or activities.[55] A number of critics, notably Sarah Lefanu and Jenny Wolmark, acknowledge the importance of women as readers and fans of sf, but generally studies of feminist sf have ignored fan readings and activities.[56]

Situating feminist sf as an element of cultural history would entail more than critical analyses of the 'feminist' characteristics of the texts alone. Feminist fans are a vital reception community whose readings should be juxtaposed with those of literary and cultural critics. A study of female fans could contribute to a broader, more inclusive history of the interaction of feminism and sf, one which incorporated the 'feminisms' evident in the extra-literary activities of the fan community. These range from the struggle for women's spaces and programming at conventions, to the engagement with feminist issues in fanzines and magazines sparked not only by feminist texts, but 'women's sf' and indeed, 'masculinist' sf. Attention to the under-utilized resources of fanzines and magazine letter columns could counter the assumption that sf was almost totally male dominated, with only the occasional, exceptional female reader before the 1960s. As early as the 1930s and 1940s, in magazines such as *Astounding*, there are letters from female readers, and avid discussion about the place of women readers and female characters.[57] Most accounts of female fandom posit a flood (or 'invasion') in the 1960s, with little agency attributed to the female fans themselves. Many critics suggest that the environment of sf changed, becoming more inclined to the 'softer' sciences, a development which 'allowed' more women to become involved as readers and fans. There is little emphasis on the efforts that fem-fans themselves made to change the environment of the sf community, such as the efforts by Susan Wood and others in organizing women-only rooms at cons, starting panels on women and sf, and founding feminist zines and women's APAs.

Additionally, attention to fan readings suggests interesting questions about the identity and positioning of sf critics, as intellectuals carrying out 'high culture' analysis on a low cultural form. While many feminist sf critics position themselves as both fan and academic, there has been little consideration of how the critic's specific reading is privileged over all other readings, or what authorizes the act of interpretation when carried out by a *critic* rather than a *fan*. Indeed, as a number of critics have observed, there are many similarities between fans and academics. Patrick Parrinder has argued that becoming a fan involves 'initiation into an unofficial field of knowledge' which has parallels with the 'official field of orthodox literary knowledge'.[58] Similarly, Jenkins points to the potential for fans to function as critics, noting that the fans' knowledge also promotes evaluation and interpretation: 'Within the realm of popular culture, fans are the true experts; they constitute a competing educational elite, albeit one without official recognition or social power'.[59] Studies of popular culture consumption would also suggest that sf fans and academics have more in common with each other than with the occasional consumer of popular fiction. Both have a commitment to engaged, critical readings, and enter into discussion of the text with others: critics publish their interpretations, while fans discuss them in zines, cons and increasingly through internet discussion groups. The process of interpretation is for both an avenue for making statements about their identity and positioning within their respective communities: for both it is a site of pleasure and a certain amount of power.

My aim in surveying some of the critical constructions of feminist science fiction(s) was to suggest the need for more interdisciplinary dialogues about feminist sf as part of a series of communities spanning feminist literature, culture and science theory. Studies of female fans by critics such as Penley have begun to legitimate the cultural and political importance of interpretations of sf from outside the academy. In the field of literary sf fandom, there exists an abundance of sources reflecting the development of feminist consciousness in sf that are vital to a detailed understanding of the cultural history of women and feminism(s) in sf. No longer situated as a transparent and passive text to be read by critics through the lens of theory, the multiplicity of feminist sf texts could begin to speak to (and for) feminist theory and cultural practice. Feminist fictions about alternative social relations of science and technology—feminist sf—is a vital part of the feminist project to deconstruct universalizing, phallocentric, scientific narratives. I would argue that feminist sf should be valued as a site for the literalization of feminist hopes and anxieties about our society which is more accessible than much of the feminist theory produced within the academy. The multiple stories of and about feminist sf, from critics, readers and authors, are a significant (and pleasurable) source for reading the intersections of feminism, science and culture in contemporary Western society.

Notes

1 While feminist sf criticism is now fairly well established, with regular articles appearing in the sf critical journals, and a growing number of book-length studies and collections by critics such as Sarah Lefanu, Jenny Wolmark, Marleen Barr, Robin Roberts and Jane Donawerth, feminist criticism of sf as a whole is still an underdeveloped area.

2 Veronica Hollinger, 'Feminist Science Fiction: Breaking Up the Subject', *Extrapolation*, 31.3 (1990), p. 229.

3 I am grateful to Sylvia Kelso for her thoughts on this issue, 'Singularities: The Interaction of Feminism(s) and Two Strands of Popular American Fiction, 1968–89', PhD thesis, James Cook University of North Queensland, 1996.

4 See, for example, Roger Luckhurst's argument that postmodernist critics of sf who claim to erase the hi/lo cultural divide ultimately always reinscribe this border; Luckhurst, 'Border Policing: Postmodernism and Science Fiction', *Science Fiction Studies*, 18.3 (1991), pp. 358–66. The lack of mainstream feminist attention to feminist sf has been most volubly criticized by Marleen S. Barr. In her recent works, Barr has abandoned her previous championing of feminist sf in favour of 'feminist fabulation', in an attempt to incorporate it into a mainstream (and thus valued) category of postmodern fiction. See, for example, Marleen S. Barr, *Feminist Fabulation: Space/Postmodern Fiction* (Iowa City: University of Iowa Press, 1992), and Barr, *Lost in Space: Probing Feminist Science Fiction and Beyond* (Chapel Hill: North Carolina University Press, 1993). For an insightful critique of Barr's position, see Jenny Wolmark, *Aliens and Others: Science Fiction, Feminism and Postmodernism* (Hemel Hempstead: Harvester Wheatsheaf, 1993), p. 25.

5 There exists quite a large, distinct body of feminist work on sf film and media; see for example, Constance Penley, ed., *Close Encounters: Film, Feminism and Science Fiction* (Minneapolis: University of Minnesota Press, 1991); Barbara Creed, *The Monstrous-Feminine: Film, Feminism, Psychoanalysis* (London & New

York: Routledge, 1993); Vivian Sobchak, *Screening Space: The American Science Fiction Film* (New York: Ungar, 1987).

6 Beverly Friend, 'Virgin Territory: Women and Sex in SF', *Extrapolation*, 14 (Dec. 1972), pp. 49–58; Mary Kenny Badami, 'A Feminist Critique of Science Fiction', *Extrapolation*, 18 (Dec. 1978), pp. 6–19; Susan Wood, 'Women and Science Fiction', *Algol*, 16.1 (Winter 1978–79), pp. 9–18; Joanna Russ, 'The Image of Women in Science Fiction', *Vertex*, 1.6 (Feb. 1974), pp. 53–57; Ursula Le Guin, 'American SF and the Other', *Science Fiction Studies*, 2.3 (1975), pp. 208–10.

7 Kingsley Amis, *New Maps of Hell* (London: Gollancz [SF Book Club], 1962 [1961]); Sam Moskowitz, *Seekers of Tomorrow: Makers of Modern SF* (Westport, Conn.: Hyperion, 1966); Sam J. Lundwall, *Science Fiction: What It's All About* (New York: Ace Books, 1971 [1969]); Brian Aldiss, *Billion Year Spree* (London: Corgi, 1975 [1973]). More obvious proto-feminist critiques had appeared previously; in a 1950s issue of *Magazine of Fantasy and Science Fiction*, Dr Richardson's 'Nice Girl on Mars' (which postulated comfort girls for spacemen) drew an impassioned response from Miriam Allen DeFord (situated as 'humanist' rather than 'feminist'). Robert S. Richardson, 'The Day After We Land on Mars', *Magazine of Fantasy and Science Fiction*, 9.6 (Dec. 1955), pp. 44–52; Miriam Allen DeFord, 'News for Dr Richardson', *Magazine of Fantasy and Science Fiction*, 10.5 (May 1956), pp. 53–57. It is also interesting to note a very early psychoanalytical interpretation of the masculinist, even misogynist implications of sf's spaceships, interstellar travel and flights from earth; see Ednita P. Bernabeu MD, 'SF: A New Mythos', *Psychoanalytic Quarterly*, 26 (Oct. 1957), pp. 527–35.

8 Sarah Lefanu, *In the Chinks of the World Machine: Feminism and Science Fiction* (London: The Women's Press, 1988), p. 93.

9 For example, Ursula K. Le Guin *The Dispossessed* (London: Victor Gollancz, 1974); Joanna Russ, *The Female Man* (New York: Bantam, 1975); Marge Piercy, *Woman on the Edge of Time* (New York: Knopf, 1976); Suzy McKee Charnas, *Motherlines* (New York: Berkley, 1978); Sally Miller Gearhart, *The Wanderground: Stories of the Hill Women* (Watertown, Mass.: Persephone Press, 1979). Russ's seminal article, 'Recent Feminist Utopias', in Marleen S. Barr, ed., *Future Females: A Critical Anthology* (Bowling Green: Bowling Green State University Press, 1981), pp. 71–85, discusses these texts along with: Monique Wittig, *Les Guérillères*; Marion Zimmer Bradley, *The Shattered Chain*; Samuel Delany, *Triton*; James Tiptree Jr. (aka Alice Sheldon), 'Houston, Houston, Do You Read?' and 'Your Faces, O My Sisters! Your Faces Filled Of Light!'.

10 The problems of canon-building in sf generally have been discussed by numerous critics. See, for example, the special issue on 'Science Fiction Research: The State of the Art', *Foundation*, 60 (Spring 1994).

11 Joan D. Vinge, 'The Restless Urge to Write', in Denise Du Pont, ed., *Women of Vision: Essays by Women Writing Science Fiction* (New York: St. Martin's Press, 1988), pp. 115–16. See also Marion Zimmer Bradley, 'One Woman's Experience in Science Fiction', in Du Pont, ed., *Women of Vision*, pp. 87–89.

12 Connie Willis, 'The Women SF Doesn't See', *Asimov's SF Magazine*, 16.11 (1992), pp. 4–8.

13 Bradley, 'One Woman's Experience', p. 84.

14 Many sf critics and authors (especially aficionados of 'hard sf') adhere to a history of the field where women's entrance into sf was made possible

only by the (negative) effects of the 'literary' influences of the New Wave, a turn to the 'softer' sciences and fantasy (and sometimes the appearance of *Star Trek* which, it is said, attracted new female fans); see, for example, Charles Platt, 'The Rape of Science Fiction', *Science Fiction Eye*, 1.5 (1989), pp. 44–49.

15 Willis, 'The Women', p. 4.

16 Willis, 'The Women', p. 5.

17 Willis' article discusses stories by all these authors including C. L. Moore, and also mentions Katherine MacLean, Leigh Brackett, Sonya Dorman, Evelyn Smith and Ann Warren Griffith. She includes a list of recommended reading (p. 49).

18 Pamela Sargent, ed., *Women of Wonder: The Classic Years* (New York: Harcourt Brace & Co., 1995); *Women of Wonder: The Contemporary Years* (New York: Harcourt Brace & Co., 1995); Janrae Frank, Jean Stine and Forrest J. Ackerman, eds., *New Eves: Science Fiction About the Extraordinary Women of Today and Tomorrow* (Stamford, Conn.: Longmeadow Press, 1994).

19 Joanna Russ, 'The Image of Women in Science Fiction', *Vertex*, 1.6 (Feb. 1974), p. 56. The story Russ is probably referring to here is Henderson's 'Subcommittee', where an intergalactic war is prevented by the wife of a high official, who has secretly communicated with one of the alien forces whose son has befriended her own. In the climax of the story, the narrator proves that she has indeed made contact with the alien mother by displaying her pink slip to the human and alien members of a high-powered military meeting.

20 See, for example, Carol A. Stabile, *Feminism and the Technological Fix* (Manchester: Manchester University Press, 1994), pp. 29–31; p. 47, n. 4. Stabile sees the claims for a female utopian literary tradition based on similarities between 1970s feminist sf utopias and nineteenth-century works such as Gilman's *Herland* as authorizing an essentialist continuum of women's writing, which allows literary critics to ignore the political and cultural circumstances of the text's production including homophobia, imperialism and even racism. On 'selective tradition', see Stabile, *Feminism*, p. 30, citing Raymond Williams, *The Long Revolution* (New York: Columbia University Press, 1961), p. 50.

21 Veronica Hollinger, 'Feminist Science Fiction: Construction and Deconstruction', *Science Fiction Studies*, 16.2 (1989), p. 226.

22 See, for example, Wolmark, *Aliens and Others*; Robin Roberts, *A New Species: Gender and Science in Science Fiction* (Urbana & Chicago: University of Illinois Press, 1993); Jane Donawerth, *Frankenstein's Daughters: Women Writing Science Fiction* (New York: Syracuse University Press, 1997). Some of the writers considered in these studies include Anne McCaffery, C.J. Cherryh and Tanith Lee, Carol Emshwiller, Phyllis Gotlieb and Cherry Wilder, and newer authors who have received little critical attention to date, including Elisabeth Vonarburg, Emma Bull, Judith Moffett and Rebecca Ore.

23 One interesting consequence of this approach is resultant change in lineage: rather than Shelley being the starting point, much earlier forbears are found, providing an immediate and substantial history, which, significantly, also provides a more venerable status.

24 As Roberts comments, 'stressing the genre's links to high art runs the risk of being complicitous with the ghettoization of most science fiction as literature unworthy of scrutiny', 'It's Still Science Fiction: Strategies of Feminist Science Fiction Criticism', *Extrapolation*, 36.3 (1995), p. 186. Roberts provides an overview of books on feminist sf, and is particularly critical of the

'mainstream' approach to feminist sf which attempts to make sf 'palatable to the academy' through strategies such as avoiding the use of 'sf' in favour of 'utopia' or 'fantastic literature', pp. 186–88. Similarly, Nicola Nixon, 'The Rebel's Progress', *Science Fiction Studies*, 21.3 (1994), pp. 421–25, argues that feminist sf needs a 'theoretical framework to facilitate its dialogue with other forms of feminist fiction', p. 424.

25 As Nixon argues, this is 'the field in which it maintains a gendered and political dialogue with other texts, and the field from which it derives and transforms its tropes, paradigms, historical resonances'. 'The Rebel's Progress', pp. 423–24.

26 Joanna Russ, 'When It Changed', in Harlan Ellison, ed., *Again, Dangerous Visions* (New York: Doubleday, 1972).

27 For this reason, many sf commentators would debate the inclusion of writers such as Atwood, Carter and Doris Lessing as part of the genre, as they do not participate in the sf community and often do not enter into the intertextual conversations with the field and its history that characterizes most 'genre sf'. Yet all three are often analysed as part of 'feminist sf', while other writers of non-realist fiction, such as Fay Weldon, are not.

28 Russ's criticism is cited fairly often (even in works which do not discuss sf in any form) and her words (or partially quoted words) often resonate uncomfortably with the pronouncements about 'sf', including her own work, that follow. For example, many critics, including those who discuss no sf or speculative fiction, cite Russ's arguments from 'What Can A Heroine Do? Or Why Women Can't Write', in Susan Koppelman Cornillon, ed., *Images of Women in Fiction* (Bowling Green, Ohio: Bowling Green University Popular Press, 1972), pp. 79–94. Russ states that there are three options for feminist writers who do not want to follow traditional 'female narratives': produce non-narrative texts, use a lyrical mode (such as Woolf did) *or* the writer can turn to genre—Russ's favoured approach. However, many critics use Russ's model here but omit the third option of genre. See, for example, Roberta Rubenstein, *Boundaries of the self: Gender, Culture, Fiction* (Urbana & Chicago: University of Illinois, 1987), p. 165.

29 Anna Livia, *Bulldozer Rising* (London: Onlywomen Press, 1988); Zoë Fairbairns, *Benefits* (London: Virago, 1979). Interestingly, studies of genre fiction rarely include Angela Carter, a literary feminist author who has more mainstream acceptability, and whose texts are often included in feminist sf critical analyses.

30 Anne Cranny-Francis, *Feminist Fiction: Feminist Uses of Generic Fiction* (Cambridge: Polity Press, 1990).

31 See, for example, Nicci Gerrard, *Into the Mainstream: How Feminism Has Changed Women's Writing* (London: Pandora, 1989), pp. 147–48; Cranny-Francis, *Feminist Fiction*, p. 1.

32 Gerrard, *Into the Mainstream*, p. 119 (my emphasis).

33 The message is clear: 'good' feminists don't like junk food! Patricia Duncker, *Sisters and Strangers: An Introduction to Contemporary Feminist Fiction* (Oxford: Blackwell, 1992), p. 125.

34 Duncker, *Sisters*, p. 99.

35 Duncker, *Sisters*, p. 99. Additionally, Duncker argues that 'all genre fiction must operate within textual expectations which are indeed clichés. To write well within a particular genre without disrupting or subverting the form

is, I believe, impossible', p. 125.

36 However, even Dunker recognizes the possible value of feminist sf: 'Feminist fiction reaches a broader audience than feminist theory. Women who might not broach Mary Daly's *Gyn/Ecology* might well read *The Wanderground'*, *Sisters*, p. 105.

37 A number of critics have pointed to the preponderance of literary criticism in studies of sf generally, with calls for different approaches, such as general histories or surveys. See, for example, Gary Westfahl, 'The Undiscovered Country: The Finished and Unfinished Business of Science Fiction Research and Criticism', *Foundation*, 60 (Spring, 1994), pp. 84–93. In his editorial for this special issue of *Foundation*, Edward James is critical of 'the way in which, with a few notable exceptions, the study of science fiction has been treated as part of the field of English or literary studies, and not as a part of cultural history', p. 3.

38 Judith Newton and Deborah Rosenfelt, 'Introduction: Towards a Materialist-Feminist Criticism', in *Feminist Criticism and Social Change: Sex, Class and Race in Literature and Culture* (New York: Methuen, 1985), pp. xvi–xvii.

39 Hilary Rose, *Love, Power and Knowledge: Towards a Feminist Transformation of the Sciences* (Cambridge: Polity Press, 1994), p. 209.

40 Donna Haraway, 'Class, Race, Sex, Scientific Objects of Knowledge', in Violet B. Haas and Carolyne C. Perucci, eds., *Women in Scientific and Engineering Professions* (Ann Arbor: University of Michigan Press, 1984), p. 213.

41 Donna Haraway, 'A Manifesto for Cyborgs: Science, Technology and Socialist Feminism in the 1980s', in Linda J. Nicholson, ed., *Feminism/Postmodernism* (New York: 1990), pp. 215–16. A similar sentiment was expressed in the 1970s by Pamela Sargent, who argued that women should not reject science and technology, and emphasized the importance of sf as a vehicle for familiarizing women with scientific advances and their possible results—a vital experience for those who were culturally induced to believe that they were not scientifically or intellectually proficient (*Women of Wonder* [New York: Vintage, 1974], p. 47).

42 Haraway, 'Manifesto', p. 220.

43 Hilary Rose, 'Beyond Masculinist Realities', in R. Bleier, ed., *Feminist Approaches to Science* (New York: Pergamon, 1986), pp. 74, 59.

44 Rose, *Love, Power and Knowledge*, p. 228.

45 Jane Donawerth, 'Utopian Science: Contemporary Feminist Science Theory and Science Fiction by Women', *NWSA Journal*, 2.4 (Autumn, 1990), pp. 535–36, 544. A revised and more detailed version appears in her recent book, *Frankenstein's Daughters*.

46 Nina Lykke and Rosi Braidotti, eds., 'Introduction', *Between Monsters, Goddesses and Cyborgs: Feminist Confrontations With Science, Medicine and Cyberspace* (London: Zed Books, 1996), pp. 1–2. The novels referred to are Marge Piercy, *Woman on the Edge of Time* and Sally Miller Gearhart, *The Wanderground*. Liz Sourbut's essay in this collection provides another example of an interactive dialogue between feminist science theory and science fiction. Sourbut examines the theoretical possibility of lesbians using technology to reproduce from female eggs alone. 'Gynogenesis' is, Sourbut admits, 'not a practical possibility. It is science fiction. But as a concept it is a way of bringing lesbians into the debates around assisted reproduction, debates which have been largely restricted to heterosexual, married couples'. Elizabeth Sourbut, 'Gynogenesis:

A Lesbian Appropriation of Reproductive Technologies', in Lykke and Braidotti, eds., *Between Monsters*, p. 227.

47 See, for example, Chris Hables Gray, ed., *The Cyborg Handbook* (New York & London: Routledge, 1995); Mike Featherstone and Roger Burrows, eds., *Cyberspace/Cyberbodies/Cyberpunk: Cultures of Technological Embodiment* (London: Sage, 1995); and the special issue edited by Thomas Foster, 'Incurably Informed: The Pleasures and Dangers of Cyberpunk', *Genders*, 18 (1993).

48 Chris Hables Gray, Steven Mentor and Heidi J. Figueroa-Sarriera, 'Cyborgology: Constructing the Knowledge of Cybernetic Organisms', in Gray, ed., *The Cyborg Handbook*, p. 8.

49 Anne Balsamo, *Technologies of the Gendered Body: Reading Cyborg Women* (Durham: Duke University Press, 1996), p. 135. Balsamo describes sf as 'works of fiction that generically extrapolate from the current moment to fictional futures [and] offer readers a framework for understanding the preoccupations that infuse contemporary culture', p. 112. See also Claudia Springer, 'Sex, Memories and Angry Women', in Mark Dery, ed., *Flame Wars: The Discourse of Cyberculture*, Special Issue of *South Atlantic Quarterly*, 92.4 (1993), pp. 157–77; and Allucquére Rosanne Stone, 'Will the Real Body Please Stand Up?: Boundary Stories about Virtual Cultures', in Michael Benedikt, ed., *Cyberspace: First Steps* (Cambridge, Mass.: MIT Press, 1991).

50 On readers of genre see Carol Thurston, *The Romance Revolution: Erotic Novels for Women and the Quest for a New Sexual Identity* (Urbana and Chicago: University of Illinois Press, 1987) and Janice Radway, *Reading The Romance: Women, Patriarchy and Popular Culture* (London: Verso, 1987).

51 Henry Jenkins, *Textual Poachers: Television Fans and Participatory Culture* (London: Routledge, 1992); John Tulloch and Henry Jenkins, *Science Fiction Audiences: Watching Doctor Who and Star Trek* (London & New York: Routledge, 1995); Camille Bacon-Smith, *Enterprising Women: Television Fandom and the Creation of Popular Myth* (Philadelphia: University of Pennsylvania Press, 1992).

52 Constance Penley, 'Feminism, Psychoanalysis and the Study of Popular Culture', in L. Grossberg, C. Nelson and P. Treichler, eds., *Cultural Studies* (New York and London: Routledge, 1992), pp. 479–94; C. Penley, 'Brownian Motion: Women, Tactics and Technology', in C. Penley and A. Ross, eds., *Technoculture* (Minneapolis: University of Minnesota Press, 1990), pp. 135–61.

53 Henry Jenkins uses the term 'textual poaching' to describe the process by which fans transform the original text, which becomes a catalyst for a series of complex interactions, interpretations and negotiations of meaning, and most importantly serves as a 'common point of reference [that] facilitates social interaction amongst fans', Jenkins, *Textual Poachers*, p. 75. See also Helen Merrick, 'The Readers Feminism Doesn't See: Feminist Fans, Critics and Science Fiction', in Deborah Cartmell, I.Q. Hunter, Heidi Kaye and Imelda Whelehan, eds., *Trash Aesthetics: Popular Culture and its Audience* (London: Pluto Press, 1997), pp. 48–65.

54 Mary Kenny Badami, 'A Feminist Critique of Science Fiction', *Extrapolation*, 18 (Dec. 1978), pp. 6–19. *The Witch and the Chameleon*, fanzine edited by Amanda Bankier (Canada, 1974–76); Jeffrey D. Smith, ed., *Khatru*, 3&4 (November) (Baltimore: Phantasmicon Press, 1975), reprinted with additional material edited by Jeanne Gomoll (Madison: Corflu, 1993).

55 Although fan writings are drawn on to provide critical material, commonly cited works include the *Khatru* symposium; Susan Wood, 'Women

and Science Fiction', *Algol/Starship*, 16.1 (Winter 1978/79), pp. 9–18; Jeanne Gomoll, 'Out of Context: Post-Holocaust Themes in Feminist Science Fiction', *Janus*, 6 (Winter, 1980), pp. 14–17.

56 Lefanu, *In the Chinks*, p. 2, mentions female authors, editors and readers of sf, referring to Susan Wood's article, 'Women and Science Fiction'; *Khatru* is also referred to as a 'fascinating document to read, not just for the wealth of ideas debated, on science fiction, feminism and women' (p.105) and Lefanu draws on the contributions by Tiptree, Russ and Charnas to illuminate her analysis of their work. See also Wolmark, *Aliens and Others*, who writes that 'fandom in sf has produced a range of informed and often innovative publications that deserve serious attention' and positions herself as a 'feminist, an academic and an avid reader of science fiction', p. ix.

57 My thanks to Justine Larbalestier for providing me with details from her research, 'The Battle of the Sexes in Science Fiction: From the Pulps to the James Tiptree, Jr. Memorial Award', PhD thesis, University of Sydney, 1996.

58 Patrick Parrinder, *Science Fiction: Its Criticism and Teaching* (London: Methuen, 1980), p. 41. See also Joli Jensen, 'Fandom as Pathology: The Consequences of Characterization', in Lisa A. Lewis, ed., *The Adoring Audience: Fan Culture and Popular Media* (London & New York: Routledge, 1992), pp. 9–29, who notes the parallel between fans' obsessions and the scholar's devotion to their research interest, which is obscured due to 'a system of bias which debases fans and elevates scholars even though they engage in virtually the same kinds of activities'. Lewis, 'Introduction' in *The Adoring Audience*, p. 2.

59 Jenkins, *Textual Poachers*, p. 86.

Vicissitudes of the Voice, Speaking Science Fiction

ROGER LUCKHURST

What, in the end, would it mean to determine the voice in its self-identity? Could the voice, in its unsullied 'pure speech', stripped of obstacles and contaminations, ever be located? And could the voice of a genre, for instance science fiction, ever be isolated in its purity? Since, for a certain strand of philosophical inquiry, the voice is the locus of identity, essence, pure auto-affection,[1] and since genre definitions seek to delineate the purest expressions of its rules, there would seem to be a structural similarity in these projects. It is a case, then, of isolating the voice in its proximity to itself; in genre terms, of scanning the 'noise' of communications traffic, before finally tuning in to that voice, which, alone, is speaking science fiction.

Almost immediately, though, problems surface in this aim. The 'inward speech' of the pure voice, speaking and listening intimately to itself, cannot be heard without being in some way 'translated': indeed, if it is to make sense, even to itself, it must partake of general language and thus be part of a signifying system which it could never, singly, own. The *im*purity of a general language, the *un*belonging in its system, are in fact the conditions on which claims to purity, 'pure speech', are founded. That is why such claims are always so anxious. The voice is always already self-divided.

It is the dream of purity and the fact of impurity that makes speaking (about) science fiction, for example within the context of a conference entitled 'Speaking Science Fiction', such a fraught and contentious exercise. For as this body of texts, this 'subjugated knowledge', emerges onto academic stages, something like the 'prudence organizations' of Philip Dick's *Ubik*, those protectors from contamination, come into operation. Who has the right to speak (of/with/for) science fiction? Who holds the authentic, self-proximate voice of the genre? Is it the writers themselves? Or is it the phalanx of fans who surround the writers? One which is otherwise degraded, rendered impure, by the secondary, inauthentic speech of academia? Despite its academic locale, manoeuvres to proclaim authenticity recur, angry fans remarking on the re-functioning of the genre for academia, academics proclaiming dual citizenship, as it were, with fandom, and thus denouncing other academics for their limited or superficial knowledge of the genre. Such arguments, however, mistake *identity* for *knowledge*,[2] or conflate genre reading for generic readers,[3] confusing the fantasm of the pure voice of the genre with the rights to speak. This is to deny, and to the very texts spoken for, fundamental impurity.

Identifiable genres do come into existence, however, and by external factors beyond the control of any putative voice (the economies of printing, publishing lists, specialist categories in bookshops, for example), as well as by the process through which texts house themselves self-reflexively within a 'generic mega-text'[4] and *re-mark* themselves *as* genre products.[5] Surely, therefore, the attempt to trace out what might be called a strategic or relative purity of science fiction, despite the inevitable contradictions attendant to genre theory, is of greater value than simply surrendering any possibility of defining the genre? Indeed it is, but we shall see that if anything identifies the voice of science fiction, it is precisely the vicissitudes and depredations of the voice.

In order to begin to unpack this assertion, let me turn to two of the most influential formulations of the specificity of the science fiction genre. Samuel Delany and Darko Suvin ultimately come to agree on the estrangement that science fiction effects: both would concur that 'the future is only a writerly convention that allows the sf writer to indulge in a significant distortion of the present that sets up a rich and complex dialogue with the reader's here and now'.[6] They agree, however, by locating the specificity of genre in what have come to be seen, in literary theory, as diametrically opposed functions: metaphor and metonymy. An opposition initially formulated by Roman Jakobson, metaphor operates by the *selection* of terms in a tension of dis/similarity, whilst metonymy works by the *combination* of terms in contiguous, syntagmatic proximity.[7] Jakobson tended to distribute poetry to metaphor and prose to metonymy; science fiction, it seems, can be located on either pole. So, for Suvin, 'it should be made clear that the sf universe of discourse presents...possible worlds as...totalising and thematic metaphors',[8] whilst for Delany the focus is on 'the most basic level of sentence meaning [where] we read words differently when we read them as science fiction'.[9] Suvin, in other words, isolates the specificity of science fiction in the rigour of its cognitive leap between levels (metaphor), whereas Delany insists that the conjunctions and disjunctions of science fiction be located as 'a specific way of reading', an *abuse* of 'particular syntactical rules' in the science fictional sentence (metonymy).[10]

Noting this distribution is not meant to cancel Suvin's or Delany's formulations. Both are extremely useful, and for science fiction criticism uncircumventable. Rather, what interests me here is the very framework on which these opposing definitions are composed, for Jakobson's literary speculations on the metaphoric and metonymic poles are, as David Lodge notes, an 'afterthought appended to a specialised study of language disorders'.[11] In 'Two Aspects of Language and Two Types of Aphasic Disturbances', Jakobson suggests that the sole operation of the metaphoric pole is a mark of a 'contiguity disorder', where sentence grammar and syntagmatic combinations collapse into 'infantile one-sentence utterances'.[12] The sole operation of the metonymic pole, in contrast, is marked by 'similarity disorder' where the aphasic cannot select new terms and can operate only within pre-given contexts.

To be reminded of this anterior focus on language disorder in Jakobson is to reflect on the peculiar effect of metaphor and metonymy being used to locate the specificity of an art form, in this case science fiction. For the 'purer' the operation of one pole is asserted the more the genre becomes, as it were, 'aphasic'. Perhaps this has less effect on Delany's assertion of metonymy,[13] but it does help articulate the sense that Suvin's theory of the genre as being 'in a final reduction…a metaphor'[14] can become a prescriptive definition, restricting science fiction to a highly limited set of 'linguistic' moves, somewhat like an aphasic.[15]

These attempts to isolate the specificity of science fiction, therefore, risk rendering it unreflectively in terms of dysfunction. It is to pursue the uniqueness of the voice into something like its *grain*, another mode of disappearance, where the grain of the voice is 'a site where language works *for nothing*, that is, in perversion'.[16] The purer the voice, the more dysfunctional and, in the end, silenced, it becomes.

Rather than retrieving the 'aphasic' patterns of these genre definitions for the purposes of demolition, however, I want to argue that they contain an important insight. Given the fragility and extreme self-reflexive anxiety attendant on speaking science fiction both in enunciations about it and within its texts, it becomes possible to track the genre, historically and materially, by its subjection to the pressures *towards* symptomatic dysfunction in its voice. In other words, the genre bears the anxieties of its perceived 'low' cultural status internally, and at the point where the voice begins to speak. Yet this tracking of the voice would not just be about lack (a simple narrative of abjection), it would also concern anxieties about the invasive *plenitude* of 'impure' voices. I propose, therefore, to discuss a number of science fiction texts which offer symptoms of this distorting pressure on the voice. My capsule readings will pursue the figure of the mute, suffering *lack* of voice, before moving to the figure of the fragile receiver of telepathic impressions, suffering *excess* of voices.

To become mute, without voice, is the most extreme form of aphasia, according to Jakobson. For science fiction texts to thematize mutism might immediately be read as a symptom of the inability to speak science fiction *tout court*. Between J.G. Ballard's 'The Sound-Sweep' (1960) and Octavia Butler's 'Speech Sounds' (1983),[17] however, there are major differences of emphasis in how their treatment of mutism asks to be read.

If Moorcock pronounced J.G. Ballard as 'the Voice' of the New Wave, it is 'The Sound-Sweep', with its complex, multiple mutisms, which suggests how that voice is only representative through its surface silences, stutterings and hesitant speech. Ballard's story ostensibly concerns the doomed relationship between a mute subordinate functionary and a rather obvious mother-substitute opera diva. Mangon's disorder is an hysterical mutism, codified in terms of a symptom of a traumatic event that might have been lifted from any of Freud's early studies of hysterics suffering from *tussis nervosa* or symptomatic throat constriction:[18] 'From the age of three, when his mother had savagely punched him in the throat to stop him crying, he had been stone dumb'.[19] The story, on one level, concerns how Mangon recovers his voice once Madame Gioconda moves from mother-figure to lover, only to return to mutism once she rejects him. But mutism recurs again and again at a series of levels: the opera singer, too, is mute in her own way, the human voice in classical music having been superseded by new ultrasonic technologies. If her able voice is silenced, Mangon's enforced silence is nevertheless full of speech, for his muteness accentuates his hearing, and his job, in this near future, is to vacuum away the uncanny traces of sounds—traffic noise, the twitter of parties—that have been found to leave persistent after-traces. The team of sound-sweeps to which Mangon belongs are described as 'an outcast group of illiterates, mutes...and social cripples',[20] who work to absorb the voices they have no access to, taking them to a kind of heterotopic space outside the city, 'a place of strange echoes and festering silences, overhung by a gloomy miasma of a million compacted sounds'.[21] In a culture tending towards silence in its art and urban surrounds, the mute Mangon is dedicated to bringing Madame Gioconda back to 'full voice' in operatic song.

Ballard evidently embeds a psychoanalytic reading in exploring these criss-crossing valences of full speech and empty voice. But at a *further* level, the relationship of the mute and the diva asks to be read as a meta-commentary on the status of the science fiction genre itself. For a New Wave text, this should come as no surprise. As part of a moment in the history of science fiction marked as formally and thematically highly self-reflexive, Ballard's story of muteness compels us to read there an allegory of the voice, speaking science fiction.

Muteness in 'The Sound-Sweep' is intertwined with a thematic of high and low art. Mangon, the subordinate, is entirely subservient to the jaded opera singer: 'You're carrying the torch for art'[22] as someone sarcastically puts it. At first it appears that we can allegorize this story as the subordination of science fiction, which masochistically absorbs the judgement of high art such that it renders the subordinate mute, except for a brief acknowledgement and return of speech entirely on the ground of high art categories. This relationship of high and low is sustained by mutual delusion: Mangon fully recognizes that his maintenance of deference to the diva is 'indispensable now to the effective operation of her fantasy world'.[23] Ballard, though, twists the lines of this allegory in allowing the mute to rebel, have his revenge, in letting the cracked and screeching tones of the deluded singer *full voice* to a horrified audience. This wry twist is in accord with the transpositions to generic value that the New Wave tried to effect: if the genre cannot speak, its muteness is nevertheless hysterical, and a patient analysis of the causes of its aphasic symptoms can allow a struggle *towards* speech, in a way which recasts the submissiveness to high art's acknowledgement, if never actually displacing the divide between high art and the low heteroglossic pleasures of the sonic dumps at the margins.

Turning to Octavia Butler's short story, 'Speech Sounds', is both to leave behind the allegorical optimism of New Wave science fiction, and to see mutism imposed by a vicissitude far more pessimistic than any temporary psychological mutism. In accord with her consistent and discomfiting concern to articulate the clash of 'hard' biological science with the 'soft' structures of the fragile *socius*, Butler has no time for the psychoanalytic frame that informs Ballard's mute.[24] 'Speech Sounds' uses a physiological model of mutism which is in tune with current definitions in cognitive science (which contain little or no reference to Freud, let alone Jakobson).[25] Here, then, a viral pandemic has attacked the language centres of the brain, leaving a population suffering a variety of forms of aphasia, aphonia and agraphia. Linguistic collapse is paralleled by social collapse, and the frustrations of speechlessness constantly spill over into silent pantomimes of violence. This is a global population in full regression towards a pre-verbal stateless state, becoming increasingly infantile (*in-fans* meaning to be 'without speech'). The agraphic heroine of this story, Valerie Rye, a history lecturer who can no longer read yet cannot quite bring herself to burn her now useless books for fuel, has a brief moment of ecstatic intimacy with a stranger before, with a jolting suddenness, she is left with his corpse and two traumatized children. Rye's first thought is to abandon them: 'They were on their own, those two kids. They were old enough to scavenge. She did not need any more grief. She did not need a stranger's children who would grow up to be hairless chimps.'[26] This rhetoric of degeneration is swept away by the first direct speech in a hitherto 'silent' text: the children can speak, and fluently, although they attempt to conceal it. Rye, too, speaks her first words of the text to them, and the story ends with a rush of speculations: 'Had the disease run its course, then? Or were these children simply immune? Certainly they had had time to fall sick and silent… What if children of three or fewer years were safe and able to learn language?'[27]

Butler's endnote to the story ascribes its writing to a general humanistic despair, the violence of a muted Los Angeles underclass typically transposed into her familiar biological registers. The story encodes a strictly scientific optimism in its ending, however: since Hughlings Jackson first noted the path of aphasia as a direct reversal of the process of the child's language acquisition, the fact that the children can speak is offered as a potential sign of linguistic (and therefore social) regeneration. Once again, though, this muteness can be read as a generic symptom, a speculation on the possibilities of speaking science fiction. If I say that the work of Octavia Butler is the silenced underside in the development of science fiction in the 1980s, this would not be quite true, given the amount of work from Donna Haraway to Jenny Wolmark that has been devoted to her, and such an assertion would risk turning Butler into a problematically idealized marginal other.[28] But it certainly is the case that the revisionist histori- ography since the eruption of cyberpunk has worked well to write the feminine *out* of the genre once more.[29] Gayatri Spivak's famous essay 'Can the Subaltern Speak?' might be relevant here. Reiterating forcefully that the subaltern 'cannot speak' because of occlusion and suppression from the historiographical record, Spivak argues that this is intensified in relation to the subaltern woman: 'If…the subaltern has no history and cannot speak, the subaltern as female is doubly in shadow'.[30] To transpose Spivak's context of (post-)colonial study to science fiction would, of course, be full of risk, but in a way it does seem that 'Speech Sounds' narrates the *doubled* occlusion of the feminine from the already 'lowly' science fiction. It is not, however, simply a text about silence, for its conclusion gestures towards the trembling emergence, in the dead centre of the genre, of a new voice appearing from the ruins of infantile mutism, a voice *in potentia* that might acquire the fluency of adult speech. The subaltern genre cannot quite speak, as it were, but a possible future of the voice is being projected beyond current vicissitudes.

To juxtapose a Ballard and a Butler short story is to register the need to consider the specific historical moments of their composition. Ballard's mute appears at the opening of the New Wave experiment; Butler's mute arrives with cyberpunk's concerted attempt to hybridize itself out of the genre. The same verbal dysfunction condenses very different scientific and allegorical meanings: the vagaries of mutism can be seen to be marking stages of the history of speaking science fiction.

Mutism is about absence of voice, an *aphasia universalis* at the end of the spectrum. Samuel Delany's *Babel-17*, written in 1967, deals with various language dysfunctions—'aphasia, alexis, amnesia'—that come to disrupt a voice still capable of speaking.[31] Another New Wave text, its self-reflexivity is again an attempt to theorize science fiction as a linguistic form. The opening description of the initially 'unreadable' Babel communication is clearly 'about' science fiction too: 'It's not a code... It's a language... A language has its own internal logic, its own grammar, its own way of putting things together with words that span various spectra of meaning.'[32] If there is an astonishing richness to the Babel language, a vertiginous re-conceptualization of the world in thinking in it that drains Rydra Wong (a child mute who has since developed an extraordinary multi-linguistic facility and become 'the voice of her age'), this is in part because the language, it seems, knows no word for the speaking subject: no 'I'. Initially, Rydra misreads this as a catastrophic aphasia peculiar to 'the Butcher', and tries to teach him the philosophical implications of 'mine' and 'thine'— this (so audaciously!) on a journey towards the tip of a space route called the Dragon's Tongue. In fact, however, reading this as a lack in language is a mistake: Babel-17 is the gateway to a telepathic relationship that has no conception of the subject as isolated monad. Rydra realizes that her own early language 'dysfunctions' and her ability to empathize with people and 'speak' their voices is due to telepathy: an *excess* of voices that dissolves the boundaries of the self. In *Babel-17*, therefore, aphasia crosses over into telepathy, and if the mute silently speaks to the status of science fiction as a genre, we shall find that telepathy, too, holds a similar function.

Telepathy is the pseudo-scientific concept coined by the psychical researcher Frederic Myers in 1882, who defined it as 'the communication of impressions of any kind from one mind to another, independently of the recognised channels of sense'.[33] It theorizes an utterly contradictory effect: it is distant touch (*tele-pathos*), intimate distance, the voice of the Other irrupting at the heart of the innermost recesses of the Self. Telepathy, therefore, dissolves the law of 'absolute isolation' of the personal self;[34] it would be something like a 'terrifying telephone', where there could be no hanging up, a perpetual babel of voices speaking in me and through me, 'me' and 'mine' being thus themselves de-railed.[35]

To seek the pure voice of a genre so obsessed with the possibility of telepathy, and from its earliest proto-generic stirrings, would therefore seem a difficult task at best: no 'I' to speak it, surely ('the Butcher' was right), because it would be traversed by a host of unlocatable 'impure' voices. The voice would always be at least *doubled*, always in excess of itself. Nevertheless, from the start the 'contaminations' of the telepathic voice have held a fascination: Kipling's 'Wireless' imbricates early radio reception with voices of the dead, whilst Stapledon's *First and Last Man* ascribes to telepathy the role as indicator of a leap in psychic evolution exactly in accord with Frederic Myers at his most utopian.[36] Once J.B. Rhine set up his experimental laboratory at Duke University, this quasi-legitimation from dubious statistical extrapolations fed into key loci of the genre, particularly through John W. Campbell's (to say nothing of Ron Hubbard's) weakness for Rhine's assertions. Indeed, by the 1950s the cadre of telepaths, misfits seeking anonymity in their hidden superiority over the mundane world, served as a figure for marginal, psychically 'gifted' sodalities of science fiction itself, from Wyndham's *The Chrysalids* to Sturgeon's *More Than Human*. Intimately connected to the emergence of science fiction, this figure, precisely of impurity, has yet been a way of corralling the genre, becoming a key *themata* or novum locating the extrapolative and fantasmatic potentialities of science fiction. Such a novum, given its powers to transgress boundaries (not least between 'hard' extrapolation and 'soft' fantasy), could not but begin to trouble generic borders, confuse the boundary of interiority and exteriority. Picking up this history once more from the 1960s, we can discern how the telepathic voice comes to foreground the very fragility of notions of 'pure' generic products.

Given that the mechanism of paranoia is the projection of interior complexes that return as persecuting voices, one would expect that the paranoid, unstable worlds of Philip Dick's fiction would be intensified in conjunction with the intimate invasions of telepathy. In *Ubik* (1969),[37] for instance, Runciter's 'prudence organisation' is meant to ensure non-contamination ('Defend your privacy, the ads yammered on the hour, from all media. Is a stranger tuning in on you? Are you *really* alone?... Terminate anxiety; contacting your nearest prudence organisation will first tell you if in fact you are the victim of unauthorised intrusions.')[38] Such purity is gained against telepathic infiltration by the blocking powers of anti-psi 'intertials'. In a text of profound ontological insecurity, however, the inertial talents appear (in one of many explanatory narratives) to be the very de-stabilizers of the 'real', sending Joe Chip into proliferating simulacral pasts. I read this text's anxiety as driven by the dream of an integral self and pure voice, even as it demonstrates the impossibility of such categories. Telepathy and anti-telepathy both serve equally to expose the shaky assertion of pure voice, indicating therefore a kind of foundational impurity. The inevitable failure to expulse impurity is foregrounded thematically in *Ubik*; it becomes a generic matter when we turn to Robert Silverberg's *Dying Inside* (1972).[39]

This novel concerns a neurotic telepath whose powers of reception are fading as he reaches middle age; the contraction of his ability passively to receive the voice of the Other has disappeared by the end of the novel. Selig moves from a sense of being assaulted by the voices of the city ('The compressed souls of those passengers form a single, inchoate mass, pressing insistently against me')[40] to a reiteration of the silence that envelops him ('Silence will become my mother tongue',[41] the last paragraph asserts). The trajectory is here towards a specific kind of silence, for the bleeding away of the telepathic voices in Silverberg's text is almost like the progressive elimination of the science fictional novum, until, by the end, we are no longer reading a science fiction novel at all: heterogeneous voices have been reduced to the homogeneity of the isolated monad of 'mainstream' fiction. This is a novel that wills the 'dying inside' of science fiction, a contemporaneous fictional account of Harlan Ellison's own pronouncement that 's—e f—n has died.'[42]

A double movement is at work in the text, though. As voices apparently retreat from him, Selig reflects on his ambivalence towards the death of his 'talent' in a way which increasingly borrows from high cultural voices: the book is saturated with T.S. Eliot's Prufrock and Gerontion, Yeats's ragings against old age, as well as references to Browning, Joyce, Traherne, Tennyson and Thoreau. An imaginary Kierkegaard exhorts Selig to 'Create silence'.[43] There are inserted mock undergraduate essays on Kafka and Greek tragedy. Also, Selig increasingly resorts to imitating other voices and writerly styles—the sermon, the epistle, the museum tour-guide.[44] The novum of telepathic receptivity may die, but at the level of generic text the intermixing of voices is positively, even anxiously, desired. The (noisy) silence which Selig enters marks a will to impurity *textually* by cancelling impure voices *thematically*.

The entry on Silverberg in the 1979 edition of *The Encyclopedia of Science Fiction* is largely dedicated to discussing Silverberg's recent 'retirement' from the genre, a retirement in effect enacted in the double movement of *Dying Inside*. The retirement proved to be temporary, of course, but this matched other voices of the New Wave, like Barry Malzberg, who were contemporaneously loudly exiting from the genre.[45] No other symptom of the death of the New Wave speaks so clearly as Michael Moorcock's disgust with the science fiction community, a field 'actively destructive to a writer's imagination and individuality'.[46] Unlike Ballard's occupation of a strange space uncertainly between science fiction and the mainstream, Moorcock has retained his dual career as fantasist and 'serious' novelist. With his ostensibly non-science fiction novel *Mother London* (1988),[47] however, these strands were woven together, and precisely by the

interruptive present absence of the telepathic voice. *Mother London* is
insistently traversed by voices—'*London's spine the district of Notting Hill is
almost entirely the product of the present generation eight years wasted suspected
poltergeists forward I the dunseye jane do chazzer all leave Jerusalem onun bugün
yüzmesi lâzum shokran merci all pork going to fry up soon no more pork*'[48]—
received telepathically by a gaggle of misfits who ultimately come to
embody the heterogeneous and occluded multiple histories of London.
Here, it is as if the tactic of retrieving 'subaltern' low cultural histories can
only be engineered by the extra-scientific, or science fictional, use of the
telepathic openness to the voices of the Other. Significantly, telepathy is
only associated with 'low' characters and 'low' discourses: of the three
'sensitives' at the centre of the text, Josef Kiss had been a music-hall mind
reader driven occasionally mad by 'little currents of electricity in the air
carrying the voices of all our times',[49] David Mummery writes popular
'hidden' histories of London, and Mary Gasalee interprets the world
through her dream engagements with Hollywood stars of the 1930s and
1940s, whilst attempting to control the telepathic blasts of voices with anti-
psychotic drugs. The italicized interruptions identify both the Babel of city
voices as well as chunks of text from *Woman's Weekly*, *The Magnet* or Captain
Marvel stories. The last of these marries science fictional content with
science fictional *medium*. In this project to recover an erased post-war
history of working-class London, therefore, Moorcock deploys the science
fictional trope of telepathy, which acts as a kind of invaginated pocket
inside a 'mainstream' text, confusing generic boundaries. Unlike
Silverberg's will-to-purity, Moorcock relies on the excess of telepathic
interruptions to suggest that the impurity and heterogeneity of the 'baggy'
novel alone can deliver a suppressed history.

The reception of the telepathic voice, its intimate distant touch, can
therefore be another productive site on which to reflect on the vicissitudes
of the generic voice. Like mutism, it is a figure that condenses diverse
potentialities. Silverberg wishes to suppress the telepathic as signal of genre;
Moorcock *enfolds* the science fictional into the framework of his text in
order to let its openness speak, impossibly, of histories beyond record. In
focusing on telepathy, that 'impure' signal of generic purity, speaking
science fiction is again displayed as possessing an inevitably self-divided
voice.

This sequence of capsule readings should indicate what I have been
trying to suggest about the voice of science fiction. From the attempts to
locate the pure voice of the genre in the metaphoric and metonymic poles
in the theories of Suvin and Delany, I have unearthed the source of these
accounts in the condition of aphasia. It is this figuration that has determined
my readings of the generic voice, one subject to symptomatic dysfunctions.

I have proposed that as far as generic specificity can be discerned, it is in the *vicissitudes* of that voice, tracked here in relation to the mute (lack) and telepathy (excess), that might prove a fruitful ground for analysis. It is my thesis that, as all genre products must re-mark on their generic identity, bear signals of their belonging to a genre, so it is that one re-mark of science fiction appears to concern its own awkwardness with its location inside a genre codified in submissive abjection to high culture, and readable in terms of an allegorical strand attached to anxieties concerning the voice. To focus on the vagaries of the voice can be a productive site on which to consider the speaking of science fiction. It is not to conclude that the genre cannot speak, but rather that *how* it speaks is subject to a mobile set of distortions, silencings and complex depredations.

Notes

1 My opening two paragraphs are directly indebted to Jacques Derrida's interrogation of Husserl's idealizing of 'the voice' in *Speech and Phenomena and Other Essays on Husserl's Theory of Signs* (Evanston, Illinois: Northwestern University Press, 1973).

2 See Gayatri Spivak: 'The position that only the subaltern can know the subaltern, only women can know women, and so on, cannot be held as a theoretical presupposition either, for it predicates the possibility of knowledge on identity... Knowledge is made possible and is sustained by irreducible difference, not identity.' *Outside in the Teaching Machine* (London: Routledge, 1993), p. 8.

3 See Steven Connor: 'Mass-market publishers and academic commentators on the fiction industry share the assumption that there are distinct groups of people in society known as romance readers, thriller readers, science fiction readers, etc. They also seem to share the assumption that the particular kinds of reading these readers undertake on every renewed encounter with their chosen genre yields them the same kind of gratification... The idea of the homogeneous reader thus conditions the assumption that this reader will always read for much the same reasons and in more or less the same way.' *The English Novel in History 1950–95* (London: Routledge, 1995), pp. 19–20. One might discern such beliefs in the 'homogeneous reader' as emanating from fandom too, although for reasons centring more on subcultural modalities of membership and identity.

4 This is Damien Broderick's highly useful term. See *Reading By Starlight: Postmodern Science Fiction* (London: Routledge, 1995).

5 The re-marking of genre is a process examined by Derrida in his 'Law of Genre', in *Acts of Literature*, ed. Derek Attridge (London: Routledge, 1993). I have discussed the re-mark at length in the opening chapter of my *The Angle Between Two Walls: The Fiction of J.G. Ballard* (Liverpool: Liverpool University Press, 1997).

6 Samuel Delany, '*Dichtung und* Science Fiction', in *Starboard Wine: More Notes on the Language of Science Fiction* (NY: Dragon Press, 1984), p. 176.

7 For Jakobson, see fn. 12 below. The best analysis of how metaphor and metonymy can serve literary theory still remains David Lodge's *The Modes of Modern Writing: Metaphor, Metonymy, and the Typology of Modern Literature* (London: Edward Arnold, 1977).

8 Darko Suvin, 'SF as Metaphor, Parable and Chronotope (with the bad conscience of Reaganism)', in *Positions and Presuppositions in Science Fiction* (London: Macmillan, 1988), p. 202.

9 Delany, *Starboard Wine*, p. 165.

10 Delany, *Starboard Wine*, p. 187 and 'Reading Modern American Science Fiction', in Richard Kostelanetz, ed., *American Writing Today* (Troy, NY: Whitsun, 1991), p. 525.

11 Lodge, *Modes of Modern Writing*, p. 74.

12 Roman Jakobson, 'Two Aspects of Language and Two Types of Aphasic Disturbances', in *Studies on Child Language and Aphasia* (The Hague: Mouton, 1971), p. 64.

13 However, Delany's argument that science fiction is a highly specific sub-language does tend to slide uncannily towards Jakobson's portrait of similarity disorder (the inability to *select* on the metaphoric pole), where the aphasic 'has lost the capacity for code-switching, [and] the "idiolect" indeed becomes the sole linguistic reality... As long as he does not regard another's speech as a message addressed to him in his own verbal pattern...[h]e considers the other's utterance to be either gibberish or at least in an unknown language' (*Starboard Wine*, p. 61). Doesn't such an assertion—there is only one idiolect, one code, and everything beyond it is 'gibberish'—sound a little like the most aggressive defences of science fiction, for instance in the essays of Robert Heinlein? 'The cult of the phony in art will disappear, so called "modern art" will be discussed only by psychiatrists,' screams Heinlein. 'Pandora's Box', in *The Worlds of Robert Heinlein* (London: New English Library, 1970), p. 17.

14 Suvin, *Positions*, p. 202.

15 For reservations on Suvin see Edward James, *Science Fiction in the Twentieth Century* (Oxford: Oxford University Press, 1994); Broderick, *Reading By Starlight*.

16 Roland Barthes, 'The Grain of the Voice', in *Image Music Text* (NY: Noonday Press, 1977), p. 187.

17 J.G. Ballard, 'The Sound-Sweep', in *The Voices of Time* (London: Dent, 1984) and Octavia Butler, 'Speech Sounds', in *Bloodchild and Other Stories* (NY: Four Walls, Eight Windows, 1995).

18 See, for instance, Freud's 'Fragment of an Analysis of a Case of Hysteria ['Dora']', *Pelican Freud Library* Volume 8 and the essay on the treatment of Elisabeth Von R in *Studies in Hysteria, Pelican Freud Library*, Volume 3.

19 Ballard, *Voices*, p. 45.

20 Ballard, *Voices*, p. 46.

21 Ballard, *Voices*, p. 61.

22 Ballard, *Voices*, p. 54.

23 Ballard, *Voices*, p. 43.

24 The clearest rejection of psychological explanation comes in *Adulthood Rites*, where a survivor of the apocalypse who had worked as a psychiatrist gives up those frameworks for the 'genetic' models proposed by the alien Oankali: 'The Oankali say people like me dealt with far more physical disorders than we were capable of recognising'. Octavia Butler, *Adulthood Rites* (NY: Warner Books, 1990), p. 259.

25 'All aphasic people have in common (by definition) that they have suffered some form of brain damage...which has destroyed neuronal cells in parts of the brain on which language seems to be critically dependent'. Ruth Lesser and Lesley Milroy, *Linguistics and Aphasia: Psycholinguistic and Pragmatic Aspects of Intervention* (London: Longman, 1993), p. 8.

26 Butler, *Bloodchild*, p. 105.

27 Butler, *Bloodchild*, p. 105.

28 See Donna Haraway, 'A Manifesto for Cyborgs: Science, Technology and Socialist Feminism in the 1980s', in *Feminism/Postmodernism*, ed. Linda Nicholson (London: Routledge, 1990) and Jenny Wolmark, *Aliens and Others: Science Fiction, Feminism and Postmodernism* (Hemel Hempstead: Harvester Wheatsheaf, 1993). More sustained thoughts on the work of Octavia Butler can be found in my '"Horror and Beauty in Rare Combination": The Miscegenate Fictions of Octavia Butler', *Women: A Cultural Review*, 7.1 (May 1996).

29 See Andrew Ross, 'Cyberpunk in Boystown', in *Strange Weather: Culture, Science and Technology in the Age of Limits* (London: Verso, 1991) for the 'masculinism' of cyberpunk. Note, too, the absence of consideration of the 'feminist' impact on science fiction since the 1970s in histories like Damien Broderick's *Reading By Starlight* or Scott Bukatman's *Terminal Identity: The Virtual Subject in Postmodern Science Fiction* (Durham: Duke University Press, 1993).

30 Gayatri Spivak, 'Can the Subaltern Speak?', in *Colonial Discourse and Postcolonial Theory*, ed. Patrick Williams and Laura Chrisman (Hemel Hempstead: Harvester Wheatsheaf, 1993), pp. 82–83.

31 Samuel Delany, *Babel-17* (London: Sphere, 1967), p. 109.

32 Delany, *Babel-17*, p. 10.

33 Frederic Myers, *Human Personality and Its Survival of Bodily Death* (London: Longmans, 1903), p. xxii.

34 William James's views on 'the personal self' held that 'Absolute isolation…is the law'. This did not preclude an enduring interest in telepathy, however. *The Principles of Psychology* (NY: Dover, 1950 [1890]), p. 226.

35 Jacques Derrida, 'Telepathy', *Oxford Literary Review*, 10 (1988), p. 13.

36 'Is it not, then, conceivable that in these direct telepathic transferences between mind and mind…we may be gaining a first glimpse of a process of psychical evolution…of some incipient organic solidarity between the psychical units we call man and man?' Myers, *Phantasms of the Living*, Volume II (London: Trubner, 1886), p. 316.

37 Philip Dick, *Ubik* (London: Panther, 1973).

38 Dick, *Ubik*, p. 12.

39 Robert Silverberg, *Dying Inside* (London: Sidgwick and Jackson, 1974).

40 Silverberg, *Dying Inside*, p. 7.

41 Silverberg, *Dying Inside*, p. 188.

42 Harlan Ellison, *Dangerous Visions* (combined edition) (London: Gollancz, 1987), p. xxiii.

43 Silverberg, *Dying Inside*, p. 115.

44 The last of these mimicked voices pauses on the tour of Selig's apartment to appraise the shelves of science fiction books, reflecting: 'These writers, gifted as they were, were the outsiders' (p. 112).

45 Barry Malzberg, 'Rage, Pain, Alienation and Other Aspects of Writing Science Fiction', *Fantasy and Science Fiction* (April 1976).

46 Michael Moorcock, 'Letter', *Foundation*, 9 (1975), p. 49.

47 Michael Moorcock, *Mother London* (London: Secker and Warburg, 1988).

48 Moorcock, *Mother London*, p. 385.

49 Moorcock, *Mother London*, p. 279.

'A Language of the Future': Discursive Constructions of the Subject in *A Clockwork Orange* and *Random Acts of Senseless Violence*

VERONICA HOLLINGER

This essay reads Jack Womack's near-future novel *Random Acts of Senseless Violence* (1993) in the context of Anthony Burgess's *A Clockwork Orange* (1962).[1] Although published thirty years apart, the latter in Britain and the former in the United States, *A Clockwork Orange* and *Random Acts of Senseless Violence* demonstrate some striking similarities. Both are the stories of very young protagonists, Burgess's 15-year-old Alex and Womack's 12-year-old Lola. Both are set in near futures of incredible violence, state violence as well as street violence. And, most strikingly, both use a language which is quite radically different from our own familiar English, a narrative strategy which results in a powerful kind of defamiliarization. My initial interest in these two novels began as an examination of the 'future' discourses which are so outstanding a feature of each text; however, over time I have become more interested in the kinds of fictional subjectivity constructed *through* these discourses, rather than in the discourses themselves.

1. Theory/Context

The theoretical context for this discussion is what has been called the 'death' of the subject, one of the most resonant of the many 'crises' which have come to be identified with the postmodern condition. This particular crisis has arisen because of redefinitions of the subject which, in the context of Enlightenment thought, has traditionally been characterized as the individual self of liberal humanism. Recent reformulations of subjectivity, however, have raised intriguing and disturbing challenges to Enlightenment positions. For instance, Fredric Jameson suggests a convincing (re)construction in his claim that the 'shift in the dynamics of cultural pathology can be characterized as one in which the alienation of the subject [a familiar concern of modernism] is displaced by the fragmentation of the subject'.[2] Within the context of the postmodern, the subject is no longer that unified self, that self-identified entity, the construction of which has been tracked by Michel Foucault in works like *The History of Sexuality* and *The Order of Things*. In one of his more apocalyptic—and frequently quoted—turns of phrase, in fact, Foucault writes of 'man' as 'an invention of recent date. And one perhaps nearing its end.'[3] Analyses like Jameson's and Foucault's are only two of many—linguistic, psychoanalytic, political, and philosophical—which have resulted in the deconstruction of notions of an autonomous and unified subjectivity.[4] And, in the novels under discussion here, we can see something of how fictional narratives undertake to maintain or to undermine the liberal-humanist illusion of the fixed subject.

My interest in the narrative subject of science fiction, or, to be more accurate, in the *narrating* subject, lies in the fact of the contradictions which arise when we look at this subject in the above terms. H.G. Wells's *The Time Machine* can provide a useful example here. In an earlier study examining, among other things, the discursive construction of the Time Traveller as I/eye witness reporter of the events in the novel, I suggested that the 'truth' of the Traveller's story is guaranteed through his own account of it, a convention used in the nineteenth century to support the fictional truths of texts as disparate as *Jane Eyre* (1848), *David Copperfield* (1850), and *Dracula* (1897).[5] At the same time, the revelation at the end of *The Time Machine*, that the Time Traveller has, in fact, been missing for three years, serves to undercut the illusion of presence which has been so carefully constructed through the use of the first-person narrative voice. Perhaps the most ironically effective signal of the absence of Wells's narrating subject is the signature written by the Time Traveller at the Palace of Green Porcelain 'upon the nose of a steatite monster from South America that particularly took my fancy'.[6] The unnamed Traveller has at last named himself, but that name exists on a monument from the past buried in a museum in the future—never in the present.

This play of presence and absence is created and sustained through language which constructs the impression of an individually realized character recounting her or his own story at the same time that the fact of a written account emphasizes the absence of any actual subject doing the story-telling. It is not only Wells's Time Traveller who is 'always already' absent from his own story; it is any first-person narrator. Thus, at the heart of even the most determinedly coherent construction of the narrating subject is the 'worm' of its own deconstruction, the potential for recognizing unified subjectivity as 'simply' a language-effect which produces the simulation of an authentic self.

2. Languages of the Future

I have borrowed the title of this essay from performance artist Laurie
Anderson, whose ironic reflections upon the vicissitudes of communication
in the postmodern world frequently take the form of satirical allegories.
In her 1979 performance piece, *Americans on the Move*, she recounts a fictional conversation with a teenage girl:

> If she didn't understand something, it just 'didn't scan.' Everything
> was circuitry...electronics...switching. We talked mostly about her
> boyfriend. He was never in a bad mood—he was in a bad mode.
> Modey kind of guy. The romance was rocky and she kept saying, 'Oh
> man like, it's like it's so DIGITAL.' She just meant that the relationship
> was on again/off again. [...] It was a language of sounds...of noise
> ...of switching. [...] One thing instantly replaces another—a
> language of the future.[7]

As Anderson's satirical account suggests, it is the young girl rather than
the older woman whose experiences are being mediated through this
'language of the future'; the artist can only comment upon it in her art.
This recalls an observation made by N. Katherine Hayles in the context of
a discussion about the nature of postmodernism:

> To live postmodernism is to live as schizophrenics are said to do, in
> a world of disconnected present moments that jostle one another but
> never form a continuous (much less logical) progression. The prior
> experiences of older people act as anchors that keep them from fully
> entering the postmodern stream of spliced contexts and
> discontinuous time... The case could be made that the people in this
> country [the United States] who know the most about how
> postmodernism *feels* (as distinct from how to envision or analyze it)
> are all under the age of sixteen.[8]

This certainly helps to explain why Russell Hoban, who, in *Riddley Walker*
(1980) creates a strong sense of the verisimilitude of his future world
through the invention of a future language, writes this novel as the first-
person adventures of a twelve-year-old narrator. As extrapolation,
Riddley's nearly illiterate language serves to characterize the post-
catastrophe world at the immediate level of the words on the page. As a
kind of allegorical tool, however, the language recapitulates the action of
the narrative, inviting the reader to participate in Riddley's quest for
meaning—represented by him, ironically, as an exercise in extrapolation,
or 'strapping the lates'[9]—through involvement in the difficulties of
decoding an almost completely foreign sign system. Hoban's narrative
motifs make of his novel an overtly self-referential text which explores the

importance of story-telling as a means of giving shape to the human situation, indeed, as a means of creating meaning.[10] Written in what Hoban extrapolates to be the language of such a far future, the novel is Riddley's self-conscious construction of his own story, filled with his comments on the act of writing itself: 'Walker is my name and I am the same. Riddley Walker. Walking my riddels where ever theyve took me and walking them now on this paper the same.'[11] Hoban's commitment in this novel to the tenets of a transcendent humanism is demonstrated in this relatively uncomplicated self-identification between name and subject—'Walker is my name and I am the same'—and in a reliable self-sameness between experience and narration.

Like Hoban's novel, *A Clockwork Orange* and *Random Acts of Senseless Violence* are *Bildungsromans*, but they are each quite different from *Riddley Walker*.[12] Unlike Hoban's far-future narration, both Burgess and Womack have written stories set in worlds not so very different from our own. Central to each is the dystopian vision of a near future in which excessive violence is both a defining feature and an inevitable response. More importantly, perhaps, while Riddley's language is common to everyone in his society and serves to create the sense of a more or less unified future world,[13] Burgess and Womack produce, not 'lingua francas' of the future, but kinds of *anti*-English representing the social, class, and generational splintering in their fictional futures.

3. Two Narrating Subjects

In *A Clockwork Orange*, Burgess's entry in the tradition of satirical British dystopias which includes Huxley's *Brave New World* and Orwell's *1984*, Alex's triumph over the forces of the political conservatism which try to 'reform' him is reinforced by his gleeful refusal to speak anything but 'nadsat', the polyglot gang-slang of 'ultra-violence' which sets him and his teenage 'brothers' apart from the mainstream society against which they define themselves. In the context of the comment by Jameson quoted above, we can read Alex as the perfectly alienated subject of modernism. Nadsat is a future teenage slang influenced by Russian, gypsy slang, and London cockney rhyming slang. The effect is a language that functions as part of the narrative material which sets the story in the future; while remaining fairly comprehensible, it is also 'foreign' enough to distance Alex's time from our own.

Alex's tone is consistently bright, breezy, humorous, cynical, confident, and amoral, as is Alex himself. This is the opening of his story:

> 'What's it going to be then, eh?'
> There was me, that is Alex, and my three droogs, that is Pete,

Georgie, and Dim, Dim being really dim, and we sat in the Korova
Milkbar making up our rassoodocks what to do with the evening, a
flip dark winter bastard though dry. The Korova Milkbar was a milk-
plus mesto, and you may, O my brothers, have forgotten what these
mestos were like, things changing so skorry these days and everybody
very quick to forget, newspapers not being read much either.[14]

The result is the satirical picture of a society moving towards an ever more
repressive future. Like Orwell, Burgess foresees a social trend toward
increasing state/government control of individual lives, culminating in a
political system which hires thugs as police and condones brain-washing
techniques to 'reform' criminals. Youth violence has reached an extreme
which is clearly fantastic; the failure of the adult world to prevent/control/
reform youth-as-psychopathic-condition reaches an equally blackly
humorous extreme. Political pragmatism reigns: venal politicians grasp at
sure and easy ways to erase crime; the police are as violent as the criminals
they battle; political reformers are prepared to destroy 'victims' like Alex
in their attempts to bring down the government. These mainstream social/
political structures try, but fail, to reduce Alex to 'a clockwork orange'.

Set against these efforts on the part of the future dystopia to reduce
individuals to conditioned objects is Alex's narrative voice, which remains
always individualistic, coherent, and resistant. Burgess reinforces the
strong subjectivity at the centre of his novel with a tripartite narrative
structure which is also strongly coherent. Each segment opens with the
words: 'What's it going to be then, eh?' repeated three times within several
pages. This repetition creates a pattern which helps to unify the story which
is, of course, Alex's story. The question itself implies the power of the
individual to make choices, something which the government's new
reform strategies, like the nefarious Lodovico Technique, are designed to
destroy.

Lest readers miss its point, Burgess's text addresses the question of choice
directly on several occasions, not least through the character of the prison
chaplain, who believes that 'Goodness is something chosen. When a man
cannot choose he ceases to be a man.'[15] The question he aims at his 'little'
charge serves to highlight the moral dilemma raised by the possibilities of
enforced 'reform': 'Is a man who chooses the bad perhaps in some way
better than a man who has the good imposed upon him?'[16] In the end, of
course, the powers-that-be fail to make any lasting dents in Alex, and
readers are left cheering for a protagonist who has overcome the forces of
repressive conservatism and managed to maintain his own strongly
individual identity. We can think of the actual narration of Alex's story as
a kind of memoir recollected in tranquillity.

In 1963, Burgess cut the final chapter of the original edition—in which

Alex decides to find a wife and begin creating more little creatures just like himself—so that most editions of the novel conclude with his hymn to music and violence, as he listens once more to Beethoven's Ninth Symphony:

> Oh, it was gorgeosity and yumyumyum. When it came to the Scherzo I could viddy myself very clear running and running on like very light and mysterious nogas, carving the whole litso of the creeching world with my cut-throat britva. And there was the slow movement and the lovely last singing movement still to come. I was cured all right.[17]

The reader's own answering exhilaration is, of course, a kind of trap set by Burgess to implicate us all in the continuing ultra-violence of this not-so-future world. Not for nothing does Alex continually draw us in by addressing his readers as 'O my brothers', making it as difficult as possible for us to remain distanced from the events he recounts and the values he represents, which, he implies, are our own values as well.[18]

The cumulative effect of *Random Acts of Senseless Violence* is very different. Like Burgess, Womack narrates the story of a young person, told in her own words, as she lives through a series of horrifically violent near-future experiences. The narrative structure, however, is not a coherent flow, but a series of disparate and fragmented diary entries. Lola begins her diary on her twelfth birthday and ends it about six months later. The story she tells is of an urban society disintegrating under the pressures of economic and social horrors which follow one another in an ever-increasing flood of disaster. These disasters impinge more and more severely upon Lola's own family until her father is dead, her mother a basket-case buried by tranquillizers, her younger sister shipped off to the right-wing Aunt Chrissie's to get her out of the increasingly dangerous New York slum in which they've come to live, and Lola herself expelled even from the tough street gang which has become her new family. In the end, she is completely alone and utterly cut off from her previous life.

Womack's science fiction writing has always been noteworthy for its imaginative use of language as the material through which he builds credible futures. In *Random Acts*, however, language does more than simply help to construct a future scenario. Equally important is the way in which the gradual shift in the discourse of Lola's diary entries, from 'ordinary' middle-class English to the language of youth subcultures and street gangs, tracks the gradual breaking down of Lola's personality. In fact, the 'future' language used by Womack's characters is suspiciously contemporary.[19] The effect of a world situated, like that of *Max Headroom*, only 'twenty minutes into the future', is inescapable; background events like the repeated assassinations of American presidents, full-scale riots on Long Island, widespread ecological devastation, and the collapse of any coherent economic system are simply extreme versions of events which we see all around us today.

When *Random Acts* opens, it is to Lola's first entry in her diary:

> FEBRUARY 15
>
> Mama says mine is a night mind. The first time she said that I asked her what she meant and she said, 'Darling you think best in the dark like me.' I think she's right. Here I am staying up late tonight so I can write in my new diary. Mama gave it to me for my birthday today. I love to write.
>
> My...name is Lola Hart. Faye and Michael Hart are our parents. We live on 86th Street near Park Avenue in New York City.[20]

Six months later, Lola's final diary entry follows on the destruction of her family and her own plunge into violence and murder. In an action worthy of Burgess's Alex, Lola beats to death with a baseball bat the psychopathic bookstore owner, Mr Mossbacher, whom she blames for her father's death and the subsequent breakup of her family. Even her fellow gang members consider her beyond the pale now and she ends her narrative completely alone, a ghost-like figure of pure and mindless aggression. In one of her last entries we can read her struggle to hold on to her sense of herself: 'When I eye myself mirrored I don't see me anymore it's like I got replaced and didn't know it but I'm still here underneath I'm still here.'[21] In fact, Lola's weakening efforts to hold on to her 'self' during this never-ending series of violent assaults might be said to constitute the main narrative motif of her story.

This is Lola's last diary entry:

> JULY 10
>
> Night's darkened full now and I spec I'm finally set to ride. Take me street take me.
>
> Lookabout people. Beef me overlong and I groundbound you express... Lookabout all you. Spec your mirror and there I be. Crazy evilness be my design if that's what needs wearing. ... Shove do push and push do shove and everbody in this world leave lovelost hereafter. Lookabout. Chase me if you want. Funnyface me if you keen but mark this when I go chasing I go catching. Eye cautious when you step out people cause I be running streetwild come nightside and nobody safes when I ride. I bite. Can't cut me now. Can't fuck me now. Can't hurt me now. No more. No more.
>
> Night night... Night night. I'm with the DCons now.[22]

Lola's 'night mind', which she mentions in her first entry, has taken over and the little girl who wrote that first entry has disappeared forever.

The text's concentration on this thematic of lost identity and disappearing subjectivity expands to include other characters as well as Lola. In fact, one important reason why Lola is unable to hold on to her self is because she experiences everyone around her changing as well. When her younger sister is sent away to live with the dreadful Aunt Chrissie, Lola complains to her diary that 'She won't be there a month before she's Chrissified... Knowing somebody so long and then they sudden change disrupts so it's not handleable anymore or at least I spec not for me.' Earlier in the novel, Lola's school friend Lori is shipped off by her parents to 'Kure-a-Kid', a kind of reform school for disruptive children. When she returns to school she hands Lola a card: 'The logo of Kure-a-Kid where they zombified her was at the top with the phone number. The only other thing it said on the card was from the Bible, we shall not die but we shall all be changed.'[23]

As Lola's life becomes infected by ever more heightened instances of violence, she begins to experience this process of the loss of self. Her first real participation in the violence which comes to define her world occurs when, after being provoked, she attacks Weez, one of the street kids she has begun to associate with: 'I stopped thinking though I didn't realize it then only after. I had pictures in my mind of the way she hit me with the bottle and she looked at me and her stupid face and the noise she made eating potato chips. It made me madder and madder and madder and I slammed harder and harder. She screamed but I didn't care.'[24] After a later fight, Lola again questions her own reactions: 'Today I suddenly felt bad about hitting that guy like I did... what's the matter with me why didn't I think of it before now? ... It wasn't like he wasn't human or anything. I could have killed him and it took me till today to care. I still remember the sound his head made when I hit it.'[25] When she finally succumbs to her own murderous rage and batters Mr Mossbacher to death, the text makes clear her now-complete division from her former self: 'When I eyed him full color again it sickened but there was no end to swinging till my arms tired and he was all broke up... What got me most was that my hands looked like somebody else's it's true when that's said.'[26] This 'somebody else' even has a new name, 'Crazy Lola', which is how her street friends begin to refer to her after she has demonstrated her capacity for participating in the violence of this new urban nightmare.

The DCons, site of the final disappearance of the little girl who becomes Crazy Lola, are one of Womack's most interesting narrative elements. Spoken of only in whispers by the other street gangs, the DCons represent the ultimate evil in this world of urban garbage. As Lola's friend Izzie tells her: 'The DCons be bad evilness, the worst of worst... They prime night-crawlers, they soulslashers, they roll when it darken and nobody see their shadow. Everybody run when the DCons come.' The DCons lie in wait for those who will inevitably join them: '"The DCons know where the lines be before people. The lines they never crossed before. They get you to cross your line. When you cross it, you with the DCons. You never come back," Iz said.'[27]

It becomes clear that the DCons are not an actual gang so much as a kind of violent ideal, the personification of the emotional and psychological state into which various of the characters sink once they've crossed their own lines, as Lola does when she murders Mr Mossbacher. Thus the end of Lola's narrative is also the end of Lola, as the middle-class young girl spirals into the black vacuum of psychopathology. Her diary recounts the disintegration of the subject of her story.

This is one of the most striking differences between Burgess's and Womack's novels: the language of *A Clockwork Orange* serves to shore up the solidity of a unified and coherent subject, while the language of *Random Acts of Senseless Violence*, as it shifts further and further away from where it began, functions as 'living proof' of the fragmentation and eventual disappearance of the subject of the narrative. The narrating self, originally constructed in the discourse of middle-class family values, becomes transformed as the discourse is transformed, to be replaced by a fragmented discourse of absence defined by the experiences and value-systems of a street culture of violence and sudden death. Rather than a tranquil recollection, therefore, *Random Acts* is characterized by the urgent immediacy of its ongoing narration and by the abrupt breaking-off of that narration.[28]

Womack's use of the diary form constructs a different kind of position for the reader as well: where Burgess builds in the reader's sympathy and, to whatever extent, her complicity, Womack's use of the diary form serves to situate the reader as voyeur, eavesdropping on a completely private story and helpless to intervene in the extremely painful events it recounts. In addition, the diary form creates a sense of the immediacy of events and actions that links Womack's narrative with the 'schizophrenic' nature of postmodern experience described above by Hayles as the sense of living 'in a world of disconnected present moments that jostle one another but never form a continuous (much less logical) progression'.[29] As Womack's title indicates, events in Lola's world are both 'random' and 'senseless', their disconnectedness the result of the world around her spiralling out of control.

It is tempting to think of Burgess's Alex as the modernist subject of liberal humanism, a coherent identity shored up by the consistency of both his narrative's structure and its discursive stability.[30] In addition, the novel's thematic concern with the question of agency, and its triumphant assertion of the power of the individual to choose and to act, serves also to maintain the sense of a coherent and active consciousness at the centre of the text. Womack's Lola, on the other hand, is the subject of a kind of postmodernism or posthumanism: her experience is mediated through the language she uses to interpret her world and her identity shifts as her language shifts. In the end, her very existence is annihilated, as her narrative voice is reduced to silence in her resolution to write no more.

Unlike Burgess's modernist classic, Womack's postmodernist sf novel represents a particular attitude about the subject and agency identified, for example, by feminist theorist Patricia Waugh, when she writes that 'Postmodernism expresses nostalgia for but loss of belief in the concept of the human subject as an agent effectively intervening in history, through the fragmentation of discourses, language games, and decentring of subjectivity.'[31] But does this make of *Random Acts of Senseless Violence* a post-modern narrative which dramatizes the illusory nature of unified subjectivity or a modernist narrative of the tragedy of destroyed identity?[32] The answer is that it is probably both. Given the level of emotional trauma with which the reader is invited to empathize, I would suggest that Womack's novel is, like most science fiction, at least partially invested in the ideology of coherent and unified subjectivity. Its story, therefore, is a kind of tragedy rather than a neutral report. Its anti-humanism is the flip side of a humanist protest against the waste of lives and personalities in the fragmented and violent condition of the postmodern.

4. Ending with Atwood

Given the effect of coherent identity which results from the use of a first-person narrator, is there a way for a narrative to construct and then deconstruct its narrating subject *without* moving the story towards tragedy, that is, without dramatizing the postmodern condition as a tragic condition, that is, treating questions of agency and choice more optimistically? The point of this brief coda to my primary discussion is to call attention to one of the few sf novels I know which both acknowledges the absence of coherent subjectivity and manages to avoid doing so in nostalgic terms. This is Margaret Atwood's *The Handmaid's Tale* (1985), which focuses on both the composition and decomposition of the subject and of identity within the context of postmodernism.[33]

At the beginning of Atwood's novel, the narrative voice is disembodied, reaching us 'from a distant place'[34] where personality has all but disintegrated under the weight of dystopian conditioning. Self-construction is a painful enterprise undertaken in the night hours of privacy and loneliness, the negative spaces of time, narrated in tones of ironic sincerity: 'I wait. I compose myself. Myself is a thing I must now compose as one composes a speech. What I must present is a made thing, not something born.'[35] Here Atwood's text both insists on the importance of such self-composition and calls attention to its artificiality. For Atwood's Handmaid, active resistance to oppression only becomes possible through this act of self-construction.

At the end, of course, *The Handmaid's Tale* proceeds to unravel the subjectivity whose meticulous construction has provided its narrative impetus. The 'Historical Notes on *The Handmaid's Tale*', a brief segment appended to the narrative proper, succeeds in casting doubt upon the very existence of the subject of the preceding narration. Like Wells's Time Traveller, we discover that, while Offred is the central presence in her own story, she has always been an absence within the text-as-a-whole. Atwood's Handmaid both exists and does not exist; she maintains a contingent presence in the play/space between the narration which composes her and the Notes which undermine that composition.

The Handmaid's Tale metaphorically undertakes an extreme deconstruction of the traditional subject of humanism, at the same time as it succeeds in constructing a strategically contingent subject capable of choice and action. Within the context of postmodernity, this kind of contingent construction takes account of theories of the 'death of the subject' while it avoids supporting the essentialism of a discredited liberal humanism.

Notes

1 Jack Womack, *Random Acts of Senseless Violence* (New York: Grove, 1995 [1993]). Anthony Burgess, *A Clockwork Orange* (New York: Penguin, 1972 [1962]).

2 Fredric Jameson, 'Postmodernism, or the Cultural Logic of Late Capitalism', *New Left Review*, 146 (July–August 1984), p. 63.

3 Michel Foucault, *The Order of Things: An Archeology of the Human Sciences* (New York: Vintage, 1973 [1970]), p. 387.

4 Reactions to this contemporary problematization of the self are by no means homogeneous, even among poststructuralists. They range from the gloominess of the Althusserian model of an ineluctable 'interpellation' to cautiously celebratory responses by feminists such as Teresa de Lauretis and Judith Butler. Paul Smith's *Discerning the Subject* (Minneapolis: University of Minnesota Press, 1988) provides a useful overview of some of the issues at stake in contemporary (re)theorizations of subjectivity and agency.

5 See my 'Deconstructing the Time Machine', *Science-Fiction Studies*, 14 (July 1987), pp. 201–21.

6 H.G. Wells, *The Time Machine* [1895], in *The Works of H.G. Wells* (Atlantic Edition, 1; London: T. Fisher Unwin, 1924), p. 89.

7 Laurie Anderson, 'From *Americans on the Move*', *October* 8 (Spring 1979), p. 48.

8 N. Katherine Hayles, *Chaos Bound: Orderly Disorder in Contemporary Literature and Science* (Ithaca, New York: Cornell University Press, 1984), p. 282.

9 Russell Hoban, *Riddley Walker* (London: Pan Books, 1982 [1980]), p. 197.

10 Hoban's efforts to imagine what language might be like in a far-future, post-literate England have been the subject of several studies. See, for example, David J. Lake's 'Making the Two One: Language and Mysticism in *Riddley Walker*', *Extrapolation*, 25 (Summer 1984), pp. 157–70. On the broad topic of language use and invention in science fiction, see Walter E. Meyers, *Aliens and Linguists: Language Study and Science Fiction* (Athens, GA: University of Georgia Press, 1980).

11 Hoban, *Riddley Walker*, p. 8.

12 This discussion would be incomplete without a mention of Octavia Butler's gripping *Parable of the Sower* (New York: Warner, 1995 [1993]). While it is only tangentially relevant here, given its virtually transparent language, it was published in the same year as *Random Acts of Senseless Violence* and also takes the form of a diary written by a young person in the near future. Seventeen-year-old Lauren Olamina writes of the catastrophes wrecking a shockingly violent and desperately impoverished California and of her attempt, as leader of a heterogeneous group of survivors, to find a place of safety where she can establish a new community according to the tenets of 'Earthseed', a kind of secular religion founded on the principle of God-as-Change. The transparent language and strong narrative voice of *Parable of the Sower* reflect Butler's allegiance to conventionally realist constructions of both character and narrative; her challenges to liberal-humanist philosophy work themselves out elsewhere, in the disruptions of hierarchies of race and gender which are so central to her science fiction.

For a general consideration of some of the ways in which the *Bildungsroman* has been integrated into genre science fiction, see Peter C. Hall's '"The Space Between" in Space: Some Versions of the *Bildungsroman* in Science Fiction', *Extrapolation*, 29 (Summer 1988), pp. 153–59.

13 See Meyers's discussion about the function of 'future' language as a unifying feature of the science-fictional world (*Aliens and Linguists*, p. 21).

14 Burgess, *Clockwork Orange*, p. 5.

15 Burgess, *Clockwork Orange*, p. 67.

16 Burgess, *Clockwork Orange*, p. 76.

17 Burgess, *Clockwork Orange*, p. 139.

18 Female readers are less likely to be enthralled by little Alex, of course, and therefore more resistant to his charms. It is obvious that the implied reader of Burgess's novel is a male reader.

While I will resist the temptation to launch into a reading of these novels from the perspective of gender issues, it is important to note that Womack's science fiction novels demonstrate a much more self-conscious treatment of these issues, at least in part, we can speculate, because of having been written more recently. Although *Random Acts of Senseless Violence* is sometimes conflicted and inconsistent in its relatively complex attempts to deal with gender issues, the coherent and comfortable gender oppositions which appear in *A Clockwork Orange* suggest that, for Burgess, gender business as usual is the rule, not the exception; indeed, misogyny is the rule, not the exception, in a world in which women's bodies are commodities to be passed around from 'brother' to 'brother'. In contrast, not only is Lola, who identifies herself as lesbian, a quite successfully delineated female character, but male characters are, to some extent, confined to the background in this text. Only female characters like Lola, her sister Boob, her girlfriends, and her mother speak directly; her father, the bookstore owner Mr Mossbacher, and other male characters are always quoted indirectly in Lola's diary.

19 For example, 'going postal', one of the most striking expressions used in *Random Acts*, is now in common use in both Britain and North America. As Lola explains, it applies to situations 'Like when people who work at the post office go crazy and kill everybody they work with' (p. 159). This invites readers to wonder to what extent Womack's future street slang is his own invention and how much has simply been gleaned from contemporary Los Angeles and New York youth cultures which, to many of us, seem already to be science-fictional constructions.

20 Womack, *Random Acts*, p. 7.

21 Womack, *Random Acts*, p. 241.

22 Womack, *Random Acts*, pp. 255–56.

23 Womack, *Random Acts*, pp. 214, 111.

24 Womack, *Random Acts*, p. 157.

25 Womack, *Random Acts*, p. 180.

26 Womack, *Random Acts*, p. 252.

27 Womack, *Random Acts*, pp. 186–87.

28 In fact, Lola's story has a kind of continuity outside the boundaries of her diary since the narratives in Womack's various novels tend to be complexly intertwined. The central voice in his previous novel, *Elvissey* (New York: Tor, 1993) belongs to a character named Isabel Bonney who remembers childhood experiences shared by 'me and Judy and poor lost Lola' (p. 24). It is clear that Isabel is the grown-up version of Lola's friend and lover, Iz, an important secondary character in *Random Acts*. I am grateful to Andrew M. Butler for drawing my attention to this particular connection between the two novels, and for the contextualizing links he traces among Womack's novels as a body of writing. See his essay, '"My Particular Virus": (Re-)Reading Jack Womack's Dryco Chronicles', in this collection.

29 Hayles, *Chaos Bound*, p. 282. See also Fredric Jameson on the postmodern condition as a schizophrenic condition (Fredric Jameson, 'Postmodernism and Consumer Society', in Hal Foster, ed., *The Anti-Aesthetic: Essays on Postmodern Culture* [Port Townsend, WA: Bay Press, 1983], p. 111–25, at p. 119).

30 Burgess's modernism is also suggested in the obvious constructedness of his future language. Nadsat is an extremely artificial language, a kind of aesthetic and intellectual exercise which bears little relation to any existent youth slang. Womack's future slang, on the other hand, as I have noted above, suggests the more 'organic' evolution of contemporary street language and, I am tempted to argue, demonstrates more of a postmodern sensibility in its deployment of popular cultural forms. I am grateful to the discussants at the 'Speaking Science Fiction' conference, especially to Jenny Wolmark, who raised this question about the 'unnaturalness' of the future language in *A Clockwork Orange*.

31 Patricia Waugh, *Feminine Fictions: Revisiting the Postmodern* (New York: Routledge, 1989), p. 9.

32 To complicate my speculations here, I should point out that this novel has been read by several of my university students as proof of Lola's achievement of heroic stature, her development into a persona strong enough to survive the horrors of her narrative world. Others have argued that Lola's descent into the psychopathology of the DCons seems, under the circumstances, to be a perfectly logical response to unbearable emotional and social pressures.

33 Margaret Atwood, *The Handmaid's Tale* (Toronto: McClelland-Bantam,

1986 [1985]). For a more detailed reading of the de/construction of subjectivity in Atwood's novel, see my 'Putting on the Feminine: Gender and Negativity in *Frankenstein* and *The Handmaid's Tale*', in Daniel Fischlin, ed., *Negation, Critical Theory, and Postmodern Textuality* (Dordrecht, The Netherlands: Kluwer, 1994), pp. 203–24.

34 Atwood, *The Handmaid's Tale*, p. 10.
35 Atwood, *The Handmaid's Tale*, p. 62.

Speaking the Body:
The Embodiment of 'Feminist' Cyberpunk

BRONWEN CALVERT and SUE WALSH

Introduction

The impetus for this paper came from our attendance at Warwick University's Virtual Futures II conference in May 1995. There, we noticed that despite the remit of the conference—virtuality—the body and its future was one of the main issues to be addressed time and again. We also noted that there was unease around the notion of bodily transcendence, expressed most commonly by feminist writers and theorists. Traditionally for feminism, being able to define clearly the subject for liberation has been vital; this may account for the reluctance to give up the body that we noted at Warwick, since the body is both historically associated with the feminine and commonly understood to be integral to self-identification. In addition to this, we were forced to acknowledge that there is as yet little in the way of female presence in the canon of cyberpunk, the literature of the virtual. Why would that be so? To find some answers we determined to focus on embodiment and transcendence, the sense of the body within cyberpunk science fiction.

Although cyberpunk is the subject of this paper, the concerns we address have not originated in cyberpunk. Science fiction, which is a literature of possibilities, has always reacted to the body as a confining space, and therefore generated the impulse to transcend the body's limitations. Classic science fiction narratives of space travel compensate for human limitation by means of the technological apparatus of the spaceship which functions as an invulnerable 'outer body' or exoskeleton. Another common expression of this theme is the immortal machinic body of the cyborg which exists at one remove from the human, experiencing neither weakness nor pain, an enabled body capable of anything that the mind could imagine.

Cyberpunk science fiction is about the mind. Technology, new inventions, computer advances, artificial intelligence and virtual reality are all staples of cyberpunk sf plotlines, and all 'in the mind'. Typically they are in a network—the 'Net', the 'Matrix'—like a giant brain that covers the entire planet and negates the need for actual, physical travel as the subject traverses the computer/neurological Net-works. What happens to this bodiless subject? And what happens to the body that is left behind? Cyberpunk literature and theorists of the 'Net' and VR are both involved in an exploration of self-identity and the question of its relation or non-relation to the body. Some commentators on the scene, whilst being fascinated and drawn by the 'troublesome' and proliferatory possibilities of the 'Net' and VR, are also ambivalent and a touch anxious about the body-loss that seems to be implied by these technologies.

Where Deleuzo-Guattarians dream of a pre-dualistic nomadic subject[1] and Nick Fox gets excited about the potential the 'Net' offers for 're-negotiat[ion of] identity untrammelled by the wetware of the body',[2] Gwyneth Jones baldly declares that 'it is through the body that we become subjects' and refuses any notion that future technologies might do away with the need for the body. She reminds us that VR is an experiential technology which therefore cannot be divorced from the body: 'virtual sex', for instance, 'quite precisely does not do away with bodies, it makes the body beautiful, puts it in a different place, but does not do away with it'.[3]

Feminist theoretical interventions on the cyberscene have also continued to worry away at the body as somehow essential to our sense of ourself, rather than exalting the new technology's alleged potential for freeing us from material presence. Donna Haraway's 'Manifesto for Cyborgs' emphasizes merging, hybridization and synthesis rather than separation; and she suggests to us the cyborg as 'a condensed image of both imagination and material reality',[4] an image that emphasizes the co-dependence of self and other, body and soul. Judith Butler in her book *Gender Trouble*[5] also stresses that the transcendental move away from the body tends to exclude women by subsuming their difference in the great universal. For her, only the explosion of categories, multiplication of versions of gender, expansion and troubling of boundaries can avoid the trap of defining and thereby restricting the subject of woman.

In her article 'Will the Real Body Please Stand Up?' Sandy Stone remarks that in the information age the split between body and subject 'is simultaneously growing and disappearing'.[6] She notes the way in which the Internet has rendered 'grounding a persona in a physical body... meaningless [since] men routinely use female personae whenever they choose, and vice versa'.[6] On the other hand, Stone also points out what seems to be the 'essential tactility of the virtual mode'[7] that comes across when 'Net' participants speak of their virtual interactions, and she is very clear that

> No matter how virtual the subject may become, there is always a
> body attached. It may be off somewhere else—and that 'somewhere
> else' may be a privileged point of view—but consciousness remains
> firmly rooted in the physical. Historically, body, technology, and
> community constitute each other.[9]

It is of interest here that we know that Stone was born male and had a
sex change operation in the 1970s. Thus we see that the 'virtual' was not
enough to express Stone's sense of herself; and her 'investment' in the
body is clear:

> ...it is important to remember that virtual community originates in,
> and must return to, the physical. No refigured virtual body, no matter
> how beautiful, will slow the death of a cyberpunk with AIDS. Even
> in the age of the technosocial subject, life is lived through bodies.
>   Forgetting about the body is an old Cartesian trick, one that has
> unpleasant consequences for those whose speech is silenced by the
> act of our forgetting...[10]

To sum up, here we have attempted to illustrate how and why women
writers and theorists might have an even more complex and confused
relationship to 'the body' than do their male counterparts. Women have
been constrained and restricted historically by their bodies (or the
perception of their bodies) and yet their close identification with 'the body'
means that it is difficult for women to see liberation in a transcendence
which effectively rubs them out.

Analysis of the Texts

In this section we will examine the manner in which Pat Cadigan, a woman
cyberpunk writer, explores through her novel *Synners* the issue of self-
identity and its relation to embodiment, and expresses a sense that
'forgetting' the body does indeed act to silence particular other bodies. We
will also refer to William Gibson's *Neuromancer* by way of comparison.

Thematic and Character Similarities in *Synners* and *Neuromancer*

Synners, first published in 1991, seven years after Gibson's seminal text
(1984), plays with similar projected situations and imaginative concepts.
Like *Neuromancer*, Cadigan's text is a multi-stranded narrative that
intertwines the trajectories of a number of characters linked by their
association (reluctant or resistant) to a multinational corporation. In
Synners the virtual-reality industry is set to be revolutionized by the
development of brain sockets that will allow information to be received

and sent directly from brain to brain. This invention is to be introduced via the commercial video industry, the video makers downloading and directly recording their imaginations.[11] Prior to this invention, the preferred method of making these VR videos was for the video maker to simulate experiences—of flying, falling or running for example—by means of a computer, a simulator suit or 'hotsuit' and a room full of props, slides and gadgets which create the effect of a bodily experience that will then be fed into the heads of the simulator 'viewers' as a 'real' experience and which they will experience as 'real'.

Gina is a synthesizer or 'synner': a person who can make virtual-reality videos from her own feelings and sensations. She and her associates (crucially Visual Mark) originally started out working for a small music video company called Eye Traxx which by the start of the novel has been taken over, first by Hal Galen Enterprises which introduces brain sockets, then by Diversifications, the multinational corporation that intends to develop the new technology. Gabe Ludovic is a disaffected and browbeaten corporation employee who spends most of his time playing VR games with two female characters he has generated (Marly and Caritha) whilst his marriage and his career disintegrate around him. Sam, Gabe's daughter, is a hacker working against the conglomerates with a community of hackers who exist in the underworld of Cadigan's novel. Just as the plot of *Neuromancer* operates to bring together as a group disparate characters such as a console cowboy (Case), a razor-girl (Molly), artificial intelligences, (re)constructed personalities, and the sub-cultures of the Panther Moderns and the Zionites, so *Synners* effects a similar move with the aforementioned characters and their associates, who include an artificial intelligence and a tattoo artist.

Similarly, the plots of both novels are primarily driven by an artificial intelligence's move to incorporate another into itself. In the case of *Neuromancer* we have two AIs, Wintermute and Neuromancer, merging; in *Synners*, Art Fish and Visual Mark's synthesis forces the plot movement. The outcome of this coming together proves, however, to have significantly different effects in the two novels.

Not only are the basic plot structures similar, there are other correspondences, some of which we, are inclined to assume, are a deliberate comment by Cadigan on Gibson's handling of certain themes. As far as we are concerned, *Neuromancer*'s most outstanding feature is its ambivalence with regard to the mind-body split that it so elaborately explores. Despite the fact that Case is said to have a 'relaxed contempt for the flesh',[12] *Neuromancer* abounds in physical descriptions that draw attention to the senses.[13] Ultimately neither body nor mind, neither coherent nor fragmented subject is privileged in *Neuromancer*, and Gibson's position remains ambiguous.

In *Neuromancer* the exploration of mind/body dualism is dramatized most clearly through the characters of Case and Molly and through the technologies of the Matrix and Simstim (Simulated Stimulation or VR). Molly is physically enhanced through surgery whilst Case is mentally linked up to transcendental cyberspace through his console. Gina and Visual Mark take up similar subject positions in *Synners*, though these are explored largely from Gina's point of view rather than Mark's.

Treatment of the Mind/Body Split in *Synners*

Gina is presented as a maverick with an outmoded way of making videos: she actually does the things she is filming, and records her real experiences of doing them. In one key sequence, she bungee jumps off a building while wired up to her VR gear. It is the effect of the jump on her body that she wants to record: the vertigo, adrenalin rush and fear. Her method of video making, though seen by the other characters as eccentric, is nevertheless presented as a somehow more valid—more 'real'—means of transmitting such experience. She is an excessively embodied character, resistant within the terms of the novel to technologically interventionist moves on the human subject and aggressively individual. Even Gina's modes of expression stress her physicality:

> She *strode* in, *planted her fists* on his desk, and *leaned into his face*. 'You're gonna be too busy to live if you don't do something about Mark. He's *fucked.*'
>
> He gave her his standard antiprofanity wince to remind her of *what an animal he thought she was.*[14]

This aggressive embodiment is associated in *Synners* with authenticity; the implication being that reality can only truly be experienced through the body, and as Gina asserts, 'in context'.[15] Gina argues again and again (with her fists too, causing 'real' pain) for the authenticity of the embodied. Recalling a late 1970s musical argument between devotees of 'real' guitar rock as opposed to 'fake' synthesizer music, Gina extols live music, whilst the author betrays her allegiance, not to punk, but to the music of the late 1960s: 'Live music, remember it? Nothing like live music, nothing like it.'[16]

By contrast, the character of Visual Mark, Gina's erstwhile partner, is based upon the Gibson-Case model. He has a 'hypertrophied' visual centre and his (pen-)name derives from an abbreviation of visualizing, since this is what he does continually; consequently he welcomes the new technology of brain sockets as a 'better way to get the pictures he saw in his head out just the way he saw them, get them out on video so everyone could see them the same way'.[17] Mark's attitude to the flesh parallels Case's closely: he too refers to his body as meat and regards it as a prison of the self, 'dragging [him] down',[18] preventing his expansion into a transcendental universe of information. Mark notes his difference from Gina in a passage which corresponds to the way in which Western epistemology has traditionally characterized the transcendent as masculine and the physical as feminine; and he also recognizes to some degree why Gina, as a woman, might not be comfortable with bodiless transcendence:

> ... He didn't understand how she could continue to cling to the heavy flesh even after knowing how the mind could be freed. But then, it didn't seem to happen the same way for her as it did for him. He knew that just by looking at her videos. Maybe her system would always be contained within herself and never spread out; *maybe there was no other way for her to keep from getting lost.*[19]

As an advocate of the body, resistant to Diversifications' use of Visual Mark in their pioneering experiments with brain sockets, Gina finds that though she is not actively silenced, she may as well be—her wishes, objections and anxieties about the procedure are ignored. And why is Gina so immune to Visual Mark's enthusiasm for the transcendence of the out-of-body 'Net'-existence? Fundamentally, she sees it as a removal from the 'real' world (Mark acknowledges that she views his video work as causing him to 'go away a lot')[20] and as a disconnection from the society of others and one's responsibility to them. Gina concurs with 'real-life' VR designer Brenda Laurel who sees computing as 'a profession...chosen by people who weren't particularly interested in social intercourse'.[21]

When Mark merges with the AI (Art Fish), the concept of individuality loses importance for him: he has the sense of becoming 'one consciousness rather than two separate intelligences. And at the same time his sense of identity intensified.'[22] Gina, however, perceives her power as being in her embodiment (Mark experiences his memory of her as though it were 'a physical blow'),[23] and hence she regards joining Mark in his virtual world as being tantamount to finally subsuming her identity to his. This is symbolically dramatized by Mark's inability or refusal to take on board Gina's pain, the symbol of his refusal to allow her to make any real impact upon him.

Gabe Ludovic, who joins Gina in the Net to help her fight the viral 'spike' (generated by Mark's stroke as he abandoned the meat of his body and merged with Art Fish), sees the disembodied nature of existence in the Net as comparable to life as an employee of a multinational corporation. He experiences comparable feelings of being swallowed up, and robbed of identity and individuality. Diversifications has stifled Gabe's creativity and initiative, and he feels his manipulation by Markt (the merged Mark and

Art Fish) in its effort to escape the 'spike' as being not too dissimilar from his treatment at the hands of his boss Manny Rivera. Coming across a projection of Rivera in the system, Gabe reflects that 'Anyone who could survive in the belly of the corporate beast would probably find this existence all but natural.'[24] Gabe's defence against the 'spike' is to remember what it is like to have a body. This affirms and asserts his individuality and self-identity, returning to him some form of agency that makes it more difficult to manipulate him. In particular he differentiates himself from Mark as a person who will accept Gina's embodied nature whilst not restricting her to that role:

> 'Oh, come on, Gina.' Ludovic sat up. The blood ran down his face in streams. 'What would become of you if you couldn't cause someone some pain, raise a few welts now and then, draw a little blood, bring up the swelling?'
>
> 'That's not all there is to me,' she said, feeling Mark try to tighten his hold on her (warm and so familiar, as if they had never led separate lives at all).
>
> 'I know that,' Ludovic said. 'The difference is, I'll take it. I have taken it. He never did.'[25]

Differences in the Treatment of Embodiment/Disembodiment in Synners and Neuromancer

The crucial difference between *Synners* and *Neuromancer* is the way in which these two novels treat the mind/body split and the question of embodiment or disembodiment. Contrary to Karen Cadora in her article 'Feminist Cyberpunk', we believe that *Synners* does not 'conflate technology and masculinity',[26] since the dualistic patterning of *Neuromancer* is complicated in *Synners* by the introduction of the characters of Sam and Gabe (amongst others) as foils to Gina and Visual Mark. Readers of cyberpunk will recognize Gina as parallelling Gibson's Molly in her embodied nature; but whereas Molly never gains access to the transcendental world of cyberspace and consequently never has the opportunity to choose between the flesh and the mind, Gina has and uses the same skills for her work as does Visual Mark; her choice of the body is an informed one.

The character of Sam acts as a foil to Gina by offering another possible version of femininity, one which is more at ease with the technological world of cyberspace, symbolized by her genuine interest in the contemporary music: 'speed-thrash', as opposed to the rock music of yester-year. Sam is a hacker virtuoso with 'an easy genius for hardware',[27] yet her most important function within the plot is to enable virus-free access to the Net through a chip reader that draws its power from her body.

The character of Gabe acts in an analogous way in relation to Visual Mark; the fact that he is a VR junky only serves to prepare him for his positional shift from virtual to 'real' suffering masculine body. His artificially generated female VR companions, Marly and Caritha, prove in the last analysis to be imaginative extensions of himself: 'Suddenly he no longer wanted to disown his thoughts and stick false names on them. He didn't have to do that right now, he didn't have to cut pieces of himself off and dress them up in masks and costumes to keep himself company.'[28]

The suggestion here is that Gabe has previously felt himself to be constrained by his gender, therefore he used Marly and Caritha as ways of 'performing' other (unallowable?) aspects of himself. This is not the only instance where gender constructions are queried. The role of the AI Art Fish is particularly interesting here:

> It was a composition of subtle and charming androgyny, the long dark hair, the classically sculpted features, the amber eyes so light in color they were luminous, the deep brown skin—definitely not one of the stock compositions you could get from Wear-Ware or some wannabee program. But he—Sam was calling it 'he' on no basis other than arbitrary—had to have spent hours mixing palettes.[29]

Time and again Sam attempts to define and thereby restrict the AI in terms of gender. Confusion and prudishness she associates with femininity;[30] and to its annoying tendency of being a know-all, Sam ascribes masculinity:

> … 'I knew it was you this time, didn't I? Even though you wouldn't identify yourself.'
> She hesitated. 'Lucky guess. Or you recognized my voice.'
> 'Have you ever spoken to me before?'
> Sam suppressed the urge to hang up on him. (Him, she thought, definitely him.) … 'You enjoy toying with other people, don't you?'[31]

This betrays Sam's frustration at not being able to pin the AI down to a particular and predictable type of behaviour based on preconceptions about gender.

Disembodiment in *Synners* does not seem to free one from the constraints of gender: Mark, for example, does not really become any less male (or for that matter less heterosexual) despite his merging with the AI. Cadigan offers instead a proliferation of different types of gender construction grounded in bodies, and refuses to allow the 'Net' to escape the reality of its own embodiment. She follows Sandy Stone's insistence that 'the virtual community originates in, and must return to, the physical'.[32] This 'fact' is illustrated in *Synners* by the way in which the LA system is protected by Sam's body and recreated by recourse to the maps drawn by Gator the tattoo artist on the bodies of the Mimosa strip. Even Visual Mark, as he gives up his body and enters the system for good, describes it in organic terms, first as 'arteries and veins' and then as 'a sewer'.[33]

For Cadigan, information has to have meaning. The 'consensual hallucination'[34] of Gibson's *Neuromancer*, with its hypnotic imagery ('... silver phosphenes boiling from the edge of space, hypnagogic images jerking past like film compiled from random frames. Symbols, figures, faces, a blurred, fragmented mandala of visual information...'[35]) is not enough for the hackers of *Synners* for, 'If it don't mean a thing, it ain't information...'.[36] What the hackers are fighting against is the restriction of information that separates people by using their differences against them:

> Biznet is the epitome of narrowcasting. As opposed to old-style broadcasting...
> '...besides being rich,' Fez said, 'you have to be extra sharp these days to pick up any real information. You have to know what you're looking for, and you have to know how it's filed. Browsers need not apply. Broke ones, anyway. I miss the newspaper.'[37]

For information to have meaning it needs what Gina calls 'context', the context of 'social relationships with cultural reference and value.'[38] Anne Balsamo suggests that Cadigan writes with an understanding of information 'as a "state of knowing" which reasserts a knowing body as its necessary materialist foundation'.[39] In *Synners* the loss of the body becomes conflated with the loss of community, and Cadigan's insistence on the body through Gina and Gabe coincides with a narrative that is driven by the forging of connections between characters.

Where the generating impulse of the plot of *Neuromancer*, the merging together of the two AIs, once accomplished allows the disparate characters of the novel to disperse, in *Synners*, as the title suggests, a longer-term synthesis of characters is achieved. This synthesis must operate on multiple levels and recognize, not subsume, difference: Gina refuses the 'spike' that attempts to swallow her being by symbolically pulling the plug on it.[40] Henceforward all connections have to be made on the basis of choice and not through dominance. Mark, Art Fish, the Eclone of Gina that she agrees to have made, and Gabe's Marly and Caritha are fused in the Netspace; whereas on the ground we are left with the newly created nuclear family of Gabe, Gina and Sam with their connections to their extended hacker family on the strip.

At Warwick's Virtual Futures conference, Peter Lamborn Wilson expressed the suspicion that enthusiasm for the information economy was a new mask for a body hatred of the old Augustinian type. His contention is supported by VR designer Brenda Laurel who regards the computer-buff fantasy of leaving the body as unsurprising, since we are referring to people uninterested in social intercourse who have therefore, on a symbolic level, already left their bodies.[41] Wilson's reaction to this state of affairs was to call for a reinstatement of the body, which is still after all the basis of wealth 'since we can no more eat information than we can eat money; someone still has to eat pears, wear shoes'. His proposed reintegration of the body and spirit into 'the one twin/diadic expression of the real' is, he argued, by extension, a defence of conviviality.[42]

Judith Butler and Sandy Stone's analyses of the contemporary cyber scene suggest that conviviality is perhaps best defended not only through merging and synthesis of body and spirit, but also through the proliferation of multiple connected and embodied subjectivities. Difference (most in view on the body) must be acknowledged: Visual Mark's initial merging with Art Fish, before the relationship is poisoned by the 'spike', is in a state of balance which recognizes them still as '*two* aspects of one consciousness';[43] nor does this merged (synthesized) entity simply conflate the inhabitants of the 'meat-world' but distinguishes 'individuals just by their input; little things, the style, the patterns, the rhythms and pauses showed variations that were no longer minuscule to him, no two ever quite the same'.[44]

To Conclude

In the dedication of *Synners* Pat Cadigan writes:

> This one is for Gardner Dozois and Susan Casper,
> who got me going on the original idea.
> For fifteen years of late nights, wild parties,
> talking dirty, and all the other stuff
> that makes life worth living
> (I've got your dedication right here)

It is a sentiment that is echoed and elaborated upon towards the end of the novel by the character Gina:

> 'Only the embodied can *really* boogie all night in a hit-and-run, or jump off a roof attached to bungi cords.' ...
> 'I guess,' he said... 'that doesn't make too much sense anymore. Doing all that just to simulate doing all that.'
> Gina burst out laughing. 'Simulate my ass! I did video just so I could do all that shit!'[45]

This insistence on the body in a virtual world is the crux of the novel and it would appear to be an impulse that Cadigan shares with others, and not only other female writers and theorists of cyberpunk. A research group led by Brenda Laurel found that in an interactive virtual reality environment, women in general preferred to have bodies whereas men preferred not to.[46]

Does Cadigan's reinstatement of the body correspond to a liberal humanist feminism still hooked on defining and delimiting a unified subject for liberation? We would argue that though there are trends in this direction within the novel, it can also be read as a radical querying and destabilizing of self-identities through the body mutable. *Synners* offers differing and multiple subject positions for both males and females: embodiment is not reserved only for the female characters of the novel, and technology is not simply conflated with masculinity. Mark's transcendental experience of the 'Net' raises some questions that are never fully and convincingly addressed; for instance, Gabe refers to the Eclone of Gina that merges with Mark as 'just a sophisticated, intelligent program. But not conscious',[47] and though Gina corrects him, stating the process of synthesis as creating consciousness, the logic of the novel up to this point suggests that 'true' consciousness is not possible for the disembodied.

Finally, whilst we feel we have shown convincingly how Cadigan's approach to the issue of embodiment in *Synners* is different at least from Gibson's in *Neuromancer*, it is worth bearing in mind that this shift towards the body and the social may be common in cyberpunk's development. Certainly in Gibson's *Virtual Light* (first published in 1993), it is the body-bound world of 'the bridge' which has centre stage as a place in which community still thrives, not the virtual world of transnational corporations or computer hackers. Freedom in *Virtual Light* is the body away from the claustrophobia of city buildings, the body exercising its physicality:

> Legs pumping, the wind a strong hand in the small of her back, sky clear and beckoning at the top of the hill, she thumbed her chain up onto some huge-ass custom ring, too big for her derailleur, too big to fit any frame at all, and felt the shining teeth catch, her hammering slowing to a steady spin—but then she was losing it.
>
> She stood up and started pounding, screaming, lactic acid slamming through her veins. She was at the crest, lifting off—[48]

Perhaps what *Synners* and *Virtual Light* actually demonstrate is a growing pessimism about the likelihood of a new freedom heralded by the communicative possibilities of the 'Net'. In as much as these seem to offer a new form of interaction, they also close down on older forms of communication. In our enthusiasm to name the late twentieth century the computer age, we should not forget that we are operating from an exceptionally privileged standpoint. The majority of people in the world are not able adequately to maintain their bodies, let alone escape them for a world of information. The history of the Industrial Revolution should tell us that new technologies habitually cause social disruption; and that the mass of people, far from being able to improve their lot, find their lives reorganized according to the needs of that technology. Now, as so often before, the new technology is not in the hands of the dispossessed.

Notes

1 Note, however, that though Deleuze and Guattari rail against *organicism*, they also delight in the material-physical: 'Amniotic fluid spilling out of the sac and kidney stones; flowing hair; a flow of spittle, a flow of sperm, shit or urine...'. Gilles Deleuze and Felix Guattari, *Anti-Oedipus: Capitalism and Schizophrenia* (London: Athlone Press, 1984), p. 5.

2 Nick Fox and Phil Levy, 'Deterritorializing the Body Without Organs: Postmodern Ethics and the Virtual Community', paper presented at Virtual Futures II: Cyberevolution Conference at University of Warwick, 26–28 May 1995.

3 Gwyneth Jones, 'Red Sonja and Lessingham in Dreamland', paper presented at Virtual Futures II: Cyberevolution.

4 Donna Haraway, 'A Manifesto for Cyborgs: Science, Technology, and Socialist Feminism in the 1980s', in Linda J. Nicholson, ed., *Feminism/Postmodernism* (London: Routledge, 1990), p. 191.

5 Judith Butler, *Gender Trouble* (London: Routledge, 1990).

6 Allucquere Rosanne Stone, 'Will the Real Body Please Stand Up?: Boundary Stories about Virtual Cultures', in Michael Benedikt, ed., *Cyberspace: First Steps* (London: MIT Press, 1991), p. 101.

7 Stone, 'Real Body', p. 84.

8 Stone, 'Real Body', p. 90.

9 Stone, 'Real Body', p. 111.

10 Stone, 'Real Body', p. 113.

11 Pat Cadigan, *Synners* (London: Harper Collins, 1991), p. 40.

12 William Gibson, *Neuromancer* (London: Harper Collins, 1993 [1984]), p. 12.

13 'He shifted on the concrete, feeling it rough and cool...'; Gibson, *Neuromancer*, p. 61; 'Smells of urine, free monomers, perfume, patties of frying krill'; Gibson, *Neuromancer*, p. 71.

14 Cadigan, *Synners*, p. 279. Emphasis added.

15 Cadigan, *Synners*, p. 290.

16 Cadigan, *Synners*, p. 209. Although she writes of a future musical genre known as speed-thrash, the musicians actually referred to by Cadigan in *Synners* include Elvis, Jim Morrison, Bob Dylan, John Lennon and Lou Reed.

17 Cadigan, *Synners*, pp. 84–85. As a comment on reading and the role of the reader/audience this is interesting, since what Mark proposes is a taking away of the reader's autonomy to interpret, endowing the author (visualizer in this case) with total pre-modernist authorial control.

18 Cadigan, *Synners*, pp. 232, 245.

19 Cadigan, *Synners*, p. 234. Emphasis added.

20 Cadigan, *Synners*, p. 84.

21 Brenda Laurel, interview
   <http//:gopher.well.sf.ca.us: 70/000/publications/Mondo/Laurel.txt>

22 Cadigan, *Synners*, p. 385.

23 Cadigan, *Synners*, p. 90.

24 Cadigan, *Synners*, p. 406.

25 Cadigan, *Synners*, p. 417.

26 Karen Cadora, 'Feminist Cyberpunk', *Science Fiction Studies* 22.3 (1995), p. 358. Cadora does qualify this statement and on the whole offers a positive reading of *Synners*.

27 Cadigan, *Synners*, p. 39.

28 Cadigan, *Synners*, pp. 201–202.

29 Cadigan, *Synners*, p. 167.

30 '…the smooth forehead wrinkling slightly. He seemed to taste the idea, as if she had suggested something rare and exotic and perhaps a little improper in some way. The expression made him look suddenly far more female than male…' (Cadigan, *Synners*, p. 168).

31 Cadigan, *Synners*, p. 169.

32 Stone, 'Real Body', p. 113.

33 Cadigan, *Synners*, p. 324.

34 Gibson, *Neuromancer*, p. 12.

35 Gibson, *Neuromancer*, p. 68.

36 Cadigan, *Synners*, p. 28.

37 Cadigan, *Synners*, pp. 51, 53.

38 Anne Balsamo, 'Feminism for the Incurably Informed', *The South Atlantic Quarterly* 92.4 (Fall 1993), p. 687.

39 Balsamo, 'Feminism', p. 687.

40 The 'spike' taunts Gina with *'That'll teach you to glory in your* separateness, *your precious* aloneness' (*Synners*, p. 424).

41 '[Computing was] a profession that was chosen by people who weren't particularly interested in social intercourse… it's no wonder that their fantasy is to leave the body. Cos it never mattered that much, they already have' (Laurel, interview).

42 Peter Lamborn Wilson, Plenary address, Virtual Futures II.

43 Cadigan, *Synners*, p. 385. Emphasis added.

44 Cadigan, *Synners*, p. 382.

45 Cadigan, *Synners*, p. 433.

46 Cadora, 'Feminist Cyberpunk', p. 365.

47 Cadigan, *Synners*, p. 432.

48 William Gibson, *Virtual Light* (London: Penguin Books, 1994 [1993]), p. 70.

Bodies that Speak Science Fiction: Stelarc—Performance Artist 'Becoming Posthuman'

ROSS FARNELL

The rhetoric surrounding science fiction attempts to persuade us that cyberpunks are the 'pragmatists and practitioners' of the posthuman future;[1] however, these fictional beings fade into phantasmagorical wish fulfilment when confronted by the reality of the performance artist Stelarc. Cyber-culture's contemporary focus on 'becoming-cyborg' has transformed this once marginalized 'body artist' into a cyber-star of cult status, embraced by the proponents of technoculture, from cyberpunk authors to theorists. But he's no cyborg-come-lately. For over three decades his art has materialized science fiction metaphor into posthuman being, 'translating' science fiction's textual and visual art, from *Frankenstein* to *Terminator* and beyond, into performative parameters. For many, performance artists such as Stelarc, Orlan, and Survival Research Laboratories (SRL) have come to represent the future of posthumanism. To others they are indicative of the apocalyptic dangers of a naïvely optimistic and untheorized approach to technology.

I propose that such performance art serves as a 'mediation' between science fiction, science, and cultural theory. A complex feedback loop of posthumanism can be traced from Artaud to performance artists, and then to theorists such as Deleuze and Guattari: from McLuhan to Virilio and Baudrillard, but also to Stelarc. The BwO, Stelarc's 'hollow body', Haraway's politicized cyborg, Prigogine's anagenesis and science fiction's fictional posthumans all intersect in a common language enmeshed in the paradigms and tropes of science fiction. Performance art attempts to offer pragmatic models for the body in future society, and possible strategies for either action, reaction, adaptation or resistance to the imperatives of information society and extra-terrestrial existence, all within a philosophy that approaches Gnosticism. Does it develop political, social and ethical strategies for survival in 'late capitalism', or is it just a symptom of the 'society of the spectacle', reducing (hyper)reality to art and image, engendering inertia and disempowerment through reductionist objectification?

Posthumanism needs to engage with a sphere of action that enables dialogue with bodies. This is provided by those performance artists who embody alterity: inscribed bodies that 'speak' science fiction. Their corporeal actualization of posthumanism generates an alternative discourse which constructs paradigms of difference from 'traditional' science fiction texts. By placing the performance events of Stelarc into the context of posthuman 'texts', I aim to illustrate aspects of posthumanism hitherto elided by the more conventional extrapolations of Otherness, such as the dominant cyborg imagery of contemporary science fiction film.

Stelarc: Reluctant Practitioner of Science Fiction

Contemporary artists like Stelarc address borders through cultural bricolage, taking different technologies and theories from various social and cultural traditions and combining them in unique border-erasing projects. This is parallelled by theorists such as Donna Haraway, whose cyborgs appropriate political, feminist, military, technological, biological and social agendas. Such willingness to raid any number of diverse cultural sources is mirrored by numerous science fiction authors. As William Gibson notes, the street finds its own use for things. So does the posthuman. Its destiny is that of bricolage, mirroring its cyborg cousin, itself a being in flux that combines the cybernetic and the organic. It is this destiny that combines art, theory and science fiction. Where Haraway is supposed to have 'literalized' the science fiction metaphor of the cyborg into a theoretical being,[2] the aesthetics of Stelarc's performances could be said to 'materialize' that same metaphor. As a performance artist existing in the no-(hu)man's-land between science fiction as art and science fiction as social/cultural reality, Stelarc is a 'practitioner' performing in an 'sf overground'.[3] Art becomes science fiction becomes awareness becomes reality becomes virtual reality becomes art/science fiction again.[4] Meanwhile, cultural 'theory' permeates the whole of this loop. Stelarc's attempt to distance himself from this cycle is futile.

Stelarc acknowledges that 'simplistically one can see similar agendas in postulating future bodies or posthuman scenarios'; however, 'praxis' forms a fundamental rupture between science fiction writers and performance artists. The importance of generating actuality, he argues, renders it 'inadequate' simply to postulate, to theorize, or to write science fiction.[5] He positions his work as an 'authentic' collapse of infinite possibilities into reality, functioning within a 'perpetual present' as opposed to science fiction which is putatively limited to the allegorical and to 'utopian ego driven future(s)'.[6] Stelarc's generalizations portray science fiction as a Cartesian fracture that ignores the body, an undeniable truth in the ethereal data existence of many fictional cybernauts. But to apply such criticism to the writing of Octavia Butler, for example, would be misguided. Though text is her medium, embodiment is anything but erased in her novels. Although grounded in speculation, writing is still a corporeal and performative practice. Stelarc's criterion amounts to a rejection of all extrapolative and speculative fiction and theory. It fails to acknowledge that his own work is also firmly enmeshed in metaphor and speculative strategy. Only a small percentage of Stelarc's ideas can be authenticated in action. His theories extrapolate from currently available technologies and social conditions, a process no different to that of writing science fiction. The difference is the medium: text versus body. However, both depend on the artist's/author's imaginative ability to convey posthuman possibilities through their respective crafts. Stelarc's body is also a 'text', inscribed by both his work and cultural preconceptions of posthumanistic metaphors— originating largely in science fiction.

While Stelarc advocates technological strategies in order to escape from our putative 'limitations', he regards science fiction's use of technology as driven by the basic 'anxiety' that it threatens our humanity: 'In science fiction...machines are always destructive and metallic...whereas human aggression, human fallibility...are romanticised as "what it means to be human"'.[7] Stelarc rejects such 'simplifications', where 'dystopian futures' function as a 'justification of the pathology of the human species'.[8] He objects to the tendency of cybernetic fiction to allay our fear that we *are* only machines, and insists instead on our body's primarily automated functioning, *remechanizing* the human 'soft machine'.[9] Stelarc again generalizes a large and diverse body of text into one narrow ideology. Not all science fiction mythologizes human fallibility while demonizing technology and symbionts.

The correlations between the images created by Stelarc's performances and those used in science fiction film are obvious. The cyborg as militaristic techno-body is the dominating presence in movies such as *Terminator, Judgement Day (T2)*, and the *Robocop* trilogy. It is impossible *not* to make comparisons between these celluloid cyborgs and the wired-in, prosthesized and turned-on Stelarc in performance. It is inconceivable that these events have not been influenced by the dominant science fiction metaphors. Many aesthetic elements of his performances, including the digital manipulation of his body's 'outputs' into a 'cyborg soundscape', are simply theatrical enhancements which emphasize similarities to science fiction.[10]

Stelarc, however, is frustrated by such comparisons, pointing for example to the chronological construction of his mechanical 'third arm' before such *Robocop*-type movies. Nevertheless, 'robotic' prosthesis is one of science fiction's seminal motifs, and any claim to primacy is misguided. For Stelarc, though, such comparisons exemplify today's propensity to evaluate society by referring to its popular culture, a strategy he is 'uneasy' about, because that popular culture is more representative of 'hype' than anything meaningful.[11] Nonetheless, he himself has become a popular icon of contemporary technoculture, a 'culture' that *is* floundering in a sea of digital hype, and yet cannot be disregarded. Despite the self-promotional excess, it is the dominant paradigm that figures such as Stelarc are inevitably and necessarily evaluated from.

Posthuman science fiction also shares with Stelarc common roots in the *Order out of Chaos* theories of Ilya Prigogine. Both Stelarc and science fiction characters such as *Schismatrix*'s Lindsay share the desire to accelerate the autopoetic drive of the biosphere through anagenetic evolution, resulting in creative multiple splits in the species that replace linear evolution with spontaneous leaps to higher levels of complexity. The similarities between Bruce Sterling's 'Lobster' characters and Stelarc's writings are remarkable: the relationship of their common borderless bodies to 'space', the embrace of both genetic and prosthetic technologies that allow a continual becoming-in-process, a 'boredom' with the 'outmoded paradigms of blood and bone', a rejection of human limitations, and a willingness to remake the body as a hollow body receptacle for technology, all point to a 'parallel evolution' of fictional character and performance artist.[12] Like Lindsay, Stelarc can be considered the 'postmodern Prometheus', a contemporary of science fiction's oldest posthuman creator, Victor Frankenstein, begetting a new artistic Creation that appropriates various technologies and applies them to the recombinant body.

Performance Art Meets the Body of the Other: Artaud

To understand Stelarc's parameters, and the importance of the artist in the construction of the posthuman, it is necessary to construct a brief history of performance body art. With the advent of cheap prosthetic, medical and even genetic technology, this art is now undergoing a revival. The aims of its protagonists, its form, substance, style, performance parameters and 'spaces', all of these have changed, helping to make this art of the body more relevant than ever to the present and future social body. The transformation of contemporary performance art from a predominantly temporal movement into a critical or theoretical performance, and its ability graphically to address issues of sexuality, gender, race and culture, has witnessed its resurgence as an important critical discourse.[13] Concurrently, performance has maintained one of its most distinguishing features: praxis. This juxtaposition of the theoretical and the practical allows it a unique place in cultural discourse.

Body art is read by Anne Marsh as primarily concerned with pre-Oedipal anxieties, as self-referential, misogynistic, and depicting 'the crisis of the subject in an advanced technological age that appears to value progress and rationality above human emotions and psychological states'.[14] For Marsh, Stelarc is the Western shaman of technology who, in a total separation of mind and body, epitomizes this valuing of 'progress and technology for its own sake'.[15] However, to dismiss such art as technotopian narcissism is to contextualize it within the Oedipal framework that many artists attempt to escape, thus limiting its potential. A more complex, perhaps anti-Oedipal approach, is necessary, rather than one which subjugates the work to desire-as-'lack' and pseudo-shamanism.[16] To point *only* to the objectification of the artist's body, as exploitation/devaluation, is to ignore both the productive body's will-to-power, and the Foucauldian inscription of the body by discourses of power.

The history of body art inevitably encounters Antonin Artaud, most popularly renowned for his 'Theatre of Cruelty'. Artaud bequeathed to performance art a phenomenological way of knowing the body. His Gnostic interpretation of the body challenges the traditional Cartesian separation of mind and body, as do many of today's performance artists. Despite the apparent paradoxes inherent within his quest to abolish all dualisms,[17] it is within the varied works of Artaud that one finds the genesis of both the theoretical and actualized schizophrenic and posthuman performative bodies. His final work, 'To Have Done with the Judgment of God', is a seminal manifesto for posthumanism, providing the source of Deleuze and Guattari's Body without Organs, and correlations with Stelarc's 'Hollow Body'.[18] Artaud's work contains all the essential elements of a body art that intersects with posthumanism: corporeality, alterity, actualization and new creation.

Genesis of Stelarc's Early Events

Having laid the historical and theoretical foundation for contemporary performance art's interrelation with alterity, my specific discussion of Stelarc's strategies begins with a précis of some of his recent theories on becoming posthuman:

> The body needs to be repositioned from the psycho realm of the biological, to the cyber zone of interface and extension—from genetic containment to electronic extrusion. Strategies towards the post-human are more about erasure, rather than affirmation... Invading technology eliminates skin as a significant site... The possibility of autonomous images generates an unexpected outcome of human-

machine symbiosis. The post-human may well be manifested in the intelligent like form of autonomous images.[19]

Stelarc has embraced the available technology of the late twentieth century to enable his 'transmutation' through corporeal means, approaching becoming Other from the outside in.

Born Stelios Arcadiou in 1946, Stelarc trained as an artist in Melbourne, then spent the 1970s in Japan, teaching and performing art. He is now once again based in Melbourne, yet is a truly global citizen, in keeping with his desire to achieve a 'planetary consciousness'.[20] He is credited with having performed one of Australia's inaugural performance events, *Event from micro to macro and the between* in 1969, incorporating projected computer images, choreographed dancers, and vision-distorting helmets. The consistency of theme within Stelarc's work, where image, technology and choreography are still of primary importance, is remarkable. In 1970 he started working with the body in suspension, and from 1976 until 1988 Stelarc experimented with controversial body suspensions achieved by the insertion of hooks into his skin.

Stelarc's own subjective reading of these performance 'texts' repeatedly rejects any significance attached to his use of hooks. He portrays them instead as a 'convenient' means by which to achieve his aim of erasing the skin as boundary and overcoming the limitations of gravity on the body, transforming the stretched skin into a 'gravitational landscape'. His fundamental aim was to demonstrate that the body as we know it is now the 'obsolete body'.[21] His amplification of internal organs and filming of body tracts further challenged the body's boundaries, prompting Stelarc to term his works 'body by-pass events'.[22] The body becomes an object of dissemination and erasure rather than of prioritization.

In 1976 he self-published *Stelarc*, a compendium of his early ideas. Beginning with and reiterating the line 'Man Must Mutate', the book heralds many of his now-familiar themes: 'Our body is a death organism', 'Man must create a being to supersede himself'.[23] By 1984, these posthuman maxims had acquired the illusion of a theoretical foundation to support their rhetoric: 'the body has created an information and technological environment which it can no longer cope with', an 'evolutionary crisis'. 'Man', continues Stelarc, has 'made himself obsolete', and must resort to a synthesis with technology to become functional in the space-time continuum he has created for himself. Information itself is an evolutionary dead-end of disconnected data, a prosthesis that merely props up the obsolete body. Consequently, Stelarc proposes various strategies of adaptation, 'necessary' for posthuman survival:

The body must burst from its biological, cultural and planetary containment. Once the body attains planetary escape velocity it will be launched into new evolutionary trajectories. ...miniaturisation creates an implosive force that hurls technology back to the body... creat[ing] the potential of life without humanity... Maintaining the integrity of the body...is not only bad strategy in terms of sheer survival, but it also dooms the body to a primitive and crude range of (limited) sensibilities.[24]

Stelarc's favourite axiom is 'Hollow, Harden, and Dehydrate', a process of replacing organic skin with synthetic data skin that supersedes the functions of our organs, allowing the body to be 'hollowed out' as a better 'host' for technology.[25] The human body is posited as having always been 'incomplete', the historical urge to extend its limited capabilities defining our very humanity.[26]

Despite what appear to be ideologically informed cultural, social, political, and post-evolutionary imperatives, art remains Stelarc's dominant inspiration. Within his theories reside the historical traditions of art as the genesis of creation. He envisages a role for the artist as an 'evolutionary guide', a 'genetic sculptor' 'transforming the human landscape'.[27] Stelarc positions this as redefining, rather than privileging, the role of the artist. He refutes the model of the posthuman as a political being designed to re-empower humanity, accusing this approach of 'perpetuating the (outdated) biological status-quo'. His emphasis is on the 'aesthetic, altruistic, or medical' choices of individuals to alter their form, on diversification rather than conformity.[28] Stelarc denies any desire to redesign the species or create a 'master race', rejecting any particular agenda of social or political control in favour of 'unpredictable' and 'multiple futures', where individuals attain the 'fundamental freedom...to determine their own DNA destiny'.[29] This attempt to remove his events from the socio-political context and contain them purely within aesthetics is self-depreciating, and aspires to an isolationism which is impossible to maintain in today's intertextuality. Consequently, he is often caught in contradiction. For example, his notion that altering one's form and functions is the real threat to 'political, social, and religious institutions' explicitly acknowledges the greater potential of posthumanism.[30]

Throughout his career, Stelarc has rejected the Cartesian mind/body duality: 'When I talk about a body, I mean this total physiological, phenomenological package... One need not refer to mind at all.'[31] As in Gnosticism, this project is fraught with difficulties. Contradictions appear when Stelarc posits the body as an 'object for designing' rather than as a subject. In reiterating the typical objectified status of the performance artist's body, rather than a Möbius strip model of body as *both* object *and* subject, Stelarc undermines his own aims. However, he does briefly remind us, as science fiction seldom does, of the 'fundamental relationship between our embodiment and our identities'.[32]

Stelarc's attempts to address his apparent contradictions reflect the difficulties faced by any challenge to existing metaphysics whilst still communicating within those parameters. He argues that by using language that is culturally coloured and contextual we are seduced into a misunderstanding of the frame of reference.[33] One must question whether this recourse to a putative difference in metaphysical conceptualization is simply a convenient escape clause to excuse apparent contradictions between theory and practice.

Becoming Posthuman Today: Technology and Image

Stelarc entered the metaphorical realm of science fiction with his construction of the 'Third Hand' in the early 1980s. This was not conceived as a prosthetic replacement, but as an enhancement of the body, capable of independent motion. His new cyborg-type image instantly caught the imagination of science fiction, itself being captured by the aesthetics of cyberpunk. In the last decade he has further extended such imagery, developing new technological body extensions like the 'Virtual Arm', which acts as a remote phantom limb. His body has become 'The Techno Self', an 'Involuntary Body' 'extruding its awareness beyond its physiology'.[34]

Recent 'Stimbod' performances have combined the third hand, virtual arm, body amplification, and computer-controlled body activation. These ideas have culminated in the recent 'Internet Body Upload' and 'Ping Body' events, both with important implications for posthuman discourses.[35] Stelarc's primary interest in combining Stimbod's remote muscle stimulator with a modem link to the Internet is to enable the body to become 'a host for remote and spatially separated agents'.[36] This challenges the putative historical, metaphysical and philosophical grounding of our humanity within individuality, the loss of which means to be 'sub-human, a machine'. Stelarc wants to explore the pathology of a body with a multiplicity of agents:

> Electronically coupled Other bodies are…being manifested in a part of your body… It's not so much an erasure of agency but rather complexity and multiplicity of operational spaces between bodies and within bodies… your awareness will neither be all here nor all there.

He is careful, however, to differentiate this aim from cyberdelic McLuhanesque or Jungian-type models of a utopian Internet global consciousness.[37]

This 'Upload' event continues Stelarc's interest in the role of *image* in posthumanism. His body's globally transmitted image becomes *operational*, its manipulation has a corporeal effect on his remotely located body. For Stelarc, this represents a significant change in the nature of bodies and images: 'Images are no longer illusory when they become interactive.'[38] If, as he asserts, the realm of the image is that of the posthuman[39] then it is important for Stelarc to empower the notion of image. Stelarc interprets the image as autonomous and Other, as 'virulent' rather than benign. He equates 'operational' images with being 'alive' in a post-evolutionary phase. This is consistent with his notion that we mostly operate as 'Absent Bodies', the genetically programmed body functioning effectively when it functions automatically.[40]

Again, Stelarc is plagued by contradiction. Operational images appear to deny corporeality in the most fundamental manner. Embodied knowledge is abandoned to the realm of the virtual, reanimating the disembodied spectre of cyberspace. His Internet 'upload' instantly invokes an image of the cyberpunk motif of neural 'jacking-in', one of the defining tropes of contemporary cyberfiction. Its phenomenological and ontological failings are well documented, and Stelarc is keen to distance his actions from this Cartesian manoeuvre.[41] The neural jack, he asserts, is little more than a metaphor for the sexual transgression of other bodies.[42] He attempts to differentiate between his notion of 'actual' virtual reality, and the 'consensual technological interface' of cyberspace. While virtual reality enables an interactivity with images, it is not, he insists, science fiction's 'hyped-up out of body experience, that's just simply a Cartesian extension, or a Platonic desire', which is more pathological than meaningful.[43] However, such differentiation is merely subjective and rhetorical. If one's image becomes operational, autonomous and eternal, then surely it too becomes an object of Platonic desire and Cartesian extension.

Stelarc's claim that images are immortal while bodies are ephemeral[44] only serves to emphasize the traditional perspective of the realm of the image as transcendental and omnipotent, reinforcing the standard cyberpunk trope of escaping from the condemned 'meat' of the body to an eternal telematic life. He unwittingly reinforces this correlation: 'religion...doesn't relate to my work directly...but it's interesting that it attempts transcendence of the human body'.[45] It is this constant resurrection of the notion of a *transcendent* after/other-life that makes comparison between religion and posthumanism inevitable. The desire for death-transcendence in posthuman extrapolation is one of the most common yet phantasmic aspects of becoming Other. For Stelarc, birth is replaced by technology, death is eliminated by it: '*The body must become immortal to adapt...* Utopian dreams become post-evolutionary imperatives.

This is no mere Faustian option nor should there be any Frankensteinian fear in tampering with the body.[46] However, simply to deny immortality as a transcendental or 'Faustian option' is inadequate. Stelarc's defence is that he suffers the 'physical consequences' of his actions, as opposed to those who 'speak in metaphors or paradigm shifts'.[47] What he 'does', though, and what he proposes, are two vastly different things.

Are Stelarc's representations of the body as electronic images the empty simulacra of Baudrillardian dystopias,[48] or can they, as Stelarc asserts, be positioned as valid operational agents? One answer is provided by Deleuze's rejection of the Western Platonic tradition that simulacra are simply copies of copies which must be banished to preserve the integrity and order of the One superior Model.[49] Rather, he argues, simulacra are images without likeness, they provide the means of challenging the traditional opposition between copy and model. The primacy of original over image is overturned. Simulacrum is the instance which includes a *difference within itself.* Stelarc utilizes such overturning of the privileged position by affirming the *image* of the posthuman as a simulacrum itself, rather than the representation of the existing 'model', his body. Deleuze also proposes that the 'virtual is opposed not to the real but to the actual. *The virtual is fully real in so far as it is virtual.*' This 'actualization' of the virtual supports Stelarc's ideas on the 'reality' of the image in the now 'operational' spaces of VR. His autonomous images can 'exist' in a spatio-temporal manner that surpasses resemblance.[50]

Stelarc Collides with Theory

1. *The Body: Technology, Art, Virtual Existence and Ethics*
For Stelarc, technology circumvents the putatively incestuous discourses of postmodern stagnation, *'bypassing'* ideological rhetoric, and generating alternative aesthetic strategies that culminate in a 'Post-human awareness'.[51] It is significant that he turns to technology for his alternative to theoretical posthuman discourses. For example, his solution to today's information overload and complexity is either to incorporate information technology within the body, or to design more effective 'inputs and outputs'.[52] He also challenges Foucault's theory of the socially inscribed body by replacing the body as site with the body as a structure to be modified.[53] However, technology *is* a social discourse that inscribes the body. Stelarc's subjective body is always already a text over-inscribed by technology, with its Western assumptions and consequences.

McLuhan's notion of externalizing the central nervous system is one of Stelarc's central tenets. His *Understanding Media* has had an immeasurable influence on the current information theories of Stelarc, Virilio, Baudrillard and others. It is based on the premise that electronic technology propels us toward the final extension of 'man', who becomes the 'sex organs of the machine world… enabling it to fecundate and to evolve ever new forms'. Where the mechanical age extended our bodies into space, the electronic age extends our central nervous system, 'abolishing both space and time as far as our planet is concerned'. McLuhan foreshadowed both the end of Western linearity in an information feedback-loop, and the 'transformation of the real world into science fiction'. Physiologically, he noted, 'man…is perpetually modified by [technology] and in turn finds ever new ways of modifying [it]'; the form of the body and of technology create a vicious feedback-loop of evolutionary mutation, where it becomes impossible to determine which is the extension of the other. While his dialectical theory of the 'Tetrad' enabled him to explore the both-and/ either-or consequences of technology and information, it appears that Stelarc and Virilio have each emphasized only one side of this model of 'effect'.[54]

McLuhan's interpretation of the Narcissus myth offers an explanation for mankind's obsession with technological extension that is readily applicable to Stelarc. McLuhan stresses that Narcissus did not fall in love with himself, but with the 'extension of himself by mirror', symbolizing human beings' fascination with any extension of their selves.[55] This constructs Stelarc's putative narcissism as that which desires the image of his *self as Other*. His performative oversignification of the body and failure to address deeper implications of alterity can result in a depreciating perception of the posthuman-*as*-fetish, reproducing the narcissistic Other-as-self rather than as empowering difference.[56] Science fiction must also address the aesthetic and narcissistic posthuman, or else face premature extinction of the species in a theoretical 'black hole'.

Virilio is the contemporary theorist who has most conspicuously criticized Stelarc's project. A self-proclaimed 'art critic of technology', he believes that after two centuries of techno-science positivism and idealism, we need to 'critique the negative aspect'. Like McLuhan, he rejects any distinction between new technology, information and war.[57] Virilio argues that one cannot 'advance technologically within the arts without first formulating critical theory commensurate with technological art', and that any 'contemporary artform that lacks a critical theory is not really an artform'.[58] Due to this perceived theoretical 'lack', one is accused of being opposed to technology in art if one criticizes it. Virilio's attempt to raise the debate on art and technology above the 'superficially positive discourses of publicity' is necessary, but he has overstated his case by arguing for the prioritization of theory *before* art and technology.[59]

Virilio portrays body art as exemplifying the brutal 'hyper-violence' of twentieth-century war machines through its symbolism of horror and mutilation. He posits Stelarc as a prophet of doom who illustrates a suicide of the body through the extension of 'the field of war into the viscera'.[60] Stelarc, argues Virilio, is a 'naïve victim' of technofetishism, unaware of the losses incurred by the disappearance of the physical body. These losses are of immense significance, whereas the *advantages* of incorporating technology into the body, as demonstrated by Stelarc, are 'so obvious, that intellectually speaking, it's of very little interest'.[61]

Virilio compares Stelarc's vision with that of Marinetti's *Futurist Manifesto*, the end of humanity in a fascist form.[62] Stelarc rejects this as a simplification of his ideas into a '*Terminator 2* kind of a cyborg'. He claims his use of technology has never been grounded in such militaristic discourse, and takes 'umbrage' at the accusation of technotopian naïveté, again grounding his self-defence in praxis: 'what I say and do is... constrained by the limitations of my body and the...hardware that I'm using... [A] theoretician like Virilio might be the one who's naïve about technology.'[63] This ignores the inherent subjectivity of his own events, elevating them to a status of objectivity that putatively resides beyond the reach of theoretical criticism. Merleau-Ponty, however, has argued that experience alone cannot be 'unproblematically taken as a source of truth, [or] an arbiter of theory. Experience is not outside social, political, historical, and cultural forces.'[64]

It can be argued that posthuman performance art is a symptom of a contemporary *l'art pour l'art* sensibility, the culmination of a self-alienation where mankind experiences its own destruction as the supreme aesthetic pleasure, 'objectifying ourselves to death' in a social and political vacuum.[65] Kroker and Weinstein maintain that, 'Technology is art to such a degree of intensity that the world becomes a violent aesthetic experiment in redesigning the cultural DNA of the human species.' We become 'voyeurs of our own disappearance'.[66] However, while Stelarc's insistence that his work is apolitical and asocial appears to confirm this analysis, such emphasis on the artist's objectified body ignores the necessarily always productive body.

Many of science fiction's posthumans are plagued by the commodification of prosthetic and genetic technology, and of the virtual spaces they inhabit. Stelarc must also address this 'commodification and elitism of access', where a body's transformational potential is indexed to its buying power.[67] He argues that the uneven dissemination of new technology is not necessarily unhelpful: 'all that it guarantees is that the experiments are going to be done on the elite', who become the lab rats of the future. However, such arguments are unconvincing, and projects such as his remain the exclusive domain of the first world. Stelarc's is not some egalitarian project divorced from the pressures of capitalist production and subjection.[68] Although he denies that his work represents desire as 'emotion and spectacle',[69] it is impossible to dismiss the global marketability of this techno-marionette-like dancer.

2. *The Phantom Body*

The symbiotic body in process of transformation is the fundamental manifestation of the entire discourse surrounding Stelarc's intersections with posthuman theory and science fiction. 'All' bodies are ever-present here: the 'objective-instrumental body', the 'subjective-animate' body,[70] theoretical, absent and recombinant bodies are all implicated in Stelarc's work. It is with some sense of vindication that he notes the contemporary interest in *'the body'*, pointing to early criticism which regarded his emphasis on the body as 'reductive'. However, while his 'theories' provide the superficial appearance of a comprehensive critical foundation to his events, in reality Stelarc's work reveals appropriated disparate fragments of contemporary discourses. This practice has resulted in the noted slippage between the seemingly Cartesian absent body of some events and writing, and the lived experiential body claimed in his 'theory'. How does he assimilate the hollow, obsolete, automatic and absent body with his claim that the body is not *'merely* this biology'?[71]

Stelarc attempts to resolve this paradox by proposing that through technology the body evolves as a 'phantom body': 'a kind of visual visceral sensation that is still coupled to a physical body', while also becoming an interactive operational image in the realm of virtual reality.[72] He projects the 'phantom image' of the body into a telematic existence, where it is *both* disconnected from, and yet simultaneously 'felt' by its corporeal 'source', allowing Stelarc to 'have his Cartesian duality and phenomenology too'. In virtual reality the spatial and temporal context of this 'phantom body image' would change as rapidly as its relationship to other bodies and objects, notably technology. Conventionally, spatiality has been 'crucial for defining the limits and shape of the body image'.[73] What happens, then, when that image becomes a 'phantom image', both located within the boundaries of its physical being, *and* a borderless virtual reality that is infinitely variable? How does the subject form a 'coherent' identity and (phantom) image when the skin is 'no longer the boundary or the container of the self'?[74] With Stelarc's erasure of the Foucaldian site of the personal and the political, identity becomes a more fluid notion. This 'self' in constant flux either 'collapses' into incoherent 'psychasthenia', or expands into a Deleuzian realm of multiple and 'schizophrenic' possibilities.[75]

3. *Stelarc and Feminist Critique: Body and Gender*

Stelarc attempts to align his theory of multiple futures with a feminist agenda of contesting futures that will guarantee diversity. He utilizes Donna Haraway's theories in an endeavour to defend his own ideas from feminist critiques of his work as patriarchal techno-fetishism, linking the objectives of her cyborg ontology to his redesigning of the human. Both are supposedly creatures in a 'postgender world' that reject pre-Oedipal symbiosis, subverting boundaries and Western origin myths.[76] Stelarc applauds Haraway's use of technology 'as a means of redefining the social role of the female...rather than seeing technology as this patriarchal construct that *purely* perpetuates male power'.[77] But his fundamentally aesthetic project is far removed from Haraway's quintessentially *political* project of feminist empowerment. More importantly, her agenda of situated embodied knowledges repudiates Stelarc's operational images. Haraway rallies against the passive, absent body, striving for the 'active' body as 'agent' rather than 'resource'.[78] It is hard to imagine two more dialectically opposed positions on the status of the body.

Any attempt to hijack feminist agenda for such a suspiciously technocratic project is fraught with contradiction. Stelarc's saving grace is the diversity of disparate theories and agenda *within* feminist criticism itself. While many feminists are hostile toward the posthuman loss of biological reproduction to 'patriarchal' technologies, Stelarc is eager to point out that one strain of feminism promotes the advantages of such a 'release' from the 'burden' of birth.[79] Another example of Stelarc's spurious appeal to feminism is his use of the performance artist Orlan to support his arguments. While her concurrence that 'the body is obsolete' and becomes its own image provides wonderful fodder for Stelarc,[80] her project is condemned by many feminists as a narcissistic performance of banal masochistic strategies that reinforces existing power discourses, rather than deconstucting them in any useful way. Consequently, her potential affirmation collapses into a reversal that ironically accentuates the criticism of Stelarc.[81]

While admitting a 'certain truth' to criticism that positions his work as a Eurocentric 'metallic-phallic' militaristic manifestation, Stelarc criticizes such condemnation as a 'simplistic assertion' that 'undermines' the 'meaningfulness of feminist critique' through an outdated polarization of male and female gender roles in a world of ambiguous gender.[82] Technology, he asserts, is not all about 'toys for the boys'; rather, it 'equalises the physical potential of bodies and blurs sexuality—revising gender roles'.[83] The potential to 'revise' gender boundaries via the 'Internet Body Upload' is keenly emphasized by him.[84] Such capacity for transgender and transracial ambiguity has been heralded as one of the most potentially liberating aspects of virtual reality. Not all critics, however, are so enamoured of these transgressions. Today's cybersex merely constitutes a diversionary (bi) product of any meaningful attempt to realize posthuman erasure. It is also dangerous to presume that such erasure of difference is desirable. The maintenance of some 'preontological', 'preepistemological' alterity is generally deemed necessary, as the insistence on sameness entails a potential disenfranchisement through the loss of the *power* of difference.[85] To ignore these issues is to leave the model of posthumanism incomplete. The (non)reproductive and technological posthuman body remains vague, untheorized, and contentious.

Despite the many important implications of Stelarc's work, it must be remembered that he is essentially a performance artist. While the contradictory juxtaposition of Cartesian practice and phenomenological 'strategy' pervades his work, within the context of performance such theory can be read as a theatrical, performance-enhancing device. It is arguable that Stelarc need not address or attempt to resolve such self-contradictory narrative and theory, as he has removed it from its critical foundations and transplanted it within an aesthetic framework. His claims to a theoretical basis can be re-contextualized within performative practices, as illustrated by his reformulation of complex theories into a series of one-line maxims that adorn the promotional literature at his performances. Theory becomes art becomes science fiction. Such a manoeuvre, however, threatens to de-politicize theory as well as art, reducing all to depth-less spectacle.

Conclusion: Performance Bodies, Posthuman Bodies, and Science Fiction

Science fiction authors, cultural and literary theorists, and performance artists like Stelarc and Orlan constantly intersect, creating a fertile interdisciplinary cross-pollination of eclectic ideas.[86] While the literal-ization of the science fiction metaphor by cultural theory has been well documented, the same literalization by performance art has not. This is not a linear model: the relationship is essentially rhizomatic. Performance artists become 'mediators' for the posthuman models of science fiction, theory and philosophy, in a creative 'mutual resonance and exchange' of concepts.[87] It is the *differences from*, rather than the *similarities to* science fiction, that make performance artists' adoption of posthuman strategies for 'becoming Other' an area that science fiction and cultural theory need to engage with, rather than simply pointing to obvious yet merely aesthetic correlating metaphors. The performative posthuman's dramatized ontology can offer new future parameters, just as science fiction provides such artists with many of their paradigms.

The posthuman is a creature of bricolage, not only of cultural themes and objects, but of genres, forms and disciplines. By drawing on the diversity of strategies in science fiction, art, theory and science, posthumanism expands its horizons. The desired and self-begotten posthuman is born of diversity into multiplicity, its options are seemingly endless. It is only by combining aspects of all these disparate discourses and models that a Tetradic vision of the posthuman can be gained, allowing the both/and, either/or consequences of alterity their necessary visibility. With typical ambiguity, performance artists provide *both* future survival strategies *and* disempowering spectacles. The premise of their work is essentially aesthetic, but within that devotion to the artistic endeavour realized through the body and its image lies their very correlation with science fiction. Merging art, image and metaphor with corporeality, they not only produce the aesthetic posthuman image, but their bodies generate knowledge that produces alternative posthuman parameters. Strategies can evolve from spectacles, actualization may derive from aesthetics. In attempting to transpose the realm of the image into the 'operational', bodies that 'speak' science fiction create an escape velocity for the image that can remove it from the confines of inertia, enabling those working within other sf mediums to incorporate a more phenomenological knowledge of the body into their posthuman extrapolations.

Notes

1 See, for example, Charles J. Stivale, 'Mille/Punks/Cyber/Plateaus: Science Fiction and Deleuzo-Guattarian "Becomings"', *Substance*, 66.3 (1991), p. 79.

2 Istvan Csicsery-Ronay, 'The SF of Theory: Baudrillard and Haraway', *Science Fiction Studies*, 18.3 (1991), p. 396.

3 Stivale posits Baudrillard, Haraway, Deleuze and Guattari and the like as 'fictional theorists' *writing* in a 'science fiction overground' ('Mille/Punks/Cyber/Plateaus', p. 79).

4 The process of creating the posthuman in a world of heightened (postmodern) aesthetics has witnessed the foregrounding of art and the artist in many contemporary science fiction texts. From the Prigoginic creators of new 'angels' in Sterling's *Schismatrix* to the 'Avatar' designers of Stephensons's *Snow Crash*, artists are always there creating the aesthetic image of the posthuman form.

5 Ross Farnell, 'In Dialogue with "Posthuman" Bodies: Interview with Stelarc', *Body & Society*, 5.2–3 (1999), pp. 129–47, at pp. 136–37.

6 Farnell, 'Interview', p. 136.

7 Nicholas Zurbrugg, 'Electronic Voodoo (An Interview with Stelarc)', *21.C: The Magazine of the 21st Century*, 2 (1995), p. 49.

8 Farnell, 'Interview', p. 138.

9 The notion of the 'soft machine' comes from David Porush's book of the same title, *The Soft Machine: Cybernetic Fiction* (New York and London: Methuen, 1985). Cybernetic fiction, argues Porush, softens the machine by justifying human pathology.

10 Stelarc's recent 'Stimbod' performances use concurrent interactive video montages, which include footage of the third hand operating in a manner

more than reminiscent of *Terminator*-type imagery.

An example of the interrelation of Stelarc's events and contemporary science fiction is provided by Pat Murphy's novel, *The City Not Long After* (London: Pan, 1989). One of her artist characters, 'The Machine', attempts to manifest the 'human/machine interface' by constructing a 'third hand'. Its description parallels almost exactly Stelarc's own account of the third hand he developed years earlier, an example of science fiction applying his actualization to its metaphors, rather than the reverse.

11 Farnell, 'Interview', p. 136.

12 Both 'Lindsay' and the 'Lobsters' are Prigogine-influenced characters in Sterling's *Schismatrix* (Harmondsworth: Penguin, 1986). The 'Lobster' Mech/Shaper symbionts first appear in 'Cicada Queen' (1983), in *Crystal Express* (New York: Ace, 1990), pp. 47–84.

13 Sarah Miller, 'A Question of Silence—Approaching the Condition of Performance.' *25 Years of Performance Art in Australia: Performance Art, Performance and Events.* Curator N. Waterlow. (Ivan Dougherty Gallery, Marrickville: RF Jones & Sons, 1994), pp. 7–12.

14 Anne Marsh, *Body and Self: Performance Art in Australia 1969–92* (Oxford: Oxford University Press, 1993), pp. 51, 95–96.

15 Marsh, *Body and Self*, pp. 107–11, 225.

16 Elizabeth Grosz traces the negative concept of desire to Plato's 'one desires what one lacks', and records its continuation through Hegel, Freud, and Lacan, among others. Alternatively Grosz proposes Spinoza as the original proponent of a positive desire: 'a fullness which produces, transforms, and engages directly with reality… a form of production, including self-production, a process of making or becoming', which finds its contemporaries in Nietzsche, Foucault and Deleuze and Guattari. Grosz notes various 'different, active, affirmative conceptions of desire'. See Elizabeth Grosz, *Volatile Bodies: Toward a Corporeal Feminism* (St Leonards: Allen & Unwin, 1994), pp. 222, 165.

17 Gnosticism such as Artaud's is putatively caught in the contradictions of 'the affirmation of the body, the revulsion from the body, the wish to transcend the body, [and] the quest for the redeemed body', an 'inexhaustible paradox' that 'transcends the limits of the mind' (Susan Sontag, 'Artaud', Introduction to *idem*, ed., *Antonin Artaud: Selected Writings* [New York: Farrar, Straus and Giroux, 1976], pp. xvii–lix [xlviii–liii]). One can question, though, whether the phenomenological body must transcend the limits of all minds, or only of those socialized by Western metaphysics.

18 The play concludes that:
    …there is nothing more useless than an organ.
    When you will have made him a body without organs,
    then you will have delivered him from all his automatic reactions
    and restored him to his true freedom. (1947)
Artaud, *Selected Writings*, pp. 570–71.

The BwO and Stelarc's hollow body are fundamentally different concepts, the former a complex notion of desire and desiring machines, the later a strategy for a 'pan-planetary physiology'. In fact, according to Deleuze and Guattari, the 'hollow body' is one way of 'botching' the BwO (Giles Deleuze and Felix Guattari, *A Thousand Plateaus: Capitalism and Schizophrenia*, trans. Brian Massumi [Minneapolis: University of Minnesota Press, 1987], p. 165).

19 Stelarc, 'Abstract: From Psycho to Cyber Strategies: Prosthetics, Robotics and Remote Existence' (Article for *Kunst Forum* issue on the body, 1994, copy obtained from author). Available on the Internet in edited form at

http://www.merlin.com.au/stelarc

20 Geoffrey De Groen, 'Barriers Beyond the Body (An Interview with Stelarc)', in *Some Other Dream: The Artist, the Artworld and the Expatriate* (Sydney: Hale & Iremonger, 1984), p. 114. A good example of Stelarc's 'global' status is provided by his itinerary for the last five months of 1995, where he performed, exhibited or spoke at 14 different 'events' in 10 different countries.

21 James D. Paffrath and Stelarc, *Obsolete Bodies/ Suspensions/ Stelarc* (Davis, California: J.B. Publications, 1984), p. 16. It is instructive to note parallels with Artaud, who felt the body's autonomy being assailed by gravitational forces, literalizing his battle with the forces of destiny. (See Jane Goodall, *Artaud and the Gnostic Drama* [Oxford: Clarendon Press, 1994], p. 157.) This corresponds with Stelarc's challenge to the destiny of the body as both Earthbound and rigid in form.

22 De Groen, 'Barriers', p. 100.

23 Stelarc, *Stelarc* (Norwood, SA: Ganesh, 1976), n.p. Lines quoted are from throughout the work.

24 Paffrath and Stelarc, *Obsolete Bodies*; De Groen, 'Barriers'. Stelarc frequently repeats such phrases as those quoted virtually verbatim in different interviews and articles. Any condensed citation of his major themes will inevitably draw widely from different sources; therefore, specific page references are not always given.

25 Farnell, 'Interview', p. 132.

26 Zurbrugg, 'Electronic Voodoo', p. 47.

27 Paffrath and Stelarc, *Obsolete Bodies*, p. 76. Similarly, Marshall McLuhan imagines the artist moving 'from the ivory tower to the control tower of society' due to a putative 'immunity' to technology (Marshall McLuhan, *Understanding Media: The Extensions of Man* [London: Routledge & Kegan Paul, 1964], pp. 64–66). Stelarc acknowledges McLuhan's influence on his work: 'McLuhan... generates the central discourse of technology in the twentieth century' (Farnell, 'Interview', p. 139).

Jeffrey Deitch also argues that art is likely to assume a central role in the move toward the posthuman, providing inspiration for new bodies and minds. This argument is based on the premise that: 'New approaches to self-realisation are generally paralleled by new approaches to art... artists have portrayed the changes in models of self-realisation that have accompanied profound changes in the social environment' (Jeffrey Deitch, *Posthuman* [New York: DAP/ Distributed Art Publishers, 1992], pp. 12, 2).

28 Farnell, 'Interview', p. 145.

29 Stelarc, 'Psycho'.

30 Farnell, 'Interview', p. 143.

31 Zurbrugg, 'Electronic Voodoo', p. 48.

32 Stelarc, 'Psycho'. Stelarc is quoting Bryan S. Turner here from *Regulating Bodies*. No other references are given.

33 Farnell, 'Interview', p. 136.

34 Stelarc, 'Towards the Post-Human (From Absent to Phantom Bodies)', in *25 Years of Performance Art in Australia*, p. 53.

35 The 'Internet Body Upload' performance was given at *Telepolis (The Interactive and Networked City)*, 10, 11 November 1995 FIL; Kirchberg, Luxembourg. 'Ping Body' was performed at the 'Digital Aesthetics Conference', Artspace, Sydney, Australia, 10 April, 1996. Further information on the strategies and logistics of these performances is available on Stelarc's home page site. The titles of other performances from around this time give an insight

into the nature of Stelarc's performances, and include: 'Voltage-In/Voltage-Out'; 'Psycho/Cyber: Absent, Obsolete & Invaded Bodies'; 'Split Body/Scanning Robot'; 'Stimbod'; 'Erasure Zone'; and 'Extruded Body/Elapsed Intentions'.

36 Farnell, 'Interview', p. 134.
37 Farnell, 'Interview', p. 135.
38 Stelarc, 'Post-Human', p. 21.
39 Zurbrugg, 'Electronic Voodoo', p. 46.
40 Zurbrugg, 'Electronic Voodoo', p. 49.
41 Among many, see for example Allucquere Rosanne Stone, 'Will the Real Body Please Stand Up? Boundary Stories about Virtual Cultures', in M. Benedikt, ed., *Cyberspace: First Steps* (Cambridge: MIT Press, 1992), pp. 81–115; Darko Suvin, 'On Gibson and Cyberpunk SF', in L. McCaffery, ed., *Storming the Reality Studio: A Casebook of Cyberpunk and Postmodern Science Fiction* (Durham: Duke University Press, 1991), pp. 349–65; Gabriele Schwab, 'Cyborgs. Postmodern Phantasms of Body and Mind', *Discourse*, 9 (1987), pp. 65–84; and Neil Easterbrook, 'The Arc of our Destruction: Reversal and Erasure in Cyberpunk', *Science Fiction Studies*, 19 (1992), pp. 378–94.
42 Farnell, 'Interview', p. 141.
43 Farnell, 'Interview', p. 140.
44 Zurbrugg, 'Electronic Voodoo', p. 46.
45 De Groen, 'Barriers', p. 105.
46 Stelarc, 'Psycho'.
47 Farnell, 'Interview', p. 130.
48 Jean Baudrillard, 'The Year 2000 Has Already Happened', in A. and M. Kroker, eds., *Body Invaders: Sexuality and the Postmodern Condition* (London: Macmillan, 1988), pp. 35–44.
49 Gilles Deleuze, *Difference and Repetition*, trans. Paul Patton (New York: Columbia University Press, 1994), p. 127.
50 *Difference*, pp. 128, 69, 67; 208–12. The danger, according to Deleuze, is to confuse the virtual with the possible: 'The possible is opposed to the real', its process is a 'realization'. In contrast the virtual 'possesses a full reality by itself', its process is 'actualization'. This difference is 'a question of existence itself'. Existence occurs in space and time, which the possible does not produce. (Deleuze, *Difference*, pp. 208–12). It is worth noting that Deleuze's challenge to the Western simulacrum in *Difference and Repetition* is inspired in part by the writing of Artaud.
51 Farnell, 'Interview', p. 143; Stelarc, 'Post-Human', p. 20.
52 Farnell, 'Interview', p. 139.
53 Stelarc, 'Post-Human', p. 20.
54 McLuhan, *Understanding Media*, pp. 63, 3, 354, 35. The 'Tetrad' is central to McLuhan's work with Bruce R. Powers, *The Global Village: Transformations in World Life and Media in the 21st Century* (New York: Oxford University Press, 1989).

Like Stelarc, McLuhan also envisaged the rise of the 'image' to the status of 'realm of action', but less optimistically (*Understanding Media*, p. 103). The digitalized posthuman, he writes, dissolves the human image. This 'creature' is no longer flesh and blood, it is an item in a data bank, ephemeral, schizophrenic, and resentful (p. 94). At that point, technology is out of control, resulting in social implosion and a loss of individualism (pp. 97–98). McLuhan's vision of a fragmented and violent (post-)humanity in identity crisis is both humanist and Cartesian. The spectre of hubris firmly opposes McLuhan to any anagenetic 'second phase' of genesis (*Global Village*, pp. 97–98).

55 McLuhan, *Understanding Media*, p. 4.

56 The reduction of the Other to the Same, where the desire for the Other is revealed as no more than desire for the Self, is noted by both Merleau-Ponty and Baudrillard. See Baudrillard's article, 'Plastic Surgery for the Other', trans. F. Debrix, in *CTheory: Theory, Technology and Culture*, 19.1–2 (22 Nov 1995) (available via email: ctheory@vax2.concordia.ca.). Baudrillard deplores today's 'hypostasis of the same', where we incestuously project 'the same into the image of the other', abolishing true alterity and difference. Plastic surgery, laments Baudrillard, becomes universal, in an 'individual appropriation of the body, of your desire… of your image… The body is invested as a fetish, and is used as a fetish in a desperate attempt at identifying oneself.' This self-production of the Other seeks to make it 'an ideal object', rejecting 'strangeness and negativity'.

57 Virginia Madsen, 'Critical Mass (An Interview with Paul Virilio)', *World Art: The Magazine of Contemporary Visual Arts*, 1 (1995), pp. 78, 82.

The city, claims Virilio, 'is the site of technology, and war is the site of super-technology' (Nicholas Zurbrugg, 'The Publicity Machine and Critical Theory (An Interview with Paul Virilio)', *Eyeline* 27 [1995], p. 14). All technology and information, notes McLuhan, can plausibly be regarded as weapons (McLuhan, *Understanding Media*, pp. 344–45).

58 Zurbrugg, 'Critical Theory', p. 11.

59 Conversely, this critical 'lack' is equally responsible for pessimistic technophobia. The incorporation of technology into art is often regarded with untheoretical suspicion that focuses upon the instrumentality at the expense of the message. The contemporary tendency to posit all technology as means without ends denies the symbiosis of art and technology any critical function. Although McLuhan has demonstrated the inseparability of the medium from the message, one needs to look beyond *only* the medium. The sensorial onslaught of images offered by Stelarc and other performance artists is commonly derided for functioning as self-promoting spectacle only.

60 Madsen, 'Critical Mass', pp. 9, 80.

61 Zurbrugg, 'Critical Theory', p. 11.

62 Madsen, 'Critical Mass', p. 80. It must be remembered that Fascist '*anti-humanism*' only portrays *one possible form* of posthumanism from a potentially endless and unpredictable repertoire. Also, not all definitions of 'anti-humanism' are regarded as necessarily negative. Structuralists and post-structuralists are often seen as productively 'anti-humanist' in their opposition to humanism.

63 Farnell, 'Interview', pp. 138, 142.

64 Grosz, *Volatile Bodies*, p. 94.

65 Walter Benjamin, *Illuminations*, ed. and intro. Hannah Arendt, trans. Harry Zohn (New York: H. & K. Wolf, 1968), p. 243; Mark Dery, 'Against Nature', *21.C: Scanning the Future* 4 (1995), p. 30.

66 Arthur Kroker and Michael A. Weinstein, *Data Trash: The Theory of the Virtual Class* (New York: St. Martin's Press, 1994), pp. 54, 77. Kroker and Weinstein argue that the personal computer now 'functions as performance art for the body electronic', replacing viscera with virtualized flesh (p. 75). This disappearance of the 'body' from 'body art' is perhaps the ironic conclusion of Stelarc's strategies, a self-annihilation of body and art in a posthuman symbiosis.

Arthur and Marilouise Kroker have appropriated Stelarc as the perfect exemplary tool with which to illustrate their theories on the 'disappearance' of the 'postmodern body'. They argue that the human body '*is* obsolete and, as Stelarc predicted, what is desperately required is a new body fit for the age of ultra-technologies'. Exemplifying the aestheticization and dissolution of the body and its organs, 'Stelarc actually makes his body its own simulacrum' (Arthur Kroker and Marilouise Kroker, 'Panic Sex in America' and 'Theses on the Disappearing Body in the Hyper-Modern Condition', in *Body Invaders*, pp. 21, 32). Stelarc translates their rhetoric into performance in the same way as he does with much science fiction, and the differences often appear negligible.

67 Brian Massumi, *A User's Guide to 'Capitalism and Schizophrenia': Deviations from Deleuze and Guattari* (Cambridge: MIT Press, 1992), pp. 136–37.

68 Stelarc's recent 'Ping Body' event utilized the data flow of the Internet as body manipulating agency. This performance is being facilitated by the 'sponsorship' of a multi-national software company providing world-wide 'home page' and Internet access facilities. This must surely raise questions of possible 'corporatization' and 'commodification/compromise' in the nature of the ensuing 'events'. The 'spaces' in which his 'autonomous/phantom' image now exists and interacts become corporate rather than public. Stelarc's 'home page' has more information on this latest performance 'mode'.

69 Farnell, 'Interview', pp. 145, 133.

70 These two distinctions are drawn from the German difference between the body as *Körper* and the body as *Leib*, as noted by Brian S. Turner, *Regulating Bodies: Essays in Medical Sociology* (London: Routledge, 1992), p. 9. Whereas *Leib* refers to the 'animated living experiential body', the 'body-for-itself', *Körper* refers to the 'objective, exterior and institutionalized body', the 'body-in-itself' (pp. 41–42).

71 Farnell, 'Interview', p. 135.

72 Farnell, 'Interview', p. 135. Stelarc is extrapolating from the amputee's 'phantom-limb' sensation, a phenomenon noted by Descartes and studied by numerous others since, especially Merleau-Ponty.

Grosz argues that the phantom limb testifies to 'the pliability or fluidity of what is usually considered the inert, fixed, passive, biological body. ...the biological body exists for the subject only through the mediation of a series of images or representations of the body and its capacities for movement and action. ...The body phantom is the link between our biological and cultural existences, between our "inner" psyche and our "external" body, that which enables a passage or a transformation from one to other' (Elizabeth Grosz, 'Lived Spatiality: Spaces of Corporeal Desire', in Brian Boigon, ed., *Culture Lab 1* [New York: Princeton Architectural Press, 1993], pp. 186–87). Accordingly, Stelarc's notion of the 'phantom body' serves his aims exceedingly well.

73 Grosz, *Volatile Bodies*, p. 80.

74 Farnell, 'Interview', p. 131.

75 According to Roger Caillois, psychasthenia is the 'inevitable' result of the loss of defining limits and the shape of the body image (Grosz, *Volatile Bodies*, p. 80).

76 Stelarc, 'Post-Human', p. 20.

77 Farnell, 'Interview', p. 137.

78 Donna Haraway, *Simians, Cyborgs, and Women: The Reinvention of Nature* (London: FAB, 1991), p. 200.

79 Farnell, 'Interview', p. 142. For example, Valie Export, in her article 'The Real and its Double: The Body', *Discourse* 11.1 (1988–89), pp. 3–27, argues that reproductive technology, such as that initiated by Mary Shelley's

Frankenstein, offers an escape for women from the reproductive 'body-as-burden' (pp. 19, 24–25). It is instructive to note that, like Orlan, Export is also a performance artist.

80 Stelarc, 'Post-Human', p. 20.

81 As Arthur Kroker asks of Orlan's art: 'Is it possible to work within the "dominant male paradigmatic codes of fetish and voyeurism" and transcend the codes?' (Sharon Grace, Introduction, 'The Doyenne of Divasection' by Miryam Sas, *Mondo 2000,* 13 [1995], pp. 106–108). Not all feminist writers, however, condemn Orlan's project. One notable exception is Kathy Davis' work on cosmetic surgery: *Reshaping the Female Body: The Dilemma of Cosmetic Surgery* (New York: Routledge, 1995). While not concerned with Orlan specifically, Davis argues that not all recipients of surgery are victims of patriarchal and cultural interpellation, or as she notes, 'cultural dopes' (p. 56).

82 Farnell, 'Interview', p. 141.

83 Farnell, 'Interview', p. 142; Stelarc, 'Post-Human', p. 20.

84 Farnell, 'Interview', p. 142. It can be argued that such 'gender erasure' is essentially meaningless, as Stelarc's body will respond to the externally initiated electrical impulses in a fundamentally male manner. Five decades of body inscription as male would not be instantly erased. Stelarc is presenting his wired-in body as the 'neutral human', whereas it is the functioning male body. The unquestioned presumption that the male body functions as a model for the sexually neutral body has pervaded the majority of science and technology, essentially erasing sexual difference and the female body. (See Grosz, 'Lived Spatiality', p. 195.)

85 Grosz, *Volatile Bodies,* pp. 208–209.

86 For example, conferences such as 'Blue Skies' at Newcastle, England in 1992, and 'Virtual Futures' (1 and 2) at the University of Warwick in 1994 and 1995.

87 The notion of 'mediators' comes from Deleuze's article 'Mediators', in Jonathan Crary and Sanford Kwinter, eds., *Zone 6: Incorporations* (New York: Urzone Inc, 1992), pp. 280–87. He proposes that in the relation between the arts, science and philosophy, there is no priority, each is creative. They interact to become each other's mediators: 'Mediators are fundamental. Creation is all about mediators. Without them, nothing happens' (pp. 283–85). This mediation is exemplified by the interrelation of posthuman discourses in sf, cultural theory, philosophy, science, and, of course, artists such as Stelarc, Orlan, and SRL.

Science Fiction and the Gender of Knowledge

BRIAN ATTEBERY

Science fiction began to be recognized in the 1960s and 1970s as a powerful tool for examining gender issues. Writers like Joanna Russ, Theodore Sturgeon, Ursula K. Le Guin, Samuel R. Delany, and James Tiptree, Jr, demonstrated just how amenable the genre was to revising relationships between (or, sometimes, among) the sexes. Yet, at the same time, feminist critiques of science fiction revealed that for most of its history, sf has generally functioned as a boys' club, excluding female characters and concerns and uncomfortable with overt expressions of sexuality. How, then, could the No-Girls-Allowed sf of the 1930s have evolved into the sort of fiction honored in the 1990s by the Tiptree Award, which recognizes the role of sf in exploring and expanding gender codes? Does the later work merely overturn the earlier, or were there features already present in early magazine sf that lend themselves to the exploration of sexual behaviors and identities?

It is not easy to read one's way back into the 1930s, to try to understand how stories from that time functioned for their readers. However, when one reads an issue of *Amazing Stories* or *Thrilling Wonder Tales* from cover to cover, complete with ads, editorials, and letters from readers, reading the hacks along with the more ambitious writers, one gets the sense that it is all one thing. Rather than being self-sufficient objects of art, the individual stories are part of a continuous stream of discourse, like the 'flow' that television programmers aim for.

The story of Professor Jones's evolutionary accelerator or Professor Brown's time machine is part of the same whole as the letter from a reader who wants to know whether electricity might be broadcast without wires. The story has its meaning within the same discourse about the ways we come to know the natural world and the place of the scientifically minded individual within society. Furthermore, this conversation about science incorporates the scantily clad maiden on the front cover and the ad for razor blades or a body-building course on the back: 'No skinny man has an ounce of SEX APPEAL, but science has proved that thousands *don't have to be SKINNY!*' declared *Astounding Stories*, April 1932, on the inside front cover. These elements suggest that the message is about gender as well as science, or rather that any statement about science also entails a message about gender.

One way to get at the message emerging from the juxtaposition of ads, illustrations, editorials, and adventure stories is to retell the stories as if they were one story, ignoring just those differentiating elements that drew readers' conscious attention and provided material for endless arguments about why the latest Stanton A. Coblenz story is or is not as good as the previous one. Take away such features as planetary climate and spaceship propulsion systems and what is left is the recurring story of a young man and his initiation into the masculine mysteries of science. The discussion that follows is based on reading the entire output of the sf magazines from a single year as if all the stories from that year were part of a single utterance. The year I have chosen, 1937, represents a point just before the message began to change. Hugo Gernsback, who created the American sf magazine format, had stopped editing in 1936. By the end of 1937, John W. Campbell, Jr, became editor of *Astounding Stories*, and his interests and tastes produced a different, though no less gender-marked, collective narrative. Campbell-era writers like Robert A. Heinlein brought to the genre a more deliberate control of language and point of view, not eliminating the sort of un-self-conscious sexual symbolism that roamed freely through the early pulps, but forcing it to clothe itself in more coherent plots and more fully developed characters. 1937 is the year before the dream went underground.

The hero of the 1930s ur-story is sometimes a student, sometimes an experienced adventurer with a checkered past. In keeping with popular romance tradition, the hero is typically virile and athletic, but he is also branded by his intellectual superiority. His difference from other young men is frequently expressed in terms of unusual perceptions: in one story, for instance, he can see into the ultraviolet portion of the spectrum. For this reason, even though 'I was normal in my desires, wanting to play and laugh as all children do ... [i]ntimate friendships were denied me, for casual friends soon came to notice my—queerness!'.[1]

The scientific world to which this hero aspires is represented by a second recurring character: the Professor. The relationship between the hero and his mentor is generally the most powerful emotional tie in the story, and is explicitly acknowledged as such: 'I loved Professor Brett Kramer at sight. He was an odd man—and I like the odd,' says the hero of K. Raymond's

'At the Comet'.[2] Unlike other emotional entanglements, to which readers responded with hostility, this tie between younger and older males was felt to enhance, rather than interfere with, a story's emotional payoff or Sense of Wonder, because the relationship between hero and mentor can be equated within the story with the love of knowledge: 'However, if my story proves the greatness of him I loved, Professor Brett Kramer, and further advances his own beloved astronomical science, I shall die content'.[3]

The Professor's research generally involves one of three related goals: personal immortality, freedom from physical limitations, or the creation of life. When he pursues one of these quests selfishly, using the hero as a tool, the story ends in combat between the two, but when he designates the hero as the one to fulfill his dream, the story results in the peaceful passing of the scientific torch. The hero becomes his surrogate son, and the pact is sealed by marrying the hero to the Professor's daughter, who is the third major recurring character.

Just how the Professor managed to acquire a daughter is a mystery, since there is rarely any evidence of his ever having had a wife. Sometimes, indeed, she is merely a surrogate daughter: an assistant or secretary who takes on the Daughterly roles of being explained to ('Seed spores? Mars?' Lucy was clearly baffled. 'Let me explain.'[4]), making coffee ('The girl busied herself at the [spaceship's] electric stove and soon they sat down to a steaming meal of scrambled eggs and coffee.'[5]), being rescued ('"Ray!" she shouted hoarsely, striving vainly to tear free from the merciless grip on her arms. "Ray! Save me! They're taking me away—to Meropolis!"'[6]), and marrying the hero.

At other times, the Daughter is herself a product of the Professor's science. The Professor tends to be scornful of ordinary reproductive methods: '"Do you mean that you can create living creatures?" "Pooh! Anybody can do that with the help of a female of the species. What I mean is that I have found the life force. I can animate the inert."'[7] Hence, he frequently seeks, Frankenstein-like, to bypass sexual reproduction, or at least woman's part in the process. 'He could produce the spermatozoon from his own body. If he could create the egg, with all its incalculable, character-determining genes, from inert matter…'[8] Whether adopted or immaculately conceived, the Daughter brings as dowry her father's secret knowledge and his blessing on the young aspirant.

The marriage and final clinch of hero and heroine is, of course, a staple of most popular genres, but it is evident in most of these stories that the bond between the hero and the Professor's Daughter is secondary to attachment between the men. 'The friendship of man for man,' states one hero sternly, 'is more enduring than love for a woman'.[9] The Daughter represents a safe form of sexuality—she helps keep the love between the men from being interpreted sexually and, by being marked as the eventual but always unconsummated object of desire, distracts us from any other sexual implications in the action of the story.

For sex is nowhere and everywhere in pulp sf. Cupid, as the title of one story intimates, is in the laboratory, even though 'the reference to "Cupid" might give rise to unfortunate misconceptions, which are hereby promptly dispelled. No—this account has nothing whatever to do with love or love-making. In fact, there is not one female in the entire story. It treats exclusively of two altogether staid and serious-minded chemists whose thoughts and efforts were as far removed from women and the unclothed little rascal with the bow and arrow as anything could possibly be.'[10]

The scientist whose sexuality is manifest only in his work, who is 'married to his experimenting' in 'virgin fields of research'[11] had been a central character in the scientific megatext long before the advent of magazine sf. Evelyn Fox Keller points out that the master narrative of science has always been told in sexual terms. It represents knowledge, innovation, and even perception as masculine, while nature, the passive object of exploration, is described as feminine. Since the time of Francis Bacon, scientists have seen themselves as seducing or ravishing Nature of her secrets.[12] Bacon, speaking in the voice of the older scientist, promises the younger acolyte that he can become both Nature's husband ('My dear, dear boy, what I plan for you is to unite you with things themselves in a chaste, holy and legal wedlock'[13]) and her master ('I am come in very truth leading to you Nature with all her children to bind her to your service and make her your slave'[14]). This equation of love with mastery, knowledge with domination, remains embedded in the scientific master narrative, affecting not merely the occupation of science, but also the knowledge produced thereby.

Scientific ideas—at least those in the physical sciences—may be gender neutral, but they can only be framed and communicated in terms of the speaker's physical being and social experience. Underlying all empirical knowledge are sense impressions conveyed through organs of the body, and the most informative of those organs—eyes, ears, tongue, lips, genitals, fingertips—are precisely those most implicated in the knower's social and sexual identity. Looking through a microscope at the inner structure of a cell is an act that carries with it associations with other sorts of looking, including the voyeur's gaze. To send out sensors to probe other worlds is to extend the sense of touch beyond the limits of the body. There is no way to imagine or to talk about such investigations without calling on the experience of the body, and the body upon which scientific knowledge is grounded in our culture is male. Indeed, it is only because science is so firmly anchored in the male experience that it can deny the traces of that body and claim to be the product of pure consciousness. In a sense, only the female body is perceived *as* a body. The male body usually lies hidden in the concept of pure mind, as in Emerson's image of the transparent eyeball.

The sf community adopted the language of hard and soft from science at least as early as 1957, when P. Schuyler Miller used the term *hard science fiction* in a review column in *Astounding*.[15] The hardness of hard science is that of the male body—or rather that body socially constructed as the opposite of female pliancy and permeability. The hard sciences are those with no meat on their mathematical bones; physics is a hard science but physiology is not, although the one is no more precise or predictive than the other. Early fans, by and large, preferred the hard variety of sf, not necessarily because of greater scientific accuracy but because such stories make the reader feel part of a technologically astute elite, someone who can contemplate the real workings of the universe without fuzzy thinking or sentiment. It is no accident that a story often considered a touchstone for hard sf, Tom Godwin's 'The Cold Equations', explicitly frames the conflict between social concerns and scientific thinking in terms of gender. In that story, the male pilot of a rescue ship is forced to jettison a scientifically naïve female stowaway. His mission is endangered by both her soft thinking and her soft body. Only the harder masculine self can successfully penetrate space.

At this point it is very difficult not to invoke Freud and begin making comments about the shape of guns and spaceships. Instead, I will try to edge my way around the issue by focussing on a less obviously male anatomical feature, the eye. The eye is the scientist's most important piece of equipment, without which it would be impossible to interface with telescopes, microscopes, graphs, or computer monitors. Unlike, say, voices or genitalia, male and female eyes differ hardly at all, and yet when eyes get adopted into symbol systems like language, the meaning of the female gaze differs dramatically from that of the male. More precisely, women are rarely represented as looking or seeing; instead even women's eyes are defined by their beauty, as something to be looked at, by men. Thus, the eye is both a sign of scientific prowess and, as Jacques Lacan and his followers have pointed out, a marker of sexual difference. Not surprisingly, 1930s sf is full of eyes and eyelike imagery.

The eyes of the scientist hero often reveal his unusual powers of observation and deduction. In Edmond Hamilton's 'A Million Years Ahead', the hero and his rival are transformed into men of the future, and the alteration is signalled primarily through their eyes: 'But the face! It was godlike in terrible beauty, the features perfectly regular, the mouth a straight, merciless line, the eyes enormous glowing ones through which looked a cold, vast mind whose shock was felt tangibly'.[16] When the two supermen fight, the weapon of choice is the eye:

> As he understood the meaning of that command, Fraham's eyes became terrible. Hellfires of furious revolt flamed in them, a surge of terrific mental resistance.
>
> But Sherill's commanding eye held steady, beating the other down again with hypnotic command.[17]

If the naked eye is not powerful enough to defeat an opponent, its power can be augmented through technology. The enhanced eye is often described as a ray or beam or light: 'The beam, no thicker than a lead pencil, stabbed into the enormous face of the ruler of Uk, drove clean into his single eye and through it into the depths of his fiendish brain'.[18]

Sometimes the eye is detachable. In Arthur K. Barnes's 'Green Hell', the hero's lost and regained rank is represented by a token of 'metal, cut in the form of an all-seeing eye, mirroring the sun and its planets... Ellerbee clutched it tightly and thrust his shoulders back. It was plain what that token meant to him—respect, honor, manhood, all those things that had been stripped from him years before.'[19]

A similar token of manhood is the Lens, 'a lenticular polychrome of writhing, almost fluid radiance' awarded to Kimball Kinnison, hero of E.E. 'Doc' Smith's *Galactic Patrol*. Like the hero's eye, the Lens's power is indicated by its size and brightness. The more mental power he brings to it, the 'tighter' and 'higher' the beam he can project. Elsewhere in the series, Smith makes an explicit connection between the Lens and gender: 'Women's minds and Lenses don't fit. There's a sex-based incompatibility. Lenses are as masculine as whiskers...'[20]

Wearing the Lens, Kinnison can penetrate thoughtscreens; enter another's mind to control his actions; perceive any object directly, 'as a whole, inside and out', without light or instruments; and eventually use his mind as a weapon to 'hurl no feeble bolts' at an enemy. The power of the Lens is only limited by the capacity of the user's mind: one must 'have enough jets to swing it'.[21]

The masculine act of seeing bestows on its object the complementary gender. As in Bacon's metaphor, the male scientist looks at a feminine universe, which thereby becomes both his mate and his property. In George H. Scheer's 'The Crystalline Salvation', the space that the scientist's gaze invades is a very feminine one indeed. It is a hollow crystalline planetoid into which the heroes' ship floats 'at very low velocity, into a rosy-hued cavern of enormous proportions'. Inside this womb 'was rest and peace and quiet, such as we had never dreamed of before'.[22]

But the feminine space can sometimes turn shy. John Edwards' 'The Planet of Perpetual Night' takes place on a world that cannot be seen. Not even that eye in the sky, the sun, can shine through its veils: 'The sun—his rays do not pierce that at all; nor do the beams of your fog-piercing headlights. It is one great mass—yet your instrument says practically no great mass near? Then what is it? What is this that gives no light, which no light can penetrate—which reflects nothing?'[23]

The male explorers contrive a ray that they hope will break through the gloom of this 'Etherless Zone'. Their employment of this ray can only be described as the climax of the story: 'Watching closely the blue beam, Dr. Davidson noted that it was slowly but surely pushing its sputtering way down to the surface below, moving and thrusting like a shaft of solid fire through the strange black shroud which obstructed its progress like a solid thing'.[24]

The act of seeing can lead not only to symbolic sexual release but still further, to impregnating the universe. 'Let us suppose,' suggests Henry Kuttner in 'When the Earth Lived', 'that a scientist has discovered a ray which creates life. He is experimenting with the atom. He turns this ray upon an atom—an extremely complex one—under his microscope. He creates life.'[25]

Because the scientific gaze is so insistently masculine, whatever it touches on tends to become feminized. Not only alien spaces, but aliens themselves must play the role of female Other to the male observer. The dark, female world of 'The Planet of Perpetual Night' turns out to be inhabited, and the narrator takes great care to mark its people as feminine. Their voices are 'treble-piping'; altogether they make 'a confused medley of thin, high-pitched notes'. They are small: 'about as high as his shoulder' with 'short plump bodies'.[26] They are, of course, blind, since their world is lightless; hence, they are not rival possessors of the masculine gaze. They must acquire knowledge by direct bodily contact, an act that has clear sexual connotations, especially when the men are obliged to reciprocate:

> The patting and stroking continued for a time to the accompaniment of soothing voices, and the two relieved men joined in by returning the implied compliments—but they were thankful for the blackness which hid their acute embarrassment![27]

The feminization of the alien can be even more explicit. The scientist of 'The Endless Chain' has used his ray machine to destroy most of humanity during a war. All that are left are himself and Soan, not a 'man of Avalon', but 'a stranger from the plateau, in the form of a true man'.[28] Soan asks Lomas, the scientist, 'How can a scientist and a madman start a new race? Eh?',[29] but that is not Lomas's greatest concern: 'Lomas stared

at the lunatic; he could change the sex of Soan without much difficulty...
But the prospect of fair Avalon overrun by a mad race who muttered
incomprehensibilities and could not feed themselves revolted him.'[30] In
other words, if it weren't for the racial problem, he would be willing to
overlook Soan's sex. (I can't help hearing echoes of Joe E. Brown, in *Some
Like it Hot*, saying to Jack Lemmon in drag, 'Nobody's perfect.')

If I were trying to demonstrate that science fiction is nothing more than
a set of male sexual fantasies decked out in exotic decor, I would stop here.
But that is not the case, even in the pulp magazines of 1937. Despite its
masculine bias and lack of sophistication, the fiction of this era already
possessed the potential to develop into a powerful tool for questioning
assumptions about gender. The picture I have drawn is as accurate a
composite as I could make it, but it needs correction on three main points.
First, there were always stories that did not fit the model: sf generates
formulas but has never been confined within them in the way that other
popular genres tend to be. Second, the audience and authorship of sf, even
in 1937, was not exclusively male. Third, the very narrative structures I
have been outlining can lend themselves to more subversive uses, and in
the hands of the more astute writers prove to be the foundation for a very
different sort of sf about gender.

Taking each of these points in turn, I must note that among the stories
in the four magazines publishing in 1937, few fit the formula precisely,
and a handful go off in different directions entirely. For instance, the 'hero'
of the story is, in a couple of instances, actually a couple, with the woman
taking a fairly active role in the adventures: examples are Jack Williamson's
'Released Entropy'[31] and Robert Willey's 'At the Perihelion'.[32] Other stories
fail to follow the standard story line at all, particularly those of the distant
past or the far future.

A surprising number of women were included among the readership
of the 1930s, or at least among those whose comments were printed in the
letters columns. Mrs Charles Bohant of Astoria, Oregon, for instance,
mentions in June, 1937, that not only is she a subscriber to *Amazing* but
that she has given a birthday subscription to her sister.[33] Women readers,
though never more than a small percentage of the correspondents, kept
their male counterparts aware that there might be other points of view on
gender issues, and indeed, starting in 1938, engaged them in a debate over
the appropriateness of women characters in sf. The redoubtable Mary Byers
took on a number of male readers over the claim, issued by a very young
Isaac Asimov, that 'When we want science-fiction, we don't want
swooning dames, and that goes double'. Byers responded that she is all for
getting rid of such 'hooey,' but that 'less hooey does *not* mean less women;
it means a difference in the way they are introduced into the story and the

part they play'.[34] The women readers' viewpoint was reinforced by the fact that a handful of the more popular writers of the late 1930s were women. Despite the unmarked gender of their bylines, Leslie F. Stone, A.R. Long, and C.L. Moore were known by at least some of the readership to be female: letters refer to 'Miss Moore', 'Miss Long', and 'our distinguished authoress, Leslie F. Stone'.[35] Of these three, the woman writer most interested in reexamining ideas of the feminine, Catherine L. Moore, published no sf stories in 1937, though readers of *Astounding Stories* were still buzzing over her novelette, 'Tryst in Time', in the last issue of 1936. Nonetheless, her presence was part of the full picture in 1937, helping to keep the discourse of sf open to alternative ways of writing and reading gender.

In fact, the presence of women in the sf boys' club reminds us that no matter how strongly the conventional images and actions of pulp sf suggest existing patterns of male domination, they *may* be read otherwise. Narrative has the power to alter any such patterns: indeed, one of the most fundamental operations of narrative is to represent change. Once the male scientist, with his phallic, nature-skewering gaze, is placed in a narrative setting, he is subject to every sort of transformation. He can be doubled, split, mirrored, inverted. The hero's role can be divided between friends; the older scientist can be a machine or an alien. Most importantly, the universe can look back. This is just what happens in one of the best stories published in any sf magazine in 1937, Don A. Stuart's 'Forgetfulness'.

This story contains many of the standard elements: a spaceship landing on an unknown planet; a heroic captain, 'tall and powerful; his muscular figure in trim Interstellar Expedition uniform of utilitarian, silvery gray';[36] a young scientist whose masculinity is less obvious and must be asserted during the course of the story; an alien race coded as feminine; a breakthrough of understanding that also implies power over the thing understood. Yet all of these elements are reshuffled by the narrative so that the ultimate effect is to question rather than reinforce standard gender codings.

There is no question that the invading spaceship stands for conventional masculinity. It is a 'mighty two-thousand-five-hundred-foot interstellar cruiser' crewed by the 'young, powerful men of Pareeth' who are led by Shor Nun, 'commander, executive, atomic engineer'. The only exception to this array of space brawn is the astronomer Ron Thule, who is set apart by being imaginative, empathetic, and self-doubting, seeing himself as a 'strange little man from a strange little world circling a dim, forgotten star'. As the group's astronomer, he has no role in the landing force: 'The men you mentioned are coming. Each head of department, save Ron Thule. There will be no work for the astronomer.'[37]

The world that is being invaded is described in terms of conventional femininity: smooth, gentle, rounded, 'a spot where space-wearied interstellar wanderers might rest in delight'. The aliens themselves are of ambiguous gender: though all are 'men', they are marked by colorful clothing and a gentle, almost passive demeanor. Their spokesman, Seun, is 'an almost willowy figure' with 'a slim-fingered hand' and 'glinting golden hair that curled in unruly locks above a broad, smooth brow'. Seun's people live in the shadow of their ancestors' city, which seems to represent their lost glory: full of mysterious machines and 'stupendous buildings of giants long dead'. Questioned by Commander Shor Nun about these monuments, Seun answers with 'feminine' indirection: 'Its operation—I know only vague principles. I—I have forgotten so much.'[38]

The turn in the story comes when Seun takes the visitors into the city and Shor Nun is overcome by the sight of machines that extend, apparently, into infinity: 'Shor Nun cried out, laughed and sobbed all at one moment. His hands clawed at his eyes; he fell to his knees, groaning. "Don't look— by the gods, don't look—" he gasped.'[39] In reponse, Seun demonstrates his power:

> 'Shor Nun, look at me, turn your eyes on me,' said Seun. He stood half a head taller than the man of Pareeth, very slim and straight, and his eyes seemed to glow in the light that surrounded him.
>
> As though pulled by a greater force, Shor Nun's eyes turned slowly, and first their brown edges, then the pupils showed again. The frozen madness in his face relaxed; he slumped softly into a more natural position—and Seun looked away.[40]

This confrontation of gazes foreshadows the story's conclusion, in which it is revealed that Seun's race has forgotten only that which is no longer necessary. They now know so much that Seun can virtually hold the universe in his mind, shifting its contents around at will. With a glance, he creates a lens-like object that is both eye and weapon:

> His eyes grew bright, and the lines of his face deepened in concentration... Quite suddenly, a dazzling light appeared over Seun's hand, sparkling, myriad colors—and died with a tiny, crystalline clatter. Something lay in his upturned palm: a round, small thing of aquamarine crystal, shot through with veins and arteries of softly pulsing, silver light. It moved and altered as they watched, fading in color, changing the form and outline of light.[41]

Using this artificial eye, Seun 'alters' the universe so that the men and ships of Pareeth are suddenly back home. They have been shifted not only through space but through time as well, to just after the expedition's departure, thereby stealing from them 'eighteen years of our manhood'.[42]

Yet Seun leaves them with a compensating gift. In place of Ron Thule's telescope, he has placed a device (a little brother to his own lens) that enables Thule to see other star systems with miraculous resolution—but only vacant systems, so that they might not attempt another invasion.

Stuart's story gets much of its effect through its subversive use of the gender code of pulp sf. If the masculine self is defined in terms of looking at the universe, then what happens when the scientist sees himself held in the eyes of the alien? When the feminine, the indistinct, the Other turns out to be the controlling Self? When the male society that the young hero seeks to join is revealed to be a group of powerless outsiders? When passivity is strength and vagueness is deeper understanding?

This story illustrates that the sexual symbolism of sf is a language, the code rather than the message. It isn't 'about' male anxiety and genital competition. Seun's crystal isn't really a phallus or even an eye. What it represents is exactly what the story says it represents: knowledge of the universe. It resembles an eye because we conceive of knowledge primarily in terms of vision, imagined to be a male prerogative. The men in the story respond to the crystal as if it were a sign of Seun's masculinity and a challenge to their own because knowledge and vision and masculinity form a complex, interrelated system of signs, each capable of standing for the others.

The scientific megatext incorporates those sign systems, but the sf version of the master narrative does not merely incorporate them; it plays with them. In Stuart's hands, the gender coding of self, universe, knowledge, and power passes through a complex set of mirrorings and reversals, with the effect of bringing underlying assumptions to the surface where they may be challenged. Every time we think we know what is happening, the story undermines our knowledge. We are even invited to misread the identities of the worlds—the world that the story places in the position of alien space is actually *Rrth*, or earth—and of the author himself. Don A. Stuart was a pen name of none other than John W. Campbell, Jr, whose stories under his own byline have little of the innovation or subversiveness of his Stuart stories. To further complicate the matter, the authorial mask that allowed Campbell to refuse 'to take the standard axioms for granted' and to 'give the feeling and humanity to his stories that had been lacking'[43] was actually the name of his wife, Dona Stuart Campbell, which suggests at least some blurring of gender boundaries if not a conscious attempt to attain a feminine point of view.

Stuart's 'Forgetfulness' was one of the first works to demonstrate sf's ability to investigate the key role of gender in constructing models of self, society, and universe. It helped point the way for later generations of sf writers, who have turned the form into a powerful tool for examining the effects of science on cultural patterns and vice versa. Looking at the story in its original context reveals that sf has this ability because of, not in spite of, its gender coding and because of the power of narrative to co-opt and destabilize other systems of meaning.

Notes

1 Eando Binder (Otto Binder), 'Strange Vision', *Astounding Stories* (May 1937), pp. 46–56, at p. 46.

2 K. Raymond, 'The Comet', *Astounding Stories* (February 1937), pp. 98–105, at p. 99.

3 Raymond, 'The Comet', p. 105.

4 John Russell Fearn, 'Seeds from Space', *Tales of Wonder* (June 1937), pp. 17–39, at p. 13.

5 Ralph Milne Farley [Roger Sherman Hoar], 'A Month a Minute', *Thrilling Wonder Stories* (December 1937), pp. 14–26, at p. 22.

6 John Russell Fearn, 'Menace from the Microcosm', *Thrilling Wonder Stories* (June 1937), pp. 14–30, at p. 22.

7 John Beynon [John Beynon Harris], 'The Perfect Creature', *Tales of Wonder* (June 1937), pp. 116–27, at p. 122.

8 A. Macfadyen, Jr, 'The Endless Chain', *Astounding Stories* (April 1937), pp. 56–72, at p. 67.

9 Nat Schachner, 'City of the Rocket Horde', *Astounding Stories* (December 1937), pp. 112–35, at p. 134.

10 William Lemkin, 'Cupid of the Laboratory', *Amazing Stories* (August 1937), pp. 79–112, at p. 79.

11 Eando Binder, 'The Chemical Murder', *Amazing Stories* (April 1937), pp. 91–114, at p. 91.

12 Evelyn Fox Keller, *Reflections on Gender and Science* (New Haven and London: Yale University Press, 1985), p. 34.

13 Keller, *Reflections*, p. 36.

14 Keller, *Reflections*, p. 39.

15 Brian Stableford, 'The Last Chocolate Bar and the Majesty of Truth: Reflections on the Concept of "Hardness" in Science Fiction (Part I)', *The New York Review of Science Fiction*, 71 (July 1994), pp. 1, 8–12.

16 Edmond Hamilton, 'A Million Years Ahead', *Thrilling Wonder Stories* (April 1937), pp. 92–97, at p. 94.

17 Hamilton, 'A Million Years Ahead', pp. 96–97.

18 Hamilton, 'A Million Years Ahead', p. 28.

19 Arthur K. Barnes, 'Green Hell', *Thrilling Wonder Stories* (June 1937), pp. 91–100, at p. 100.

20 E.E. 'Doc' Smith, *First Lensman* (1950) (rpt New York: Pyramid, 1964), p. 38.

21 E.E. 'Doc' Smith, *Galactic Patrol*, in *Astounding Stories* (1937–38) (revised 1950 and rpt New York: Pyramid, 1964), pp. 103, 182, 141.

22 George H. Scheer, 'The Crystalline Salvation', *Amazing Stories* (June 1937), pp. 92–119, at p. 113.

23 John Edwards, 'The Planet of Perpetual Night', *Amazing Stories* (February 1937), pp. 15–57, at p. 24.

24 Edwards, 'Perpetual Night', pp. 45, 52.

25 Henry Kuttner, 'When the Earth Lived', *Thrilling Wonder Stories* (October 1937), pp. 90–100, at p. 94.

26 Edwards, 'Perpetual Night', pp. 28, 29.
27 Edwards, 'Perpetual Night', p. 29.
28 Macfadyen, 'Endless Chain', p. 66.
29 Macfadyen, 'Endless Chain', p. 63.
30 Macfadyen, 'Endless Chain', p. 64.
31 Jack Williamson, 'Released Entropy', *Astounding Stories* (August 1937), pp. 8–30.
32 Robert Willey [Willey Ley], 'At The Perihelion', *Astounding Stories* (June 1937), pp. 52–71.
33 *Amazing Stories* (June 1937), p. 136.
34 *Astounding Science Fiction* (December 1938), pp. 160–61.
35 *Amazing Stories* (February 1937), p. 137.
36 Don A. Stuart (John W. Campbell, Jr), 'Forgetfulness', *Astounding Stories* (June 1937), p. 140.
37 Stuart, 'Forgetfulness', pp. 139–44.
38 Stuart, 'Forgetfulness', pp. 140–45.
39 Stuart, 'Forgetfulness', p. 149.
40 Stuart, 'Forgetfulness', p. 149.
41 Stuart, 'Forgetfulness', p. 157.
42 Stuart, 'Forgetfulness', p. 163.
43 Lester del Rey, 'Introduction: The Three Careers of John W. Campbell', in *idem*, ed., *The Best of John W. Campbell* (Garden City, NY: Doubleday, 1976), p. 3.

Corporatism and the Corporate Ethos in Robert Heinlein's 'The Roads Must Roll'

FARAH MENDLESOHN

Robert Heinlein's 'The Roads Must Roll'[1] is startling in its unselfconscious advocacy of technocracy. As Heinlein has been described by some as expressing the 'complex populism of the United States',[2] and became in later years a libertarian, this opening statement is distinctly at variance with the widespread understanding of Robert Heinlein's work amongst science fiction critics, an understanding which has been based on his selection of the frontiersman, whether space man, farmer or trader, as the quintessential American hero.[3] However, what distinguishes these characters from populist iconography is that each is the possessor of specialist knowledge and has a technological and scientific education. For Heinlein, the proof of intelligence was the ability to manipulate a slide rule. His farmers and tradespeople are technocrats and progressives.

This traditional misinterpretation of Heinlein by science fiction critics is critical to an understanding of the development of science fiction as a genre and an understanding of its history. Because Heinlein is perhaps *the* most important writer in the development of science fiction in the 1930s and 1940s, both in terms of his own fiction and the theories which he developed for the genre, categorizing Heinlein as a populist assists the misconstruction of science fiction as 'popular' culture rather than the middle-class culture which most science fiction critics now recognize it is. This mis-understanding can be traced essentially to an ahistorical critique of Heinlein and of science fiction, which confuses 'populist' with fashionable, and assumes the fashion amongst Heinlein's readership and their wider social group (middle-class America) to be equally popular with other social classes. The irony is that Heinlein himself attempted to draw attention to such distinctions, whilst arguing for the dominance of the ideology to which he and many of his readers subscribed. This paper, focussing on one particular story, seeks to illuminate Heinlein's beliefs and his position within the cultural politics of science fiction.

In 1940, when 'The Roads Must Roll' was published in *Astounding*, Heinlein had been active for several years in a genre which had rejected rural populism in favour of corporatism and technocracy, and this becomes evident both in the world he created and in the competent hero he developed. That Heinlein tapped into the culture and values of his audience is attested to by this story's status as a classic. 'The Roads Must Roll' is one of the stories collected in *The Science Fiction Hall of Fame*, an anthology published in 1970 of magazine science fiction originally printed between 1934 and 1963 and voted the 'best' by the Science Fiction Writers of America.[4] This is the case despite the fact that the technology at the centre of the story is unlikely to work, as is explained later in this article. Such sloppiness is usually an unpardonable offence in science fiction, and that it is ignored by most commentators is a testimony to the degree to which Heinlein's world reflected and illuminated the world of his readers, reinforcing their belief in the guiding role of scientific objectivity and in their importance as 'expert' managers, engineers and professionals.[5] The main focus of this article, therefore, is the extent to which Heinlein built upon the social expectations of his 'professional' community and by doing so exposed the attitudes and concerns of this community. In the story under consideration the principal concern is the role and behaviour of America's unions. The solution which Heinlein offered is the application of objective rationality by scientifically trained experts.

The article will focus on two main themes, one textual (attitudes towards labour unions) and one sub-textual (attitudes towards the corporate ethos), in order to illuminate the extent to which it is unacceptable to typify Heinlein as a populist.

The Plot

In 'The Roads Must Roll', the main form of transport in future America is along massive, many-stripped conveyor belts running at speeds ranging from 5 miles per hour to 100 miles per hour. These rolling roads carry both freight and passengers across America. Passengers either walk on the strips, hopping from one to another until they reach one travelling at the required speed, or they settle down in one of the roadway facilities such as 'Jake's Steak House No. 4' until such time as their section of the road reaches their destination. The rolling roads which Heinlein describes are essentially conveyor belts but on these conveyor belts are fixed structures such as diners. There are two ways in which these conveyor belts can turn around, either by travelling over and then under the rollers, in which case presumably these structures are conveyed under the rollers, or the roads operate as the luggage conveyors in airports, and the above-mentioned steak house would have to be flexible in order to cope with both the straight stretches and the curves.

America has become totally dependent upon these moving roads. Urban, and increasingly suburban, America has shaped itself around this steel skeleton. As the story opens, the Rolling Road mechanics in the Sacramento sector are planning a strike and part way through the story stop the roads, causing turmoil in the transport system and death and injury to the passengers. The mechanics are demanding the right to leave a job without giving three months notice, the right to elect engineers, and parity with the engineers produced by the quasi-militaristic training college. Mr Gaines, the chief engineer, stops the strike and eventually thwarts a workers' revolution with the aid of the cadets, the new generation of corporate engineers, who are imbued with a strong sense of loyalty to the company and a sense of duty to the public. Throughout the story, his rationality, his use of scientifically trained personnel, and his knowledge of scientific psychology are contrasted with the irrationality and psychological susceptibility of the strikers.

Labour Unions and Labour Relations

The focus of the plot in 'The Roads Must Roll' is a strike on America's most essential service: the roads. The story reflects the growing concern of the American middle class over the power which certain sections of the labour force appeared to have acquired to disrupt the economy. The rail strikes of the late nineteenth and early twentieth century had alerted Americans to the extent to which a single industry could, potentially, disrupt the entire economy of the United States. Traditionally, railroad strikes had been violent, in part because the railroads had early been recognized as part of the country's essential infrastructure and therefore a Federal Government concern. In 1877, when President Rutherford B. Hayes authorized Federal troops to intervene, it had been on the grounds that interference with train movements was not only an assault on property rights, but a rebellion against the government. The concept that the railroad occupied a special place in the nation's industrial system was reinforced in 1884 in the Wabash railroad receivership case. The Federal Court of the Eastern District of Missouri consented not only to place the road into receivership prior to actual default (thus securing its funds from creditors) but also appointed receivers close to the owner in order to ensure the continuing operation of the railroad. At stake, beyond the interests of the bond holders, was a new notion of public interest.[6]

By the mid-1930s, the railroads had experienced a number of different attempts at control by the Federal authorities. These attempts were aimed at mediation between the unions and the employers but, on the whole, the Federal authorities were firmly on the side of the employers and willing to deploy troops if necessary. Under the Railway Act of 1934, however, the National Mediation Board assured labour of the right to organize within certain limits. By the time Heinlein was writing, therefore, his fears were somewhat outdated. Heinlein's fears, like those of certain sections of the middle class at large, were grounded in beliefs which had developed over more than twenty years: that there was something essentially un-American about unionism and fundamentally 'irrational' about mass action.

American unions in the years before the Second World War were as successful as they had ever been. During the First World War, the AFL, through the efforts of Samuel Gompers, had secured a reasonable amount of influence with the relatively sympathetic Wilson government, but the collapse of the socialist movement in America in the 1920s, and Gompers' adamant belief that unions should not entrench themselves in party politics in the manner of the British unions in the period, undercut union strength in the years after the war. Without a major political party tied directly to union support, industrial labour rapidly lost what few gains in the matter of wages and conditions it had made during the war years. With the Depression, employers had regained the upper hand and this was reflected in rapidly deteriorating conditions, despite the presence of a friendly government under Roosevelt. Although a reasonable number of workers benefited from minimal social security legislation, many were left outside these provisions, and outside the Fair Labor Standards Act of 1938.

Yet despite the AFL's disavowal of electoral intentions, and the attempt to completely disassociate from the Socialists and other independent labour movements, the AFL found that it too was affected by the anti-left rhetoric of the 1920s. The 1920s and 1930s saw a struggle between corporate America and representatives of labour to gain control of the concept of 'Americanness'. In the late 1930s, the Ladies Garment Workers of Los Angeles felt obliged to declare in their publicity: 'Remember you are free Americans. It is your right to join the union and go on strike... Don't let your employer or anybody else threaten you, frighten you, hold you or stop you.'[7]

Those outside the unions saw this 'right' as a threat. In 'The Roads Must Roll' membership of a union is a matter for suspicion. When Gaines asks Harvey why he did not inform on the union in the preparatory stages of the strike, Harvey replies: 'you can't refuse to work with a man just because he holds different political views. It's a free country.'

Gaines responds: 'You should have come to me before... No, I guess you are right. It's my business to keep tabs on your mates not yours. As you say, it's a free country.'[8]

Whilst reassuring on the surface, it reinforces the sense that there is something fundamentally 'wrong' with unions. Clearly, freedom has distinct boundaries. Increasingly, to be involved in union activities was to invite suspicion of one's patriotism. The National Association of Manufacturers and other employer groups attacked Labor's Non-Partisan League and the American Labor Party in New York under the slogan, 'Join the CIO and Help Build a Soviet America.'[9] The problem for American unions was that as long as strike action was regarded as fundamentally un-American, strikers were either accused of radicalism or labelled the victims of outside agitators. Despite initial sympathetic reporting, at the end of the San Francisco General Strike in 1943 Russell B. Porter reported in the New York Times:

> ...the younger and more radical leaders had swayed a strongly articulate minority of the rank-and-file into a reckless demand for direct action... The great majority of the rank-and-file of the strikers...had let their leaders vote them into the general strike, and had gone out without understanding the suffering it might bring upon them and their families, as well as on the general public, and without the slightest idea of the implications of a general strike as a revolutionary movement against the existing political, economic and social system.
> They did not want to overthrow the government or to establish Soviets and were as shocked as anybody else when it was revealed that some of the agitators who had been working with them did have such aims.[10]

This is the scenario which Heinlein employed. Brother Harvey tells Gaines, 'You know how it is, there are a few soreheads everywhere'.[11] The few radical leaders influence their elders, and thoughtless workers follow outside agitators on strike. The illogicality of this appears to have passed the 'rational' Heinlein by. Heinlein's workers, however, in contrast to the 'moderation' shown by San Francisco's strikers, were taking on notions of revolution.

Early on, Heinlein's strikers are unexpectedly joined in their demands by Mr 'Shorty' Van Kleek, chief deputy engineer for Sacramento, a man liked by the mechanics, who declares: 'I always feel more comfortable here in the guild hall of the Sacramento Sector—or any guild hall for that matter—than I do in the engineers' clubhouse.'[12]

In transgressing the 'natural' social boundaries Van Kleek offers an indication of his later irrationalities. As is made explicit later in the story, Van Kleek has rejected the ethos of technocracy which exhorts the managers to manage and the workers to acknowledge the supremacy of the properly trained. Technocracy, with its emphasis on training hierarchies, is clearly hostile to democracy, but approaches its attack, as here, by presenting democracy within certain situations as 'manifestly' absurd. On the other side, the strikers—or at least their leaders and certainly Van Kleek—have adopted the doctrine of 'Functionalism'. Heinlein interrupts the flow of events to give us a little lecture on 'Functionalism'.

> It claimed to be a scientifically accurate theory of social relations. The author, Paul Decker, disclaimed the 'outworn and futile' ideas of democracy and human equality, and substituted a system in which human beings were evaluated 'functionally'—that is to say, by the role each filled in the economic sequence. The underlying thesis was that it was right and proper for a man to exercise over his fellows whatever power was inherent in his function, and that any other form of social organizations was silly, visionary, and contrary to the natural order...
>
> Functionalism was particularly popular among little people everywhere who could persuade themselves that their particular jobs were the indispensable ones, and that therefore, under the 'natural order' they would be top dogs. With so many different functions actually indispensable such self-persuasion would be easy.[13]

Ironically, despite Heinlein's dismissal of 'Functionalism' as irrational, it is remarkably close to the ethos which is imbued into his cadets, as I will discuss later. In fact, the notion that certain people are more essential than others is central to the concept of 'expertise', and that those with it should both wield power and gain social status and equivalent power is clearly a fundamental rule within both corporate structure and capitalist society. However, dismissing the opposition as irrational allows Heinlein to grant to his hero the moral high ground and the position of scientific objectivity, thus avoiding close analysis of his hero's motives and actions.

On the side of businesslike management and scientific reasoning, then, we have the coolly rational Mr Gaines who takes time to consult Personnel for the psychometric reports on Van Kleek before confronting the man. Gaines is the chief engineer of the Diego-Reno Roadtown and when we meet him is showing around a representative of the Australian government which has expressed an interest in the roads project. The representative is a cipher, whose role is to be somebody to whom Gaines can explain things, filling the audience in with the requisite 'future science' and history (a common strategy in sf but one which the mature Heinlein was at pains to discourage). Assisting Gaines are Brother Harvey, the 'good' worker whose true union credentials are asserted by his participation in the strike of '60, and a cast of engineer cadets in dungarees and braided caps.

Harvey's role is crucial. It is he who betrays the union in such a way as to make it seem a rational thing to do. He doesn't survive the strike: his martyrdom is a useful catalyst for Gaines' anger but also serves the essential purpose of excusing Heinlein from having to worry about his fate once the strike is over. It is Harvey who argues that the strike is unreasonable,[14] not Gaines, thus apparently relieving Gaines of the moral obligation of defining the strike as wrong and reinforcing the notion that this is not a union struggle against injustice, but a battle between the forces of scientific modern objectivity and populist irrationality. In reality, it is Gaines who has abrogated to himself the right to justify the workers' grievances. His sympathetic role in an earlier strike is trotted out a number of times just to reassure the audience that this is not straightforward union bashing. Harvey and Gaines between them allow us to accept Heinlein's view of the trade unions, one which is clearly rooted in middle-class America's attitudes towards the trade unions as they had been developing during the previous fifty years. In 1937, Russell Porter, commenting on the spread of sit-down strikes after the Akron rubber-workers' actions in 1935 and 1936, had warned against

> the boomerang consequences of the spirit of lawlessness encouraged by the sit-down. The promiscuous use of sit-down strikes...has led to abuses in which racketeers and ex-convicts have taken over labor unions and seized plants...
>
> The demonstration of how effective a minority may be in such a strike has also created a problem for labor, which may be faced some day with sit-downs called by a minority of Communists or others seeking to take over control of the union leadership as a means toward seizing power in the government.[15]

This fear of labour revolution was firmly connected to the fear of 'un-American', that is, foreign influence. Yet, even with the growth of the sit-down strike, there was little evidence that American workers were looking towards the type of revolutionary theory which Heinlein feared. As Porter pointed out in the above article, the American workers who employed the sit-in neither tried to operate the factories nor used the sit-in to direct pressure on the government. When Heinlein's workers threaten revolution, his explanation was that it was at the behest of an 'outsider' (to the union), someone who has rejected the corporate ethos of consensus capitalism and who, therefore, was clearly irrational.

Exploring Corporate America
An important question is why Heinlein made this equation of corporate organization and scientific objectivity. The corporate ethos which the

unions faced had been emerging in the later decades of the nineteenth century. By the 1930s, Taylor's scientific management had become the legitimating theory behind current trends in industry and in social order. Heinlein, in 'The Roads Must Roll', took on this ethos almost completely. Like much of the science fiction community he embraced Taylor's arguments that only disinterested engineers and 'objective' professionals could create efficient business conditions. The assumption was that business and politics could be understood and administered with objectivity.[16] Such faith in objective scientific management could serve to obscure its own inadequacies. Thus, Gaines' men had been appointed by trained personnel teams. They had been certified by the 'Wadsworth-Burton' method of psychological profiling[17] and were, therefore, both expert and stable. When Van Kleek proves faulty and unstable, it is the implementation of the tests that proves to be at fault, and not the scientific method itself. The technocrat cannot allow that the tools he or she uses be faulty.

One aspect of the emergent corporate ethos which we see quite clearly on the rolling roads is the emphasis on rank, on lines of command and on the formal qualifications which are required by 'modern' industry. For the readers of *Astounding*, many of whom were a part of this newly professionalized middle class, such a stress on the necessity of formal training was comforting.[18] The growing necessity of formal qualifications protected this new class from other upwardly mobile groups by placing in the way barriers that only those with access to formal education—the sons and in some cases daughters of this established social group—could surmount. Once a technocratic middle class had been created over the course of a generation, it was no longer necessary to look for talented recruits amongst the labouring classes. Such recruits might even be thought dangerous, bringing with them aspirations not of the right corporate quality. Van Kleek, then, the 'talented tinkerer', the man of the earlier generation rapidly being superseded by the corporately minded cadets, was not merely becoming anachronistic: he was potentially dangerous. His identification, as he explains, is with the labourer and not the company. For the company, it was the development of the engineer corps that would, in the long term, counter this threat. As Gaines argued: 'When the oldest engineer is a man who entered the academy in his teens, we can afford to relax a little and treat it as a solved problem.'[19]

By creating a separate and separated corps of engineers, the company achieves a vital split in worker solidarity and provides itself with an in-house force of potential strike breakers. This need to reinforce status divisions in the corporate world is reflected thoroughly in 'The Roads Must Roll'. Mechanics and technicians are not encouraged to socialize, and a clear sense of public responsibility is seen as essential to the moral character of the middle manager.

> The technicians in the road service are indoctrinated with the idea that their job is a social trust. Besides, we do everything we can to build up their social position. But even more important is the academy. We try to turn out graduate engineers with the same loyalty, the same iron self-discipline and determination to do their duty to the community at any cost, that Annapolis and West Point and Goddard are so successful in inculcating in their graduates.[20]

This analogy with the military was not coincidental. The split between the technicians and the engineers illustrated in 'The Roads Must Roll', whilst emulating the pattern of corporate recruitment, also picked up on Heinlein's naval past. His engineers wear braided caps with their dungarees, salute and are called 'cadets'. Before dismissing this as entirely militaristic and beyond the bounds of the corporate mentality, it is worth remembering the serried ranks of ushers in the great movie houses of the 1930s, dressed in quasi-military uniforms and subjected to drills and moral checks, a humiliation also enforced on the Ford workforce. This type of corporate ethos, embracing notions of military-style loyalty, seems to have been uncomfortably pervasive in the 1930s.

One visible aspect of the new industrial order which I have indicated above was the extent to which management was willing to join forces to avert or destroy industrial action. The line drawn between management and the labouring classes enabled the new middle class to see its interests as lying with the employers and with the material prosperity identification with the employers could bring. As illustrated in the previous quotation, Heinlein recognized the importance of high social status as a means of controlling managerial level employees. We should not be surprised, therefore, that Gaines goes himself to break the strike. Far from being simply action-adventure hyperbole, managers throughout the late nineteenth and well into the twentieth century, as Zunz points out,[21] regarded it as their duty to their employers to be present in person when strikes were to be broken violently. When managers on the railroads began to take a hard line against labour in 1877, they were increasingly defining themselves as public servants, despite their employment by private companies. The tendency was for companies to encourage this trend, encouraging status divisions within the workforce by setting management to spy on the morals and politics of labour, as at the Ford factories, and by encouraging all possible identification with the company. As Gaines has said, it was his role to keep an eye on the men.

The fictional strike is eventually resolved when Gaines takes a force of loyal cadets into the Sacramento sector. Harvey is killed on the way, as mentioned earlier, and his death provides the excuse for an increase in the level of violence. A number of cadets have previously been excluded from the raid because they have indicated a desire for vengeance, an 'irrational' motive. But, when Harvey is shot down by a striker whilst engaged in a solitary negotiation, both Gaines and the cadet captain momentarily lose control and shoot back, although neither is in immediate danger. Harvey as a martyr, his 'face set in a death mask of rugged beauty',[22] is both a testimony to the character of the true American working man and a symbol of the 'deep sense of loss of personal honour' which Gaines feels at having lost control of both the strike and the strike breaking.

The denouement, however, does not depend on the gun but on the superiority of the 'rational expert' over the irrational labouring man. I mentioned earlier that Gaines takes time out to consult the personnel profiles. His discovery is that the tests Van Kleek took revealed him to be a 'masked introvert' with an inferiority complex, slightly unstable but with the ability to attract and handle workers.[23] Van Kleek had been retained on the basis of this ability and granted promotion, which he had used to ensure that only the most 'unstable' workers were placed in his sector. Gaines, in possession of this knowledge, undermines Van Kleek's self-confidence and reduces him to a gibbering wreck on the floor. Gaines, on the other hand, retains his cool composure throughout. His expertise has carried him through, and in future greater reliance must be placed on the scientific method, and less on individual people.

The Car and American Individualism
Perhaps the most striking aspect of this story, to contemporary eyes, is the extent to which Heinlein visualized a future dependent upon public transport. In the context both of Heinlein's later much vaunted individualism, and of the rapid spread of the motor car in the inter-war period (approximately 26 million automobiles were on the road by 1929), this requires some explanation. In the text, Gaines recalls that by (the fictional) 1945 'there was a motor vehicle for every two persons in the United States'.[24] What more could the middle-class family want? However, it was Heinlein's commitment to a view of the future which embraced the logic of objective management of resources which enabled him to envisage a world in which the motor car contained the seeds of its own destruction. In this story, but not necessarily elsewhere in his work, he argued: 'Seventy million steel juggernauts, operated by imperfect human beings at high speed, are more destructive than war'.[25] In his future-alternative 1945 the premiums paid for compulsory liability and property damage insurance by automobile owners exceeded in amount the sum paid to purchase

automobiles. In Heinlein's future, it was no longer safe to drive in crowded metropolises, pedestrian accident rates soared, and cities became choked with cars.

> From a standpoint of speed alone the automobile made possible cities two hundred miles in diameter, but traffic congestion, and the inescapable, inherent danger of high powered, individually operated vehicles cancelled out the possibility.[26]

The cessation of automobile expansion in Heinlein's future does not, however, occur because common sense and individual reason prevail. Instead, the only branch of the Federal government of which Heinlein (not unlike many other middle-class Americans) appears to approve intervenes. In a future 1947, a National Defense Act is passed which declares petroleum 'an essential and limited material of war'. Although it is not made clear that there is a war actually going on, with seventy million vehicles facing deprivation a solution was required to meet the new demand for transport. Solar driven conveyor belts are Heinlein's solution.

In 1939, it is questionable whether the vision of a car-dependent culture which Heinlein creates is based on any contemporary reality. True, the car-owning population was expanding rapidly, but the Depression had hit the automobile industry heavily, and although there had been a rapid recovery, sales again fell by almost 50 per cent in the recession of 1937–38. Heinlein's faith in the rapid expansion of the automobile seems somewhat misplaced in this context, but, even though he presents a picture of its rapid obsolescence, the means by which he does this is essentially optimistic. A reasonable amount of the science fiction of the 1930s contains scientifically qualified but unemployed heroes. A significant part of the readership which Heinlein was addressing had seen its economic security and the value of its education and qualifications undermined by the Depression. It needed reassurance. That the car would die from prosperity was a note of reassurance offered to this section of the magazines' readership.

But this explanation is not enough. Heinlein's analysis still seems out of place. However, in predicting gridlock, I would argue that Heinlein was looking not just to the rising numbers of cars on the road, but at the failure of the road system to keep pace. In *Cities of Tomorrow*, Peter Hall makes the crucial point that although car ownership in the United States reached the highest level in the world prior to the Second World War—as many as one car to every two families before the Depression hit—the USA, unlike countries such as Germany, was reluctant to use public works projects to their full potential. As counties and states were equally reluctant to use their financial resources to fund road-building projects, a national road network failed to emerge until after the war.

> Apart from a longer distance extension of the New York Parkway system into the neighbouring state of Connecticut...America's first true inter-city motor way, the Pennsylvania Turnpike through the Appalachians from Carlisle near Harrisburg to Irwin near Pittsburgh, opened only in 1940. December of that same year marked another milestone in the automobile age: Los Angeles completed its Arroyo Seco Parkway, now part of the Pasadena Freeway... Thereafter war intervened: at its end Los Angeles had precisely 11 miles of freeway.[27]

Heinlein, therefore, was seeing cars running on roads intended for very different forms of transport, for a far lighter transport load and yet with the capacity to increase living distances for many miles. He predicted: 'The great cities of Chicago and St. Louis...[will stretch] out urban pseudopods toward each other, until they...[meet] near Bloomington, Illinois'.[28] Interestingly, he was enough in tune with current trends towards suburbanization that he also expected that the cities themselves would begin to shrink. Heinlein's heart was with rural America, and like Frank Lloyd Wright, Heinlein saw the expansion of the transport network, in whatever form, as a liberation from the town. His roads would develop a 'prototype of a social pattern which was to dominate the American scene for the next two decades: neither rural nor urban, but partaking equally of both, and based on rapid, safe, cheap, convenient transportation'.[29] Heinlein envisaged a social pattern which, despite its dependence on public and therefore communal transport, had the potential to liberate the individual into the countryside. In this Heinlein represents one very clearly defined section of the science fiction community, which would always see technological advance as a means to return to a pastoral arcadia. As a contrast, one could examine the alternative visions of Isaac Asimov. In his *The Caves of Steel* (1954), he employs Heinlein's own rolling roads to make possible a world totally covered over and enclosed, the ultimate in urbanization.

But shortage of road space is not the only reason which Heinlein offers for the move towards a less individualistic mode of transport. In a standard sf assumption, the 'masses' are dismissed as too self-interested to take on board either the necessity of rationed supplies or the dangers of the individually controlled mobile engine. Despite the dangers and difficulties outlined above, the masses are not sensible enough to take the obvious decision. Nor will they necessarily be motivated by pecuniary factors. Heinlein implies that even excessive insurance charges will not deter the would-be automobile buyer, such is his/her enthusiasm for the excitement and illusion of liberation which the automobile offers. Instead, the knowledgeable and the objective manager must step in to rectify the situation. But as Heinlein never approved of central government interference in peacetime he had to create a military emergency which abrogated power over the oil supplies. In later years, Heinlein was to come to rest most of his personal philosophy on a complicated mixture of militarism and libertarianism in order to preserve both his belief in the rights and power of the individual, and his faith in corporate action, but even in 1939 he was prepared to hand over the rights of the individual without qualm to the military. Interestingly, the roads themselves are constructed on that same compromise as the American railroads, as private companies supported by Federal goodwill. Presumably, for the Federal authorities to actually build them, in whatever guise, would constitute unwarranted interference. Whilst Heinlein has no faith in the 'masses' to make sensible decisions he is happy to see the 'experts' in the form of the military planners and the engineers step in to regulate develoment.

Clearly, Heinlein's identification is not with the 'little man' of American society. The ordinary, uneducated individual is irresponsible, selfish, self-interested and incapable either of identifying the common good, or of making decisions to advance that good. Instead, in the 1940s Heinlein was undoubtedly committed to a progressive ethos of scientific and managerial education and governance by the professional. To most science fiction critics this is evident, but what has has not yet been accepted is that it does not support the continuance of the description of Heinlein as any sort of 'populist'.

Notes

1 First published in 1940 in the pages of *Astounding Science-Fiction*, the most successful of the early American science fiction magazines. Robert A. Heinlein, 'The Roads Must Roll', *Astounding Science-Fiction*, ed. John W. Campbell (June 1940), pp. 2–22, British edition.

2 David Pringle and John Clute, in *The Encyclopedia of Science Fiction*, ed. John Clute and Peter Nicholls (London: Orbit, 1993), p. 556.

3 See, for example, *Space Cadet* (first published, New York: Scribner's, 1948), *Red Planet* (New York: Scribner's, 1949), *Farmer in the Sky* (New York: Scribner's, 1950), *Space Family Stone* (New York: Scribner's, 1952), *Time Enough for Love* (New York: Putnam's, 1973).

4 John Huntington, *Rationalizing Genius: Ideological Strategies in the Classic American Science Fiction Short Story* (New Brunswick: Rutgers University Press, 1989), p. 16.

5 For a detailed analysis of the socio-economic construction of the science fiction community see Albert I. Berger, 'Sf Fans in Socio-Economic Perspective: Factors in the Social Consciousness of a Genre', *Science Fiction Studies*, 4.3, (1977), pp. 232–46. For a wider discussion of the impact of this on science fiction see Albert I. Berger, *The Magic That Works: John W. Campbell and the American Response to Technology* (San Bernardino, CA: Borgo Press, 1993) and Huntington, *Rationalizing Genius*.

6 Oliver Zunz, *Making America Corporate, 1870–1920* (Chicago: The University of Chicago Press, 1990), p. 35.

7 Michael Kazin, *The Populist Persuasion: An American History* (New York: Basic Books, 1995), p. 146.

8 Heinlein, 'The Roads', p. 16.

9 Patrick Renshaw, *American Labour and Consensus Capitalism, 1935–1990* (London: MacMillan, 1991), p. 32.

10 Russell B. Porter, 'General Strike Called Off', *New York Times*, July 20 1943.

11 Heinlein, 'The Roads', p. 16.

12 Heinlein, 'The Roads', pp. 3–4.

13 Heinlein, 'The Roads', p. 14.

14 Heinlein, 'The Roads', p. 3.

15 Russell B. Porter, 'The Broad Sit-Down Challenge', *New York Times Magazine*, April 4 1937, pp. 94–95.

16 Zunz, *Making America Corporate*, p. 35.

17 Heinlein, 'The Roads', pp. 19–20.

18 Berger, 'Sf Fans'.

19 Heinlein, 'The Roads', p. 9.

20 Heinlein, 'The Roads', p. 9.

21 Cf. *Making America Corporate*, pp. 61–64.

22 Heinlein, 'The Roads', p. 18.

23 Heinlein, 'The Roads', p. 20.

24 Heinlein, 'The Roads', p. 6.

25 Heinlein, 'The Roads', p. 6.

26 Heinlein, 'The Roads', p. 6.

27 Peter Hall, *Cities of Tomorrow: An Intellectual History of Urban Planning and Design in the Twentieth Century* (Oxford: Blackwell, 1994), p. 282.

28 Heinlein, 'The Roads', p. 6.

29 Heinlein, 'The Roads', p. 6.

Convention and Displacement: Narrator, Narratee, and Virtual Reader in Science Fiction

DANIÈLE CHATELAIN
and GEORGE SLUSSER

Analysis of the science fiction narrative has, in general, been restricted to the areas of themes or ideas, where it makes its claims to innovation and newness. Sf offers a large body of narratives. Its narrative *forms*, however, have yet to be systematically analysed. Indeed, it is only by examining how sf functions in terms of the system it shares with narrative in general that we can determine how, and in what ways, these new thematic situations generate significant structural transformations.

To suggest a way to examine sf in terms of the larger narrative system, we focus on one aspect of that system—the relation between narrator and narratee. Gerald Prince defines the narrator as 'the one who narrates as inscribed in the text,' and the narratee as 'the one who is narrated to as inscribed in the text.'[1] In a narrative the process of telling can involve one or more senders of messages and one or more receivers. The sender is the narrator—one or many, declared or undeclared—who at the narrative instance has already witnessed, at a greater or lesser degree of 'distance' in space and time, the events and objects he recounts. This narrator addresses a narratee, the receiver of his discourse, who again may be declared or undeclared. But it is the distance or closeness between narrator and narratee, in terms of space, time, culture, learning, and so on, that seems to determine the kind and amount of information that is conveyed in a narrative. For example, the less familiar the narratee is with the world told by the narrator, the more need there is for the narrator to comment on actions and surroundings.

In fact, control of this distance between narrator and narratee appears to be the means by which the author of any narrative can convey, or refuse to convey, information about his fictional world to a reader. But who is this 'reader'? It is not the real reader, for any given narrative has n number of these, who vary so widely in terms of spatiotemporal and cultural distance that an author cannot control them.[2] Nor is it the so-called 'implied reader', who for Gerald Prince, is 'the real reader's second self, shaped in accordance with the implied author's values and cultural norms'.[3] In fact, this is a shadow pair, whose presence between narrator-narratee and author-reader is both speculative and unnecessary for the analysis of basic narrative structures. It is simpler to speak of a real author, who writes for what we will call his 'virtual reader'. This reader is, in the dictionary sense, 'potential', the reader empowered by the author as the one he initially wrote for, and who is contemporaneous with the instance of the first publication of the narrative work. We have then a schema of relationship where narrator is to narratee as author is to virtual reader. Both the narratee and the virtual reader receive information the narrator and author are conveying concerning the world of a given narrative.

Sf narratives, by definition, talk about unknown worlds. These may be the not-yet-known worlds of some extrapolative future; or they may be less obvious and more tenuous parallel or 'alternative' worlds. For all degrees of 'unknown', however, it is obvious that some information needs to be conveyed. Indeed, it has become a cliché to say that up to 90 per cent of the content of a given sf narrative is information imparted for the sake of 'world building', which is simply the author, by means of discourse between narrator(s) and narratee, making the unfamiliar familiar to his virtual reader. Clearly, this process of making known the unknown, through conveying information, is a matter of degree not kind, and is found in traditional and sf narratives alike. Given this, sf as conveyor of unknown worlds appears to function in two main situations:

(1) The situation where the narratee (and virtual reader) initially do not know the world in which the actions and events of the story take place. In the course of the narrative, however, the author, through the narrator, will either explain this unknown world in a way that is understandable to the virtual reader via the narratee, or the narrator will give information that seems to satisfy the narratee, but does not satisfy the virtual reader. In the latter case we see the author playing with the virtual reader's expectations.

(2) The situation where the narratee knows the world in which the actions and events take place, but the virtual reader does not. In such a case, the narrator has no need to convey any specific information to his narratee. It is by means of this lack that the author keeps his virtual reader voluntarily in the dark. By widening the distance between the narrated world and the world

of the virtual reader, the author creates an effect of estrangement. The question seems to be, however, just how much such estrangement between narratee and virtual reader can the sf narrative bear and remain sf?

By focusing on these two situations—the narratee needs information about the world being narrated, or the narratee does not need information—we can see how the sf narrative develops out of the use or transformation of older narrative forms, forms which themselves have focused on the conveying of information from the narrator to the narratee, in order to inform in indirect manner a virtual reader. What follows is an attempt to classify these forms in terms of the role they play in the development of an sf narrative.

I. The Unfamiliar Made Familiar
1. The Traditional Travel Narrative
This form, traditionally in the first person, is at the basis of numerous sf narratives. Here, the narrative of a traveler, who tells of his travels to some distant, not previously known place, conveys information to a narratee who has not traveled, thus does not know the place in question. By doing so, the author informs his virtual reader, who also has not 'been there'. In this case, the traveler who has returned 'home', his narratee, and the virtual reader are all contemporaries, all sharing a common cultural milieu, so that what informs the narratee informs the virtual reader at the same time. At the basis of the travel narrative, certainly, are logs and accounts of real travels, explorations of places that are distant from narratee and virtual reader primarily in terms of space. A notable example is the *Journal* of Captain Cook, in which he describes 'His First Voyage Round the World, Made in H.M. Bark "Endeavor", 1768–71'. Much of the journal is a factual sea log, with dated entries. Arrival at far-off ports of call or places, however, generate lengthy descriptions of landscape, vegetation, customs of inhabitants.

As a fundamental form of storytelling, such narratives have, from the beginnings of written record, been associated with imaginary voyages, travels to 'made up' places or fabulous countries of the mind. There is the narrative of Gilgamesh's voyage to the place of eternal life; there are Greek and Roman seafarer tales, the Indian wonder stories of Ktesias and others, and later Lucian's blatant fantasy *A True History*. More's *Utopia* offers a significant version of this form. The primary narrator, 'Thomas More', becomes in turn the narratee of the secondary narrator, Raphael Hythloday, who has returned from a voyage 'under the equator', beyond vast deserts to the temperate lands of the Utopians. His narrative, as with that of Captain Cook, is one of descriptions of geography, customs and (even more clearly) of morals. Hythloday (from the Greek *huthlos*, nonsense) is described by a second narratee, Peter, as a sailor who 'has sailed not as the sailor Palinurus [Aeneas's pilot] but as Ulysses, or rather as Plato'.[4] The implication is that the nature of the information conveyed, and the observations set forth, go beyond those of a Ulysses, known to be a keen and pragmatic observer of men and manners. This narrator rather is one who moves in Platonic or ideal realms; his telling is of *ou-topos* or 'nowhere', the realm of the dreamer. This narrative is not meant to be purely informative. Playing on the irony of a place name that designates, at one and the same time, a good place and no place, the telling here forces both narratee(s) and virtual reader to make comparisons between Utopia and contemporary England, provoking a sense that neither is a wholly adequate world. But whatever the irony, or the 'reliability' of the narrator's discourse, the fact of the great spatial and ideational distance between Utopia and the explicitly contemporary situation of narratee(s) and virtual reader require that Hythloday give a detailed account of the nature of the place.

2. *Travels to Outer Space in SF*

This same travel narrative paradigm is at the basis of any number of *near* space voyages of the kind that flourished in the 1950s and 1960s, from the influential Heinlein juvenile *Rocket Ship Galileo* (1947), to works of Arthur C. Clarke such as *The Sands of Mars* (1952), and stories like 'The Sentinel' and (moving farther out in the solar system) 'A Meeting with Medusa'. In these works, an undeclared third-person narrator replaces the traditional first-person narrator. In *Rocket Ship Galileo*, the narrator has clearly witnessed this 'first trip to the moon'. And comments such as the following, for example, reveal the narrator speaking to a narratee who, though he clearly finds the voyage wondrous enough to be told in detail about it, shares the narrator's world and its stage of technological proficiency: 'It is common enough in the United States for boys to build and take apart almost anything mechanical, from alarm clocks to hiked-up jalopies.'[5] Like the narratee (and virtual reader) of a Captain Cook, the narratee here awaits the tale of the witnessed moon, and, seen in the lack of any visible resistance to the telling on his part, clearly finds the information as conveyed plausible and satisfying.

Clarke's narrator, in *The Sands of Mars*, takes space exploration one small step further, to the first landings on, and colonization of, Mars. Moon settlements exist: they are outposts, last ports of call before the uncharted. Space 'ships' have names (here the *Ares*) like Captain Cook's *Endeavor*. And within the narrator's story of protagonist Gibson's travels, we hear stories of further explorations, such as those of the legendary Hilton to Saturn:

'He had seen the incomparable splendor of the great rings spanning the sky in symmetry... He had been into that Ultima Thule in which circled the cold outer giants of the Sun's scattered family.'[6] As in the classic travel narrative, much information is conveyed to the narratee of these far-off places, information which, though slightly extrapolated into the future, all remains plausible in terms of technology and do-ability within the virtual reader's lifetime. Clarke himself emphasizes this in the Foreword to the 1967 re-edition: '*The Sands of Mars*...was written in the late 1940s—when Mars seemed very much farther away than it is today. Reading it again after a lapse of many years, I am agreeably surprised to find how little it has been dated by the explosive developments of the Space Age.'[7] The same holds true 30 years later, in light of the discovery of fossil remains in possible Martian rock.

3. *Naturalist Worlds*

In the midst of the 'positivist' nineteenth century, we find an avatar of the voyage narrative in the realist and naturalist novel in France. The explicit purpose of these narratives, in light of the 'scientific' pretensions of writers from Balzac to Zola, is to explore milieux that are assumed to be unknown to the standard middle-class narratee and virtual reader of the day. Again a narrative mechanism is put in place for conveying information about places on the urban and cultural map. Because these places have not been visited, or in some cases even imagined, information about them, to the virtual reader and to the narratee, appears new and in some cases fabulous. Rather than horizontal, the direction of exploration is vertical: a 'cut' into the strata of society. Zola in *L'Assommoir*, for example, takes his bourgeois virtual reader on a exploration of the *bas-fonds* of working-class life in contemporary Paris, conveying information of places of drink and tenement houses that must seem quite strange. In *Germinal* he takes a similar reader into the 'world' of miners, conveying that world in great detail, by having his narrator tell the narratee of unfamiliar actions and places, of unfamiliar speech habits and patterns of behavior.

Curiously, the narratives of Zola's contemporary Jules Verne, on one important level, function in like manner. In their initial aspect, novels *De la terre à la lune* and *Autour de la lune* seem to be travel narratives in the traditional 'horizontal' sense, narrating in great detail travel to the moon and back. Information about this unknown world is conveyed both by the undeclared, third-person narrator, and by talkative character-observers. But within this travel frame, fully half of these narratives recount another unknown world, one located this time in the 'vertical' sense at the centre of the narrator's home world itself. The narrator here is not (as he would be if this were a traditional travel narrative) a Frenchman who has gone to the US, then to the moon, and then back to France to tell his tales to a contemporary French narratee. Verne gives this role instead to a character—Michael Ardan. Rather, like the narrator of a Zola novel telling of a world beneath the surface of the familiar world that he both knows and has researched extensively, Vernes's narrator recounts the world of American industry—a place he claims to know in depth and detail—to a narratee and virtual reader who are, in the primary sense of editor Hetzel's project to 'educate' his countrymen, contemporary Frenchmen.

In the same manner as Zola's narrator narrates the Parisian *bas fonds*, Verne's narrator tells in great technical detail how the Baltimore Gun Club functions. He takes the narratee (and by association the reader) into state-of-the-art factories, makes him witness to dialogues among 'experts' who lay bare the industrial processes by which the fabulous moon rocket is made. In like fashion, the idiolect of the American technocrat is presented with all its distinctive speech mannerisms, just as naturalist novelists claimed to 'record' the exact idioms of a given social milieu. Verne does not, via narrator and narratee, take his reader 'downward' to exotic places below the normative level of social discourse. He brings the French technophile instead up to the level of American industry, upon which like processes of industrialization were seen to function in a freer, more efficient manner. If travel to the moon is the subject of a traditional travel narrative, description of the American factory system that enables the adventurers to get to the moon is an extension of the naturalist narrative, which explores the exotic that lies just a reach beyond the normal world of 'home'. In the sense of the naturalist novel then, the great detail of the telling is justified by the fact that neither narratee nor virtual reader (in Verne both can be identified—through the kind and nature of details related—as middle-class Frenchmen who are technologically disposed) has personally visited an American factory or board meeting, whereas the narrator (by the intimacy with which he presents his information) must be assumed to have done so.[8]

4a. *Historical Worlds: The Past*
The historical novel, like the travel story, is the other fundamental narrative form that is at the basis of innumerable sf narratives. In travel narratives and in naturalist explorations of unknown milieux, whether the distance be purely physical or social and cultural, the narrator has 'been there', and the narratee has not, thus needs to have information, the conveying of which allows the writer to inform his virtual reader who has not been there either. But in the historical narrative, there is a temporal factor to be considered as well. For now, distance is measured from what is a clearly indicated contemporary narrative instance, to the telling of some

chronologically dated past historical epoch. The narrator here, in some way or other, has knowledge of this past place and time, and conveys information to a narratee who does not have this knowledge. This, in turn, is a means whereby the author informs the virtual reader, who needs the information as well.

The opening statement by the narrator in Walter Scott's *Ivanhoe* clearly indicates this distance between the pastness of the events and places he is recounting and the time of the narrative instance: 'In that pleasant district of merry England which is watered by the river Don, there extended in ancient times a large forest...'[9] Scott's narrator drifts back in history to finally settle on a period 'towards the end of the reign of Richard I'. Likewise, in Balzac's novel *Les Chouans, ou la Bretagne en 1799*, the narrator positions himself even more precisely in relation to the time in which the events of his narrative took place: 'During the first days of the year VIII, at the beginning of vendémiaire, or, in terms of the actual calendar, toward the end of the month of September, 1799...'[10] The chronological markers place the narrative instance after the abandonment of the revolutionary calendar, and thus locate it closer to (if not totally contemporaneous with) the actual moment of the author's writing the story (itself dated). In order to inform his virtual reader, the author uses a narrator who conveys information about the past to a narratee who seems to be contemporary to the reader.

4b. *Historical Worlds: The Future*
A common form of sf is simply to invert the form of the historical narrative, and to substitute a future world for a past one. This reversal however leads to some interesting variations on the traditional relationship between narrator and narratee (and thus the virtual reader). For example, in a work like Frederik Pohl's 'Day Million', the narrative begins with a troubling use of the future instead of the past tense: 'On this day I want to tell you about, which will be about a thousand years from now, there were a boy, a girl, and a love story.'[11] The events take place on 'day million', which on our calendar would be 2740 AD. The narrator, imprecisely, refers to this time as 'a thousand years from now'. By his manner of speech (he uses expletives like 'cripes!' and phrases like 'you don't give a rat's ass') and topical references (to Crisco and Relaxaciser chairs), he is identifiable, despite his own fuzzy sense of chronology, as an American man circa 1960, contemporary to the period when the story was written (1966). The narrator then is conveying information about a far-off future time and place that he has somehow, mysteriously, witnessed, for he tells about it in the past tense. He methodically relates things about an almost totally alien future, but to a narratee who is like himself a man contemporary to

the period of the publication of the book, and thus contemporary to the author and to the virtual reader. This is made obvious when the narrator makes explicit comparisons between future events and things he and the narratee both share. Except for the small matter of temporal paradox, this narrative functions in the same manner as the historical narrative of Balzac or Walter Scott.

Many of the best known space epics of sf, though set in futures far more distant than day million, offer, in terms of information conveyed by a narrator to his narratee, a significant variation on the conventional historical narrative. In narratives like Asimov's *Foundation*, Herbert's *Dune*, or even Delany's *Nova*, both the narrator and the narratee now belong to the future. In such a case, what the narrator tells is the past for himself or herself and the narratee. For the virtual reader, however, these things and actions take place incredibly far in the future. In such a situation, co-location of narratee and virtual reader appears unlikely, for the former would have vastly different information needs than the latter, given the span of millennia that separates them. But by placing the future narrator and narratee themselves in the situation of the conventional historical narrative, telling about events in their past, the author in a sense dupes his or her reader into identifying with the narratee, who in his context also needs information about a distant world, if only in his near past.

Part I of *Foundation*, for example, has as epigraph an entry in the *Encyclopedia Galactica* on Hari Seldon, main protagonist and founder of the Foundation: 'HARI SELDON—born in the 11,988th year of the Galactic Era; died 12,069. The dates are more commonly given in terms of the current Foundational Era as –79 to the year 1 F.E.'[12] A footnote tells that the quote comes from the 116th edition of the *Encyclopedia*, published in 1020 F.E. The quote itself announces a crucial meeting between Seldon and Gaal Dornick that occurred two years before the former's death. The ensuing narrative recounts this meeting. If the narrator is the one citing this edition, then he is telling his narratee a story that took place 1022 years earlier. Because of this 'historical' distance, the narrator is justified in informing his narratee in great detail about the collapse of the Galactic Empire, the science of psycho-history and the creation of the Foundation. At the same time, the author is informing the virtual reader, for whom these fictive events will take place 13,089 years in the future.

Herbert's *Dune* uses the same device of epigraphs from 'historical' documents in order to locate events that (for the virtual reader) are in the far future in a time that constitutes the narrator's and his narratee's past: 'To begin your study of the life of Muad'Dib, then, take care that you first place him in his time: born in the 57th year of the Padishah Emperor, Shaddam IV. And take the most special care that you locate Muad'Dib in his place: the planet Arrakis.' It is the Princess Irulan's document here that provides historical information (and directives) for the undeclared narrator. That narrator conveys information about Dune and its savior to a narratee who is obviously of his later period. The *Dune* narrative conveys information from an eclectic mix of times and places—future technology, Imperial Islamic history (in the same way Asimov's narrative draws details from Gibbon's *Rise and Fall of the Roman Empire*), 'modern' ecology—that confounds the reader's attempts to place the complex intergalactic civilization in clear relation to his own place and time. Only in the Appendix does Herbert provide more 'historical' documents that make this link, by dating the births and deaths of the protagonists in terms of our contemporary chronological system: Shaddam IV (10,134–10,202).[13]

4c. *Tales of the Last Man*

Sf also offers one future-historical scenario—the 'last man' story—that generates a significant variation in the relationship between narrator, narratee, and virtual reader. This form is a conflation of two forms of historical finality—the end of *kairos* or religious time, and the end of purely human time, here in terms of total destruction of the race. In these works, a single survivor narrates the final moments of human existence, whether this results in extinction (Mary Shelley's *The Last Man* [1826]), or in evolutionary transformation, or even transcendence. Yet if this is so, then for whose ears is such a narrative destined? Much detailed information about these final moments in human history is conveyed, but to whom is it conveyed? If the last man himself is the narrator (imagine Wells's Time Traveler witnessing the death of our Earth and Solar System, but deciding to stay in that world, to tell its story and die with it), is his recounting a soliloquy, a narrative like an interior monologue, something overheard rather than heard? If this is the case, then the role of the narratee as receiver of information (thus the conduit that feeds the same information in parallel fashion to the virtual reader) is effaced.

But what happens in this situation when the narrator is a third-person narrator, who was not an actor engaged in the events, but merely a witness of the final scene who now tells it as a *past* event to a narratee who, given his need to be informed, has to be located even farther in the future? An example is J.H. Rosny aîné's *La Mort de la Terre* (1910). Here a third-person narrator recounts the last words and actions of Targ, the sole remaining human being on Earth. Targ's final gesture is told thus: 'Refusing euthanasia, he went out from the ruins, and lay down at the oasis among the ferromagnetics. Then, humbly, a few atoms of the last human passed into the New Form of Life.'[14] The past tense of this narrative locates the instance of narration after the death of Targ.

Who then is this narrator, and to whom is he speaking? His narratee could perhaps be part of this New Form, the so-called ferromagnetics, who are a non-organic life form. But would they, plausibly, need information about the death of the life form they have incorporated? In any event, for the virtual reader, this is a narrative about humanity's farthest future and beyond. But for the narratee, whoever it is, it *has to be* a historical narrative.

It seems, however, in the case of these terminal narratives, that a formal concern of science fiction is to seek some means of mediating the otherwise total estrangement between the virtual reader, and the narrator and his ultimate narratee. Arthur C. Clarke's *Childhood's End* offers an ingenious attempt to do so. In this third-person narrative, Earth's children ultimately pass into an autism that isolates them from all verbal communication, and in this state form an energy system that joins the alien condition of Overmind. Clarke however gives his character Jan, in the position of Last Man on Earth, a path of communication to an alien race called Overlords. These beings place him in the role of observer, and narrator, of the destruction wrought by the transformation of Earth's children into Overmind, then capture his narrative via radio from outer space. In terms of evolutionary history, which determines past and future, these aliens occupy an ambiguous position in relation to the dying humanity. Technologically more advanced than humans, they are at the same time, as beings with wings and tails, associated by past humanity with devils, reprobate beings, somehow an evolutionary dead end, unlike humanity unable to accede to the Overmind. Because Jan's narratee is a member of this alien race, the otherwise vast distance between virtual reader and silent narratee is mitigated. On one hand, for the Overlords, collectors of cosmic museum specimens, Jan's narrative of human passing is a bit of oral history. Given the Overlords' curiosity, the reader is left to ask whether the third-person narrator was not of their race, bounded by its lack of access to the state of the Overmind? It appears (as if Jan's narratee now takes the narrator's role) impacted by the story told. Indeed, the story of humanity's courage in the face of extinction seems to have given them (and with them perhaps the virtual reader) new hope, or at least passed on a trick or two to help them circumvent *their* dead-end status: 'They would serve the Overmind because they had no choice, but even in that service they would not lose their souls.'[15]

5. *An SF Hybrid: Travel Narrative/Historical Narrative*

In sf, travel narrative and historical narrative seem to combine naturally into a hybrid form. Probably the most famous early sf narrative to combine these two forms is H.G. Wells's *The Time Machine*. This narrative literally reverses the traditional historical novel by having the narrator relate to his narratees, contemporaries of the virtual reader, information about the future, not the past. At the same time, if the unknown world lies in the chronological future of narrator, narratee and reader alike at the instance of narration, it belongs *at the same time* to the narrator's past at the moment he tells it. Pushing the paradox farther, the narrator tells his story to narratees who want to know what *had* happened, not what will happen, for in terms of theirs and the Traveler's biological time line all the future events he recounts occurred *before* the narrative instant, thus in the past of narrator and narratee alike, as was exactly the case in Walter Scott and Balzac.

Wells's narrative—with its possibility of actual time travel—forces its reader to ask a question that previous readers, simply accepting the convention of the historical novel, did not ask: how did the narrator become so familiar with the most intimate details of a past era (as with the narrator of Ivanhoe's England) if he or she had not been there himself? The time machine makes literal the temporal 'voyages' implicit in historical narratives. Indeed, by allowing a narrator to travel to the past or the future, then return to tell the tale, the machine brings about a conflation of historical narrative and travel narrative. A number of time travel stories—those that concern a time loop 'anchoring' the narrative in a 'now' instant formed by the contemporaneity of narrator and narratee—allow their narrator, either as traveler or as witness who has been there and returned, to inform the listener (and the contemporary virtual reader) about places in spacetime that are unknown to them.

Wells's Traveler went physically into the future. His announced second voyage, into the past, the true realm of the historical narrative, where things have already happened, thus in terms of common sense, cannot be changed, is never narrated, for the Traveler never returns. A slightly earlier novel, Mark Twain's *A Connecticut Yankee at King Arthur's Court* (1889), purports to move the narrator (the 'Yankee' of the title) physically into the past. He lives and acts among sixth-century people, introducing late nineteenth-century technology, and finally slaughtering an entire social class with a Gatling gun, before he finds his way back to his 'now' in place and time. But how could this narrator really travel to the past, where his changes would of necessity alter the course of history? Was all this, a common device in earlier historical narratives, just a dream?

The primary narrator (a conventional 'editor' figure) sets the time of the events for his narratee in the opening line of the book: 'It was in Warwick Castle that I came across the curious stranger whom I am going to talk about.'[16] The stranger speaks a 'sixth-century' English, talks with intimacy of knights of the Round Table ('exactly as I would speak of my nearest personal friends'), and tells his interlocutor he was responsible for an inexplicable bullet hole in a piece of armour on display. He then vanishes, only to reappear that evening in the room of this narrator, interrupting his reading of Malory. The stranger first narrates in person, telling of how he was hit on the head in this century, and awakened in medieval England. Then he hands his listener, the primary narrator who has become his declared narratee, a manuscript containing a detailed account of his stay in the past. Exchanging this document for Malory, this declared narrator becomes declared reader within the fictive world.

Things further complicate. On one level, as the Yank's narrative is read by this primary narrator, it functions as a historical narrative, a narrative reacted to at a distance, as something either true or false. Just as the bullet hole in Sir Sagramore's armor is historically 'questionable' (Cromwell's soldiers could have done it), so the manuscript, described as a 'palimpsest' with Yankee handwriting over old monkish script, is no proof of authenticity. At the end of this manuscript (whose title is 'The Tale of the Lost Land') our primary narrator learns, in 'Clarence's Postscript', that the Yank was put to sleep by a spell from Merlin, and laid to rest in a cave with the manuscript. The assumption is to be made that he slumbered there for 13 centuries, and awoke again in his own time. Questioning this, the sceptical narrator is in fact indicting the conventions of the historical narrative. These demand that narratee (and virtual reader) suspend disbelief and accept as true information about the past given by a narrator in their time who could not have been there to observe it, let alone act in it. Twain's narrator, telling of his visit to the dying Yank, overhears the continuation of his historical narrative only to declare it an 'effect', the work of an actor.

The body of the novel, however, the Yank's narrative itself, calls for a different narratee, that of the traditional travel narrative, whose conventions require that the narrator physically had gone to the place he tells about. When Hank describes men and women as having 'long, coarse, uncombed hair that hung down over their faces and made them look like animals', he expresses the cultural codes of his time, codes understood by a *contemporary* narratee and virtual reader alike. The fact of a conventional travel narrative operative within the frame of the historian's scepticism seems to say that the 'Lost Land' is not mere dream or historical fabrication, but perhaps a real physical place. Perhaps Hank *was there*. Perhaps, once he returns to his own time, it is physically impossible for him to go back there. In this narrative context, his final grievings for the loss of Sandy, rather than mad ravings, become a tragic expression of physical dislocation: 'Yes, I seemed to have flown back out of that age into this of ours... with an abyss of thirteen centuries yawning between me and you! Between me and my home and my friends.'[17]

The complexity of Twain's narrative is seen when measured against a modern version, L. Sprague de Camp's *Lest Darkness Fall* (1941). De Camp makes literal what was possibly dream or narrative ambiguity in Twain: his traveler goes physically to a past time. His actions in the past change the course of history as we know it. Carrying this logic to its conclusion, then, once an alternate history is created, there could be no Merlin's spell or manuscript come through time. It would never reach a narratee in the author's world, for that world would be elsewhere, inaccessible. De Camp's narrative however does not take this into account. A third-person narrator tells how archaeologist Martin Padway, hit by lightning in the virtual reader's contemporary Rome, slips back on history's 'fourth-dimensional web' to Rome in the sixth century AD. Though Professor Tancredi tells Padway before the slip that 'the web...is tough. If a man did slip back, it would take a terrible lot of work to distort it', Padway (like Hank) proceeds to do such history-changing work. The narrator however continues to convey information to a contemporary narratee *in our time*, though at some point, due to the distortion of the web, that time must cease to exist, or to be accessible to communication. The narrator tells of Padway's initial dislocation—'All sorts of things might have happened in the meantime. He might have blundered into a movie set. Mussolini, having long secretly believed himself a reincarnation of Julius Caesar, might have decided to make his people adopt classical Roman costume.'[18] Ignoring growing temporal dislocation, he continues up to the end to address this same narratee, in logical contradiction to the non-historical tense of the final statement: 'Darkness would not fall.'

Among nineteenth-century time displacement narratives, one work stands out because it does not bring (as in Wells and Twain) its narrator back to the author's and reader's present, but leaves him forever in the future to which he has physically been relocated, if not of his own volition actually 'traveled': Edward Bellamy's *Looking Backward: 2000–1887*. A young Bostonian, Julian West, sinks into mesmeric sleep one evening in 1887, and (like a Rip Van Winkle who does not age) awakens in the year 2000. Unlike Hank, his future direction loses him to the virtual reader's time, to which he never returns. On the opening page of his narration, he begins telling the story of the reader's time to narratees in the year 2000: 'I first saw the light in the city of Boston in the year 1857. "What!" you say. "Eighteen fifty-seven? That is an odd slip. He means nineteen fifty-seven, of course?"'[19] The incredulity of these future narratees, who have difficulty at first with this literal displacement backward, is mirrored by that of the virtual reader, for whom West's future location is equally troubling. West, as he utters these words, is thirty years old. If he were born in 1857, as he says, then this should (for the virtual reader) locate the moment he tells the story precisely at 1887, the date of publication of Bellamy's book.

Once West's twentieth-century narratees accept his mode of transport, he becomes for them a man from the past, and his narrative takes on the historical currency of document. Bellamy prefaces West's narrative with a short Preface, precisely dated: 'Historical Section, Shawmut College, Boston, December 25, 2000', thus a document dated *after* his account, looking explicitly back on it as history.[20] Both for West's declared narratees, Dr Leete and his daughter Edith, and for the author of this Preface, it is the contrast between their present and his tale of an 'ancient industrial system with its shocking social consequences', that allows them to extrapolate the course of progress in their future: 'It seems…that nowhere can we find more solid ground for daring anticipations of human development during the next thousand years, than by "Looking Backward" upon the progress of this last one hundred.'[21]

But if West's narrative, recounting the world from 1857 to 1887, is history to his future narratees, it is also history for the virtual reader as well. In light of Dr Leete's comments, however, what would otherwise for this reader be near history, myopically seen, takes on critical distance from the constant comparison with this world and its utopian 'future'. In a sense, there are two distinct narrators here. West's story, though it is of contemporary times, is made history, and information about it can be conveyed as such, by the fact that its narrator addresses his remarks to future narratees, providing the otherwise familiar with historical distance and estrangement. Leete's story, on the other hand, is a narrative about travel to a future world. Leete is the man who has been there. This time however he does not have to return to a shared present, for that present has come to him. When he conveys information to West, a *displaced* man of 1887, he conveys it at the same time to the virtual reader of that same date. West is physically in the future, but not mentally there. The virtual reader is neither.

In Bellamy, we see an early attempt to mediate what will later become an increasing problem for sf narratives—too great a distance, in terms of information flow, between narrator and his narratee, both vastly displaced in terms of space and time, and a virtual reader 'left behind' in the author's present. Space and time work together here to expand the range of the sf travel narrative. The range of space travel, in a work like *Rocket Ship Galileo* for example, is limited (in a manner analogous to the traditional travel narrative) by the technology available at the time when the novel is published. But by displacing the narrator and narratee into a distant future, the author can simply assume new technologies (such as Asimov's FTL 'jumps') which in turn enable further and further voyages into deeper spacetime.

Towards the other end of the spectrum from Bellamy, but still involving mediation between displaced narrators and narratees, and the author's virtual reader, is a novel like Poul Anderson's *Tau Zero* (1970). A generational starship begins to accelerate out of control, ultimately reaching the 'impossible' barrier of light speed. But despite the incredible voyage, the narrative begins in a time and place easily conceivable by the reader circa 1970: a near-future Stockholm, sometime in the twenty-second century. Located in this future, the narrator nevertheless easily links his narratee to the virtual reader by making references to monuments that were *built in the latter's past*, for example terraces that 'were empty of everything except the life that Carl Milles had shaped into stone and metal, three centuries ago'.[22] Thus, though the narratee is in the virtual reader's future, that future becomes closer when the narrator connects its present with past events, that are both within the narratee's collective memory, and at the same time encompass the virtual reader's present. An unbroken historical line is created, forging continuity if not identity between narratee and virtual reader.

II. Extrapolative Narratives

As we have seen, the themes of sf create situations of extreme temporal displacement in relation to traditional narrative. In taking literal account of these displacements, sf brings about significant formal transformations in the two narrative forms traditionally used to convey information about distant, hence unknown worlds to an author's reader—the travel narrative and the historical narrative. In this case, the author's reader is made to accept the fact that, if a narrator and narratee are displaced in space and time, that narratee will not get the same amount or kind of information that the virtual reader needs if he or she is fully to understand the world conveyed. As the narratee naturally knows the extrapolated world, he or she does not need as much, but *less* information than the reader about how it works. Sf, as extrapolated narrative, operates in a zone between two conventional forms. On the one hand, there is the realist 'novel of manners', where a narrated world is intimately shared and known by all parties—narrator, narratee, and virtual reader. On the other hand, there is the fantastic narrative. In Franz Kafka's 'The Metamorphosis', for example, the narrator conveys information that, though from the outset it cannot be reconciled with the experience and expectations of the virtual reader, is heard without reaction, in accepting silence, by the narratee. The uncomprehending reader is increasingly alienated. Where rupture between narratee and virtual reader, blocking transfer of information about a given narrative world, remains so unrelenting, we move outside the formal limits of sf, toward the fantastic.

1. *Minimal Extrapolation*

This form would seem singularly unsuited to sf. And yet many of the most effective sf works, from the so-called 'Golden Age', make creative use of the form of the novel of manners in terms of the narrator-narratee relationship. Such narratives, in sf, are usually described as narratives of 'minimal extrapolation'. In them, the writer creates a world that is located, in relation to his virtual reader's clearly contemporary world, slightly in the future. The effect of these narratives comes from stretching but not breaking the thread of shared understanding that links narratee to virtual reader. This occurs when the narrator presents an action or thing that is different from what exists in the contemporary world, and does not explain it. The virtual reader does not know this thing or event, but the fact that it is given without explanation implies that the narratee does. The virtual reader is forced to make the mental adjustments that allow him to 'catch up' with the narratee, to familiarize himself or herself with that which is provisionally unfamiliar or strange.

Examples among the 'classic' stories of the 1950s are many. The first line of Lester Del Rey's 'Helen O'Loy' reads: 'I am an old man now, and I can still see Helen as Dave unpacked her.'[23] The narrator sees no need to comment to his narratee on the fact that women, in this world, are unpacked. The author here, it seems, wants his virtual reader to experience a moment of mental adjustment, to realize that a new Helen of Troy can be made of alloy. Once the initial surprise passes, the virtual reader accepts the comfortable story of fatal love that follows. We have another example in Heinlein's 'The Roads Must Roll'. Here are its opening lines:

> 'Who makes the roads roll?' The speaker stood still on the rostrum and waited for his audience to answer him. 'Who does the dirty work "down inside" so that Joe Public can ride with ease?'[24]

Narrator and narratee clearly share the same world. But Heinlein is playing on the virtual reader's reaction, calculating an initial effect of quasi-estrangement. The virtual reader can envision 'rolling' roads as a figure of speech. But he is not prepared for the next statement, where metaphor becomes literal statement, with actual people doing work 'down inside', physically making the roads roll. Yet once this fact is accepted, the world of this narrative becomes as negotiable for the virtual reader as it is for the narratee.

If one leafs through the stories in the famous Volume I of the *Science Fiction Hall of Fame*,[25] one will see that in many of these works, Hugo Award winners from the 'Golden Age', the narrator addresses a narratee who neither requires nor gets information about its future world. In a story like Jerome Bixby's 'It's a *Good* Life', the virtual reader, despite an initial disorientation, easily enters its world. But in stories such as Cordwainer Smith's 'Scanners Live in Vain', the thread that links virtual reader to narratee is stretched almost to breaking point. The first line proves baffling: 'Martel was angry. He did not even adjust his blood away from anger.'[26] The continuing narrative however is even more so. The narrator continues however to present things and actions that, because of the sparse, declarative manner of their presentation, are assumed to be totally familiar to the narratee. But to the virtual reader attempting to become familiar with the ways of this new world, the lack of information is increasingly perplexing. The author however does not intend silence to become total alienation. On the contrary, in this and like stories (Alfred Bester's 'Fondly Fahrenheit' is an example), enough coherent patterns are given that the virtual reader is able eventually to familiarize himself or herself, and join the narratee in apprehending this future world, if with a lesser degree of familiarity and comfort. In sf, it seems, to exclude the reader totally violates its generic imperatives, where some 'knowing' must take place even if only as shared or half-grasped impressions, rather than absolute rational certitude. A narrative, then, where actions and things are presented as and for themselves, with no information *about* them conveyed, would appear impossible in sf.

2. *Extended Extrapolations*
Some sf writers appear to have been challenged by this exclusionary possibility. There are examples, as in Samuel R. Delany's *The Einstein Intersection*, of unknown worlds recounted in near-hermetic collusion between narrator and narratee. The intended effect is to produce not only temporary bafflement but sustained, radical disorientation in the virtual reader.[27] We have here Lo Lobey's telling of his never-explained quest across a broken land of cultural artifacts left behind by some future human society that has experienced an unnamed holocaust. What we have, in a sense, is a travel narrative that begs for information to be conveyed about its strange world. And yet Lobey's narratee, because he seems so familiar with what is being told, neither requires nor exacts commentary on that world. There are a few moments where a description is given, or where discursive dialogue occurs, as in Lobey's famous discussion with Spider about the 'Einstein intersection'. Yet these speak of things and concepts that, though apparently of human origin, are uttered in ways that remain oblique to the virtual reader's own system of codes, myths, or knowledge. If Delany's narrative remains sf, it is because the reader finally must conclude, despite its narrator's persistent near-behaviourist telling things that are 'different', that the logic of this future fictional world *is* systematic difference. Once he grasps the principle of Lobey's narrative, the virtual

reader makes cognitive contact with the narratee, and thus to some extent is brought to share his strange future.

Here, in this unfeasibility of a totally exclusionary narrative about an unknown world, we rejoin the limit of sf as narrative implied in Darko Suvin's term 'cognitive estrangement'.[28] As we have seen, estrangement results from a more or less broad disparity between the world known to the narratee and that of the virtual reader. But because the thread of understanding is never totally broken, the reader is urged to overcome, to a sufficient degree, this distance between worlds. Suvin comes closest to describing this process in his remarks on the sf narrative as 'novum': 'The essential tension of sf is one between the readers, representing a certain number of types of Man of our times, and the encompassing and at least equipollent Unknown or Other introduced by the novum.'[29] In the case of sf adaptations of the narrative of manners (with its 'types of man of our times'), the new world is invariably a future or alternate world. Indeed, in cases where narrative is pushed to extremes that maximally alienate the virtual reader, it appears that such narrative, as sf, only pushes the reader all the more forcefully to strive to know if the world in question really lies in some eventually understandable, materially locatable, other place. This defines the essentially materialist nature of Suvin's sf reader. Such a reader is unwilling (if through generic rather than ideological imperatives) to accept a narrated world as some artfully contrived 'other', or play formal games with obfuscation and alienation.

However, if a totally estranging sf narrative of a future world is unfeasible, what of such a narrative of the past? The distant past has left archaeological traces, objects and visual forms and images, that may still be visible, but are perhaps no longer cognitively understood. In contrast, we have no 'future things' under our eyes, only extrapolated possibilities, with minimal reach into the not-yet-known, beyond which the thread breaks, and 'new' objects can only be given strange-sounding names, phonemes that point to nothing conceivable. Arkady and Boris Strugatsky, in *Roadside Picnic*, go about as far as possible in the direction of future archaeology. In this narrative, a 'Zone' appears, which contains a number of strange objects whose origin, nature and functions remain unknown. They seem to have come from some advanced civilization, so advanced that these miraculous objects are as common and disposable to them as litter would be to us at a roadside picnic. The narrative advances as humans, on 'archaeological' expeditions, find these objects, name them (giving them names that reflect their level of culture—'witch's jelly'—or cognitive perplexity—'full empties') then try to reconstruct their purpose or use, a process that rapidly degenerates into personal quests for wealth or power.

Filmmaker Federico Fellini has argued, in his essay 'From the Planet

Rome', that a narrative of the future (i.e. science fiction) cannot estrange by overextending the distance between narratee's and reader's world, because no things exist by which to measure that distance. Fellini uses the example of his film *Fellini Satyricon*.[30] Unlike words, in the medium of film one cannot call things into existence by naming or describing them. For future 'things', models or visual simulations must be constructed, and these are necessarily limited in their future strangeness by our present incapacity to see what is not yet there. The past however, in this regard, offers what the future does not—visual vestiges of 'worlds' almost incomprehensible today.

As for the vestiges that surround Fellini in 'planet Rome', these (like the text *The Satyricon*) are fragments. Petronius' narrative was originally a novel of manners, where the narrator recounts the morals of his time to a narratee of that time, thus a contemporary of the virtual reader. This narrative, however, has come down to us in as hopelessly fragmentary a state as the Pompeian mural paintings that provided the film's visual décor. Fellini's camera narrates *his* Satyricon with raw images of scenes and objects that, to a narratee and virtual reader of Nero's time, might have seemed familiar and meaningful. But in the 1970 film, Fellini conveys words, gestures, and objects *of that time* without mediating information, as if his narrator addressed a narratee of Nero's time who needed none. The effect on the virtual viewer is perplexity that goes beyond cognitive estrangement. Fellini proves his point: the past can, with its mute objects, offer the alienating silence of the thing-in-itself. But in doing so he reveals that Rome is not (as he claims) a planet at all, and that this filmic exercise in viewer alienation is not a science fiction narrative. As with Kafka's 'Metamorphosis', its premise is to render the known unknown.

There are many more combinations and variations of this basic relationship between narrator, narratee and virtual reader to be explored in sf, just as there are in narrative in general. We have tried to demonstrate ways in which the sf narrative has used, and made significant alterations to a number of traditional forms. Sf in its narrative structures is neither conventional nor radical; it offers formal variants on a system shared by all forms of storytelling. Sf however, in its insistence on telling unknown worlds, calls attention to the channel of conveying information that exists between narrator and narratee within the text, and author and virtual reader outside that text. In the traditional forms sf adapts to its purpose—the travel narrative, historical narrative and the narrative of manners—the co-location of narratee and virtual reader, as point at which information passes from one domain to another, remains unquestioned, even when logically (as in the historical narrative) it is problematic. Sf's insistence, however, both on temporal displacement of narrator and narratee, and on treating this displacement as physical fact, as material part of the story, calls attention to the necessity of this formal artifice in narrative, and by doing so calls for new strategies to keep this channel of communication open—a necessity if sf is to tell of worlds unknown because distant in the future or in an alternate past.

Notes

1 Gerald Prince, *A Dictionary of Narratology* (Lincoln, NE: University of Nebraska Press, 1987), pp. 57, 65. We are indebted to Prince's discussion of the 'narratee' published in 'Introduction à l'étude du narrative', *Poètique*, 14 (April 1973); English version in Jane P. Tompkins, ed., *Reader-Response Criticism* (Baltimore: Johns Hopkins University Press, 1980), pp. 7–25.

2 Prince (*Dictionary*) sees the 'real or concrete reader' as 'not to be confused with the implied reader of a narrative or with its narratee and, unlike them, [as] not immanent to or deductible from the narrative' (p. 79).

3 Prince, *Dictionary*, p. 43.

4 Thomas More, *Utopia* (ed. Edward Surtz; New Haven: Yale University Press, 1964), p. 26.

5 Robert A. Heinlein, *Rocket Ship Galileo* (New York: Charles Scribner's Sons, 1947), p. 19.

6 Arthur C. Clarke, *The Sands of Mars*, re-edition with Foreword by the author (New York: New American Library, 1967), p. 27.

7 Clarke, *The Sands of Mars*, p. v.

8 Verne was clearly fascinated by the rapid pace of American industrialization, and by its laissez-faire nature—fascinated and, increasingly, weary as well, as one can see in later moral tales featuring American heroes and an industrial setting, such as *Robur le conquérant*. Interestingly, in contrast with the narrator of a work like *De la terre à la lune*, who displays such an intimacy with the processes of American industry, as if he were an American born and raised, Verne himself never spent more than two weeks on US soil in his entire lifetime—a quick voyage to New York and back, where he got barely 200 miles from the big city. America was on the one hand a country of the mind; but a country that, by clear analogy with what Verne perceived to be contemporary industrializing France, was on the other hand merely an extension, in the quantitative sense, of his native milieu, and thus that of his reader.

9 Sir Walter Scott, *Ivanhoe* (London: The Penguin English Library, 1985), p. 7.

10 Honoré de Balzac, *La Comédie humaine*, VII (Paris: Bibliothèque de la Pléiade, 1955), p. 765: 'Dans les premiers jours de l'an VIII, au commencement de vendémiaire, ou, pour se conformer au calendrier actuel, vers la fin du mois de september 1799, une centaine de paysans...'

11 *The Best of Frederik Pohl*, introduction by Lester Del Rey (Garden City, NY: Doubleday), 1957, p. 56.

12 Isaac Asimov, *Foundation* (New York: Avon Books, 1966), p. 7.

13 Frank Herbert, *Dune* (Radnor, PA: Chilton Book Co., 1965), Appendix.

14 J.H. Rosny aîné, *Récits de science-fiction* (Verviers: Marabout, 1975), p. 177: 'Ensuite, humblement, quelques parcelles de la dernière vie humaine entrèrent dans la Vie Nouvelle.'

15 Arthur C. Clarke, *Childhood's End* (New York: Ballantine Books, 1953), p. 218.

178   DANIÈLE CHATELAIN and GEORGE SLUSSER

16 Mark Twain, *A Connecticut Yankee at King Arthur's Court* (London: Penguin English Library, 1971), p. 33.

17 Twain, *Connecticut Yankee*, p. 409.

18 L. Sprague de Camp, *Lest Darkness Fall* (New York: Ballantine Books, 1974), p. 6. The original version of this work was published by Street and Smith Publications, 1939.

19 Edward Bellamy, *Looking Backward: 2000–1887* (New York: Signet Classics, 1960), p. 25.

20 It is interesting that this date, December 25, is one day before the birth of West in his past time and place: 'It was about four in the afternoon of December the 26th, one day after Christmas, in the year 1857, not 1957, that I first breathed the east wind of Boston...' (*Looking Backward*, p. 25). Could Bellamy be suggesting that, despite the information loop that links past, present and future in this narrative, it might in fact all be a Christmas fantasy, the dream of a yet unborn man?

21 Bellamy, *Looking Backward*, p. xxii.

22 Poul Anderson, *Tau Zero* (New York: Berkley Books, 1970), p. 124.

23 Lester Del Rey, 'Helen O'Loy', in Robert Silverberg, ed., *Science Fiction Hall of Fame: The Greatest Science Fiction Stories of All Time* (New York: Doubleday, 1970), p. 42.

24 Robert A. Heinlein, 'The Roads Must Roll', in Silverberg, ed., *Hall of Fame*, p. 52.

25 See n. 23 above. The 'greatest' stories are stories chosen for Hugo Awards from the late 1930s to the early 1960s, thus the authoritative statement of the title is more than advertiser's hyperbole.

26 Cordwainer Smith, 'Scanners Live in Vain', in Silverberg, ed., *Hall of Fame*, p. 288.

27 Samuel R. Delany, *The Einstein Intersection* (New York: Ace Books, 1967).

28 Darko Suvin, *Metamorphoses of Science Fiction* (New Haven: Yale University Press, 1979). 'Sf is, then, a literary genre whose necessary and sufficient conditions are the presence and interaction of estrangement and cognition, and whose main formal device is an imaginative framework alternative to the author's empirical environment' (p. 7).

29 Suvin, *Metamorphoses*, p. 64.

30 Here is Bernard K. Dick on the title of this film, which juxtaposes the names of interpreter and author (or is it narrator and author?): 'In the arts, one is accustomed to possessives that fuse work and interpreter into a unique kind of authorship. But a solecism like *Fellini Satyricon* seems alien, even pretentious; *Il Satyricon di Fellini* would have been worse, as the director admits. Actually *Fellini's Satyricon* was the preferred title, but Gian Luigi Polidoro got to Petronius first and produced a quickie *Satyricon* (1969) with Ugo Tognazzi. The courts upheld Polidoro's right to the title...and Fellini was forced to call his version *Fellini Satyricon*—hyphenated in Italy, unhyphenated elsewhere.' (Bernard K. Dick, 'Adaptation as Archeology: Fellini Satyricon', in *Modern European Filmmakers and the Art of Adaptation*, ed. Andrew S. Horton and Joan Magretta [New York: Frederick Ungar, 1981], p. 145.)

The essay 'Planet Rome' is published in *Fellini's Satyricon*, ed. Dario Zanelli, translated by Eugene Walter and John Matthews (New York: Ballantine Books, 1970), pp. 46–60.

Aphasia and Mother Tongue: Themes of Language Creation and Silence in Women's Science Fiction

NICKIANNE MOODY

This consideration of the uses of silence and language creation in women's science fiction is drawn from a much larger study which examined popular fiction, marketed as science fiction in Britain, during the 1980s. At the beginning of the 1980s, quite a drastic change occurred in the look, content and form of print science fiction in Britain. Partly this was due to deeper structural changes in the British publishing industry and book production, especially in the context of multi-national and multi-media leisure corporations. It was also due to the way that the publishing industry began to perceive science fiction as a commercial genre. To generalize, this change resulted in the term 'science fiction', as a category for selling popular fiction, losing its prominence in the bookshop. It was replaced initially by fantasy and increasingly by horror and these generic distinctions adopted a new iconography for their titles and cover designs.

Defining science fiction is a quagmire, especially when considering how it was redefined by publishers, writers, booksellers and readers during the 1980s. The definition used by this study was therefore Norman Spinrad's infamous statement that science fiction is whatever is sold as science fiction. The study's main focus became two groups of writers, one predominantly male and the other a group of women writers who continued to write and had their writing signified as science fiction. They wrote fiction which addressed and explored contemporary science and scientific practice, new technology and social change. Both groups, that is cyberpunk and feminist science fiction, were recognized by critics and readers from outside a specialist interest in the genre. Both prospective futures featured imminent and far-reaching social change. Cyberpunk proposes an urban high-tech dark future medievalism, which was not denied by the feminist fiction. However, in contrast women writers offered the possibility of a collective pastoral guild-ordered life in the fictional future which may nor may not utilize new technology.

In order to consider the representation of silence in this fiction we are going to look at a smaller group of the feminist science fiction writers. It is a pleasing peculiarity of the genre that feminist writers could appropriate science fiction forms, conventions and marketing for their critique of contemporary society and social relations. Dystopian representations of technological transformations in culture, society and the experience of the working environment become dominant themes in science fiction of the 1980s. Utopian and dystopian writing built on the tradition of New Wave in the 1970s to provide an informal site for debates concerning the nature of contemporary experience and extrapolative contingencies in near future patterns of social organization. During the same period cyberpunk considered postmodern identity and corporate capital, by focussing on the city and re-employing the conventions of hardboiled detective or mystery fiction. Whereas these narratives concentrated on the experience of the individual and their actions, women's science fiction visualized a 'post-industrial' society from a very different perspective. Their response to the evolution of such a society was to propose alternatives to patriarchy and effect speculative transformations of society through communal will.

The meeting of language and patriarchy raises critical debates in this fiction which directly address the prospect of social change. Suzy McKee Charnas' opening to *Walk to the End of the World* (1979) is a good example of the general premise shared by these novels: 'They [the men] forbade all women to attend meetings and told them to keep their eyes lowered and their mouths shut and to mind their own business, which was reproduction.'[1]

Either through cataclysm, ecological disaster, war or the social change wrought by alien contact, a sharp division has arisen between men and women, with women existing in a state not just of inequality, but of powerlessness. The novels commonly envisage a state of post-feminism. Central to Haden Elgin's (1984) construction of society in the late twenty-second century is the 1991 amendment to the United States Constitution which revokes women's rights.[2] In consequence they are declared to be legal minors who must have male guardians. In *The Handmaid's Tale* (1985) we witness the passing of the feminist movement that is our past as it is suppressed by religious fundamentalism in the wake of a future nuclear war.[3]

Themes of language and its relationship to the physical and cultural environment have long been popular topics in science fiction. Since the 1930s the problem of alien contact in linguistic terms has been seen as more than just the need for a universal translator. It has also figured prominently in future extrapolations of human society. Katherine Burdekin published *Swastika Night* in Britain in 1937, under the name Murray Constantine. In the narrative's fictional world the Nazi Reich has endured for 700 years and Burdekin offers a feminist critique relating power politics to gender politics. Women have been reduced to empty vessels, with no name, no voice and no language of their own. The narrative forewarns that women will eventually cease to exist in a world totally populated by men, leading to the demise of the species. However, Burdekin sees the women's complicity in keeping silent at the beginning of this assault on their civil rights as the cause of the tragedy.[4]

In Lefanu's (1988) history of women's science fiction writing, she demonstrates how feminists turned to science fiction to analyse social and literary constructions of women as gendered subjects. Marge Piercy's *Woman on the Edge of Time* (1974) is often taken as the prime example, for Piercy enters the genre to engage with Shulamith Firestone's views on gender and technology. Piercy uses science fiction conventions to bring the theoretical debate into sharper relief.[5] Twenty years later, Piercy's *He She and It* (1992) can take on the cyberpunk of male writers and respond in fiction to Donna Haraway's cultural interrogation of the cyborg.[6] Other writers such as Margaret Atwood (*The Handmaid's Tale*) and Zoë Fairbairns (*Benefits*, 1979) also found the dystopian aspect of the near future diegesis ideally suited for their exploration of sexual politics, feminist debate and cultural anxiety.

In the 1980s more authors became interested in linguistic theory and researched it as they would any other 'science'. Feminist writers began to use feminist linguistic theory as a premiss for a science fiction narrative—a way of disseminating that theory in a popular form and a process of extrapolation both to test and to explore the theory. For example, Miller Gearhart in *The Wanderground* (1979) experiments in the first part of the text with her use of language.[7] Cyberpunk writers (or Burgess in *A Clockwork Orange*, 1962)[8] use a similar technique to produce a futuristic argot. Miller Gearhart invents words and expressions complementary to the society of women that she is outlining, gradually drawing together an interconnecting series of narrative and purely descriptive chapters. The prose only becomes clear to the reader when the action is imperative and the language used to describe the city, the purges and the hunts is startlingly contemporary. Therefore the experience of our own time intrudes directly on to the previous rhythm of the text which has been constructed by the utopian writing.

A common motif used by the group of writers that we are considering is the examination of the role of language in the construction of institutionalized oppression. Aphasia and speech are central metaphors

which are used recurrently in woman's science fiction. At the beginning
of the novels women are rendered mute or knowingly speak a language
which is not their own. They exist as a dispossessed or subjugated
indigenous population. Some narratives respond to this situation by
constructing or promoting a language spoken by women, which can
express the experience of women and thus empower them. Others foresee
an increasingly gendered stratification reaching a point where the two
sexes are unable to communicate with one another. Language is seen as
something which is always in a state of change and these societies are
themselves in flux.

These novels are neither utopian nor dystopian. I would call them
eutopias, which adapt the discourse for constructing an alternative future,
allowing them to debate a range of contingencies. Social change and a new
society in this fiction necessitate a new language. The novels are
challenging, they distance and disconcert their readers. Moreover, the
narrative conclusions are not necessarily certain, especially as the fictive
future is often only present in fragments and snatches. There are
inconsistencies and elisions which require active reading. Novels such
as Margaret Atwood's *The Handmaid's Tale* use pseudo-documentary
discourse which provides ample room for speculation on the part of the
reader. This appears to be a very important aspect of the novels'
presentation. In this way the writer draws attention to the fact that she is
using a construction of the future to examine the past and contemporary
experience. The issues that are constantly reiterated are presented as moral
concerns firmly rooted in economic, social and physical power relations.

Frequently the starting point for these novels is the recreation of classical
attitudes to the speech of women, the founding tradition of Western
political thought. For in Plato's *Republic* women are silenced. The private
speech of the household, the speech of women, is judged to lack either the
form for philosophical argumentation or the force for poetry. It was
therefore seen as without meaning, unformed, chaotic, the speech of doxa
and mere opinion and not truth. Moreover, household speech could
neither be heroic nor part of the philosophic male quest for wisdom through
dialogue. Thus women were excluded from politics and from participating
in philosophic discourse. Women had no place to bring their thoughts to
a public arena. And as one sex was confined to the private sphere and the
other had access to the public, the two could not speak to one another.
This is a dramatic premiss which is taken literally by writers such as Sheri
Tepper in *The Gate to Women's Country* (1988).[9]

The aphasia found within these texts is partially brought about by
characters physically being prevented from speaking, but frequently the
silence is self-imposed. The novels consider an older definition of aphasia,

of being unable to voice thought in words. Although the ability to voice thought enables autonomy, as the inability prevents it, it is often a rite of passage. Silence is seen as productive and not just a prelude to confession or evil, its signification in Greek drama. Silence, contemplation and self-knowledge are seen as strategies to confront patriarchy.

A direct example of this is the plot to Joan Slonczewski's *A Door into Ocean* (1986). A patriarchal society attempts to colonize a matriarchal one. The invasion of the planet is justified by a colonial discourse of protection and order, with the objective of bringing patriarchal law to a backward society of women. The *Sharers* of that planet are seen as a valuable resource as they possess knowlege of life science lost to the patriarchy through a major and destructive war. A large number of these feminist futures see a return to rural order as capitalism collapses under its own weight. The *Sharers'* response to the invasion is collective silence and not individual speech:

> Day by day, a wall of deafness crept inexorably from raft system to raft system, cluster to cluster. All around the globe, natives were shutting their ears and mouths to Valian troops, Iridian and Dolomite alike. Nothing seemed to break that silence, not shouting, beating, imprisoning. [10]

In other narratives passive resistance comes in the form of language creation. *Native Tongue*, written by a doctor of linguistics, is the prime example of this approach.

> These women, the women of linguists for years back, had taken on a task of constructing a language that would be just for women. A language to say things women wanted to say, and about which men always said 'Why would anybody want to talk about *that*?[11]

Linguists in this diegesis have risen to the top of the professional and social hierarchy. The economic necessity to trade with alien worlds relies on the skills of translators which are at a premium. In order to retain one professional group's monopoly over this essential service, their wives and daughters become a working resource and gradually come to recognize themselves as such.

In *Native Tongue*, silence or being silenced forces women to take action and to learn to speak for themselves. In *A Door into Ocean* silence, or as it is referred to in the text, *unspeaking*, has great cultural significance. It is seen as a form of violence and in this fictional society it is the ultimate deterrent. As well as being violent it is a response to violence. Unspeaking can be undertaken between individuals and groups and it is an action to settle differences. In an extreme form silence is a response to pain, a way of controlling pain called *whitetrance*. *Whitetrance* is complete silence and withdrawal to the extent that if you talk to a person in *whitetrance* the 'mental invasion' will kill them. The experience of many changes in social behaviour is not necessarily harmony, but conflict, debate and discussion which is resolved or mediated by speech rather than physical violence. Frequently speech and violence in these narratives are interlocked by cogent imagery.

Alternatively, quite a lot of the women's writing moves towards giving women a voice denied by patriarchal language. The language created by Haden Elgin in *Native Tongue* called *Láadan* provides the following terms. The women have used their science to create a language which will voice their feelings and facilitate collectivity. For example:

radema:	to non-touch, to actively refrain from touching
rademalh:	to non-touch with evil intent
radéela:	non-garden, a place that has much flash and glitter and ornament, but no beauty
radiidin:	non-holiday, a time allegedly a holiday but actually so much a burden because of work and preparations that it is a dreaded occasion; especially when there are too many guests and none of them to help.[12]

However, this writing is not just amelioration, neither should it be seen as writing for comfort. Its goal is not to provide space for the fantasy of autonomy. Irigary sees the silence of the female other as ensuring the auto-sufficiency of the male.[13] She raises the question just as these writers do: what would happen if the other wanted to speak? Not all of the writers are certain, but they are quite aware of the responsibility attached to the freedom to determine one's actions. Aphasia takes many forms in this fiction and it is generally seen as part of a process through which women learn to value themselves and learn to contribute to and work as a community. The narratives are set within or acknowledge a harsh dystopian future as part of their diegesis. Language and the power of speech are seen as holding counter-cultural potential. In the cyberpunk novels language is often referred to as a virus. In *Native Tongue* it is unknown what releasing a new language will do.

> All right, then suppose we begin to use it, as you say we should do. And then as more and more little girls acquire Láadan and begin to express the perceptions of women rather than those of men, reality will begin to change, isn't that true?[14]

Language is seen as something more complex than a social variable, a magic cure or a narrative resolution. It reveals complicity and the responsibility of the speaker or listener. The fiction combines a representation of women's experience in a male-dominated culture with linguistics as a central speculative concept. Women's autonomy is seen to exist within the reciprocated relations of a community—a community which can operate because it can communicate clearly and freely. The books address a need for women to challenge the patriarchal base of language if they are to change the patriarchal base of society. Silence is a major part of that imaginative process.

In Greek the term *ataxeria* makes a connection between silence and freedom from anxiety. The anxiety predominant in these narratives is pain and death, which is one of the ways that Slonczewski's *whitetrance* is used. There is however also a fear for the loss of agency. Silence is not just the result of fear: it allows protagonists to conquer fear and thus escape their social incapacitation. Le Guin acknowledges this duality in one of her 'sayings from the valley' in *Always Coming Home* (1985):

> When I'm afraid I listen to the silence of field-mice
> When I'm fearless I listen to the silence of the mousing cat.[15]

The creation of a new language and the freedom to explore history and the possibility of change allows women to share collective experience. This new language is used to illustrate a democracy where all can speak. The feminist texts view social change as a long-term plan. This is very much the case in *Always Coming Home* (1985) where Le Guin sets out her society by examining its imaginary form through a melange of ethnographic and anthropological data. A decisive moment in the history of this future post-nuclear war Northern California society is the confrontation between a patriarchal and a matrilineal society. The distinction between the two forms of social organization is examined in terms of culture, and the management of resources, ineffective economies and land use result in personal and societal impoverishment. One of the most effective contrasts between the two societies is found in their use of language:

> The Dayao [patriarchy] seemed never to decide things together, never discussing and arguing and yielding and agreeing to do something before they did it. Everything was done because there was a law to do it or not to do it, or an order to do it or not to do it. And if something went wrong it seemed never to be the orders, but the people who obeyed them who got blamed. [16]

As Burdekin has already acknowledged the relationship between silence and complicity, these novels negotiate the relationship between action and responsibility. They do so by extending metaphors around the power of language, silence and speech. As Offred in *The Handmaid's Tale* is able to remember her mother's stories about the feminist movement in the 1960s and 1970s, she also remembers the Commander's wife Serena Joy from an Evangelical television programme:

> She wasn't singing then. She was making speeches. She was good at it. Her speeches were all about the sanctity of the home, about how women should stay home... She doesn't make speeches anymore. She has become speechless. She stays at home, but it doesn't seem to agree with her. How furious she must be, now that she has been taken at her word.[17]

The conclusion to these novels is not decisive. Speech has often been created and the aphasia of women has produced wise counsel. However, the new status quo is seen as fragile and only sustainable if the members of the community are committed to talk and to engage in the continual creation of language and the shared experience this engenders.

Once more the clearest example of this is the conclusion to *The Handmaid's Tale*, where we are returned as readers to Atwood's framing device for the novel (i.e. the lecture being given to the Twelfth Symposium on Gileadan Studies). The text that has just been read by the reader (or heard in the fiction) is now addressed as something which requires interpretation. We do not know what happened to Offred, but like the characters at the symposium we can celebrate the consignment of Gilead to a future past. However, for Atwood this is a precarious course, and we need to be vigilant in public speech and private study.

In exploring these diegeses with clear dystopian or utopian contingencies the eytmological, legal and social construction of language forms part of the way in which these narratives return to the grim realities and histories of gendered experience. This is a practice which is unwelcome in the hegemonic consensus of a post-feminist, consumer-orientated society.

Notes

  1 Suzy Mckee Charnas, *Walk to the End of the World & Motherlines* (London: The Women's Press, 1989), p. 1.

  2 Suzanne Haden Elgin, *Native Tongue* (London: The Women's Press, 1985).

  3 Margaret Atwood, *The Handmaid's Tale* (London: Virago, 1987).

  4 Katherine Burdekin, *Swastika Night* (London: Lawrence and Wishart, 1985 [1937]).

  5 Sarah Lefanu, *In the Chinks of the World Machine: Feminism and Science Fiction* (London: The Women's Press, 1988), p. 59.

  6 Margaret Piercy, *He She and It* (New York: Knopf, 1991). N.B. this novel was published as *Body of Glass* in the UK.

  7 S. Miller Gearhart, *The Wanderground* (London: The Women's Press, 1979).

8 Anthony Burgess, *A Clockwork Orange* (London: Heinemann, 1962).

9 Sheri S. Tepper, *The Gate to Women's Country* (New York: Doubleday, 1988).

10 Joan Slonczewski, *A Door into Ocean* (London: The Women's Press, 1987), p. 274.

11 Haden Elgin, *Native Tongue*, p. 93.

12 Haden Elgin, *Native Tongue*.

13 L. Irigary, *This Sex Which is Not One* (New York: Cornell University Press, 1985).

14 Haden Elgin, *Native Tongue*, p. 250.

15 Ursula K. Le Guin, *Always Coming Home* (London: Gollancz, 1986), p. 312.

16 Le Guin, *Always Coming Home*, p. 348.

17 Atwood, *The Handmaid's Tale*, p. 56.

'My Particular Virus': (Re-)Reading Jack Womack's Dryco Chronicles

ANDREW M. BUTLER

There is a moment in Jack Womack's *Terraplane* which describes a fault that I am liable to indulge in this chapter: the narrator Luther observes: 'The love of plot is my disease'.[1] It is in the nature of the following analysis to be plot-driven. But this invocation of disease leads me in turn to refer to a virus. In the afterword to *Heathern*, Jack Womack notes 'If *Heathern* is the first or, for that matter, second exposure that you have had to my particular virus, I should recommend that you now read, or reread, in this order, *Ambient* and *Terraplane*'.[2] Of course, a disease is 'an ailment' and a virus is something which is transmitted, but in popular usage, the two can be interchangeable. The plot transmits, reproduces and mutates like a virus through the Dryco Chronicles.

Womack's Dryco Chronicles is projected to be a six-book series consisting of *Ambient* (1988), *Terraplane* (1988), *Heathern* (1990), *Elvissey* (1993), *Random Acts of Senseless Violence* (1993) and the book which completes the sequence, which has yet to be written. This chapter will investigate the different ways in which they can be read, according to the order in which they are read, and will examine the position of these books within post-*Neuromancer* sf.

Many of the books come with cover endorsements from William Gibson. In one quotation, Gibson describes the book's impact as 'A jarringly potent kick in the head.'[3] In another he compares it with his own work: '[*Terraplane*'s] mostly set in an unbelievably bad New York of the near future. If you dropped the characters from *Neuromancer* into his Manhattan, they'd fall down screaming and have nervous breakdowns.'[4] This suggests that, even if these books are not actually cyberpunk, then the reader who likes cyberpunk will approve of them. But whether these books are cyberpunk or not surely depends on how we define the genre.

In my paper on Neal Stephenson's *Snow Crash* and Jeff Noon's *Vurt*, given at the Strange Attractors conference in 1994, I isolated three areas of supposed novelty in cyberpunk that critics, often critics new to sf, seemed to have latched onto: a computer-generated realm, language and character. I will quote what I said about the second and third areas, as I have not altered my position on these:

> Cyberpunk was supposed to be linguistically dense, but that was there in Alfred Bester and Pohl and Kornbluth in the 1950s. Finally cyberpunk was meant to be streetwise, featuring pushers and prostitutes rather than rocket scientists and their beautiful, dutiful daughters. But even this is prefigured in something like Samuel R. Delany's *Dhalgren*.[5]

Certainly the linguistic density applies to Womack's writings; referring to *Terraplane* I suggested that 'through time travel, rock and roll met James Joyce with the ultraviolence and linguistic excess of *A Clockwork Orange*'.[6] The characters in several of the books speak an odd combination of slang, abbreviations and nouns converted to verbs:

> Aiming Bronxward up Broadway our car carried us home; through smoked windows we eyed tripleshifters deconstructing the walls between Harlem and Washington Heights as the northern, higher parts of Manhattan underwent their own regooding... I'd lived there as a child. We'd grown together in Washington Heights, me and Judy and poor lost Lola, inloading info, streetsmarting, grasping our world's way in a moment's breath if and when essentialled; I regooded myself, once I left.[7]

The use of 'Aiming Bronxward up Broadway' sets it within a New York which should be at least faintly familiar to almost all readers: the Bronx, along with Manhattan, Harlem and Brooklyn, is an area known from its depiction in countless American films and television programmes, and Broadway is familiar to those with a knowledge of theatre and musicals. Indeed, Manhattan and Harlem are mentioned later in the sentence, along with Washington Heights, a less well-known area which would now be associated with New York by the reader: a mental map of their journey is being built up. However, the coining of 'Bronxward' abstracts a particular district into a direction or tendency, as much as a place which it is possible to visit. The passivity of being 'carried' by the car suggests either that they are being driven by a chauffeur—and are perhaps so familiar with this as not to notice—or that technology is such that cars operate on automatic pilot.

'We eyed' is an acceptable usage already in existence, carrying connotations of suspicions or a wariness on the part of the one who is looking. A 'tripleshifter' is also an existing coinage, given in the *Oxford English Dictionary* but not defined. It presumably works on the model of 'doubleshifting', where two sets of workers work alternating periods in a mine or factory. 'Tripleshifters' presumably work with three groups, of eight hours each. This suggests a shorter shift, and therefore an improvement on the real world. (On the other hand, if Womack is using it on the model of working a double shift, in the sense of working two shifts on the trot, then tripleshifting is much worse.)

'Deconstructing' is unlikely to be used in the precise sense that Derrida would have used it; it is far more likely to be taken to mean taking apart down to the smallest brick, rather than any deeper philosophical invocation of unsettling binary oppositions and double readings. 'Regooding' is, however, a term that has the paradoxical sense that deconstruction often carries: it is referring to a kind of salvation, of returning to the good from an evil past, or rather of returning to the status of a prior golden age before the current evil-tinged one. This relies upon a nostalgic yearning for a world that never was, and a naïve trust in the possibility of salvation that is unlikely to be borne out by experience. As we shall see, the possibility of salvation is crucial to the sequence, as indeed is the impossibility of yet achieving it.

'Inloading info' is a rather dehumanizing metaphor for learning and education; 'streetsmarting' a rather clumsy yoking to imply that the characters were streetwise. 'Smart' perhaps suggests the importance of living on one's wits, outsmarting others, adapting to situations as they occur rather than the much drier idea of being wise. This is supported by the rather poetic feel to 'grasping our world's way in a moment's breath'. This could be taken to mean that they were ready to adapt in an instant to a new situation, 'a moment's breath' being even shorter in feel than a moment. 'Essentialled' is another coining, transferring an adjective into a verb.

The language here both creates a world for the reader, who is constructing an imagined environment from what she is reading, and emphasizes how different this environment is from the real world. At the same time, the individual reader obviously makes parallels with her own usages and experience, and is always comparing the fictional with the real. In *Elvissey* the language is arguably at its most complex; in the following novel Womack returns to a style which is more familiar from the present. However, as *Random Acts* is told from the point of view of a teenage girl, it never quite becomes 'standard' American English. The language does develop, but as the character (the 'poor lost Lola' referred to in the above extract) ages, she begins to learn the street speech and slang of the future rather than grammatically correct English.

The central characters in Womack are often security guards and mistresses rather than heroic scientists, and in *Random Acts of Senseless Violence* the three main characters are part of the gang from the above extract. This is, as I have noted, suggestive of a cyberpunk sensibility. What prevents Womack's sequence from becoming cyberpunk is the lack of computers and cyberspace.[8] But what cyberspace represents—a kind of 'consensual hallucination',[9] another realm different to yet overlapping with our own, a hell into which characters enter to rescue someone or something in order to solve a problem in the 'real' realm—is here. If not entirely cyberpunk, then the sequence is, as Geoff Ryman wrote in his review of *Vurt*, 'cyberpunk-seasoned'.[10]

Put at its simplest, the sequence presents a future history of the world, centred on the Dryco Organisation, founded by Thatcher Dryden, who is a former drug dealer. America's decline into violence is matched by the rise of this corporation, despite the corporation's various attempts to improve society for the good of the corporation—despite attempts to regood it. But rather than writing a book followed by five sequels, Womack has alternated between sequel and prequel. The internal chronology of the sequence is such that the events occur in the order: *Random Acts of Senseless Violence, Heathern, Ambient, Terraplane, Elvissey*.

This tactic is hardly new. Asimov's original Foundation trilogy is not published in the order that it was written; it begins with a novella on Psychohistory which was written last. C.S. Lewis's Narnia books were completed by *The Magician's Nephew*, a prequel to *The Lion, the Witch and the Wardrobe*. Nowadays it is published as if it is the first of the sequence. Cynically, we could argue that once a series is successful, then the author can make more money by selling a prequel, a prologue or a prelude, particularly if it is written much later than the rest of the sequence and can therefore be labelled 'The long-awaited overture' or some such designation. In Womack's case, the decision to write prequels came early in the process: 'After I started *Ambient*, I realized I needed to get the rest of the picture. The whole concept came to me about half-way through, but I knew I'd have to write four to five books to cover the rest... The reason I did them non-chronologically was just that *Ambient* was the first one I did, and that came right in the middle of the series.'[11]

In the case of the Foundation trilogy and the Narnia chronicles, the tendency is to read these in the internally chronological order. Womack, in the afterword to *Heathern*, seems to argue that we should do the same; but two books later he is suggesting that we should start with *Random Acts of Senseless Violence*: 'I've slightly altered the reading order; I would say *Random Acts of Senseless Violence* and *Heathern* take place concurrently, I would recommend, to those readers who haven't come to me before or

the readers who read me again to start read *Random Acts* first.'[12] The novel
is written in diary format, supposedly by an upper-middle-class twelve-
year-old girl living in New York on Saturday 15 February 1997.
Unfortunately Lola's fortunes are going to change: her father's living as a
screen writer is increasingly precarious, their servants have been made
redundant, and they have to move to a less wealthy neighbourhood, the
Lower East Side. There Lola's father gets a job working in a bookshop,
under a psychopathic boss. As her family disintegrates around her, Lola
finds company in a gang of African-American girls, including Isobel and
Jude. It is a violent time, with five presidents killed in one year, and Lola
herself commits one coldblooded act of revenge as she loses her sanity.
Evidence for her failing abilities might be found in the dating of the novel—
whereas it clearly starts in 1997 on p. 8, by p. 13 it has 23 February as a
Saturday, rather than a Sunday. Some dates are a day late. On balance
1997 is the most likely year. Alternatively, of course, Womack may have
miscalculated.[13]

  Heathern takes us into the world of Dryco, and its leader Thatcher
Dryden's attempts to jockey for power in, according to the blurb, 1998.
Told from the point of view of Joanna, Dryden's mistress, it is an account
of Dryco's failed attempt to use school teacher Lester Macaffrey as a
messiah. Macaffrey has been performing miracles, and is seen as a potential
asset to Dryco: world salvation is a sellable commodity. This plot is tangled
up with Japanese rival Otsuka's corporation, which appears to have
infiltrated Dryco. The messiah plan fails, and the novel ends with Joanna,
apparently transformed into a messiah herself, flying from the top of a
building.

  Ambient is set sometime in the teens of the twenty-first century, once
more within the Dryco Organisation. But here Thatcher Dryden is Thatcher
Dryden Jr, the idiot son who briefly appears in *Heathern*. Seamus O'Malley,
one of Dryden Jr's bodyguards, falls in love with his boss's mistress Avalon,
and is caught up in a plot to assassinate Drydens Sr and Jr. Dryden Sr's
paranoia was such that he has programmed a computer named Alice—
glimpsed briefly a couple of times in *Heathern* as something designed to
help Dryden Jr—to have a fifty-fifty chance of setting off the nuclear
weapons in orbit, thus wiping out life on earth. The novel closes with
Dryden senior dead and Alice running through her program, the future of
humanity hanging on the toss of a virtual coin.

  In *Terraplane*, Avalon and Seamus are running Dryco. The novel
concentrates on events arising from their Russian interests. Luther
Biggerstaff is looking for a Russian scientist Alekhine, who has some sort
of device Dryco desires, and who has gone missing. Instead Luther takes
Alekine's assistant, Oktobriana, and is pursued back to America. Under

attack, they engage Alekhine's device, and travel in time back to a parallel 1939, where racism is rife and blues singer Robert Johnson has not been murdered. Luther eventually returns to the twenty-first century, but his bodyguard Jake commits suicide in transit after his lover Oktobriana has died of a mystery disease. The disease here is perhaps that he is now unnecessary to the plot.

Elvissey, set in 2033, combines the plots of *Heathern* and *Terraplane*: using the time travel machine Dryco kidnaps Elvis Presley from 1954 to bring him to the present to be used as a messiah for the many believers in Elvis's divinity. Again, Dryco sees salvation as a commodity which will give them power, but, again, the plan fails. There is an elegiac tone to the book, a tying up of threads. We finally work out what happened to Joanna: 'She'd suicided as well... yet another mindaddled.'[14] A portrait of the Dryden family is described: 'Mrs Dryden lounged in a wingbacked chair, squeezed twixt her men fore and aft, glaring at her onlookers with eyes appearing borrowed for the occasion... Mrs Dryden's hand rested in semblance of blessing atop her teenager's brow, who sprawled on the carpet before her, his head brushing her knees ... His leggings' shadows revealed an untoward bulge, as if mother's touch comforted more than was proper... Thatcher Dryden stood behind his wife as if he'd crept up to surprise.'[15] The narrator of *Elvissey* is Isobel, who we learn grew up in the Lower East Side with Crazy Lola and Avalon,[16] who was then called Jude or Judy. Dryco is attempting to reform—regood—itself, and to improve the world, particularly by rebuilding New York. But Dryco still has a long way to go before it is an ethical organization, as Isobel finds to her cost.

Read this way, the sequence tells of a New York descending into barbarism, with occasional attempts at resurrection from despair. From a depressing start of Lola's shattered world, we witness murder, racism, double-crosses and Machiavellian activities of all kinds. But read in the order that Womack wrote them, new patterns emerge. For example, *Ambient* opens with Thatcher Dryden's visit to a bookstore, *Random Acts of Senseless Violence* ends with Lola's bloody revenge on the bookstore owner who abused her father.

Elvis, a character in *Elvissey*, appears first on the first page of the first book, *Ambient*: 'Mr Dryden, like his father, loved E.'[17] The C of E or Church of Elvis features, but it is not until *Elvissey* that it takes centre stage. In *Elvissey*, we can see Jude and Isobel's troubled relationship; if we proceed to the next book, *Random Acts of Senseless Violence*, we can watch their childhood traumas and view the two in a deeper light.

This childhood is invoked at a slight remove in a sequence in chapter seven of *Heathern* when Thatcher Dryden, the narrator Joanna and bodyguards go to visit the Japanese Otsuka, in order to sign a deal with him. Joanna remembers the landscape they are travelling through as being once much friendlier: 'Brick apartments, fifteen or sixteen stories high, would have stood at the avenues... The shopkeepers of the street would know you as a customer as they'd known your mother; as they believe, and believed, they'd know your daughter.'[18] This is a childhood very much to be contrasted with that described in *Random Acts*—understandably, as it is set more or less contemporaneously with *Heathern*. On the other hand, it does not fit with the parallel pasts glimpsed in *Terraplane* and *Elvissey*, written either side of *Heathern*. But the scene does fit in with the information given in a scene already quoted from above: Isobel travelling north along Broadway in *Elvissey*. Here, in *Heathern*, we are told something of the history of this throughfare: 'the car [was...] swinging north onto Broadway. Once the avenue ran one-way from Columbus Circle; Thatcher, surely for no reason other than to show that he could have it done, decreed that its traffic should race salmon-like upstream.'[19] No matter in which order the reader comes to these sequences, the journey up Broadway is associated with memories of childhood. The reader who progesses from *Heathern* to *Elvissey*, whether on internal or external chronology, will realize at that point how far the landscape has been controlled by the Drydens. Should a reader come to the lines in the other order, then the effect is less striking: the world of the Drydens is well established in *Elvissey* and petty changes seem par for the course.

Prior to this journey, Joanna learns from a conversation with Bernard, one of Dryden's advisors, that a supercomputer is being constructed to oversee operations: '[A generation] number twelve, or what in theory is called, I believe, the Algorithmic Logistical Interactive whatchamacallit hoozis.'[20] In addition to being a slight tip of the hat to *2001: A Space Odyssey*'s HAL (Heuristically programmed ALgorithmic computer), it provides a history for the computer which has been mentioned as featuring in *Ambient* and *Terraplane*: ALICE. For the reader who comes first to *Terraplane*, and then *Heathern*, there is a sense of history being opened out, of Womack providing a richer history for his world. The reader who comes to it the other way round will find a throwaway line or idea developed into an actual invention.

Otsuka's conversations with Dryden revolve around racism, and memories of an enmity between the States and Japan dating back to Pearl Harbor, reinforced by a distrust of all races Asiatic following the Korean and Vietnam Wars. Otsuka makes a link between the American and Nazi ways of life: 'In some ways Americans would be ideal Nazis, but in the long run it would never work. Every man would insist upon being his own Führer.'[21] In *Elvissey*, the prospect of a Nazi America is explored in some depth, as the political basis of the parallel 1954 from which Elvis is to be kidnapped. This in turn is a plausible descendant from the tendencies of a racist country depicted in *Terraplane*'s 1939. The reader who reads *Heathern* early on in a reading of the sequence is thus alerted to look out for instances of Nazism, reaching a zenith in *Elvissey*. If *Heathern* is read after *Elvissey*, then a frisson of irony will be felt.

The encounter with the Japanese is a follow-on from the encounter with the Soviet world in *Terraplane*. In *Heathern* the signing of the treaty is followed by the killing of Otsuka, who Dryden knows is involved in events in Costa Rica that threaten Dryco, and may yet be planning to kill Dryden: retaliation occurs in advance. The treaty holds; even though Dryco and Japan are effectively at war, there are some points on which they can co-operate for mutual gain. A reader who then reads *Terraplane*, where co-operation between Dryco and some elements of the Soviet Union is going on despite thirty years of war between America and the Soviet Union, is immediately suspicious. Luther and his bodyguard Jake are dealing with Skuratov, who is able to carry on a conversation with them loyal to the state, whilst communicating with them in a code about kidnapping a scientist. Eventually Skuratov is indeed revealed to be an agent of the Dream Team, an equivalent of the KGB, and thus part of some greater conspiracy. A reader who progresses from *Terraplane* to *Heathern* would have a similar suspicion of the encounter with the Japanese, but the suspense is not so drawn out.

Along with Otsuka, the bodyguard Gus is killed, and a new recruit, Jake, stands as the saviour of the Drydens. Jake acquires a samurai sword: 'Taking up Otsuka's sword from the desk, where the associate had dropped it unsheathed, he tied its strap around his waist.'[22] In *Ambient* and *Terraplane* we have already met the bodyguard Jake, with his samurai sword, and see him die. To progress from *Heathern* to *Ambient* to *Terraplane* is to watch the career of a bodyguard from start to finish. On the other hand, to progress from *Terraplane* to *Heathern* is almost to watch a character being resurrected. His past is being fleshed out, adding a richness not previously apparent to the character.

The idea of salvation or resurrection recurs, in one form or another, throughout the sequence, particularly when dealing with messiah figures. In *Ambient*, mention is made of Macaffrey, Godness, and Joanna; in *Heathern* we finally meet them. The book mentioned in *Ambient*, *Visions of Joanna*, consisting of 'the messages of Macaffrey as told by Joanna',[23] should be perhaps thought of as a fraud if Joanna dies at the end of *Heathern*, as suggested in *Elvissey*—when did she have time to write them down? But then this should not be a surprise: Macaffrey and Joanna's followers use parts of the Bible, which by then we know is not as it seems:

The Q documents ... were the long-lost original gospels. They detailed how Jesus, a trusting sort, was hired by Pilate to spread confusion among warring Jewish factions; how Judas found out and so betrayed his betrayer; how Jesus, pulled from the cross in time's nick by those wishing to use the affair for their own effect, recovered and was by accident seen by his horrified followers; how some of his followers were so horrified that they wished to kill him—again; how Jesus escaped with his wife, Mary Magdalene; how he died, at an advanced age, somewhere far from Gethsemane.[24]

From the start, then, Womack describes a world in desperate need of salvation, and one where salvation myths have great currency. In real life, Womack is a bit more cynical about salvation: 'The fun about sinning is that you can repent, and vice versa, and sometimes it seems to me that's been the whole of human history, just a question of like, "OK, I'm going to do better now," and it does better until it just can't control itself and then does worse again.'[25] The worlds described in the Dryco Chronicles are in a moral trough, forever waiting for the improvements to come.

At this point I want to return to the idea of cyberpunk-seasoned fiction, and my paper on *Snow Crash* and *Vurt*. In that, I noted that both were retellings of the myth of the visit to the Underworld. In Noon's *Pollen*, published since then,[26] this becomes even more obvious with a character called Persephone, and a visit to an underworld complete with a three-headed dog and a river to cross.

This link was first made by Joan Gordon, who argues in her essay 'Yin and Yang Duke it Out' that cyberspace represents a communing with the dead, a visit to the Underworld. Writing specifically of feminist sf, she argues that cyberpunk has an 'extensive and gritty handling of the motif of the journey to the underworld... In every case, the trip reveals the underside of the human condition... A version of the mythic journey...will help us capture our dark side.'[27] Seen in this way, cyberpunk, far from being a new genre in the 1980s, has its roots in stories dating back at least as far as the third millennium BC. As Graham Dunstan Martin pointed out to me,[28] another version of this story is the Harrowing of Hell where Christ, according to legend, descends to hell to rescue the dead. Cyberspace is any space beyond the everyday ontological one: there is no actual up and down, no actual volume. The computer-generated realm is a virtual one, outside of the body, the underworld/afterlife realm is beyond the body. But both the computer-generated and the afterlife realms are treated *as if* they *are* spatial.

The visits to the underworld to rescue Eurydice, Desdemona (*Vurt*) and Juanita/Inanna (*Snow Crash*) involve a male hero rescuing an idealized female; but the rescue seems not as important as the transformation of the hero through an increased knowledge of his self or of the nature of reality.[29] The effect of the transformation is in some degree dependent upon the success of the rescue and the return of the rescuer. Perhaps a more apt model is that the fictional environment is faced by a problem which cannot be solved in the 'actual' realm. The solution is to be found by entering into a different realm, at great risk to the travelling hero.

In the Dryco Chronicles, the problem is the disintegration of law and order, along with the basic fabric of society. In a realm of assassinations, random violence and self-interested multinational corporations—first delineated in either *Ambient* or *Random Acts of Senseless Violence*, according to taste—solutions must be found elsewhere.

In *Heathern*'s Macaffrey we have a messiah in contact with forces beyond the real world, but he is killed before Dryco can make use of this. The action remains in 'this' fictional realm. In *Terraplane* and *Elvissey*,[30] a trip is made to another realm, one in the past, which is in an entirely different universe, and thus must surely be of a different order of being. No matter how bad the realm of Dryco gets—and it gets pretty bad—this alternative realm is even worse. With Churchill and Roosevelt dead, and Stalin assassinated, nothing stops Hitler in his march across Europe. The visit here is surely one to hell, from which Elvis is rescued. In both cases a messiah is sought, and with it a sense a transcendence, of something beyond this world— something perhaps we seek in sf, a conversation with the other, the radically different and strange.

Of course, it fails; it has to for the sake of the sequence. Book six is yet to come. *If* the world is to be saved, *if* Dryco regoods itself with the rest of the world, then the sequence has been closed. Gaps and elisions in the history may be filled in, but anything further will be a mistake. The regooding so far has been misguided, a kind of 'forced moral rearmament'. Dryco has become so large, so smug in its position as dominator of the world that it cannot be controlled from the centre any more. The back-to-basics policy, as borne witness to in the real-world counterparts to the United States and Britain, only succeeds in revealing more sleaze, more immorality. If salvation is to be seen as a product, it is a commodity that must be demanded from a broad-based, grass-roots market, rather than being supplied from a dominating corporation.

I wish to close with some speculation on the nature of the sixth book. If we follow the sequel-prequel-sequel-prequel pattern we should expect a sequel, probably set in the mid-2030s—we have two novels set in 1997–1998, two set in the teens of the twenty-first century and one set fifteen years later in 2033.[31] It will surely tell of a true messiah—or as true to a messiah as the sequence can have—and will probably involve more time travel and musicians. Will Buddy Holly be the next messiah?

Hopefully not.[32] The task of pulling off a convincing solution to the Dryco Chronicles which brings a credible salvation seems a difficult one, and perhaps explains why Womack put off writing it. All that Womack has revealed so far is that most of the characters seen so far will not be returning, with the possible exception of Joanna: '[She] has essentially been sitting on Long Island for six years, waiting to know exactly what it is a messiah is supposed to do.'[33] I hope the book, entitled *Going, Going, Gone*, is worthy of the words which will no doubt grace its cover: 'the long-awaited conclusion'.

Notes

1 Jack Womack, *Terraplane* (New York: Tor, 1990), p. 188.
2 Jack Womack, *Heathern* (New York: Tor, 1991), p. 215. As I will explain later, Womack now recommends that the reader start with *Random Acts of Senseless Violence*.
3 Jack Womack, *Elvissey* (London: HarperCollins, 1993).
4 Jack Womack, *Random Acts of Senseless Violence* (London: HarperCollins, 1993) and *Terraplane*.
5 Andrew M. Butler, 'Being Beyond the Body? Neal Stephenson's *Snow Crash* and Jeff Noon's *Vurt*', in *Strange Attractors*, ed. Mark Bould (Plymouth: Mark Bould, 1995), p. 66.
6 Butler, 'Being Beyond the Body?', p. 66. Veronica Hollinger made a link between the teenaged narrators of *A Clockwork Orange*, Russell Hoban's *Riddley Walker* and *Random Acts of Senseless Violence* in her paper at Speaking Science Fiction. Without rejecting the validity of the comparisons, it must be noted that Womack does not like these particular two novels, as he admitted to me in an interview on 29 January 1997:

> AMB: What about Anthony Burgess's *A Clockwork Orange*?
> JW: I had read that but not liked it; in fact I never finished it. I loved the movie, but the book I could just never really get through… [laughter]
> AMB: It's always being mentioned in relation to your work.
> JW: Oh, they stuck it on early, early on, and it's just like, but I liked Burgess's nonfiction writings, his writings on music, his essays on Joyce but his fiction never really caught me. And *Clockwork Orange* was… I was just so, it was like *Riddley Walker* which also crops up periodically –
> AMB: Yes, that was next on the list!
> JW: I've just never been able really to get through either of those books. I just don't have the patience, I suppose, to do the sort of things I subject my own readers to on a smaller scale.

Andrew M. Butler, 'Tomorrow Had Already Happened: An Interview with Jack Womack', *Vector*, 123 (May/June 1997), p. 5.
7 Womack, *Elvissey*, p. 24.
8 Although a large computer named Alice does play a role in some of the action. When asked about this omission, Womack replied: 'Computers—thinking about it, looking at it, what I suspect it'll be like in the future, what has certainly been the case as I've gotten my laptop and worked on it—it's just computers, will be just one of those things that you just don't notice in thirty years. It'll just be like, I think I've seen a description one time, where you

worry about your computer in the same way you'll be really deeply concerned about the motor in your refrigerator. They'll be everywhere but just not noticed.' ('Tomorrow Had Already Happened', p. 6).

9 William Gibson, *Neuromancer* (London: Grafton: 1986), p. 67: 'Cyberspace. A consensual hallucination experienced daily by billions'.

10 Geoff Ryman, '*Vurt*', *Foundation*, 61 (Summer 1994), p. 90. More accurate would be 'cyberpunk-flavoured' on the model of 'chocolate-flavoured'—it looks and tastes like chocolate, but is in fact something else, it is a simulated chocolate.

11 Jack Womack, 'Random Acts: Jack Womack', *Locus* # 413, 34.6 (Jan. 1995), p. 73.

12 'Tomorrow Had Already Happened', p. 6. But note he has written elsewhere: 'it's best to read *Heathern* first, because stylistically *Random Acts* is where the language goes from the straight English in *Heathern* to the more futuristic style in *Ambient*' (*Locus*, p. 73).

13 In conversation Womack suggested to me that it was something he had either not bothered to look up or had accidentally got wrong. He attributed no special meaning to it.

14 Womack, *Elvissey*, p. 50.

15 Womack, *Elvissey*, pp. 72–73.

16 Compare Avalon's words in *Ambient* (London: Unwin, 1989), p. 31: 'Crazy Lola. We grew up on the same block. She's fuckin' psycho.'

17 Womack, *Ambient*, p. 6.

18 Womack, *Heathern*, p. 110.

19 Womack, *Heathern*, pp. 107–108.

20 Womack, *Heathern*, p. 104.

21 Womack, *Heathern*, p. 115.

22 Womack, *Heathern*, p. 12.

23 Womack, *Ambient*, p. 157.

24 Womack, *Ambient*, p. 80.

25 *Locus*, p. 74.

26 Jeff Noon, *Pollen* (Greater Manchester: Ringpull, 1995).

27 Joan Gordon, 'Yin and Yang Duke it Out', in Larry McCaffery, ed., *Storming the Reality Studio: A Casebook of Cyberpunk and Postmodern Science Fiction* (Durham and London: Duke University Press, 1991), pp. 201–202. It would seem in this case that the 'our' is gendered female; Gordon advocates a female cyberpunk to counter 'The boys' club'.

28 In the question and answer session following the paper at the University of Reading.

29 It must be said that *Snow Crash*, befitting its parodic inclinations, resists this. It is difficult to believe that Hiro/Hero has here learned anything. His enemies still undefeated, Hiro remains behind in the Metaverse and takes refuge in the economic solution of advising hackers about the snow crash virus. Meanwhile the female protagonist Y.T. quietly gets on and saves the world.

30 In the former the trip is almost accidental, in the second it is planned. In the latter, the rescue variant of the visit to the underworld motif is unusual in that it is a husband-and-wife team rather than a lover seeking his or her loved one. In *Terraplane* Luther returns with a 'rescued' loved one and Jake loses himself with the dead Oktobriana between the two realms.

31 Womack has written: 'At some point in the future I will wrap it all up with a volume that takes place 15 years after *Elvissey*', *Locus*, p. 74.

32 AMB: Is Buddy Holly next on the list?

JW: No, no, I could never do that, I would never do that, nor will there be any reintroduction of Elvis, or the Big Bopper, Gene Vincent or Eddie Cochrane.

AMB: Bob Dylan?

JW: I'm going to avoid him, though at some point you might get a brief glimpse of The Velvet Underground, anyway.

'Tomorrow Had Already Happened', p. 6.

33 Given that she is last seen at the end of *Heathern*, set in 1998, this suggests that part of the action will take place in 2004.

Aliens in the Fourth Dimension

GWYNETH JONES

When Two Worlds Collide

The aliens can always speak English. This is one of those absurdities of pulp fiction and B movies, like saucer-shaped spaceships and hairdryer machines that track your brain waves,[1] that might well come true—suppose the visitors avoid those disconcerting forms of long-haul space travel that whisk you across the galaxy and dump you in the concourse of Lime Street station before you have time to say 'Non-Smoking'. If they come in slowly they'll spend the latter part of their journey travelling through a vast cloud of human broadcasting signals, which they'll easily pick up on the alien cabin TV. They'll have plenty of time to acquire a smattering of useful phrases. Or so the current received wisdom goes—I'd love some expert to tell me if this idea makes sense, by the way. By now it's not completely inevitable that they'll speak English, and with a United States accent, in the traditional manner. They might get hooked on Brazilian soap opera. But whatever formal, articulate language our visitors use in real life, all the aliens we know so far speak human. They speak our human predicament, our history, our hopes and fears, our pride and shame. As long as we haven't met any actual no-kidding intelligent extraterrestrials (and I would maintain that this is still the case, though I know opinions are divided) the aliens we imagine are always other humans in disguise: no more, no less. Whether or not hell is other people, it is certainly other people who arrive, in these fictions, to challenge our isolation: to be feared or worshipped, interrogated, annihilated, appeased. When the historical situation demands it science fiction writers demonize our enemies, the way the great Aryan court poet[2] who wrote the story of Prince Rama demonized the Dravidian menace, in India long ago. Or we can use imaginary aliens to assuage our guilt. I think it's not unlikely that our European ancestors invented the little people who live in the hills, cast spells and are 'ill to cross'—who appear so often in traditional fiction north of the Mediterranean and west of Moscow—to explain why their cousins the

Neanderthals had mysteriously vanished from public life. I see the same thing happening today, as science fiction of the environmentally conscious decades becomes littered with gentle, magical, colourful alien races who live at one with nature in happy non-hierarchical rainforest communities. Even the project of creating an authentically incomprehensible other intelligent species, which is sporadically attempted in science fiction, is inescapably a human story. Do we yet know of any other beings who can imagine, or could care less, what 'incomprehensible' means?

More often than not, the aliens story involves an invasion. The strangers have arrived. They want our planet, and intend to wipe us out. We have arrived. The native aliens—poor ineffectual technologically incompetent creatures—had better get out of the way. The good guys will try to protect them: but territorial expansion, sometimes known as 'progress', is an unstoppable force. This pleasant paradigm of intra-species relations obviously strikes a deep chord. We, in the community of science fiction writers and readers at least, do not expect to co-exist comfortably with other people. Whichever side is 'ours', there is going to be trouble, there is going to be grief, when two worlds collide. And whatever language everyone is speaking, there is definitely going to be a breakdown in communications.

When I invented my alien invaders 'the Aleutians' I was aware of the models that science fiction offered, and of the doubled purpose that they could serve. I wanted, like other writers before me, to tell a story about the colonizers and the colonized. The everlasting expansion of a successful population, first commandment on the Darwinian tablets of stone, makes this encounter 'the supplanters and the natives', an enduring feature of human history. Colonial adventure has been a significant factor in the shaping of my own, European, twentieth-century, culture. I wanted to think about this topic. I wanted to study the truly extraordinary imbalance in wealth, power, and per capita human comfort, from the south to the north, that came into being over three hundred years or so of European rule in Africa, Asia and the Indian subcontinent: an imbalance which did not exist when the Portuguese reached China, when the first British and French trading posts were established on the coasts of India, when European explorers arrived in the gold-empire cities of West Africa.[3] I also wanted—the other layer of the doubled purpose—to describe and examine the relationship between men and women. There are obvious parallels between my culture's colonial adventure and the battle of the sexes. Men come to this world helpless, like bewildered explorers. At first they all have to rely on the goodwill of the native ruler of the forked, walking piece of earth in which they find themselves. And then, both individually and on a global scale, they amass as if by magic a huge proportion of the earth's wealth, power and influence, while the overwhelming majority of those native rulers are doomed to suffer and drudge and starve in the most humiliating conditions. But why? I wondered. How did this come about? Why do most of the women get such a rough deal?

I felt that my historical model would be better for throwing up insights, mental experiments, refutable hypotheses about sexual politics, than other popular 'alien invasion' narratives based on the history of the United States. The possibilities of an outright lebensraum struggle would soon be exhausted; a situation involving any extreme division between master race and slave race would be too clear cut.[4] I needed something in a sense more innocent. A relationship that could grow in intimacy and corruption: a trading partnership where neither party is more altruistic than the other, whichever manages to win the advantage. Most of all, I needed something slow. I needed to see what would happen to my experiment over hundreds of years: over generations, not decades. So, the Aleutians appeared: a feckless crew of adventurers and dreamers, with only the shakiest of State backing, no aim beyond seeing life and turning a quick profit; and no coherent long-term plans whatever.

Interview with the Alien
Some stories about meeting the aliens are recruiting posters for the Darwinian army. Explicitly we're invited to cheer for the home team, or enjoy the pleasurably sad and moving defeat of the losers. Implicitly we're reminded that every encounter with the other, down to office manoeuvring and love affairs, is a fight for territory: and the weak must go to the wall. Some people invent aliens as a utopian or satirical exercise, to show how a really well-designed intelligent species would live and function, and how far the human model falls below this ideal. I confess to adopting elements from both these approaches. But above all, I wanted my aliens to represent an alternative. I wanted them to say to my readers *it ain't necessarily so.*[5] History is not inevitable, and neither is sexual gender as we know it an inevitable part of being human. I didn't intend my aliens to represent 'women', exactly; or for the humans to be seen as 'men' in this context. Human women and men have their own story in the Aleutian books. But I wanted to make them suggestive of another way things could have turned out. I planned to give my alien conquerors the characteristics, all the supposed deficiencies, that Europeans came to see in their subject races in darkest Africa and the mystic East—'animal' nature, irrationality, intuition; mechanical incompetence, indifference to time, helpless aversion to theory and measurement: and I planned to have them win the territorial battle this time. It was no coincidence, for my purposes, that the same list of qualities or deficiencies—a nature closer to the animal, intuitive

communication skills and all the rest of it—were and still are routinely awarded to women—the defeated natives, supplanted rulers of men—in cultures north and south, west and east, white and non-white, the human world over.[6]

They had to be humanoid. I didn't want my readers to be able to distance themselves; or to struggle proudly towards empathy in spite of the tentacles. I didn't want anyone to be able to think, why, they're just like us once you get past the face-lumps, the way we do when we get to know the TV alien goodies and baddies in Babylon 5 or Space Precinct 9. I needed them to be irreducibly weird and, *at the same time*, undeniably people, the same as us. I believe this to be a fairly accurate approximation of the real-world situation—between the Japanese and the Welsh, say, or between women and men; or indeed between any individual human being and the next. Difference is real. It does not go away. To express my contention— that irreducible difference, like genetic variation, is conserved in the individual: not in race, nationality or reproductive function—I often awarded my Aleutians quirks of taste and opinion belonging to one uniquely different middle-aged, middle-class, leftish Englishwoman. And was entertained to find them hailed by US critics as 'the most convincingly *alien* beings to grace science fiction in years'. Now it can be told...

Since they had to be humanoid I made a virtue of the necessity, and had someone explain to my readers that all those ufologists can't be wrong. The human body plan is perfectly plausible, for sound scientific reasons. This led me into interesting territory later on. Whether or not it's true that another planet might well throw up creatures much like us, I don't know. But humanoid aliens certainly make life easier for the science fiction novelist. The control our physical embodiment has over our rational processes is so deep and strong that it's excruciating trying to write about intelligent plasma clouds—if you're in the least worried about verisimilitude. It's a trick, it can be done. But the moment your attention falters your basic programming will restore the defaults of the pentadactyl limb, binocular vision and articulated spine. You'll find your plasma characters cracking hard nuts, grappling with sticky ideas, looking at each other in a funny way, scratching their heads, weaving plots and generally making a third-chimpanzees' tea-party of your chaste cosmic emanations.

They had to be humanoid, and they had to be sexless. I wanted a society that knew nothing about the great divide which allows half the human race to regard the other half as utterly, transcendently, different on the grounds of reproductive function. I wanted complex and interesting people who managed to have lives fully as strange, distressing, satisfying, absorbing, productive as ours, without having any access to that central 'us and themness' of human life. I realized before long that this plan created some aliens who had a very shaky idea, if any, of the concept 'alien'—as applied to another person. Which was a good joke: and like the cosmic standard body plan, it led to interesting consequences. But that came later.

Once my roughly humanoid aliens reached earth, interrogation proceeded along traditional lines. I whisked them into my laboratory for intensive internal examination, with a prurient concentration on sex and toilet habits. In real life (I mean in the novel *White Queen*) the buccaneers resisted this proposal. They didn't know they were aliens, they thought they were merely strangers, and they didn't see why they had to be vivisected before they could have their tourist visas. The humans were too nervous to insist, but a maverick scientist secured a tissue sample... With this same tissue sample in my possession, I was able to establish that the Aleutians were hermaphrodites, to borrow a human term. (I considered parthenogenesis, with a few males every dozen or so generations, like greenfly. But this was what I finally came up with.) Each of them had the same reproductive tract. There was an external organ consisting of a fold or pouch in the lower abdomen, lined with mucous membrane, holding an appendage called 'the claw'. Beyond the porous inner wall of this pouch, known as 'the cup', extended a reservoir of potential embryos—something like the lifetime supply of eggs in human ovaries, but these eggs didn't need to be fertilized. When one or other of these embryos was triggered into growth—not by any analogue of sexual intercourse but by an untraceable complex of environmental and emotional factors—the individual would become pregnant. The new baby, which would grow in the pouch like a marsupial infant until it was ready to emerge, would prove to be one of the three million or so genetically differentiated individuals in a reproductive group known as the 'brood'. (I should point out that I'm going to use the human word 'gene' and related terms throughout, for the alien analogues to these structures.) These same three million people, each one a particular chemically defined bundle of traits and talents, would be born again and again. In Aleutia you wouldn't ask of a newborn baby, 'is it a boy or a girl?'. You'd ask, 'who is it?'. Maybe there'd be a little heelprick thing at the hospital, and then the midwife would tell you whether you'd given birth to someone famous, or someone you knew and didn't like, or someone you vaguely remembered having met at a party once, in another lifetime.

So much for reproduction, but I needed to account for evolution. How could my serial immortals, born-again hermaphrodites, have come to be? How could they continue to adapt to their environment? It was a major breakthrough when I discovered that the brood was held together by a living information network. Every Aleutian had a glandular system constantly generating mobile cell-complexes called 'wanderers' which were shed through the pores of the skin, especially in special areas like the mucous-coated inner walls of the 'cup'. Each wanderer was a chemical snapshot of the individual's current emotional state, their status, experience, their shifting place in the whole brood entity: a kind of tiny self. The Aleutians would pick and eat 'wanderers' from each other's skin in a grooming process very like that which we observe in real-life apes, baboons, monkeys. To offer someone a 'wanderer' would be a common social gesture: *'Hello, this is how I am...'*. Once consumed, the snapshot information would be replicated and shuttled off to the reproductive tract, where it would be compared with the matching potential embryo, and the embryo updated: so that the chemical nature of the person who might be born was continually being affected by the same person's current life. It was a Lamarckian evolution, directly driven by environmental pressure, rather than by the feedback between environment and random mutation, but it looked to me as if it would work well enough. Nothing much would happen from life to life. But over evolutionary time the individual and the whole brood entity would be changing in phase: growing more complex, remembering and forgetting, opening up new pathways, closing down others. I noticed, when I was setting this up, that the *environment* to which my Aleutians were adapting was the rest of Aleutian society, at least as much as the outside world. But that's another story...

I had done away with sexual gender. But if I wanted a society that seemed fully developed to human readers, I couldn't do without passion. I had no wish to create a race of wistful Spocks, or chilly fragments of a hive-mind. The Aleutians must not be deficient in personhood. Luckily I realized that the wanderer system gave me the means to elaborate a whole world of social, emotional and physical intercourse. The Aleutians lived and breathed chemical information, the social exchange of wanderers was essential to their well-being. But they would also be drawn, by emotional attachment, infatuation, fellow feeling or even a need to dominate, to a more intense experience: where the lovers would get naked and *lie down* together, cups opened and fused lip to lip, claws entwined, information flooding from skin to skin, in an ecstasy of chemical communication. They would fall in love with another self the way we—supposedly—fall in love with difference. Romantic souls would always be searching for that special person, as near as possible the same genetic individual as themselves, with whom the mapping would be complete.

More revelations followed. The whole of Aleutian art and religion, I realized, sprang from the concept of the diverse, recurrent Self of the brood. Their whole education and history came from studying the records left behind by their previous selves. Their technology was based on tailored skin-secretions, essentially specialized kinds of wanderers. Their power to manipulate raw materials had grown not through conscious experiment or leaps of imagination, as ours is held to have developed, but by the placid, inchworm trial and error of molecular evolution. Arguably there was only one Aleutian species—if there had ever been more—since this process of infecting the physical world with self-similar chemical information had been going on for aeons. The entire Aleutian environment—buildings, roads, furniture, pets, beasts of burden, transport—was alive with the same life as themselves, the same self.

Once I'd started this machine going, it kept throwing up new ideas. I realized their society was in some ways extremely rigid. Any serial immortal might be born in any kind of social circumstances. But no one could change their ways, or even retrain for a new job, except over millennia of lifetimes. An Aleutian couldn't learn to become a carpenter; or to be generous. You were either born with a chemically defined ability or it was not an option. Aleutians, being built on the same pattern as ourselves but with a highly conservative development programme, revert easily to a four-footed gait. This is good for scaring humans, who see intelligent alien werewolves leaping at them. The obligate cooks use bodily secretions to prepare food: a method quite acceptable in many human communities, where teeth and saliva replace motorized food mixers; and Aleutians all use toilet pads to absorb the minor amount of waste produced by their highly processed diet. I made up this because I liked the image of the alien arriving and saying '*quickly, take me somewhere I can buy some sanitary pads...*'; but then I noticed this was another aspect of the way they don't have a sense of the alien. They don't even go off by themselves to shit. Aleutians live in a soup of shared presence, they are the opposite of Cartesians. They have no horror of personal death (though they can fear it). But things that are intrinsically not alive—like electrons, photons, the image in a mirror or on a screen, they consider uncanny... I could go on, but I won't. We'd be here forever. I believe the elaboration, the proliferation of consequences, could be continued indefinitely. It all goes to show, if anyone needed another demonstration, how much complexity, and what a strange illusion of coherence within that complexity, can be generated from a few simple, arbitrary original conditions.

It's said that the work of science fiction is to make the strange familiar and the familiar strange. I often find that what we do is to take some persistent fiction of contemporary human life, and turn it into science. By the time I'd finished this phase of the interrogation my Aleutians had all the typical beliefs and traditions of one of those caste-ridden, feudal tropical societies doomed to be swept away by the gadget-building bourgeois individualists from the north. They were animists. They believed in reincarnation. They had no hunger for progress, no use for measurement or theory, no obsession with the passage of time. They were, in short, the kind of people we often wish we could be, except we'd rather have jet transport and microwave ovens.[7] But in the Aleutians' case, everything worked; and their massively successful ambient-temperature bio-technology was exactly tailored—as if by a malignant deity—to blow the mechanizers away. They were on course to take over a world, although they didn't know it. Not because they were sacred white-faced messengers from the Sun God or what have you: but because they were *not* weird. By chance they had arrived at the historical moment when that jaded mechanist paradigm was giving out, and they had the goods that everybody on earth was beginning to want. They could do things the locals could do themselves, they had skills the locals could well understand, and they were just that crucial half a move ahead of the game.

Speech and Silence

I interrogated my aliens in the language of science, looking for differences that would work. Eventually I became uneasy about this process. If the Aleutians were in some sense 'supposed to be women', it was disquieting to note that I'd treated them exactly the way male-gendered medicine has treated human women until very recently—behaving as if their repro-ductive system was the only interesting thing about them. I approached their own speech and language with more humility, deliberately trying to remove the division between experimenter and experiment. I had travelled, fairly widely. I had been an alien in many contexts, not least as a girl among the boys. I had observed that though the colour of my skin and the shape of my chest would always be intriguing, I could often be accepted and treated like a person, as long as I made the right gestures. Wherever you go there will be busfares, light switches, supermarkets, airports, taps, power sockets, street food, TV cartoons, music cassette players, advertising hoarding, motorway landscape. Watch what the locals do, and you'll soon adjust to the minor variations in the silent universal language.

One can look on the sameness of the global village as an artefact of cultural imperialism, another bitter legacy of White European rule in all its forms. But I felt that these narrative signs of a single human life, repeated the world over, must be connected to that animal-embodiment we all share, or they would not survive. I had invented new forms of difference, now I wanted to celebrate sameness. I made my Aleutians silent, like dumb animals, for many reasons, but first of all because I knew that I could pass for normal in foreign situations as long as I didn't speak. And I made human body language intelligible to them, on the grounds that just as our common humanity makes and recognizes the same patterns everywhere, the aliens' wordless natural language had been deeply shaped by the same pressures as have shaped the natural languages of life on earth. The whole bio-chemical spectrum is missing, from their point of view, because we have no wanderers, no intelligent secretions at all. But every human gesture that remains is as intelligible to them as another brood's dialect of the common tongue, that everyone shares at home. To make sure of my point I raised and dismissed the possibility that they were time-travellers returning to their forgotten planet of origin; and the other possibility that they had grown, like us, from humanoid seed sown across the galaxy by some elder race. They were an absolutely, originally different evolution of life. But they were the same because life, wherever it arises in our middle dimensions, must be subject to the same constraints, and the more we learn about our development the more we see that the most universal pressures—time and gravity, quantum mechanics, the nature of certain chemical bonds—drive through biological complexity on every fractal scale, from the design of an opposable thumb to the link between the chemistry of emotion and a set of facial muscles. This sameness, subject to cultural variation but always reasserting itself, was shown chiefly in the aliens' ability to understand us.

In line with my model of Aleutians as 'women' and 'native peoples' it was right for them to be wary and rather contemptuous of spoken language. I wanted them to be silent like the processes of cell-biology, like social insects exchanging pheromone signals: like larger animals conversing through grooming, nuzzling, eye-contact and gesture. I wanted the humans, convinced that the barrier between self and other was insur-mountable except by magic, to be deeply alarmed by these seeming telepaths—the way characters in classic male-gendered science fiction are so absurdly impressed at an occult power they call *empathy*, whereby some superbeing or human freak can *actually sense* the way other people are feeling (God give me strength: my cat can do that). But I didn't want to do away with spoken language altogether. Words are separation. Words divide. That is the work they do. I know this because I've felt it happen: whenever I open my mouth and speak, and prove by my parlous accent and toddler's vocabulary that I don't belong; whenever I make a public, female-gendered statement in a male group. Everything else that we think we use language for we can handle without what the Aleutians call 'formal speeches'. But for the Aleutians not to have this means of separation, this means of stepping out of the natural cycles would have made them less than people. So I invented a special class of Aleutians, the 'signifiers', who were obligate linguists the way other Aleutians were obligate food-processors or spaceship-builders. Of course they assimilated human articulate languages with dazzling speed. (This is another of the space-fantasy clichés that I think has been unfairly derided. I wouldn't be able to do it. But then, nobody would sign up an obligate monophone such as myself on a trading mission to another planet, would they?)

It also transpired that the aliens did have a kind of no-kidding alien-life-form telepathy for long-distance contact: another proliferation of the wanderer system. But that's another story. There was no problem with the mechanics of speech, by the way. I gave them teeth and tongues and larynxes more or less like ours: why not?

I had made the Aleutians into self-conscious intelligences who still manipulated their surroundings the way bacteria do it; or the even simpler entities manufacturing and communicating inside our cells. In their use of all forms of language I elaborated on this conservatism. They were beings who had reached self-consciousness, and spoken language, without abandoning any of the chronological precursor communication media. All life on earth uses chemical communication; then comes gesture, and vocalization comes last. Humans have traded all the rest for words—so that we have to rediscover the meaning of our own gestures, and the likely effect of the hormone-laden scent-cells we shed, from self-help books full of printed text. To the Aleutians, by the way, this lack of control gives the impression that all humans have Tourette's Syndrome: we're continually babbling obscenities, shouting out tactless remarks, giving away secrets in the common tongue. I pictured my Aleutians like a troop of humanly intelligent baboons, gossiping with each other silently and perfectly efficiently, having subtle and complex chemical interactions: and just occasionally feeling the need to vocalize; a threat or boast or warning, a yell of 'Look at me!' It only occurred to me later that I'd made the Aleutians very like feminist women in this: creatures dead set on having it all, determined to be self-aware and articulate public people, without giving up their place in the natural world.

But inevitably, insidiously the 'signifier' characters, the aliens with the speaking parts, became an elite. I had already realized that I had to 'translate' the wordless dialogue of Aleutian silent language into words on the page. In this I was up against one of the walls of make-believe. Science fiction is full of these necessary absurdities: I accepted it with good grace, the same way as I'd accepted the human body-plan; and used some funny direct speech marks to show the difference, which the copy-editor didn't like. But now I felt that the male-gendered mechanist-gadget world was sneaking back into power, with historical inevitability in its train, in the Trojan Horse of articulate language. I did everything I could to correct this. I began to point out the similarities between the Aleutian silent language, and our spoken word as it is used most of the time by most humans. I found myself listening to human conversations and noticing the gaps: the unfinished sentences, the misplaced words, the really startling high ratio of noise to signal. I realized that most of our use of language fulfils the same function as the grooming, the nuzzling, the skin-to-skin chemical exchange that other life-forms share, but which with us has become taboo except in privileged intimate relations. I further realized that everything humans 'say' to each other, either in meaningful statements or in this constant dilute muttering of contact, is backed, just like Aleutian communication, by a vast reservoir of cultural and evolutionary experience. We too have our 'soup of shared presence', out of which genuinely novel and separate formal announcements arise rarely—to be greeted, more often than not, with wariness and contempt.

Reinventing the wheel is a commonplace hazard in science fiction. It makes a change to find one has reinvented poststructuralist psychology. I recognized, some time after the event, that in the Silence of Aleutia I had invented the unconscious in the version proposed by Lacan, the unspoken plenum of experience that is implicit in all human discourse. Then I understood that my 'signifiers' represented not a ruling caste but the public face of Aleutia; and the Silent represented all those people who don't want to 'speak out', who 'just want to get on with their lives': the group to which most of us belong, most of the time. In Aleutia, as in human life, the 'signifiers' may be prominent figures. But who is really in charge? The intelligentsia, or the silent majority? Which is the puppeteer? The fugitive, marginal latecomer, consciousness? Or the complex, clever, perfectly competent wordless animal within?

Convergent Evolution
It's now several years since I started writing about the Aleutians, and nearly a decade since I first outlined the project... on a beach in Thailand, one warm summer night in 1988. A lot of history has happened in that time, and much of it somehow affected the story. The 1989 revolutions in Europe made a great difference to *White Queen*. The war in the former Yugoslavia had a grim influence on the second episode, *North Wind*. The nature of the enduring low-intensity conflict in Northern Ireland had something to do with what happens between human men and women in all three books. The third instalment, *Phoenix Café*, is bound to have a *fin de siècle* feel. I've read and shakily assimilated lots of popular science, and science itself has become more popular, so that concerns which were completely science-fictional and obscure when I began are now topics of general interest; and that's made a difference too. Even the battle of the sexes has changed ground, both in my mind and in the real world. I'm not sure how much, if any, of my original plan survived. But this is okay. I intended to let the books change over time. I wanted things that happened at first contact to

appear later as legends that couldn't possibly be true. I wanted concerns that were vitally important in one book to have become totally irrelevant in the next. I wanted phlogiston and cold fusion in my science, failed revolutions and forgotten dreams in my politics. I thought that discontinuity would be more true to life than a three hundred years' chunk of soap-opera (or so, it's difficult to say exactly how much time has passed, when the master race finds measurement boring) that ends with everybody still behaving the same as they did in episode one. It's true to the historical model too. I don't think anyone would deny that the European empire builders had lost the plot, sometime before that stroke of midnight in 1947, climactic moment in the great disengagement.

My son Gabriel tells me stories. Not surprisingly, given his environment, he tends to tell me science fiction stories. I'm delighted when he comes up with some motif or scenario that I recognize as a new variation on a familiar theme: and he's furious (like some adult storytellers I could mention) when I point out to him he's doing something that's been done countless times before. Always, already, what we say has been said before. A while ago he came up with an adventure where the characters kept being swept away into the Fourth Dimension, an experience that transformed them, partially and then permanently if they stayed too long, into horrible gargoyles. That was where I found the title of my paper. Sadly, I can't fault his argument. There's no getting away from it, the Fourth Dimension makes monsters of us all. My Aleutians, though, have managed to change the process around. There's a sense in which aliens can represent not just other people, but some future other people; some unexplored possibility for the human race. Maybe my Aleutians fit that description. It has been a surprise even to me to see how human they have become, how much I've found myself writing about the human predicament, about the mysteries of self and consciousness. But that's the way it has to be, unless or until the great silence out there is broken. Until we meet.

Notes

1 Saucer-shaped flying machines: hypersonic flying saucers driven by microwaves are at present the goal of serious researchers in the US (reported in *New Scientist* No 2017, 17 February 1996). MRI imaging of brain activity, involving something oddly similar to those old skiffy hairdryers, is already reality.

2 Valmiki, writing in the third century BC, Christian chronology.

3 Mungo Park travelling in Africa in the eighteenth century was staggered by the size of the cities he found, comparing urban conditions very favourably with those in Britain (Mungo Park, *Travels in the Interior of Africa*, 1799).

4 Although Octavia Butler's trilogy 'Xenogenesis' develops a 'slavery' narrative of alien invasion of great complexity.

5 Pleasingly, for me, a quote from a Porgy & Bess lyric (George Gershwin

and Dubose Heyward 1935) sung by a black American who finds refuge from cultural domination in this defiant thought.

6 Annie Coombes, *Re-inventing Africa* (New Haven and London: Yale University Press, 1994).

7 Joanna Russ, in the *The Female Man* (New York: Bantam, 1975), makes a similar observation about idyllic separatism.

Freefall in Inner Space:
From *Crash* to Crash Technology

SIMON SELLARS

> The narrator must be a metasubject in the process of formulating
> both the legitimacy of the discourses of the empirical sciences and
> that of the direct institutions of popular cultures. This metasubject,
> in giving voice to their common grounding, realizes their implicit
> goal. It inhabits the speculative university. Positive science and the
> people are only crude versions of it. The only valid way…to bring
> the people to expression is through the mediation of speculative
> knowledge.
>
> Jean-François Lyotard, *The Postmodern Condition*

> Can't you see I'm making this up as I go?
> 'It seems then,' I said, 'if pewter dishes, leaves of lettuce, grains of
> salt, drops of water, vinegar, oil and slices of eggs had been flying
> about in the air for all eternity, it might at last happen by chance that
> it would come a salad.'
> 'Yes,' responded my lovely, 'but not so nice as this one of mine.'
>
> Johan Keplar, *Die Stella Novae*

In seeking to answer the question 'Who Speaks Science Fiction?', we
should make some attempt at least to define this most knotty of categories
and the assumptions underlying its usage.

As is well known, the 'Father of Scientifiction',[1] Hugo Gernsback,
envisioned his *Amazing Stories* publication in the 1920s as an outlet for
'charming romance[s] intermingled with scientific fact and prophetic
vision'.[2] The emphasis on science (or at least, the illusion of science) and
a shared set of assumptions surrounding this type of knowledge endured,
crystallizing into a genre with its own codes and precepts for operation.
For that initial heady mixture—the privileged will-to-knowledge

previously unavailable, white-hot heat sandwiched between the tail-end of the Industrial Revolution and the imaginary landscapes beyond—seems to persist at the heart of much subsequent genre sf. This Golden Age represents an eternal adolescence, a bygone era when increased leisure was channelled into a few outlets, gleaming and magnificent in their singular devotion to a new evolution in thought. Its allure is understandable, perhaps even necessary, to our postmodern age, in which nostalgia and traditional values are pre-packaged as marks of authenticity in a secret-less world, a world without depth.

As Carl Freedman argues:

> ...much sf, especially of the more conformist sort, is a kind of historical fiction in disguise: witness the nostalgic reconstructions of the entrepreneurial in Heinlein's novella *The Man Who Sold the Moon* or in the section on merchant traders in Asimov's *Foundation*, both classic works of 'Golden Age' sf which, however liberal in overt ideology, do find Utopian traces in the entrepreneurialism which the monopoly capitalism of the postwar US was, at the time of writing, rendering more and more obsolete.
>
> ...historical fiction, paradoxically, is the more vulnerable to an unhistorical fetishism of the past...in which the merely aesthetic relish of costume and exoticism triumphs over the genuinely conceptual issues of historical specificity and difference...[3]

Certainly, the *popular* perception of science fiction—as romantic retro-futurism—is tied to a superficial reading of the Gernsbackian formula.[4]

A second original characteristic needs to be noted: namely, a shared belief in the power of the genre as a superior kind of cognition, from Gernsback to Dick to Ballard to cyberpunk.[5] However, it was cognition that rigorously sought to patrol its own boundaries, extrapolating from the mainstream methodologies and criteria for 'reality' that must be applied to fantasy and speculation:

> While a rigorous definition of 'hard sf' may be impossible, perhaps the most important thing about it is, not that it should include real science in any great detail, but that it should respect the scientific spirit; it should seek to provide natural rather than supernatural or transcendental explanations for the events and phenomena it describes.[6]

In today's cyber-culture the machinations and methodology of current technology are becoming increasingly invisible and unfathomable, 'unnatural' in their process. Yet the Gernsback legacy (modified by John W. Campbell and others) appears intact. Indeed, the success of *Star Trek*—

as a kind of 'Melrose Space'—indicates the genre's rude health; yet it remains a 'trainspotter's' pursuit (albeit with enormous commercial clout), where moral uncertainties and ethical dilemmas are flattened into simple dichotomies, usually revolving around good and evil. In part, this is an effect of the way visual renderings of science-fictional scenarios have come to displace their literary counterparts in the popular consciousness.

Paul Virilio writes of the proliferation of images in the electronic era of reproduction as

> a kind of seeing without knowing; a bedazzlement, a pure seeing... Images contaminate us like viruses... They are not informative images which inform us in the sense of feedback, and of comprehension, but in the sense of an epidemic, in the sense of contamination.[7]

Virilio believes that this bedazzlement arises from an ever more sophisticated visual and virtual technology. Even if we temper some of the more apocalyptic aspects of his argument, it is clear that the concurrent advances in cinematic special effects perform a similar function, since the temptation is to privilege the image, to showcase it and fetishize it, as 'science fiction' becomes a commodity, validated by the progressiveness of its means of production.

Consider the following advertisements, merely two of many in which the gleaming surface of technological progress becomes the newest currency. These were commissioned by Telstra, the Australian telecommunications concern. In the first a man is led into a room containing multiple banks of TV monitors. He watches computer-enhanced studio trickery, as the wonders of advanced telecommunications are demonstrated to him. Awe-struck, he comments: 'This was all science fiction not so long ago.' In the second, two small children swing through trees and jump huge chasms—feats obviously beyond the capacity of their years—as they act out their Indiana Jones-type fantasies. Suddenly they happen upon the entrance to an underground Telstra facility, where they are greeted by a Telstra worker. Awe-struck, they wonder aloud about his actions. The worker proudly proclaims: 'I'm laying cables for the information superhighway.'

These signify much more than the arrogance of a major conglomerate with advertising dollars to spare and unlimited cultural resources to plunder. Here the Telstra company, in one (thoroughly researched) fell swoop, announces the death of science fiction as an extrapolative, speculative genre, by acknowledging that the tropes of estrangement and inversion typically utilized by sf are in fact reports from the coal-face of the media landscape, the air we reflexively breathe. Telstra acknowledges the evolution of the media-savvy consumer, armed with intimate knowledge of the methodology of the media landscape, while also legitimizing the calm nihilism of critical theorists such as Virilio and Baudrillard. For the ads' message is clearly this: we live inside a mediated fiction, our only reference points those fictions we consume—why not trust someone, Telstra, whose fictions are more life-like, more wraparound, more real than any other? Passivity is presented as a choice, a loopback failure in which all roads lead to Telstra. Or do they?

Freedman writes that sf privileges

> the telos of critical theory: the elaborate and powerful demystifying apparatus of Marxist (and Freudian) thought exist, ultimately, in order to clear space upon which possible alternatives to the existent can be constructed.[8]

However, it should be clear by now that in the invasive realm of late capitalism the machine must be turned against itself. This represents the radical change from standard forms of socially aware science fiction, typically presented in films such as *The Omega Man*, *Soylent Green*, *Rollerball* and *THX 1138*. Such sf depicted a 'one man against the system' scenario: typically, the hero's rebellion was brutally crushed and his broken body used as a totemistic warning for the rest of society. Now the system fights back in very different ways: the time-lag between innovative culture and flaccid cliché is almost infinitesimal.[9]

Accordingly, a kind of twice-removed sf has become the ideal paradigmatic form. Virilio comments upon key themes of 'science-technology-other worlds':

> Science fiction narrative, in effect, shows most of us turning in circles like the blind before the very obviousness of the familiar universe. A kind of incompatibility between our physical presence in the world and the different degrees of nocturnal anesthesia of consciousness [lapsing] into short or prolonged, mild or serious states of absence which may indeed bring about...our sudden immersion in other universes—parallel, interstitial, bifurcating...[10]

In this regard, it is instructive to note a mid-1980s manifesto from Bruce Sterling, where the central themes of cyberpunk science fiction are identified as 'body invasion' (prosthetics, implants, gene splicing) and 'mind invasion' (artificial intelligence, mind-machine interfaces). Again, the focus on a type of post-humanism is depicted as resulting from technological advance. Crucially, however, Sterling roots this identification in *experience*:

The cyberpunks are perhaps the first sf generation to grow up not only within the literary tradition of science fiction but in a truly science-fictional world. For them, the techniques of classical 'hard sf'...are not just literary tools but an aid to daily life. They are a means of *understanding*, and highly valued.[11] (my italics)

Clearly, there are still valuable lessons to be learnt from sf's passage into public consciousness. The cyberpunk movement, such as it was, self-destructed with the release of the William Gibson-scripted *Johnny Mnemonic*, a film which lazily drew upon mediated versions of cyberpunk for its stylistic and thematic basis, becoming in effect a simulacrum—a copy with no original.[12] This outcome was always assumed in Sterling and Gibson, intensely media-savvy writers. Yet their imaginings became trapped within their own rhetoric: the extrapolative, hard sf techniques employed by the cyberpunks have become so much a part of Western lore, with the technological future collapsing into the ever-accelerating present, that it becomes increasingly difficult for Gibson in particular to write without reading as a parody of himself. If anything, the cyberpunks were too aware, becoming victims of their own iconic power. As Benjamin Long discusses:

> The language of Silicon Valley tech-heads is straight out of the realm of cyberpunk...and many of their ideas have been borrowed directly from Gibson... Since the late 1980s a number of software companies have been developing Spatial Data Management Systems...that would allow them to visually navigate through virtual structures of data, much as Gibson's characters do in cyberspace, a move that brought a swift letter from Gibson's lawyers, and, supposedly, a threat by Gibson to trademark the name of one of those involved. At a NASA laboratory, researchers named a 'slaved binocular remote camera platform' after Molly, a character who performs that function in *Neuromancer*. In...*Virtual Light*, Gibson completes the art-imitating-life-imitating-art loop by having his protagonist, Berry Rydell, watch a telepresence set tuned to 'servo-mounted mollies on the outside of the plane'.[13]

Accordingly, Gibson yearns to produce a different kind of fiction:

> On my tour for *Virtual Light*, I was...saying that the next logical move was to write a novel that would do everything that you would expect a William Gibson novel to do, but would be set in the real world and would involve no fantasy elements whatsoever. On second thought, I decided that it would be awfully hard to do...[14]

Despite best intentions, then, there is reason enough to argue that the term 'science fiction' has become meaningless, merely a marketing category, a quaint throwback to a romantic, bygone era. Just as obviously, however, in this culture there is a real need for a literature of ideas, translatable into the action and practice of everyday life. Indeed, the 'attention given to science fiction by cultural theorists and the world of information technology' signifies a collective cultural desire to make sense of the rapid changes occurring around us, replacing the flights of fancy which once obsessively rocketed us into space.

In an essay on the similarities between 'postmodernist fiction' and sf, Brian McHale argues that these 'two ontological sister-genres...have been pursuing analogous but independent courses of development', obliterating sf's past as a medium for scientific extrapolation, undermining its future, according to that particular track, but at the same time claiming relevance for the genre by returning to Darko Suvin's well-known formulation of sf as a 'literature of cognitive estrangement'.

This is a useful starting point, for genre-policing is in itself a pointless pursuit, available to those unwilling or unable to confront the fluidity of a discourse that threatens to envelop us, at the same time as it liberates. Advertising and the media explosion have taught their receivers to become a writerly audience, through the targeting of precisely such stimuli,[15] but only according to a framework tightly controlled by the designers of these fictional worlds. 'Choice' must still conform to stricture. Just as perform-ance artist Perry Hoberman utilizes a 'karaoke' mode, or participatory model, in his installations (as opposed to the standard 'interactive' paradigm) so cultural improvisation must be encouraged, rather than mapping or navigation. The user must be allowed to remould existing forms practically in order to envisage, in Suvin's words, '...an imaginative framework alternative to the author's empirical environment'.[16]

As Carl Freedman reminds us, critical theory-aligned-with-sf is well-equipped to articulate these strategies. Yet the 'cultural theorist' branch of sf remains a hermetically sealed environment, much like its generic cousin. Consider Veronica Hollinger:[17]

> While I do not at all mean to suggest that postmodernist cultural production cannot also be an effective means of political resistance and perhaps even of political change, it would seem that the particular allegorical formula that produces specular sf[18] arises from an impulse to negate such effectiveness.
>
> ...This quality of numbness is...evident in the final moment of Ballard's *Crash*, in which the narrator, mesmerized by the iconography of violent, technologized death, and 'already...

designing the elements of [his] own car crash,' meditates on the image of 'a thousand crashing cars.'

Hollinger continues, subsequently quoting and commenting upon Zoe Sofia's description of our 'contemporary science-fiction culture':

> ...Sofia's analysis bears significant resemblances to Baudrillard's theoretical allegorization of contemporary sociopolitical reality as sf catastrophe. However, the point of her analysis is not passive acceptance but an aggressive feminist resistance to and rejection of those science-fictional aspects of the present that threaten to foreclose the future.[19]

Like many of her contemporaries, Hollinger has a political agenda to serve, a border to patrol. Her reading of J.G. Ballard's 1973 novel *Crash* is an ideological decision, serving no useful purpose once outside this domain: it deceitfully renders the text inert by the very act of plundering its resources, its world-view, in order to spruce up a parallel text. To paraphrase Freedman, she privileges 'aesthetic relish' over 'conceptual issues of specificity and difference' by refusing to acknowledge and work through the shifting nature of postmodern cultural production. The rest of this essay will demonstrate that such a reading can be of no interest to those who do not read science fiction, merely live it in everyday lives.

*   *   *   *   *

It is worth looking at *Crash* in further detail, since it is a text which encapsulates much of the aesthetic and philosophy of the cyber-culture (the 'present') that has come to replace the imaginings of science fiction (the 'future').[20] Like the hyperreal landscape in which it is set, *Crash* occupies an ambiguous space, somewhere between critical theory and cyberpunk sf; the psychological impact of the writing leaves it open to various interpretations. In the hands of Mark Pauline's Survival Research Laboratory, for example, *Crash* is depicted as a cyborg fantasy, a Benjaminesque sense of the destruction of the self conceived as aesthetic pleasure of the highest order.[21] *Concrete Island* (1974) and *High-Rise* (1975) have been written about in similar terms. Yet, these works—Ballard's 'urban disaster' trilogy—are about accepting the implications of post-industrial society, and of evolving an imaginative response to the resulting technological and societal relations. In this mode, *Crash* avoids the various limitations normally imposed by science fiction's passage into popular consciousness. In an essay on William Burroughs, Ballard identifies the generic weight which so often stifles sf. Still struggling under the expectations of the Gernsback legacy, the vocabulary of the genre long ago passed into the collective popular imaginary. Superseded by the high-tech grandeur of the Space Age, these fictional elements are, according to the author, 'now valid only in a kind of marginal spoofing'.[22]

Here Ballard is prescient: as we have noted, hard sf is destined to be overtaken by the technological developments of the real world, refiguring itself again and again as a future that never happened, a victim of our postmodern society and its peculiar focus on the present: a compressed moment devouring the past and future, and regurgitating it as mere surface texture, at the whim of the vogue. Taking his cue from Burroughs, Ballard's own work utilizes these self-satirizing figments to construct an alternative mindspace, drawing upon the recombinant power of the imagination and its ability to construct a kind of hypertextual key to our fractured and displaced technological identity. His use of sf metaphor clears ground for positive action, linking this imaginative response to new technologies: simulacra become ripe for inscription with brand-new auratic powers, as sf provides a language for understanding technology, rather than being seen merely as a product of this technology. Thus the characters in *High-Rise* are presented with

> a model of the world into which the future was carrying them, a landscape beyond technology where everything was either derelict or, more ambiguously, recombined in unexpected but more meaningful ways.[23]

Ballard's trilogy inhabits the space between perception and recognition. The author has always been fascinated by the view of reality which our mental and nervous systems perfect for us: the simple fact of objects appearing smaller as they recede distance-wise would make absolutely no sense to a blind person suddenly given sight. To sighted people it is a commonplace, barely given a second thought. Clearly the media landscape plays upon this instinctive tendency to compress reality into manageable frames, neatly flattening difference and co-opting diversity. Numerous commentators, including Ballard and the theorists mentioned previously, have refigured the television screen as a 'third eye', perceiving images and processing information on our behalf. In this sense, it is difficult to disagree with Fredric Jameson, who notes that:

> The postmodern viewer…is called upon to do the impossible, namely, to see all…screens at once, in their radical and random difference… and to rise somehow to a level at which the vivid perception of radical difference is in and of itself a new mode of grasping what used to be called relationship: something for which the word collage is still only a very feeble name.

> [These] cultural products...[stand] as something like an imperative to grow new organs, to expand our sensorium and our body to some new, yet unimaginable, perhaps ultimately impossible dimensions.[24]

This view of postmodern existence aligns itself to the universe of *Crash*— Ballard's introduction to the French edition of his novel identifies the 'death of affect' as the 'most terrifying casualty of the twentieth century'.[25] This demise of feeling and emotion is linked to the demise of the self, as Jameson describes it,[26] and the same process is inscribed in the values and stylings of the motor car, a twentieth-century advertising phenomenon, and its attendant technology. In a recent article architect Steve Whitford described his intentions when designing two retaining walls forming part of a road link:

> Our first important contribution to the discussion about the design of road hardware was to argue that concerns for human scale were irrelevant when these elements were being viewed from a scale modifier; a fast moving vehicle. The car makes large distances small, steep hills flat, and compresses events isolated in time and space into connected events occurring almost simultaneously.[27]

Aligned with the advertising of lifestyles which invariably accompanies the car, the result is a kind of virtual reality, in which the consumer becomes enmeshed within the signs and values of the communications landscape, and the flattened space that remains. Similarly in *Crash*, the characters are defined by this metallized skin; the body is fragmented and subsequently held together by signs and symbols, as in the following excerpt, which describes the aftermath of a road accident:

> His hand had struck some rigid object as he was hurled from his seat, and the pattern of a sign formed itself as I sat there, pumped up by his dying circulation into a huge blood-blister—the triton signature of my radiator emblem.[28]

Automotive advertising consistently reminds us that cars can buy status, wealth, power, respect, attraction to the opposite sex, peace of mind, and so on. At the same time violent, thrill-a-minute, State-sanctioned mini-dramas (in Australia, at least) warn us of the underside of this technological construct—the seductive, destructive power of speed. What of the unfortunate consumer, flattened into the non-space connecting these simultaneous universes? To make the conceptual leap from 'violent weapon' to 'sexy accessory' requires us to disregard our 'traditional' sense organs in true Jamesonian fashion and to accept the type of oxymoronic information so often disseminated through advertising media, in which 'fresh frozen', 'light, yet filling' and 'virtually spotless' products abound. Such tactics exhort us to suspend disbelief: 'Your reality will be superseded by ours.'[29]

For Jean Baudrillard, 'true sf' must therefore 'seek to revitalize, to reactualize, to rebanalize fragments of simulation—fragments of this universal simulation which our presumed "real" world has now become for us.'[30] *Crash* fulfils this function: indeed, Baudrillard perceives in Ballard's work a vision of humanity simultaneously fascinated and numbed by its technological environment, emptied of all value judgement.

These arguments are persuasive. In a culture in which surveillance cameras betray our secrets to the public sphere, everyone from hooligan footballers to shoplifters expresses surprise and outrage when their actions are relayed to a wider audience. *Caught In the Act*, a new British TV programme, has spent months buying surveillance film from various operators: gas-bagging grannies in the street and semi-naked women in changing-rooms share air-time with vicious thugs conducting smash-and-grab raids... Mick Jagger, onstage with the Stones at some monstrously large and impersonal stadium, catches a glimpse of himself on the Sony Jumbotron to his left. For the first time, he sees what the audience sees, a hyper-active stick-figure engaging in the most ludicrous prat-falls. For an instant, his face ripples and stains with bewilderment. But the show must go on... On air, chat-show host Oprah Winfrey refers to her televisual persona as the 'Oprah-Oprah Thing', and wonders aloud why an audience would confuse 'it' with 'me'. As Ballard observed early in his career, Earth is truly the alien planet.

Thus, the elements in *Crash* explicitly couched in sf mythology are stripped of finality, of a finite futurism, the real world becoming 'rebanalized' by their metaphoric invocation, as in the following excerpts:

> The distant headlamps, refracted through the soap solution jetting across the windows, covered their bodies with a luminescent glow, like two semi-metallic human beings of the distant future making love in a chromium bower.
>
> The bones of my forearms formed a solid coupling with the shift of the steering column, and I felt the smallest tremors of the road-wheels magnified a hundred times, so that we traversed each grain of gravel or cement like the surface of a small asteroid.[31]

Ultimately such passages, with their language of alien-ation and disruption, remind the reader of the irreal nature of the media landscape and of ourselves, as technology-infected subjects: once this position is recognized, the automobile is then refigured by Ballard as a prosthesis, a technological object under human control.

Clearly Veronica Hollinger errs in dismissing the role of the imagination in this universe-without-secrets. The character Vaughan is obsessed with planning a car crash involving the actress, Elizabeth Taylor, with altering and transforming her public persona mediated through the world's camera-eye. Previous celebrity automotive deaths involving Jayne Mansfield, Albert Camus and James Dean also preoccupy Vaughan; his aim is to restage these accidents, in a way that will make sense to his disordered consciousness. As Baudrillard highlights, the camera dictates the intensely visual language of *Crash*—accordingly, Vaughan's perception of these events is couched in the terms of the media landscape, in the paradoxical 'nightmare marriage of sex and technology'. As the filmed version of *Crash* reminds us, James Dean's violent death forever froze him as an icon of youthful rebellion and lust; he now exists as a kind of digital ghost, cruising the media terrain, at the beck and call of whomsoever chooses to call up his image. Thus the sexual act in Ballard's work, so often invoked in film and literature as a guide to 'essential' humanity, becomes merely a commodity, free-floating, a violence imposed on the absent body:

> Elements of her body...were framed within the cabin of the car. As I pressed the head of my penis against the neck of her uterus, in which I could feel a dead machine, her cap, I looked at the cabin around me. This small space was crowded with angular control surfaces and rounded sections of human bodies interacting in unfamiliar junctions, like the first act of homosexual intercourse inside an Apollo capsule.[32]

Couched in unemotive, abstracted biological-medical terminology, descriptions of this most intimate of acts are explicitly linked to a kind of pornographic reality. As TV news presents violent acts as fetishized emblems of humanity—human behavioural patterns unencumbered by moral or social obligations, just 'televisual'—so too, sexuality becomes fused with its machines, an artificial response to an artificial situation.[33] Seduced by this miasma, Vaughan seeks to construct his own 'celebrity death' and in the process plummets to destruction and apparent failure:

> ... he died on the flyover as he tried to crash my car into the limousine carrying the film actress whom he had pursued for so long. Trapped within the car after it jumped off the rails of the flyover, his body was so disfigured by its impact with the airline coach below that the police first identified it as mine.[34]

Vaughan's dream of resurrection, on the news-loops which would have captured the proposed crash with Taylor, is dashed. However, in reaching this point he re-asserts a long-lost subjectivity as he negotiates a landscape 'without limits, without referentiality'. In this mortal shock, this body-rending event, Vaughan and his symbolic car-crash confront, and maintain escape-velocity from, the disempowering death of affect underlying the tensions in *Crash*. For Ballard, the absence left by the simulation model—by the destruction of technology as it traditionally appears to us (refracted through scientific models and therefore 'Frankensteinian', threatening)—is seen as a chance for joyous reclamation of a techno-body previously thought to be erased forever:

> The destruction of this motor-car and its occupants seemed, in turn, to sanction the sexual penetration of Vaughan's body; both were conceptualized acts abstracted from all feeling, carrying any ideas or emotions with which we cared to freight them.[35]

More and more we find ourselves within a literal media landscape, bombarded by icons of film, television, the presence of digital technologies and the changing nature of info-transmission. 'Fictionalized' and 'real' world events commingle with gleaming sexuality in advertisements, politics, and entertainment—all products of a system, a model of reality, which has imploded, and is haemorrhaging uncontrollably. Stretched to infinity, invading the imaginary. Global events couched in the logic of dreams, mediated by cinematic, visual language; angles and fields of vision alternated, transmitted via textual pans and zooms, a multi-televisual universe.

Acceptance of media fictions requires a certain willingness to accept the rhetoric of the image and the natural inclination of the imaginative realm to conventionalize reality, to blend the illogical with the familiar. Ballard's work blends several levels: public, personal and fantastical, and according to the author, allows the simultaneous examination of 'the different strata that make up our own experience of the actual world'.[36] Although written in linear fashion, *Crash* is as demonstrative of the process as its 'cut-and-paste' predecessor *The Atrocity Exhibition*. Couched within a realist form, the work undercuts the psychological expectations normally derived from this type of structure. For realist literature operates within a self-referential articulation of form—referring back to itself or similar narratives. *Crash*, however, is stripped of narrative omniscience. In its mingling of frames—scientific, medical, pornographic with realist techniques, and the reader-reception each requires—*Crash* avoids finality. As Baudrillard would observe, it is without referentiality, without limits. But *Crash* is more than simply 'without'. It is transformed as a subversive agenda, the negative value seeping in and invading the commercial, that is conventionalized, shell.

Clearly the implications are important and far-reaching: in an age in which technology is geared to capturing and re-working information and data (digital sampling, Photoshop, morphing, multi-media systems), a new form of expression arises—one which alters what it means to be 'original' and externalizes reality as a playground for the imagination. To paraphrase Ballard, in a world in which any original response to experience has been pre-empted, the most effective method for dealing with that world is to assume that it is a complete fiction—our task must therefore be to invent the reality. These are strategies gaining much currency today, from the Alt. X and Avant-Pop manifestos on the World Wide Web to the gushing tomes of media analyst Douglas Rushkoff, with his 'media viruses' and infected 'datasphere'.

More substantially, musician Brian Eno has cited the example of classical Thai music. To the untrained Western ear, it will be quite an experience to learn that certain parts of these scores are designed to be 'melancholy' or 'uplifting', when they sound merely baffling or utterly discordant, infused with no emotion whatsoever.[37] In order to sever this golden noose, Eno advocates found-sound samples or alternative rhythm and melody lines in what can be an often totally random juxtaposition. If the listener approaches it with an open mind, then hopefully the parts can re-assemble themselves into a meaningful whole, based directly on the experience of the listener. The thrill of recognition when hearing a sample from one's cultural imaginary—a chart-topping song, for example—can be superseded, or illuminated, when that same bite is speeded up, aurally stretched to breaking point, or replaced by the jarring grate of an inept bass-line and poorly constructed drum rhythm. The thrill of recognition— and therefore of enjoyment—is wrenched from its warm womb, as the consumer is invited to reflect upon their relationship to commodity culture: how can one decide which is 'good' or 'bad' music? Certainly, these types of strategy may tap into something completely beyond such dichotomies.

Musicians practising techno and drum 'n' bass stylings up the ante by reflecting the hyper-kinetic nature of inner-megacity life, stretching and distorting the spatial and temporal dimensions of this environment through similar techniques. The so-called distance senses, seeing and hearing, extend the body out perceptually; they are now in danger of being lost forever, caught amidst a welter of cross-signals. In these forms of music, everything is equal in the mix, inviting the listener/viewer/consumer to fight against sensory fascism. In denying access to the normal modes of sensorial alignment, the body is brought back into play, feeling and groping its way around a strange, yet hauntingly familiar space.

Recording artists Negativland discuss the psychological impact arising from the act of selection and juxtaposition, as their music recontextualizes fragments from the media landscape, 'chewing them up and spitting them out' as 'a new form of hearing the world around us'. For Negativland, this is the inevitable consequence of the 'electronic age of media saturation' and the technology of reproduction available on a widespread basis.[38]

Psychologists are now identifying ailments and strains which arise from 'information overkill', attacking and debilitating the body: Information Fatigue Syndrome is a recent coinage. The sum total of all printed information doubles in increasingly shorter amounts of time, as the human cost arising from the processing of this material increases exponentially. As Ballard writes: 'Science and technology multiply around us. To an increasing extent they dictate the languages in which we speak and think. Either we use those languages, or we remain mute.'[39] These musical examples represent positive and practical applications of this philosophy, countering the 'Black Shakes' of information overload.

In the attempt to define the essence of sf, we should remember the words of Michel Foucault:

> ...as our society changes...polysemic texts will once again function according to another mode... one which will...have to be determined or, perhaps, experienced.
>
> We would no longer hear the questions that have been rehashed for so long: 'Who really spoke?... With what authenticity or originality?' Instead there would be other questions, like these: 'What are the modes of existence of this discourse? Where has it been used, how can it circulate, and who can appropriate it for himself? What are the places in it where there is room for possible subjects? Who can assume these various subject-functions?' And behind all these questions, we would hardly hear anything but the stirring of an indifference: 'what difference does it make who is speaking?'[40]

Applying a similar philosophy to a mass-cult aesthetic—the popular genre of science fiction—Ballard reclaims the techno-body, fused with technology as an aid to perception. In the broken-down community of his high-tech high-rise, where social order has dissolved into apparently primitivistic tribal warfare, the residents use their hyper-bodies as a cognitive map, each with its individual beacons of pain and desire guiding them across the thin, reflective surface of the techno-sphere:

> As he inhaled the stale air he was refreshed by his own odor, almost recognizing parts of his body—his feet and genitalia, the medley of smells that issued from his mouth. He stripped off his clothes in the bedroom, throwing his suit and tie into the bottom of the closet and putting on again his grimy sports-shirt and trousers. He knew now that he would never again try to leave the high-rise.[41]

In the turn from the outer space of Ballard's early career as a science fiction writer to the inner space of today, *Crash* and *The Atrocity Exhibition*—with their formulation of an alternative mindscape within the framework of sf—remind us that we all speak science fiction, and that questions regarding the health of the genre are trivial, at best: better left to the fanboy networks and the coded precepts found in films such as *Star Wars*.

For the rest of us, there is work to do.

Notes

1 'Scientifiction': a phrase later to mutate into the catchier 'science fiction'.

2 Brian Stableford, 'Definitions of SF', in John Clute and Peter Nicholls, eds., *The Encyclopedia of Science Fiction* (London: Orbit, 1993), p. 311.

3 Carl Freedman, 'Science Fiction and Critical Theory', *Science-Fiction Studies*, 14.2 (1987), p. 187.

4 As Gary Westfahl notes:

...science fiction in the 1930s seemed to be evolving into a literature about space travel... Gernsback was simply responding to this new reality—one which, ironically, he neither desired nor directly inspired. (Gary Westfahl, 'Wanted: A Symbol for Science Fiction', *Science-Fiction Studies*, 22.1 [1995], p. 10.)

5 And suitably illustrated by a 1964 short story from Dick, entitled 'Waterspider', the writing of which represents an act of some conceit. Its central premise revolves around the veneration by a future society of twentieth-century pre-cog[nitive]s—those gifted with the ability to predict the future. The names of these 'pre-cogs'? Wells, Anderson, Asimov, van Vogt, and so on... In cold outline, 'Waterspider' had much in common with the Gernsbackian mind-set.

6 Peter Nicholls, 'Hard SF', in Clute and Nicholls, eds., *The Encyclopedia of Science Fiction*, p. 542.

7 Paul Virilio, Jean Baudrillard and Stuart Hall, 'The Work of Art in the Electronic Age', *Block*, 14 (1988), p. 5.

8 Freedman, 'Science Fiction', p. 188.

9 The following pop-cultural artefact summarizes the situation perfectly:

It's difficult to say which came first, real lesbian chic or the media hype about it, but the question is largely immaterial—the two are now feeding back on each other. The snowball effect went something like this: lesbians got sick of the militant-dyke dress and behaviour codes and lashed out, sexually and stylistically. The progressive media picked up on this. Trendy 'straight' women picked up that lesbianism is hip, as did tv producers, glossy-mag editors, and scriptwriters. Now, hip shows, hip mags and hip young things are falling over themselves to get a piece of the lesbian action. And so it grows... (Karen-Jane Eyre, 'From the Editor', in *black + WHITE* [October, 1996], p. 2.)

10 Paul Virilio, 'Moving Girl', *Semiotext(e)*, 1.4 (1981), p. 242.

11 Bruce Sterling, 'Preface', in *idem*, ed., *Mirrorshades: The Cyberpunk Anthology* (London: HarperCollins, 1994), p. xi.

12 A good example is the rock 'n' roll aesthetic of the genre, all

mirrorshades, chrome, and black leather, refracted through a visually descriptive, cut-up and canted prose. Incorporated into MTV graphics and numerous music video clips, for which it is ideally suited (this being Gibson's intention, after all), the culmination seems to be the characterization and visual framing of *Johnny Mnemonic*'s Ice-T role, a badass-by-rote. But perhaps the clearest example is Gibson's descriptions of cyberspace—information as a solid, conceptual graphic-interface—which, in the latest spurt of cyber-films, has become little more than an excuse for a fast-paced ride through Silicon Valley. *Mnemonic* appropriates this visual style, seemingly at random, causing the narrative to become messy and incoherent. The intention seems to be not so much plot-driven, as to provide a reference point for the film's target audience—hip, young, MTV cyber-junkies.

13 Benjamin Long, 'Flash Gibson', *Black and White*, 5 (February 1994), p. 86.

14 Toby Redd and Anna Nervegna, 'The William Gibson Interview', *Transition*, 47 (1995), p. 84.

15 An example would be the Australian lemonade commercial which asks the viewer to concentrate on a clear glass of the fluid, and look for the 'naked woman' outlined in the gaseous discharges rising to the surface. Of course, it is a normal glass of lemonade: the ad is sending up—with a self-conscious wink to the eagerly receptive audience—the trusted advertising maxim 'sex sells'.

16 Brian McHale, *Postmodernist Fiction* (New York and London: Methuen, 1987), pp. 65; 59.

17 Veronica Hollinger, 'Specular SF: Postmodern Allegory', in Nicholas Ruddick, ed., *State of the Fantastic: Studies in the Theory and Practice of Fantastic Literature and Film* (Westport and London: Greenwood Press, 1992), p. 33.

18 'Specular sf simulates sf, but is not itself sf. A work of specular sf, then, is a reflection of sf, but it is not itself the "real thing". It is not im-mediate, but is mediated... by whatever specific allegory underlies any particular text.' (Hollinger, 'Specular SF', p. 29).

19 Hollinger, 'Specular SF', p. 34.

20 Since this essay was conceived and then delivered at the 'Speaking Science Fiction' conference, David Cronenberg's film version of *Crash* has been released. The film, although faithful in adaptation, is conceptually weaker than its source and therefore presents a less coherent world-view. This derives mainly from a subtle shift in the central narrative conceit of the film. As the narrator of Ballard's *Crash* confides, 'It's not sex that Vaughan's interested in, but technology'. However, it's not technology that Cronenberg's interested in, but sex. This of course makes for a very different sensorial experience to that provided by Ballard's original. And of course, sex sells. England, one of the last territories to view the film, must be whipped into a frenzy by now...

21 Jim Pomeroy describes an SRL performance, offering his own slant on Ballard's work:

> Playing to the pit and dancing on the edge, SRL begs many questions, offers few answers, and moves off the stage leaving smouldering ruins and tinny ears in its smoky wake. SRL is boys' toys from hell, cynically realizing the masculinist fantasies of J.G. Ballard and William Burroughs. (Quoted in Scott Bukatman, *Terminal Identity: The Virtual Subject in Postmodern Science Fiction* [Durham: Duke University Press, 1993], p. 292.)

22 J.G. Ballard, 'Mythmaker of the 20th Century' (1964), in V. Vale and Andrea Juno, eds., *J.G. Ballard* (San Francisco: Re/Search, 1991), p. 107.

23 J.G. Ballard, 'Some Words about Crash!', *Foundation: The Review of Science Fiction*, 9 (November, 1975), p. 47.

24 Frederic Jameson, *Postmodernism, or The Cultural Logic of Late Capitalism* (London: Verso, 1991), pp. 31, 39.

25 Ballard, 'Some Words . . .', p. 45.

26 'Since there is no longer a self present to do the feeling' (Jameson, *Postmodernism*, p. 15).

27 Steve Whitford, 'Cocks Carmichael Whitford: Road Hardware Projects', *Transition*, 39 (1995), p. 40.

28 J.G. Ballard, *Crash* (London: Vintage, 1995), p. 20.

29 Another example: here in Melbourne, by the side of the Flinders St. railway overpass, pedestrians have the opportunity to glimpse an advertisement hoarding touting a 'Gamblers' Anonymous'-type service. The accompanying picture is of a distressed family man, his partner's arm lovingly draped over his shoulder. This image plays upon recent media hysteria regarding abandoned children found in the casino carpark, their parents happily gambling inside. Rising into the skyline above the overpass is the drab and grey World Trade Center, home of the Crown Casino, with an over-size Crown logo proudly glinting in the sun. Its attendant cultural baggage belongs to the realm of State-sponsored propaganda, extolling the economic worth of the Casino (the Victorian Premier's rhetoric states that to argue against this worth is to be most assuredly 'anti-Victorian'—he wants us to be one big, happy family, whatever the cost). In this compressed dimension, the 'new sensorium' Jameson seeks—perhaps the split-brain syndrome of Philip K. Dick's *A Scanner Darkly*—beckons more than ever before, as our cultural imaginary switches from the concept of the 'broken family' to the 'happy family', and backwards and forwards time and again, according to whichever media invocation is in vogue. Umberto Eco neatly sums up:

> ...profit defeats ideology, because the consumers want to be thrilled not only by the guarantee of the Good but also by the shudder of the Bad... Both at the same level of credibility, both at the same level of fakery. Thus, on entering his cathedrals of iconic reassurance, the visitor will remain uncertain whether his final destiny is hell or heaven, and so will consume new promises. (Umberto Eco, *Travels in Hyperreality* [London: Picador, 1987], pp. 57–58.)

30 Jean Baudrillard, 'Two Essays: 1. Simulacra and Science Fiction. 2. Ballard's *Crash*', *Science-Fiction Studies*, 18.3 (1991), p. 311.

31 Ballard, *Crash*, pp. 161–62; 196–97.

32 Ballard, *Crash*, p. 80.

33 After the Port Arthur massacre in Australia, in which 30 people were shot dead, the debate around violent films has become even more confused. Do these films influence events in real life? Fudging the issue, our TV stations continue to show graphic footage from such events, with one eye on the ratings, while their entertainment arm proceeds to pull suspect films from the airwaves, replacing them with bland and supposedly inoffensive 'family' entertainment. In this realm, the strict policing of frames renders pointless any attempt to define televisual violence, and its supposed effects. Couched within the protective shell of 'reality', violence exists as a touchstone for our emotions— simultaneously repellent and mesmerising.

34 Ballard, *Crash*, p. 220.

35 Ballard, *Crash*, p. 129.

36 Ballard, 'Some Words . . .', p. 51.

37 Brian Eno, 'Resonant Complexity', *Whole Earth Review* (Summer, 1994), p. 42.

38 Negativland, *Fair Use: The Story of the Letter U and the Numeral 2* (Concord: Seeland, 1995), pp. 121, 129.

39 Ballard, 'Some Words . . .', p. 47.

40 Michel Foucault, 'What is An Author?', 1969, in David Lodge, ed., *Modern Criticism and Theory: A Reader* (London and New York: Longman, 1988), p. 210.

41 J.G. Ballard, *High-Rise* (London, Flamingo, 1993), p. 104.

Notes on Contributors

Brian Aldiss, over twelve months of 1999–2000, received a Prix Utopia at Poitiers, was made Grand Master of Science Fiction by the SFWA, and was awarded an honorary DLitt by the University of Reading. Obviously this sort of thing cannot go on. His recent books include *White Mars: The Mind Set Free*, a utopia written in collaboration with Sir Roger Penrose. A new collection of short stories, *Supertoys*, is due to be published in Spring 2001.

Brian Attebery has written extensively on fantasy and is currently finishing a book on gender and science fiction. With co-conspirators Ursula K. Le Guin and Karen Joy Fowler, he edited *The Norton Book of Science Fiction*. He lives in Pocatello, Idaho, in close proximity to mountains, wild rivers, cowboys, and (Shoshone-Bannock) Indians, and teaches at Idaho State University.

Andrew M. Butler lectures in film and media studies at Buckinghamshire Chilterns University College, High Wycombe. He is the membership secretary of the Science Fiction Foundation and features editor of *Vector*. He is the author of the Pocket Essentials volumes *Philip K. Dick* and *Cyberpunk*.

Bronwen Calvert is a PhD student in American Studies at the University of East Anglia. She is researching issues of embodiment in cyberpunk fiction, with particular focus on 'feminist' cyberpunk.

Danièle Chatelain is Professor of French at the University of Redlands. She is the author of *Perceiving and Telling: A Study of Iterative Discourse* (San Diego State University Press, 1998), and is writing a book on Flaubert and the laws of phenomena.

Candas Jane Dorsey is a Canadian writer, editor and publisher of speculative and other literature, living in Edmonton, Alberta. Her story '(Learning About) Machine Sex' has been widely anthologized. Her first novel *Black Wine* (1977) won the Tiptree, Crawford and Aurora Awards. Her latest book is *Vanilla and Other Stories* (NeWest Press) and the novel

A Paradigm of Earth is forthcoming from Tor in 2001. She is currently co-editing (with Judy McCrosky) *Land/Space*, an anthology of speculative writing on prairie themes.

Ross Farnell has recently been awarded a PhD for his thesis 'Mediations and "Becomings": The Posthuman Condition in Contemporary Science Fiction and Cultural Theory'. He has written extensively on science fiction and related issues including representations of the body in text and theory. *Science Fiction Studies* has recently published articles on both William Gibson's *Virtual Light* and *Idoru* (25.3) and Greg Egan's *Permutation City* (27.1). He teaches science fiction part time at Monash University, Melbourne, manages a cultural centre and indigenous art gallery, and when time allows pursues his other passion, composing and recording electronic music.

Veronica Hollinger is Associate Professor of Cultural Studies at Trent University, Ontario, Canada. She is a co-editor of *Science Fiction Studies*, and has published widely in areas related to speculative fiction. With Joan Gordon, she is currently editing a collection of essays for the University of Pennsylvania Press, *Edging into the Future: Speculative Fiction and Contemporary Cultural Transformation*.

Gwyneth Jones was born in Manchester, studied the History of Ideas at Sussex University, and started writing science fiction while on a three-year trip to south-east Asia. Recent publications include a collection of essays, *Deconstructing the Starships*, and, under the pseudonym Ann Halam, a teenage horror story called *Don't Open Your Eyes*.

Roger Luckhurst lectures in nineteenth- and twentieth-century literature at Birkbeck College, University of London. He is the author of *'The Angle Between Two Walls': The Fiction of J.G. Ballard* (1997) and co-editor of *Literature and the Contemporary* (1999) and *The Fin de Siècle: A Reader in Cultural History c. 1880–1900* (2000).

Farah Mendlesohn is a lecturer in American Studies at Middlesex University and Features Editor of *Foundation: The International Review of Science Fiction*. Recent work includes writing on Terry Pratchett and a range of television sf. Currently, she is writing a book on post-war utopian fiction with Edward James (University of Reading).

Helen Merrick is Acting Director, Centre for Western Australian History at the University of Western Australia. She is co-editor of *Women of Other Worlds: Excursions through Science Fiction and Feminism*.

Nickianne Moody is Principal Lecturer in Media and Cultural Studies at Liverpool John Moores University. She is also convenor of the Association for Research in Popular Fictions for which she edits the journal *Diegesis*. Her current research includes an oral history of Boots Booklovers Library and an examination of the representations of plague across nineteenth- and twentieth-century media.

José Manuel Mota is Professor of English at the Faculty of Letters, University of Coimbra, Portugal. His PhD dissertation discussed Philip K. Dick as a science fantasy writer. He has also published articles on Ursula K. Le Guin, J.G. Ballard and H.G. Wells.

Josef Nesvadba (b. 1926) is the best-known living Czech sf writer. A doctor of medicine since 1950, he specializes in psychiatry, especially group psychotherapy. He is the author of twelve books, six films and one TV serial, mostly translated into German. English translations of his short story collections are: *Vampires Ltd* (1964), and *In the Footsteps of the Abominable Snowman* (1970, published in the US as *Lost Face*). More recently, short stories have been published in the British sf magazine *Interzone*.

Andy Sawyer is the librarian in charge of the sf collections at Liverpool University Library, including the Science Fiction Foundation Collection. He teaches on Liverpool's MA in Science Fiction Studies and has published articles on John Wyndham, telepathy in sf, Babylon 5 and Terry Pratchett.

David Seed is Professor of American Literature in the Liverpool University English Department. He has written books on Thomas Pynchon, Joseph Heller, and other writers. Among his latest publications are *Imagining Apocalypse* and *American Science Fiction and the Cold War*. He is series editor for Science Fiction Texts and Studies (Liverpool University Press).

Simon Sellars, formerly of Monash University, Victoria, Australia, is Special Events Coordinator, RMIT Union Arts, and a writer/editor.

George Slusser is Professor of Comparative Literature and Curator of the Eaton Collection at the University of California, Riverside. He has written and/or edited 28 books. His most recent book is *Stalkers of the Infinite: The Science Fiction of Arkady and Boris Strugatsky* (Xenos Books, forthcoming).

Sue Walsh has lectured in English and American Literature at the Universities of Reading and Central Lancashire. She is a PhD student at the University of Reading, where her research on the construction of the wolf in children's literature continues her engagement with how and to what ends ideas of the 'real' are produced in literature. She has an article entitled 'Child/Animal: It's the "Real" Thing' forthcoming in the *Yearbook of English Studies*, no. 32, special issue on 'Children in Literature' (February 2002)

Index